The Huntsman of Alba

Huntsman of Alba Series - Book 1

Dr. Doug Chapman

A Tiree Publishing House LLC novel

Cover Design: David Colón
Cover Illustration: Caius Augustus

ISBN: 978-1-959958-03-1 (Paperback)
978-1-959958-04-8 (E-Book)

First edition February 2023

www.drdougchapman.com

CHAPTER ONE

E very instinct the huntsman had told him that the kill
edged closer. Hawk moved alone through the forest,
gliding past the towering trunks. He searched for signs of
his target. Beams of sunlight tried to penetrate the thicket of
conifer needles swaying in a quiet breeze. The branches blocked
the light, casting muted shadows in a dark and twisting dance
along the ground. *It had to be here, a sign. But where?*

Hawk stalked forward, stepping lightly in his onyx leather
boots. Despite the summer's heat, an uneasy chill danced along
his neck and arms, his hair standing on end. The normal vibrato
raised by the forest's birds was noticeably absent. His trained eyes
scanned the ground and trees, yearning to glimpse his prey. Hawk
couldn't fail. He had to find it. No other option existed.

A red squirrel darted up Hawk's path and jumped over a
fallen log. That's when his prey revealed itself on the forest floor.
A tuft of snow-white fur drew his eyes like a fiery beacon on a
stormy ocean bluff. It clung tightly to the fallen log. Hawk inched
closer, reaching out to grasp it with a gloved hand. He glanced at
his fist, the mustiness of decaying wood wafting to him. He
turned his hand palm up and opened it. The piece of fur caught

the breeze—hair from the white stag he hunted. Hawk allowed the twitch of a smile to play on his lips. He was on the right path.

Hawk studied his surroundings. The breeze shifted the fallen orange needles about the ground, revealing sporadic hooved tracks. They dotted the soft earth in front of him. Hawk followed them, inspecting their indentations. The cloven hoof prints dug deeper into the dirt, kicking up debris while shifting their direction. The stag must have turned to run. But run from what? Hawk scanned the woods for a clue of what might have made the stag flee. His eyes caught a single print in the mud, much different from the cloven hoof of a stag.

Impossible, Hawk thought. *A print like that shouldn't be anywhere near here.* Seeking a closer examination, he bent over. Out of the corner of his eye, the red squirrel fled up the nearest pine. Hawk rose, then turned toward the rumbling thunder in the distance. The approaching roar of horses' hooves echoed through the valley.

Hawk gritted his teeth and spun to face the approaching hunting retinue. There was no chance of finding the stag nearby with so many horsemen. He knew the retinue stretched obscenely large down the wooded road. But what hunting party isn't large when in the king's company?

The lead rider raised a plated metal hand. He signaled a halt to the party as his horse came to rest above the tracks Hawk had followed, smearing the details. The cavalcade of hunters and servants behind him stopped, but the king's banner, a white cross on a blue field, never ceased wavering in the breeze.

Hawk stepped up to bow before King David, the First of Alba. An azure cloak floated behind the king, rippling in the air. His suit formed a protective mail around his upper body. A thick, plated piece protruded from his chest, decorated with the holy cross. The king's style might have been more at home on a battlefield than the neighboring hunting grounds, but Hawk wouldn't mistake anyone else for the king.

The king raised the front hinge of his helmet, crowned with

two mighty antlers. Hawk kept his eyes on the ruined tracks but sensed the king's glare.

"Why haven't we seen anything yet? I didn't expect to find the prize straight away, but I thought we'd have seen a stag or doe, or damn it, even a hare jumping across the path. Instead, shite. I sent you ahead to scout. Are you a huntsman or not?" King David demanded, steadying his position in the saddle.

The stallion attempted to correct its stance, shifting the monarch forward and backward while its hooves made sense of the uneven rocks.

Hawk shifted his gaze to the king. Hawk's brown eyes and stern face betrayed no uneasiness in the presence of royalty. A tree shadowed the huntsman's bronzed complexion. His raven-colored hair didn't move despite the wind's intentions. Instead, it spiked stiffly skyward in a short row down the middle of his head.

"Well, Huntsman? Do you want your payment, the information you asked for? What do you suggest?" the king exclaimed, spinning his gray stallion toward Hawk.

"Your Grace, you hired me to help you hunt the stag. So that's what I mean to do. I can't do that with this *military parade* announcing our presence to every living creature in Edinburgh. Eighty hooves thunder through this valley, and it's enough for every animal to scatter before we get within half a mile of them. Do you want to hunt this beast? Get off your saddle and come with me. We leave the retinue behind."

The king scoffed, then scoffed once more. Hawk turned to him, and the king's mouth twisted up, assessing the predicament. Or assessing Hawk's insolence.

"You're right, Huntsman," the king said, as the desire to hunt must have won out. He pivoted his horse to face the eager hunting party. "Squire, come here. Squire! Yes, you, you bumbling fool. Come. Take my horse. We're going on ahead through the woods. It's impossible to hunt whilst we're all bumping into each other like this. The huntsman and I shall carry on and claim our prize."

A young boy reached over his mare's mane to grab the king's

reins and steady the horse. The king's hinged helmet clanked shut as he slid off the horse's saddle. Hawk watched in amusement as the king's seal-skin boots sunk into the trail's mud from the excess weight of his armor.

"Take my steed and remain here in case we have need of you," the king commanded the squire before glancing back at the huntsman.

Hawk didn't wish to push his luck. Crossing limits with a king never ended well, and the hunt was too important to fail. He nodded approvingly.

"Y-yes, Your Grace," the young boy stammered.

The squire's left hand trembled, and the reins slipped. But, leaning quickly, he snatched them with his right.

"Steady, Robert," King David barked.

The king removed his helmet and fixed it to his saddle, the ornamental antlers leaving a dozen tiny indents in the leather. He unfastened a calf-skin canteen from his horse and tied it to his belt, letting it dangle on his right hip. The king slung a quiver and wooden hunting bow over his back.

"It's Ralf, Your Grace," the squire corrected, his tone suggesting he didn't even know his exact name.

Hawk ignored the hunting retinue and turned his attention to the path in front of them. He led the king down the road ahead.

They went on further down the path before turning left and veering off the trail, following the tracks. Their steps brought them higher up the sloping terrain. The huntsman's steps made no sound as they walked. The king's, however, had a slight metal jingle from his loose mail armor.

It wouldn't make their hunt any easier.

Hawk certainly dressed the part of a huntsman. He wore leather boots with dark wool trousers. His torso sported a matching thick woolen gambeson equipped with leather shoulder pads. Steel chain mail, pressed securely into the leather so it didn't move or rattle, covered the pads. It would halt a sharp arrow or the piercing thrust of a blade. Hawk had wrapped a four-piece buckskin kilt around his waist, protecting his thighs and hips without limiting his movement. And the silence. The huntsman made no sound as he moved.

The king broke the silence. "Those battle axes on your back, Huntsman, I've seen nothing like them in my life. Where in God's good name did you get such fine steel?"

Hawk reached back with his left hand. He brushed the tip of the steel, sliding his finger down to the polished metal shaft. He repeated the motion on the second blade.

"They were my family's," he said.

The axes, with their handles secured crisscross on Hawk's back, had their blades facing outward and ready for action.

"Truly? Such fine steel to wield."

"They work for me."

"Yes, so I would hope," the king said, resting his hand on the trunk of a tree. Hawk watched the king use it to propel himself further up the mountain. "Think we'll get the beast? Holyrood Abbey won't be complete until we feast on the white stag in its halls, and . . ." King David paused, catching his breath ". . . and how I wish to have his head above my hearth."

The huntsman, having heard the tale many times since arriving in Edinburgh, didn't ask about the now-famous hunt. The king didn't waste any time jumping into the story, however.

"I set off on a hunt a few years ago, into the same woods we're in now. I rode ahead of my hunting party, of course. It wasn't long before I was out of sight and came across a white stag. I dismounted and unsheathed my sword as the white stag charged at me, the devil. You wouldn't have guessed, but I tripped, stepping on my new cloak, and fell straight to the ground. I could do naught but reach out and try to grab the white stag."

"Did it thrash you?"

"Remarkably, no. I grabbed the antlers. However, in place of the stag's antlers, a holy cross appeared. The holy cross saved my life, but the beast escaped, as you know. Within a year, I constructed Holyrood Abbey to commemorate the miracle I witnessed that day. Truly a miracle. You could not imagine my joy upon the rumors of the white stag's return to my forest of Drumselch. Oh, how I wish to have the white stag in my grasp."

"You'll have your wish," Hawk said, continuing up the slope.

He wanted to ask the king if he imagined the holy cross or why he still wore his cloak despite tripping over it in his story. Hawk decided to leave it. His focus stayed on the hunt.

A tree caught Hawk's eye as they walked. He moved closer to the pine's aged gray bark. Removing his glove, Hawk brushed a hand against two parallel scrapes at eye level on the trunk.

Curious, he thought, tracing the grooved scratches on the tree.

"The stag marks his return," the king said with joy.

"Not like any stag I've seen," Hawk replied, puzzled with concern.

"That's because you've never seen my stag. Come, lead on, Huntsman."

The men moved on up the path toward the peak. Hawk replaced his glove, but his mind lingered on the marks.

They walked on a mountain known as the Seat. The incline headed endlessly upward. Hawk continued hiking with ease, pushing them further through the trees.

The wooden area broke into heather as Hawk approached a crest halfway up the mountain's northern side. Wading through the brush, he stood on a rock jutting out from the surface. Hawk peered over the edge. King David, out of breath from the no doubt unusual bout of exercise, placed a hand on the huntsman's shoulder.

A prominent stone castle crowned a jagged hilltop in the distance. Auburn, stony cliffs surrounded the fortress on three sides, cascading hundreds of feet before meeting the tangled depths below.

"Edinburgh Castle," the king said between breaths. "Magnificent. Its lofty turrets stand guard over the kingdom. The kingdom of Alba is beautiful, but there's no greater beauty than Castle Rock. Take it in, Hawk, for you'll see nothing as glorious as this."

The huntsman remained still, despite agreeing with the king. Few places in the world could take a man's breath away, both metaphorically in the huntsman's case and literally with King David, as Alba.

Contrasted against the steep-edged pinnacle of Castle Rock, the remaining side gently sloped into a mile-long hill. Along the hill's spine lay the main roadway filled with the bustling markets of Edinburgh. Feathering off from the main road stood houses, tofts, and farmyards, making up the growing city.

"Can you see the abbey?" the king asked. "There, to your right, at the end of the road from Castle Rock? Holyrood Abbey. Yes, there you go. The valley nearly hides it."

The valley, which led up a forested part of another large hill, held a set of crags just beyond. Hawk knew, having seen the other side of this hill before the hunt, they formed a semi-circular barrier and a natural border to the Drumselch forest they traveled through.

"He won't travel over the cliffs," Hawk declared. "The heat of the day rises, and the beast will seek water in the valley."

They set off down the other side of the Seat into the gorge. The king followed Hawk closely, the ringing metal aggravating the huntsman's focus.

Hawk pressed onward, picking up the fresh trail of cloven-hooved tracks leading between the tall trees. He surveyed the shadowed forest methodically. Where he needed to go was clear, but Hawk hesitated.

A ruffled breeze blew at their backs, urging the two men into the forest. Hawk nodded to the king, assuring he understood as well as Hawk did. They needed to be on their guard as they entered the wood. The king nodded back.

Hawk trod through the dense bracken, shifting it to spot the stag's tracks while keeping a close watch for further signs on the trees. His eyes noticed it effortlessly. More snow-white hair clung to a tree trunk. Hawk studied the bark. There were no grooves, only a round patch of stripped wood bearing fresh sap like the blood of a seeping wound.

The stag is close. Hawk could sense it. Glancing at the ground, he noticed the scuffled prints of hooves. Moisture swelled in the tracks. They were fresh. *The stag is close.*

He crouched and nodded to King David to follow suit. The king, holding a bow in one hand, imitated the huntsman's stance. The two hunters followed the stream deeper into the valley. They rounded a rocky bend and glimpsed the stream's destination: a pool of fresh water.

At the edge of the water, on the opposite bank, lay a magnificent specimen. Hawk's eyes dilated as the prize appeared. Even lying down, its enormity gave Hawk pause. Its antlers sprouted back from its head like two branching trees in a leafless winter. The beast's coat, the color of snow, spanned from its nose to its tail—King David's white stag. Despite resting next to a considerable boulder, the shadowless white fur glistened. But the coat was tarnished. Blood hemorrhaged from a shredded abdomen. Entrails cascaded from the stag and reached toward the pool of water, leaving little doubt of the stag's fate.

No, this can't be it. It cannot happen this way, Hawk cursed, abandoning his crouch to get a better look. He followed the edge of the pool, tracing the semi-circular bank to the fallen stag. His pace quickened with every step, trying to outmaneuver the sinking pit growing in his gut.

Hawk reached the animal, and a rank odor of wet fur, like a dog trapped in a rainstorm, crept in. He removed a large obsidian knife from his belt. The huntsman sank to one knee next to the head of the animal and slashed the beast's neck. A crimson flow confirmed the white stag had recently died. The blood seeped into the nearby pool, poisoning the serenity of the water.

King David stared, unable to remove his eyes from the scene in front of him. Tears formed in the king's eyes.

"My dear God . . ." The king swallowed, wiping away the teardrop that formed.

A choking realization crept into Hawk. King David tasked him with hunting the white stag as a trophy, and in exchange, Hawk would receive the information he sought. His end of the deal lay in jeopardy. Something else had killed the stag. He tried to think of a way to maintain his agreement, to keep his end of the bargain.

"My God," the king gasped again. "This moment is not how I imagined it. What is this madness? What could have done such a thing? And in my woods?"

Hawk cleaned his black blade on his trousers, about to speak, when it happened.

King David's head snapped up, looking behind Hawk. His eyes widened, his frown evaporating as his jaw dropped open.

A mighty grip squeezed Hawk's right shoulder and grasped tightly onto the mail armor. Hawk turned toward the hand. But it wasn't a hand. Its fingers ended in gnarled claws with wild, dark-black fur. He followed the hand up, scanning past the forearm and hairy biceps toward the face of the beast holding him. Muscles swelled over the body, possessing the same wiry dark hair. It stood taller than anyone Hawk had seen, and he'd once met Towering Hjalmar Gronvold, the Norse bodyguard of King Sigurd the Crusader. His captor's eyes wouldn't have belonged on a man's head. They glowed like fiery suns, darkened only by slit-like pupils. The head wasn't that of a man's, but a wolf's.

The wolf revealed a muzzle full of fangs. Drool poured from between the monster's canine teeth as it emitted a low growl. There was no time to react. The claws dug through his armor before the beast hurled him to the side. He crashed onto a root, pain jolting across every rib that made contact.

Hawk cursed for letting the dead stag distract him. He had abandoned his senses—his instincts—too easily. He hadn't expected a monster in the forest. But his reflexes returned immediately, and he spun off the ground to his feet.

The beast stepped forward and grabbed at the king, throwing him into a nearby tree. King David clanked to the ground, his mouth gaping open, unable to make a sound and gasping for breath.

"Werewolf!" Hawk shouted, drawing the monster's attention.

The axes appeared in a flash. They were perfect extensions of his reach, his hands welcoming the familiar grip of the handle. The huntsman readied himself, arms spread wide as he circled the beast, putting it between him and the water.

The monster crouched, coiled to attack, but sprang straight up, its muzzle pointing to the sky, and howled. The shrill cry echoed over the water as the king scrambled to cover his ears.

Hawk, unaffected by the wail, lunged and swung his right ax at the werewolf's shoulder. It stepped backward, sensing the blow and staying out of reach. Hawk, spinning from his weapon's missed strike, carried his momentum with a left-handed backward attack. But he missed again.

Hawk marveled at the werewolf's speed—perhaps the quickest he'd seen. But the huntsman was quicker.

The monster shifted back on one foot. It launched at the huntsman and reached out with its massive paws. Hawk danced to the left with a quick pirouette and dodged the brunt of the attack. The wolf landed on all fours and didn't stop. It galloped in a circle and positioned itself next to the fallen stag. Hawk gripped his axes tighter.

The werewolf placed its grungy hands on the carcass and snarled. Its eyes moved between the two hunters and the stag. It dragged the body away from the edge of the water, attempting to round the large boulder.

Adrenaline coursed through Hawk. He held an ax over his head, perfectly lined up with his thin strip of hair. The huntsman groaned, hurling the ax toward the beast before it could get behind the boulder. The ax spun end over end and found its mark in the monster's thick, muscular shoulder.

The monster roared, releasing the carcass and falling on its side. It writhed, kicking the ground in anguish. The beast finally gathered its composure. It grasped the shaft of Hawk's weapon and dislodged the blade in its shoulder, dropping the weapon to the ground.

The huntsman charged the beast, every step a precise, calculated motion bringing Hawk ready to strike. But the werewolf whimpered, turning its tail and sprinting away upright.

Hawk halted his momentum and spared a moment to assess the king's condition. King David rose from the ground and hobbled toward him.

"Did you see that?" Hawk asked excitedly. "I thought he was going to throw the ax at me the way he gripped that handle. Fastest one on two legs I've seen too. He's long gone now. Are you alright?"

The adrenaline proved too much for King David—an overwhelming systemic response. The color drained from the king's face, and he bent over, hands on his knees. He took a few more deep breaths.

"You've seen that before? What was that monstrosity?" the king managed.

"A lycanthrope. A werewolf."

"What is it doing in my forest?"

"I haven't the faintest idea, Your Grace. It's peculiar, given how close it was to the city."

"You say you've seen these before, have you?" the king asked, repeating his question.

"I am a huntsman," Hawk said, simply wiping his blade clean on his gambeson and placing both axes into their resting spot on his back.

He approached the fallen stag with King David. Four long gashes marked the torso's skin. A large section of tissue and fur over the caudal rib cage peeled back from where the monster tried to escape with the prey.

"Can it be stopped?" the king asked.

"Of course. It's like any beast." Hawk heard the muffled sound of hooves coming over the valley.

The hunting retinue no doubt heard the commotion and were investigating. The king turned toward the sound as well.

"Huntsman, I am in need of your services. And this time you must not fail me. You must track this . . . this . . . God, I can't believe I am saying this in Edinburgh, but you must track down this werewolf. You must stop it before it commits any savagery like this on my people. But take heed: no one, and I mean absolutely no one, can know of this. It was just a *wolf*, after all . . ." King David slowed to emphasize the detail. "Do this, and I'll give you anything! Name it and it is yours."

"Why, Your Grace," Hawk replied, smiling, "you already know my price. It hasn't changed. For stag or monster, it is the same. The Norsemen—I want that information."

CHAPTER TWO

The feast's commencement was at hand. Candelabras lit the room, and tapestries of blue and white hung on the stony engraved walls. The pews of Holyrood Abbey stood pushed to one side. A half dozen wooden benches and tables stretched underneath the fanciful vaulted ceilings. Each guest sat in front of a hard-breaded trencher. Most brought their favorite drinking vessel with them. But the food—well, the king would provide the food.

Prayers led to grace, the eager guests waiting for their promised meal. The smell emanating from the victualing yard's cooking pit wafted in through the open windows and doors. Fresh scents of smoked mutton and swine drifted around the room, rivaled only by the aroma of freshly poured ale.

Hawk sat toward the rear of the hall, in the row furthest away from King David's high table. He wouldn't have fit in with the nobility. Hawk wore the same onyx outfit he had on the hunt that morning. His axes remained secured in an *X* on his back. As only a mere huntsman, Hawk received no such luxuries as sitting close to royalty anyhow. But as the king's current huntsman, he was one of the few guests allowed to carry his weapon to the feast openly.

Hawk's seating choice gave him little worry. He sat closer to the musicians strumming lutes and whistling flutes. But his seat had another benefit. He preferred, at a banquet, to not have to watch his tongue when speaking and instead occupy it with eating. Endless courtly courtesies grew tiresome.

He looked around at his companions licking their lips in anticipation of the best meal they'd have all week. Hell, the best meal they'd have all year.

The large wooden doors of the church opened, and, one by one, servants ushered in the feast. Platters of charred lamb with kettles of a brown broth stew decorated the tabletops. Hawk stared in awe at the servant balancing a tower of manchet. Her hand fixed to the platter, which swayed back and forth, keeping the tower of loaves steady as she passed bread out to the seated nobles.

The lass smiled as she approached, swinging her head and flicking away a stray lock of red hair. She handed him some bread. She must have realized Hawk was the end of the line, as she rolled her eyes with the completion of her task, the smile evaporating. He thanked her, knowing she'd likely spent the entire day baking the bread for the king's feast, only for it to be consumed within a few moments of serving it.

Hawk wasn't wrong, either. The sound of dining guests filled Holyrood Abbey, groans of satisfaction reverberating with wholesome laughter through the hall. Guests gnashed on meat ripped from the bone and clanked their goblets of ale on the table.

Hawk grabbed a hunk of charred lamb and put it on his trencher. Then he ate. He tried every food presented to him, pausing only to take a swig of ale and wash down the bolus of bread and meat.

"So you're the huntsman I've heard so much about," said the man dressed in a blue silk tunic next to Hawk.

Hawk moved a healthy portion of seared, salty lamb from one side of his mouth to the other and, not wanting to speak, nodded.

"Kenneth Olifard of Linlithgow. This man here," the man in a blue tunic pointed to a large burly man sitting across from

Hawk, "is my good man, Gerard. And what do they call you, Huntsman?"

"Hawk," said Hawk.

"So you hunted with the king? Tell me? Is it true? Did he really shoot his famous white stag? Or was it painted so afterward? Thirty-some years I've been hunting, and I've never seen a white stag. Yet he's seen the same one twice!" Kenneth shook his head in disbelief, then grabbed the last bite of his roll and threw it in his mouth.

"It's real indeed." Hawk hesitated, swallowing the rest of his lamb. "I'll let the king talk about his hunt."

"Hmm, yes. Well, we have yet to see the beast anyhow. The king sure likes to make an event of the beast, waiting until we've all supped before the reveal. Heh, no doubt so he can save the venison for himself."

Gerard leaned forward. "That hart, was it the same white beast from which this abbey takes its creation? It must've been quite old. So old, in fact, that I'd guess the beast would've fallen if the king had walked up to it and blown on it."

Gerard pursed his lips together and imitated the gesture. Hawk smiled at the joke, but it rapidly faded with the memory of the stag's shredded abdomen.

"I'd believe that," laughed Kenneth. "I've seen something like it happen before, only with sheep. I walked with a farmer and his dog out to see the lambing prospects for the year. We crested the hill of the pasture to see the entire flock together, save one. It stood alone against the border of the field. Well, two whistles, and the dog ran after the sheep to bring it in. One bark from that mutt and that was it. The sheep keeled over, dead as can be. The broken-mouth ewe had nearly twenty years on it, well, so the farmer said anyway. But sometimes a bark will do it."

A young servant walked past, holding a keg. She poured the ale into the goblets of the surrounding feasters and continued down the line. Across the hall, the roar of two men shouting rose above the feasting guests. A tussle ensued as the men tried to apprehend each other. Hawk sat too far away to make out their claims, but enjoyed the spectacle all the same. Before the men reached fisticuffs, the shout of a monk, decorated with a large cross tattoo over his temple, ceased the roused guests.

"Probably Clan Donnchadh reminding those who sided with Máel Coluim's claim to the throne that they haven't forgotten, eh? Clan Olifard has supported the king since Cumbria, but convincing those northern Highland clans to kneel to a southern king is a waste of time. It always leads to swords, and it won't end, Huntsman. Pay them no mind," Kenneth said. "Well, speaking of swords . . . Hawk, it troubles me greatly, so I must ask. Those peculiar axes on your back, what are they? I have never seen the likes of them before."

The huntsman shifted on the bench, pondering how best to answer the question. He put a hand through his black spiked hair, remembering the word his father used for them: *tummahegan.*

Hawk hadn't met anyone in any kingdom whose tongue could grasp the word, so he simplified it. "Tomahawks. They're called tomahawks."

"Tomahawks, eh? Erm, eh, so, Master Hawk. Where are you from? You're not from Alba, or even all of Britannia. That skin of yours, and that accent—where is home for you?" Kenneth asked.

Hawk met the eyes of the local lord. He stared into them and through them to his past. He wasn't from Alba or Britannia, true.

Where am I from? I hardly remember myself.

He could barely see it. He sat on top of a large, lichen-covered boulder. The flakes of pale green peeled off as his hands brushed against the coarse granite. From above, the red-and-yellow leaves moved and twisted, like they set aflame the forest. The chill of autumn clung to his skin. He took in a deep breath. The alluring smell of the campfire drew him back home. His home, a wooden barked hut, had a single smokestack sticking out of the top. He reached out, grabbing the deer pelt flap, feeling the fur glide through his fingers as he pushed it open and stepped in. A woman stood there, her raven hair down to her shoulders. Hawk looked up at her, but her face . . . it wouldn't form. He reached a hand out to touch the figure. The woman darkened, the world around growing dim, the memory fading away.

"Attention!" yelled a short herald in a yellow doublet at the front of the hall, snapping Hawk from his thoughts.

The man's voice reverberated over the stone walls, and the room went silent at once.

"King David, king of Alba . . ."

"Yes! Yes. Alright, thank you," the king said, cutting off the man.

King David moved from behind his high table toward the guests' benches. His blue-clothed shirt fit snugly around the royal's chest, but swayed prominently around his outstretched arms, giving an almost clerical appearance.

"Welcome, everyone. I hope you are enjoying the food."

Hawk spun on the bench, turning around so he faced the king. Relief flooded him, having been saved from Kenneth Olifard's small talk. Hawk watched the king as he spoke and noted the position of power King David held suited him well. The king spoke with grand words and even grander hand gestures.

A king should be a brilliant orator, Hawk thought.

Once, when Hawk ventured through Heinafylki, he met with the local lord on commission, Lord Albjorn the Bitter. The lord had hired Hawk and his companion, Garrett, to put an end to a lynx that had gained a taste for human children. After two days of tracking, the two huntsmen brought the grizzled feline before Lord Albjorn. The lord slumped on his throne and grunted approval, and a servant presented them with their fee. The huntsmen left without uttering a word to the Norse lord. "Some ruler," Garrett had mocked.

King David, however, was a magnificent storyteller indeed.

He spoke of the hunt, embellishing every detail. The crowd listened intently, gasping and awing at the appropriate times. To his crowd, King David had tracked and mastered the stag himself. Only Hawk knew the truth, that the king killed no stag that day. The king also neglected to mention the werewolf. Again, only Hawk knew the truth. It didn't matter to Hawk, so long as he got the promised information.

King David's speech approached a close. "I'm afraid I'll be enjoying the bounty of the beast all to myself in the castle. But, my good people, I assure you it is truly a sight to behold. To gaze upon the white beast is to gaze upon the heavens themselves. But do not take my word for it. Look upon the white stag for yourself. Let us raise our goblets and give thanks to the Lord God, Almighty."

A resounding amen ushered from the dinner guests. As if on cue, the main doors burst open. Four brutish men carried in a large platter adorned with the white head and antlers of the fallen stag. Hawk turned around to catch sight of the trophy once again.

The men paraded the hart's head around the room for all to bear witness to the creature's death. The stag's eyes, shriveled and shrunken, couldn't meet the guests' gaze as they reveled in the sight of its demise. Its tongue hung just outside the muzzle, dried and purple.

"My word, it's as white as snow," said Gerard, his mouth agape.

"I would not have believed it if you told me a hundred times," said Kenneth. "Ha! You may be a huntsman, Hawk, but the king has gotten himself the prize of eternity with that. You will never be able to top that one!"

Hawk feigned a smile, knowing the truth of the hunt.

"Eh, but nevertheless, before I had asked you, Huntsman, where are you from?"

"I traveled north from England at the start of spring, but I grew up near Heinafylki in the kingdom of Norway," Hawk finally managed.

"You don't look to me to be a Norseman," Gerard retorted.

"What does a Norseman even look like?" Hawk asked without effort—a response given countless times before when pressed on his appearance.

"Heh ha," coughed Kenneth in amusement. "You hear that, Gerard? Have you even seen one yourself? No? Well, I have, and they certainly weren't as bronze as you, Huntsman. Nor did they sound like you either."

Hawk's face fell. He certainly stood out in the crowd. He knew what questions followed, and he dreaded answering them again and again. But Hawk didn't expect what came next.

Kenneth leaned in closer to speak to the huntsman. "In truth, we should be thankful you haven't seen a Norseman recently. Dangerous folk, it would seem. I've heard talk of a raid on a village carried out by Norsemen right under the king's nose at Rosslyn."

Hawk's eyebrows climbed higher. He set his goblet on the table and turned to Kenneth attentively.

"Heh, I see by your interest, you've heard naught of this. Well, our gracious king has done his best to keep it hidden. But my friends in court tell me of a Norse raid on Rosslyn no more than three days past."

Hawk couldn't hold back his curiosity. "What happened? Where did they go?"

"Not much on details, I'm afraid. But they be Norsemen, sure as that. I think the king is embarrassed it happened on his lands and they escaped. He's trying to keep it hushed."

"A pox on it," spat Gerard, reaching to his left and taking the unfinished roll from his neighbor's plate.

He bit into it quickly before his actions garnered any notice. But Kenneth stared at his friend until the message, *Do not, under any circumstances, do that again*, grew evident.

Hawk paid them little attention and instead mulled over what Kenneth had revealed. Was there really a raid on a local village by a pack of Norsemen? Could it have been them? The ones he pursued? Hawk didn't wish to waste any more idle thoughts on the matter. He had to hear it directly from the one man in the hall who knew the truth.

"Many thanks for your company, my lords. Forgive me," Hawk said as he rose abruptly, stepping over the bench.

He made a straight line for the high table at the hall's front. King David caught his eye immediately as the huntsman approached.

"May I have a word, Your Grace? Of Rosslyn?" Hawk said, straining to be heard over the feast patrons.

The king's brow furrowed, then released its tension in a jovial smile.

"For you, Huntsman, of course. Come, I, too, need to talk."

The king stepped briskly from the stage and strode toward a dark oak door in the hall's rear. Hawk quickened his pace to catch up just before the door creaked shut.

The room, cramped in on all sides, housed only a desk and some small shelves. Light through a stained-glass window dominated the opposite wall, painting the room like a royal tapestry in a plethora of dim hues. The glass, in exuberant colors, depicted King David stopping the attacking white stag with a holy cross, a solemn angel overseeing them.

Although the hour grew late, the sun remained high enough in the sky to illuminate the stained glass. Candles weren't needed just yet.

The king went directly to the chair behind the desk and sat down. The huntsman stood at ease, folding his arms across his chest. He eyed the king, noticing the tension building in the king's face even when he wasn't under an audience's gaze. King David's brows furrowed as he stared through the huntsman's armored jacket, as though unfocused.

Finally, the king sighed loudly and raised his hands in an exaggerated shrug. "What kind of arsehole hosts a feast to celebrate a hunt but does not serve the venison at the feast? Only me, it seems. By God, I'll not eat the meat that wolf touched. I had the men burn it. The hide? Ripped to shreds. I'll barely make a small cloak from it, let alone the massive rug I desired. Do you know how priceless that rug could've been, Hawk? How can I sit here and eat when that, that monster is out there? How can you?" The king slumped in his chair like a child, not the ruler of a kingdom.

Hawk leaned against the wall, his tomahawks clanking in contact with the stony surface. "We agreed I'd leave first thing in the morning. I can't track it through the night. Do you remember how fast he moved? I'll not outrun a werewolf."

"Of course I bloody remember how fast he moved! It was, as you say, a werewolf, damn it. I'll remember that for the rest of my life." The king rubbed his temples. "When we first met, I asked you if you were a godly man, Huntsman."

"I've been baptized," Hawk said, repeating the words every lord and king wished to hear when they looked at him—when they only saw his otherness.

The truth was another matter.

"Good. God works in mysterious ways. This morning, I woke up with no notion of a thought for such monsters in this world. That—" the king scratched his crowned head

"—that werewolves were just fables. Tall tales to frighten children. Monsters may have existed long ago, but praise God, they were driven out not long after the Romans left."

"You've no notion of such creatures?"

"Stories exist, to be sure. But that's all they ever were—stories. Reports come of creatures still prominent, deep in the wilderness, but it's hard to distinguish folklore from fact. A man claims he's seen a beast in the forest. But they're peasants. How can we discover the truth? Those stories go on, passing into legends. But this isn't some deep wood. This isn't a lost cave of the Highlands. This is Edinburgh!"

"It won't head to the city, that I can assure you," Hawk said, brushing aside the king's ramblings. "With that wound, it'll seek shelter, in a cave or the woods, just as you assumed. Rest easy; I will find it."

The king pushed the chair back and stood facing the window.

The window mirrored King David's reflection, the face twisted in thought, arms resting on its hips, and his eyes piercing the stained-glass king.

"Tell me, Hawk, have you killed a werewolf before?" the king asked.

"Yes. I have."

"What? That's all?" the king said, his voice growing pricklier.

Hawk shrugged, unsure what the king was prodding. "As a huntsman, I've been asked to hunt all sorts of animals. It could be an alderman asking for an elk to feed a starving family. A wild boar, which having uprooted all the crops on a farm, must give itself back to feed the farmers. I've been asked to kill a bear that terrorized a village. But laymen could kill elk or boar, even a bear if they're lucky. Every so often, there are beasts that require a professional: a huntsman. A werewolf slaughtering horses on the outskirts of Hundorp. A draugr in Eystridalir, which, guarding its ancestral grave, decided the local villagers visiting their departed loved ones were a threat. A grindylow that grabbed six children before the duke considered hiring me. Yes, Your Grace. I have killed a werewolf. I've hunted many and more of its ilk that haunt your nightmares. I am a huntsman. It's my profession."

King David continued pondering his reflection in the colored glass. He removed the golden crown from his head and spun it around in his hand, inspecting each of the sapphires emblazoning its thorny points.

"Your Grace . . ." The huntsman hesitated, leaning back on the wall, his weapons clanking again. "You promised information for the stag. I fulfilled my end."

"That's right. The Norsemen raiders you seek. And now you want to ask me about Rosslyn? How did you come by information concerning Rosslyn? Well, I suppose you would've made the connections once news got out. Yes, my constable was made aware of the urgency of your request. And it just so happens that Norsemen raiders made landfall to pillage Rosslyn. Can you believe that? Mocking me right under my nose. They have since fled back to the sea, the cowards. But where to, you wonder? That answer would be hard to track by a huntsman like yourself. But you shall have what you desire from me, only if I have what I desire. Do you understand?" The king turned from the window and sat back in the chair with a sigh.

"Do I understand?" Hawk asked, stepping away from the wall. He walked up to the desk with his mouth ticked to one side. "I understand you're withholding what we agreed as payment. I want what I'm owed. I want that information. I won't let it slip away from me. Do I understand?"

"Yes, do you? You're talking to a king. Need I remind you? You surely saved my life in that forest, and for God's will, I shall forgive your tone. I promised you information for the white stag trophy. Instead, some foul creature tore and shredded my trophy. Sure, I received the head, but that's only half of the prize. So your task is only half done."

"Your Grace . . ." Hawk gritted his teeth.

The king's bitter expression warned Hawk that any argument would bite off more than he could chew. He needed to collect himself.

"The matters of arrangement have changed, as we already agreed in the woods. You agreed to undertake the hunting of the werewolf. The Norse have escaped, but my men have leads on where they went, Huntsman. Bring me the head of the werewolf, and you, too, shall know."

"That would suffice, bringing you the werewolf's head?"

"Indeed, a promise."

"Will you provide coin enough for my travels?"

"And some," the king said, parting his mouth to reveal a toothy grin as he slid his tongue along their surface.

"Thank you, Your Grace. I would leave now, but—" he knocked on the wood with his leather studded gloves "—I'm afraid I can't see in the dark, and night is approaching."

Just then, the door swung open. A man in a white doublet backed into the room, blissfully unaware of the place's current occupation. He had company, too. A fair-haired lass, dressed in the cloth of the king's servants, wrapped her arms around the man's neck. Their eyes were closed. Their lips intertwined. The door slammed shut, and the man swiftly pressed the girl against it.

Hawk looked toward the king, assessing his reaction. King David rubbed his bearded chin, scrutinizing the couple. Then his head bowed as his hand slid up to his forehead. The shrill of giggles and moans emanated from the new entrants. Hawk snorted.

The white-suited man kissed down the girl's neck, hoping, it would seem, to find his way further south. The girl checked her surroundings for a suitable location for lovemaking. Her eyes widened as she saw the king sitting at a desk, and a tall man in black armor, both with their eyes fixed on her. She slapped her partner on the shoulder.

"S-s-s-stop," she stammered.

The man, unaware of his current predicament, and no doubt eager to continue, went on downward.

She pushed him away. "Stop, I said."

"Whaddya mean? C'mon," he pleaded.

"No, please continue," the king jested sardonically. "By all means, barge in without looking and make love right here. Right here in the house of God. *My* house of God."

The king leaped up, the chair flying back against the windowsill.

"Get out! By God, get out of here!" the king shouted.

The two bowed apologetically and hurried out of the door back into the hall. The cacophony of music and chattering guests carried through the open door before it closed again. Then the room fell silent.

Hawk brushed a hand through his hair. He didn't want to break the silence and busied himself with studying the stained-glass window. The colors, less vibrant than before, gave the room a cobalt glow. Only then did Hawk notice that the sun had dipped behind Castle Rock. The room darkened, and the light faded softly.

Before either man spoke, the door whooshed open a second time. A knight strolled in, carrying a thick stench of sweat and horse.

"Your Grace," he breathed.

The knight wore plated armor, although he had no helmet. He fell to one knee and bowed his head.

This man reeks, thought Hawk, *and he's stretching that plate out.* Indeed, the plated knight bulged out of his armor's joints. The man's immensity flattened the regularly convex surface of the plate. *He probably got the chest plate when he was a young boy and has used it his whole life.* Hawk noticed the cloak, sky blue with the white cross. The man was a knight in the service of King David of Alba.

"Your Grace," the knight repeated, "a report has come in. I was patrolling the outer Grange when I came across a rider from the south." He paused again, allowing himself a moment to gather his words between breaths. "He claims a ravenous wolf prowls his lands and is preying on his sheep. Each morning they awake to more losses. It was Baron Sinclair, Your Grace."

"Sir Miller, what's happened?" the king ordered. "Did you run all the way here from the Blackford fort?"

"No, Your Grace. I rode my horse to the stables."

"Did the rider describe the wolf?" Hawk asked, cutting the monarch off before he scolded the unfit knight.

"Eh, no, my lord. They hadn't seen the wolf. But it cannot be more than one. The rider said there's no returns to its howls from the pack. It sounds like a stray to me, broken off from the others and hounding the baron at Rosslyn."

"Yes, a lone wolf ravaging the local sheep at Rosslyn. It sounds like you need a huntsman, Your Grace," Hawk finished, smirking at the king. Hawk reached over his shoulder and ran a finger down his tomahawk blade. "I know just the one."

The king made his way to the open door. "Guard!" he yelled.

A page, no more than sixteen, shuffled in.

"Your Grace?" he asked.

"This man requires the best horse in our stable for first light on the morrow," King David said, gesturing to the huntsman. "Give him whatever else he requires. Send in the constable. And when you're finished, report back. I have a message for Commander Cormac."

"Your Grace," Hawk said, nodding slightly in respect as he took his leave.

Before closing the door, Hawk looked back to see the knight, still on one knee, the king's eyes remaining fixed on Hawk.

CHAPTER THREE

He pushed the deerskin aside and stepped out of the wigwam onto the soft dirt. He wiggled his exposed toes, burying them into the dry, powdered soil. He stretched the muscles of his legs, arms, and back, bending backward and peering at the sky. The full moon glowed white-hot, ornamenting the black abyss. The stars flowed like embers from the moon, illuminating his surroundings.

A village of bark-covered huts formed a circle around a central fireplace. A young girl leaped out and surprised him—his big sister. She laughed, pushed him back, then darted away amongst the huts. A game of chase. His weaving through the village concluded with the giggling capture of the girl before she made her way to the fireplace.

He followed into the village's embrace. Fire twisted and turned, blazing in a dance to the booming drums of the villagers. Sparks cracked, shooting up and raining down as more fuel was thrown into the inferno.

The rhythm traveled through the ground. The drum's beat rushed through his toes, into his knees and hips, and on up. His body lost control. He stepped with the sound. He moved with ferocity. He jumped. He spun. He flowed in with his sister, family, and friends as they gave thanks for the coming of spring. He glided to the pulse of the song. Howling. Singing. Dancing.

They danced into the night. He danced until sweat gripped his flesh and his raven hair stuck to his back. He danced until his feet and limbs ached. He danced until he could no longer give thanks to the Creator.

He sat on a nearby log and faced the fire. The fire, too, had become tired, and its dancing ceased. He stared into the glowing orange embers. His mother sat down next to him, but he continued watching the glowing coals. He liked the way they shimmered, changing colors from orange to red to blue and back again. The flames enthralled him. She put an arm around his shoulder. Her touch was warm against his back, which had cooled in his own shadow. He could've stayed there, in that moment, forever.

His mother jerked backward, and a thin red mist covered his side. He sprang toward the fire in surprise, then glanced back at what had happened. A demon gripped the top of his mother's head, vibrating with a burst of deep throaty laughter.

A glistening suit of shiny rings, shimmering in the firelight, covered the demon. The same shiny material crested the demon's head. Its right eye glowed a ghastly pale while darkness shrouded its left. The only recognizable feature on the demon was the brown bear pelt resting on its shoulders. Its weapon was long and slender, but sharper than any arrow point or ax he'd ever seen. No rock could make that.

The weapon glowed liked the demon's skin in the fire, save for the red blood, which trickled down the point. It bellowed in a mysterious tongue. "After them!"

He scrambled backward, stepping on the coals and jumping in pain. He turned around and ran for the huts.

All around him, more demons sprung out of the darkness. They cackled and screamed as they fought, their shining shells rattling as they moved. Fire glowed and grew along the wigwams. It resumed dancing, but its dance was different. The fire, out of control, raged through the village. He stopped. The dancing flames trampled his village, burning down the wigwams.

A man sprung out in front of him, his uncle, a stone tomahawk glinting in his grip.

"*Kuhkuhqi qaqiq muhtuqash*—run up the trees." His uncle gestured to the darkened woods.

Turning back around, the boy's uncle looked over his shoulder. His pupils dilated even in the firelight, and he shoved the boy toward the woods, crying out like a warrior. The boy brushed the dirt off his knees and turned to see his uncle's stone meet a demon's armored metal plate. The rock shattered, unable to penetrate the demon's metal hide. The monster grasped the man with its talons and pierced him with the long, slender blade. Blood washed out over the man's wound. Blood dulled the demon's weapon's shine. Blood. Blood.

The boy couldn't move. Fear gripped hold of him. He stared at the carnage engulfing his home, his family. Chaos danced in the night, but he couldn't find this rhythm. The fire, the screaming, and the chaos were music unknown to him.

Something picked him up. He squirmed in its embrace. The talons seized him. The demon spun him around. The demon who cut his mother down breathed on him. But it was no demon. Up close, he could see it was a man. A pale man, but still a man. Brown hair grew out of his chin like a bull moose. The man's two different eyes filled him with terror. That one eye, pale as a full moon, bore into him.

The demon man flashed his fangs, and his grip grew tighter. The boy struggled. He looked at the man's armor. A canvas of dark blue and adorned with a golden, winged cat breathing fire covered it. The cat's eyes frightened the boy, and he looked back at the man. Tighter, the talons seemed to grip. The man's pale eye never left his gaze. Tighter, they gripped. Tighter.

CHAPTER FOUR

The sun's first light reached through the stable's square wooden window. It spread over the hay, caressing the golden grains and straw. It spread further over Hawk's black gambeson as he lay motionless. The light continued up to the huntsman's chest. It traversed his honey-colored skin and up his muscular neck. The light went on, emboldened, extending over the huntsman's chin to his eyes, his open brown eyes.

Hawk had barely slept, thanks to the terrible nightmares that shook him awake. Nightmares—or memories he hadn't thought of since becoming a huntsman—the same ones that frequented his sleep.

Hawk rolled off the straw pile, brushing off the flaky remnants of his makeshift bed that lingered on his black woolen trousers. The seeds and filings floated in the rays of sunlight. He stood in the light, absorbing and replenishing the heat that slipped away in the chilly night.

The page had spoken with him the night before. "The king has asked me to take you to the castle, Sir Knight. You're to have your own bed and hearth."

The huntsman, having spent most of his nights sleeping on the trail, had become unaccustomed to the luxury of a bed. He declined the offer, preferring to be beyond the walls. The royal livery's loft, piled with fresh summer straw, provided all needed amenities. The straw contoured and cushioned, while the stable roof sheltered him from rain. The horses, wary of any disturbance, would cry out, alerting him of any danger. But they couldn't warn Hawk of the danger of dreams.

Hawk dipped a finger into a pungent pine resin, oil, and wax concoction. He ran it through his hair, remembering his uncle's spiked roach headdress. Hawk then belted his thick buckskin kilt across his waist and ran a finger up and down the tanned surface. The tomahawks, resting in the hay pile next to where he slept, fit smoothly into the X-shaped sheathes on his back, the blades extending above his shoulders like two watchful guardians. He slipped on his studded onyx-colored gloves and descended the ladder to prepare his horse.

Hawk stepped out of the barn and into the bright, warm sunlight. He closed his eyes, pointing his nose directly at the sunlight, and smiled.

"Cursor, is it not? It isn't too often we get two sunny days together in this land," he told the horse, rubbing its burgundy muzzle.

It didn't answer but tossed the bit around in its mouth.

"I'll need you to be on guard today, Cursor. Sleep hasn't been kind to me. I don't feel as ready as I should before a hunt."

Hawk spoke the truth. He'd scarcely gotten a full night's rest in more than a month. It seemed the closer he got to the raiders, the more stressed his dreams became. He hoped his sleep was enough for the day.

The huntsman set off at a trot, leaving the stables, Holyrood Abbey, and the castle road behind him.

He passed the stone structures of Edinburgh's growing city, which would soon wake with the rising sun. Hawk passed empty market stands adorned with colorful bunting, a blacksmith's forge with coals cooled black, and a shop that must've sold baskets or pottery, judging by the painted shape plastered on its door. The buildings gave way to toft farmland. Sprawling fields of barley, wheat, and grass coated the hillsides. The grain, ready for harvest, glowed a ripe yellow. Only the speckling of serf houses, springing up like boats on a golden lake, broke the endless sea of fields.

The sun rose over the Seat in the east, the mountain's shadow shrinking by the minute. Hawk headed south toward Rosslyn and Baron Sinclair.

Less than a day's ride, I hear, Cursor, even through the woods, he thought. *There and back, and I'll be on my way.*

They rode on, cresting a small hill. A rider on a chestnut mare approached from the opposite direction. Hawk continued his pace, holding the reins in one hand, keeping the other free if needed. The approaching rider wore the same plated armor as a knight in service to King David. The knight had a closed-plated helmet, ornamented with a blue feather. The rider drew closer and raised a hand in greeting.

"Hail, my good man. That saddle. That steed. Do you come from the king's stables?" the knight asked, his voice metallic and hollow, ringing through the eye slits in his helmet.

Hawk cocked an eyebrow at the man for not raising his helmet to speak. A simple courtesy, yet this knight somehow forgot it. Hawk tamped down his annoyance, but only to not delay his trip any longer.

"I am indeed. You have a keen eye, Sir . . ."

"Sir William Maurice of Holyrood," replied the knight, puffing out his chest and placing an arm over his heart. "And you are?"

"Hawk. Huntsman."

"Where might you be taking the king's horse, Hawk the huntsman? And alone at that." A light breeze blew the knight's feather from one side to the other.

"King David required a huntsman. A baron has requested help with a wolf in nearby Rosslyn, as you've no doubt heard from your compatriots."

Hawk's mount stretched out his neck and, unfurling its

upper lip, tasted the air. Hawk shifted in his saddle, his annoyance at having to explain himself building. Hawk's stallion sniffed the back end of Sir William's mount. The mare stirred in agitation.

"Yes, indeed. I heard of this plight from Sir Miller's watch. Well, may luck be with you. I must continue my patrol," the knight said, seeming to recognize he was close to losing control of his horse.

Sir William clicked his heels and set off toward Edinburgh center. His mare leaped forward, eager to be out of reach of Hawk's stallion.

Hawk leaned forward in his saddle and stroked Cursor's neck, thankful for the help in ending the conversation. He trotted down the path, repeating to himself that he owed Cursor an extra ration of oats at Rosslyn. To avoid further delays, Hawk rode south past the Blackford fort, away from any more curious knights.

They trudged up a long, sloping hill. The barley gave way to green grasslands, and sheep flocked to the edges of their paddocks, away from the passing horse and rider. The two marched to the top of the hill, leaving a wake of hoof imprints in the grass, filling with the clinging morning dew. The hillside valley on the southern face spread for miles, covered in forest. A vast range of rolling hills reached across the horizon. Beyond, Hawk could barely make out the start of farmlands and Rosslyn. The ancient forest swallowed horse and rider as they traveled on toward their hunt.

They rode on through the trees and under the forest's canopy. Even with its protection, the sun and heat still weighed on the huntsman. Despite the abundant watery sweat building under his armor, his mouth continued to dry.

A magpie cawed from a low bent branch. Cursor stumbled for a moment and nickered a return. The sound made Hawk's hair bristle across his neck and arms.

"*Ciqunapuq*. Quiet, Cursor. It's only a bird," Hawk whispered, patting the horse's neck and urging it forward.

The magpie glared down from the branch as they passed, its eyes black and hollow.

They continued onward, the horse's hooves crunching the conifer needles on the ground. Cursor, a horse built for great speed on the road, required extra planning in his hoof placement. The horse and rider, cautious of tripping over the sprawling gnarled roots crawling out of the forest floor from beneath the trees, maneuvered carefully through the thick foliage.

At last, the huntsman came across a small stream. He dismounted, grabbed the reins, and walked the horse to the stony bank. After he released the reins, the horse took two more steps into the water before dipping its muzzle into the refreshing liquid.

Just like a king—withholding the Norsemen's whereabouts from me. Why did I deserve this punishment? I can't control werewolves or beasts. Hawk knelt at the edge of the stream and removed the cap of his canteen, submerging the clay bottle.

After soothing his throat with a swig of pure water, he closed his eyes and pondered the dream from the night before—his sister's dance. The rhythm of the babbling current flowing past the horse's legs, the trill of birds chirping overhead, and the nearby owl's hooting tones gave music to her dance. The stallion stamped, splashing the huntsman.

Perhaps I'll learn all I need to know in Rosslyn, and I'll have no need of the king. And if not, I'll simply find the werewolf and bring the king its head as promised. Hawk hesitated at the splashing, then plunged his hands into the water, washing his face. The stallion's black hooves continued to stamp and splash before the trampling dissipated into the forest behind him.

Hawk sprung up, water dripping down his puzzled face. He followed the fleeing horse for a moment before turning back to see what it had fled from. Across the brook, on the opposite bank, the bracken swayed. Black fur rose from the brush, encroaching on the river. A dark shape emerged from the undergrowth.

Is this the werewolf haunting the farmers? It'll be quicker to get its head to the king now. I don't even need to make it to Rosslyn.

Anticipation coursed through Hawk's veins as his eyes narrowed on the shape in the rustling bracken. It paused in the undergrowth, still hidden, waiting for the precise moment to spring.

The huntsman took a step back, splashing in the shallow depths of the river's edge. His legs were spaced shoulder-width apart, his posture lowered, ready to dive out of the way of the beast's lunging attack. The black tufts of fur moved closer to the edge of the ferns.

The snout emerged first, revealing the dark creature's intentions with an evil grin of sharp bared teeth. It moved, paws stepping lightly with its head lowered, toward the river's edge. The canine's yellow-green eyes, accentuated by the smooth black coat, glowed in the dim forest light. Its bushy tail whipped to the side as it fully left the thicket. The beast was no monster, however, but a normal, albeit substantial, wolf.

Hawk hesitated. It certainly looked threatening, but it couldn't be the monster he sought. He reached behind to grab his tomahawk. His hand didn't find the weapon. A force seized, twisted, and thrust his hand straight into his back. A knife appeared, as if from nowhere, and pressed under Hawk's chin with a cold, malicious embrace.

"Dinnae move," said a voice behind him, the words cold and calculated. "Ye were goin' tae kill my wolf, weren't ye?" the voice accused, pressing Hawk's hand further into his spine.

It was a woman's voice, a cunning voice. Hawk glanced at the pale arm holding the knife, then back at the wolf. He clenched his dangling left hand.

"I said dinnae move." The knife bit deeper, a twitch away from sticking Hawk's windpipe.

"Your wolf?" Hawk choked, the words sticking on the blade. The wolf crossed the river, growling low and inching closer to Hawk's boots.

"Looked tae me like ye were about tae put an ax through Tiree. That's nae very nice. Why should I nae let him finish ye here and now?"

The voice hooted like an owl, and Tiree's growl deepened into an open snarl. The wolf recoiled, ready to launch at the huntsman.

"I'm hunting a wolf, a big wolf, that's attacking the farms of Baron Sinclair. I thought your dog was a—"

She cut him off. "Sinclair? Ye're headed tae Rosslyn?"

"Yes. Baron Sinclair needs a wolf slain."

"They need help with a simple wolf? Why did they ask for ye?"

"Let me go and I'll explain," Hawk gritted through clenched teeth.

"Explain tae me why someone dressed as yerself is out in the wood alone. Ye dinnae look like yer from this land. Are ye a raider, strayed from the pack, eh?"

"No. I'm not a raider. I've already told you. Let me go and I'll explain."

The voice whistled, and the wolf relaxed, panting before drinking from the stream. Hawk spun away from the sound and, with his hands free, removed his two weapons in a flash. Tomahawks drawn, Hawk stared at a young woman.

"Calm down," she laughed, walking over to pet her furry companion.

Hawk stood, ready to strike. His heart pounded through his chest, surprised.

How could I let that happen? I let myself be distracted by the thought of finishing the hunt early. The nightmares from the night before had finally caught up with him. Hawk wouldn't drop his guard again.

The lass was wild. She tied her hair in a plait, with a waterfall of tangled dark waves flowing freely past her shoulders. A thick, black hide mantle covered those same shoulders. A green and blue tartan scarf wrapped around her waist and crawled over one shoulder, buckling securely across her chest. A skirt, matching the black hide of her mantle and trimmed with green and blue wool, swayed as she stepped back.

She cleaned the knife across her chest and holstered it back in her boot. Her tall boots showed the wear of hundreds of miles of marching. Hawk knew he stood before a warrior.

Only then did Hawk notice the recurve bow across her back. "That's not a simple hunting bow," he pointed out.

The warrior returned the observation with a mocking smile, acknowledging his astute deduction.

"Well, what's this about Clan Sinclair?" the warrior directed.

Hawk glared at her, allowing only a half-truth. "The baron needs help with a lone wolf attacking his sheep. I saw it yesterday hunting in the woods of Edinburgh. The king has commissioned me to bring down the beast," Hawk explained, still standing in the rushing stream.

He remained locked into position, tomahawks still out, unable to trust his former captor. She didn't seem to notice or care.

"A wolf, ye say? Did ye get a good look at it?"

"Pretty good. I know a wolf when I see one." He gestured at her companion.

"And the king hired ye? Who are ye?"

"Who are you?"

"Ha!" she chuckled, stepping out of the water and back onto the stony shore. "That's fair. I'll go first. I got the jump on ye."

Tiree left the water and shook, raining droplets all around him. The young woman mimicked her companion, swinging and shaking water free from her legs, one boot at a time.

"The name's Mòrag," she said, adjusting her boots.

"Hawk," he answered.

"Hawk?"

"Yes."

"Your name is Hawk?"

"Yes."

"Well, Hawk, it seems ye're in luck. I, too, am headed to Rosslyn. I'm nae much a fan of the southern clans like Sinclair, but I've heard a lot of rumors about Rosslyn—about yer wolf and the baron's woes. I mean tae ask a few questions and *help* as I can. Someone plundered Rosslyn. Norsemen from the talk. Hence, stopping ye. Ye dinnae dress like a man from Alba. I thought ye were one of them. Clearly naw. I think I could help ye and yer commission. Especially since yer headed in the wrong direction. Ye'll hit the hills soon, and they'll trap ye west of Rosslyn. It just so happens I ken where tae go. Now, ye can stand in the water all day, or we can go there together."

Mòrag walked over and grabbed a bag from behind an oak tree. She threw the bag over her shoulder and strode back to the water's edge. Her emerald eyes locked with his. Hawk stared back, trying to uncover any deception, trying to reveal any hint of malice. There was only stern determination.

"Well? Are ye coming?" she asked, a smile parting her expression.

The water seeped into Hawk's boots, soaking his toes. He wiggled his foot as he stood in thought.

Competition isn't necessary, Hawk thought. *I don't need the help, but two against a werewolf is better than one. Not to mention her presence would force the werewolf to split his attention. Besides, she knows about the raid on Rosslyn. She might help me get more information.*

And he had had enough of standing in the river.

"Fine," Hawk replied, sliding his axes onto his back. "But you better have something to eat in that bag. You scared away my supplies." He waded through the water and grabbed his canteen off the shore. He splashed his way back across to the other side of the stream. Not hearing her footsteps, he mocked, "Well? *Are you coming*?"

"Let's go, Tiree," she called. The wolf ran ahead of the huntsman and disappeared into the forest. Mòrag hopped from rock to rock, avoiding the water, and caught up to Hawk. "It's good that horse ran off. If it wasnae afraid of wolves, I would've taken it and left ye behind," she snorted.

Hawk didn't find it as funny. He trudged on ahead, his boots squelching out the last of the water with every step. Uneasiness rose inside Hawk with every one of those steps.

How could I let this happen? If it had not been for Cursor running away, I might be lying in that river. Cursor must be halfway to Edinburgh by now.

Hawk wanted to search for Cursor, but in the end, his desire to keep moving forward prevailed. To go back and search would cost him more time, time he couldn't spare. Instead, he brewed in silence as they walked, keeping occupied with careful glances over at the warrior, Mòrag.

The valley forest seemed ancient and untouched. Rocks, which hadn't moved since the melting of the last glaciers, lay strewn across the organic floor. Primordial wooden giants enveloped in green moss had fallen all around, frozen amidst the arduous process of melting into the earth. Through the leaves of the towering upright trees, the speckled blue of the sky shone. The sun hung directly overhead.

They continued in a reserved calm toward their destination. The wolf would periodically circle back to check on its master's position, panting all the while. Mòrag would run her hand through its thick black fur and scratch behind its ears before Tiree vanished into the bracken again.

They continued walking for some time. Hawk kept a cautious eye on the wolf that, only moments before, threatened him in the river. How could he focus on finding a werewolf if he had to keep one eye on the two travelers? Not to mention that the wolf's presence muddled any chance of tracking the monster. The prints in the dirt, the low canine panting in the distance, tufts of black fur scraped against the pine tree. Any of it could be Tiree or the werewolf. Meanwhile, Mòrag could be waiting to stab him in the back or set her companion on him. Hawk walked on warily.

I just need to finish the werewolf, gather what I can of the Norsemen in Rosslyn, and I'll escape from her, Hawk swore to himself.

The forest eventually opened into a small meadow of green

grass. Tiree's tail stuck out of the tall stalks. Hawk noted the wolf's head lowered to his paws. The huntsman took a second to sit on a stump and grab a drink from his canteen.

Mòrag left the woods and stopped at the wolf. She investigated what held his attention, then moved to stand next to the huntsman.

The heat of the day lingered in the meadow. Hawk delighted in the feeling of his hair standing off his head, spiked, bare, and cool. Both his companions wore thick dark manes. Sweat dripped from Mòrag's temple, and she wiped it away with her hand.

In Hawk's experience, female warriors often replaced the brute strength of men with a harsh, crass approach to life. He looked up at her, wondering if she truly knew the way to Rosslyn. He hoped she wasn't lying, but couldn't begrudge the truth she shared and what he realized during their silent travels. Alone, he might've walked in the wrong direction, extending his trip for hours while searching for the beast. They had at least avoided the hills she mentioned, the ones that would've led to his delay.

"We should keep moving," Hawk said, breaking their long silence.

"Gi'e us a minute," Mòrag said, unslinging the single leather strap of her woolen sack and setting it on the ground. Her hand rummaged blindly while her eyes shifted from the wolf to the meadow and then to Hawk.

Mòrag's face lit up. She removed a dried chunk of red meat from the bag and took a large bite, clenching her jaw to tear off a single piece. She offered the rest to Hawk.

"Here, payment for the horse," Mòrag bid.

Hawk examined the meat. It certainly looked better than the nothing in his possession, and stopping to hunt for dinner would only delay him even longer. He took the peace offering.

The huntsman gave a begrudging, "Thanks," and ripped off a chunk of his own. The beef slice was surprisingly rich, with a salty flavor of smoke. He munched on the stringy meat.

"Not bad," he mumbled between chews.

"Aye, and it'll last longer than bread," she added.

"You said you heard rumors of Rosslyn?" he finally asked her more about it.

"Aye, I heard some things on the outskirts west of Edinburgh. Norsemen raiders from the sea attacked Clan Sinclair. Naebody kent much else. So I headed this way."

"What else did the rumors say?" Hawk asked. "Where did the raiders go? What else did they tell you?"

"Nae much, I dinnae ken any of that," she replied.

He paused for a moment, still working the leathery meat in his mouth. "Your accent. How far north are you from?"

"Have you been up north?"

"No, I haven't."

"Then I'm just from up north," she jested. "What about ye? From a distance, I thought ye were a raider lost in the wood. That accent, then. Yer skin. Ye're nae from here either, I'd wager."

"Fair enough. I'm not."

"So where are ye from then?"

"I come from a land far away, west and across the sea."

"I have seen men from Ireland. They dinnae look like ye do."

"I'm not from Ireland," he corrected.

He took another bite of the dried meat, grinding down the salty fibers.

"Then where? The Isle of Ice?" she guessed.

"Further."

Hawk swallowed the remaining morsel. He watched as the wolf returned to meet his master. Tiree's tongue ran over his muzzle and cleaned off the red blood of a fresh kill.

"It would seem ye are well traveled," Mòrag declared, rubbing underneath the wolf's chin.

The young woman examined her gloves, newly painted with the crimson of fresh blood.

"He'll nae share," she laughed.

Tiree continued cleaning his muzzle. But his eyes lingered on the huntsman. Hawk met the wolf's gaze. An uneasy tension filled him. Hawk leaned back before his feet compelled him to stand from the stump, breaking the canine's stare.

"How did you two meet?" Hawk asked, cracking his back and stretching his arms.

"He was just a wee pup when my da found him alone in the snow. Our ewes fed him, and he picked up on training in nae time. Tiree is smarter than me. He watches my back, and I watch his. We're good like that."

"Do you always go around holding strangers at knifepoint in the woods?"

"Nae. Only stupid ones who stop tae get a drink alone with a perfectly good horse," she rebuffed. Then, with a sheepish grin, she added, "Sorry about that back there. Hey, if ye're a knight of the king's service, where is yer banner?"

"I'm no knight. I am a huntsman," Hawk replied, folding his arms across his chest.

"A huntsman?"

"A huntsman, yes."

"What's that mean? Are ye the only one allowed tae hunt around here?" she asked, scrunching her brow at him.

"No. I'm simply a man of the hunt. I travel from village to town to burgh, taking commissions on whatever needs hunting. Sometimes it's a few deer to feed a starving family. Sometimes it's a wolf attacking a shepherd's flock. I go where I please, and where I'm needed."

"And people pay ye for that?" she laughed. "Hunting?"

"The world is modernizing. A man used to do it all. Now, a farmer must choose where to spend his expertise: on crops or on sheep and cattle. He no longer needs to harvest for just his family, but the entire village, and cart his goods to the market. If he doesn't, the king's taxman will come and tan his hide.

"So the farmer doesn't have time to learn to track down a deer in the woods. Instead, he only can focus on his farm and livelihood." Hawk glanced from Mòrag to the wolf and back again. "And when the bear enters the village and starts eating the farmer's sons, the local magistrate knows that means less tax money for his future estates and fewer soldiers in his army. So that's a problem that needs dealing with by a professional immediately. I'm that professional, a huntsman. And you, what do you do?"

The young woman blinked at Hawk and wiped the sweat from her brow again. She pushed a brown lock of hair behind her shoulder and took a drink from her canteen.

"I dinnae have a profession. I'm just me," said Mòrag.

The wolf cocked his head toward the other side of the meadow. His ears flashed their pinnae in the same direction. *What caught Tiree's attention?* Without warning, the wolf ran off across the tall grass and vanished into the conifer trees beyond the clearing.

"We should go. Rosslyn's nae far now," Mòrag said, grabbing her bag and throwing it over her shoulder. She snuffled. Hawk did the same. A shepherd, having run out of fields to use over summer, had set his sheep to graze near the forest edge, the faint scent of sheep blowing in through the trees.

"Always trust your nose," Hawk said, and they set off toward the trees and the awaiting settlement.

CHAPTER FIVE

"So let me get this clear," Hawk clarified. "You first noticed the sheep disappearing about four weeks ago. There were six dead in three nights, was it? Then it vanished for a month's time, and now it's begun all over again, which is why you've sent for the king's help. Is that right? How many dead this time?"

"Err, this is the second sheep, sir. And two hounds. Poor ol' Bess. The bitch was to whelp in a fortnight, the devil take it," replied a well-dressed man.

Bronze buttons decorated his red-and-yellow doublet. The clean and barely worn fabric belied the man's actual occupation, however. He reached a calloused hand up and removed a canvas hat. He wiped a hand across his hairline, streaking a line of dirt along his forehead. The man had red, sunburnt skin and crisp lines radiating from the eyes. The aged wrinkles sprouted from a lifetime of labor.

Hawk and the gentleman sat at a wooden table in the Rosslyn farmhouse. Behind them, leaning against the opposite wall, stood Mòrag. Her face stretched hard and sullen as she studied the farmer.

The two had agreed that taking Tiree, a lone black wolf, onto the estate of a farmer seeking to kill such a beast, wouldn't be wise. Tiree had obediently remained at the edge of the forest.

"You haven't seen the wolf yourself, Baron Sinclair?" Hawk asked.

"No, sir. I have a wife and family, and I'll not stick my neck out to glimpse a ravenous wolf. I thought the bloody beast was gone. When it came back, I thought it would go again, same as before, and that my hounds were enough to drive it off. Though, apparently, they proved not.

"'Great,' I thought, 'just what we needed after this cursed week.' I made my farmhand, Thomas, stay out for a night. He's a bull of a man, mind you, and I've seen him swing a pitchfork. I thought, at the very least, he could sound the alarm. Come the morning, the bastard was asleep, and a ewe lay strewn about the field. This wolf is taunting me, I tell you."

"You believe it's one wolf and not the work of a pack?" pressed Hawk. "How are you sure if no one's seen it?"

"I've seen wolf packs before, sir. They howl, they bark, they devour the corpse at the scene. This wolf howls alone."

"Did anything about the attack seem strange to you?" Hawk asked, trying to piece the attacks and the werewolf together.

"Well, yes. How many lone wolves can take on two hounds? And don't get me started on the corpses," Sinclair scoffed. "Strewn about the field. Horrifying, I tell you. Horrifying. I threw the hounds and sheep from last night into the barn. I locked my family in the house. Customarily, I'd rally the village and kin, but well, you see, sir . . . It will be difficult to do anything of the sort after this week. I suppose a wolf pales to burned houses from the Norsemen's attack."

The baron looked at the ceiling, collecting himself. Hawk twitched involuntarily at the mention of the raid. It took all of Hawk's patience not to jump into questions about the raid.

Baron Sinclair continued, "But that's just it, Sir Knight. We need some order, some normalcy. I can't have a lone wolf destroying what's left of our food provisions. I can't have it, sir."

"I'm no 'sir.' I wasn't knighted, nor am I royalty. I am a huntsman commissioned by the king," Hawk corrected.

"Begging your pardon, sir . . . eh . . . my lord? I'm just glad you two huntsmen came so quickly," stammered Baron Sinclair.

"I'll have a look at the mess myself, if you don't mind, Baron." Hawk got up from the chair and made for the door.

"I'll show you to the barn myself, my lord."

"We have a few more questions," interrupted Mòrag, finally emerging from the shadowed wall.

"Y-yes, m'lady. Anything you'd like. Simply name it, and I'll endeavor to do what I can. I cannot spend another night knowing a wolf is terrorizing my lands," the baron pleaded.

Mòrag's emerald eyes glinted in the dim light, her face cold and hard as if carved from ice.

Mòrag speaking up surprised Hawk. He deliberately informed her he would lead the discussion. He listened cautiously as they moved toward the exit, uneasy about where the conversation may wander.

"Good. Let's go then," she said, opening the door and ushering the trio through.

Hawk stepped into the blue sky. Soft wisps of clouds appeared over the western horizon, dipped in the orange-and-purple paint of the setting sun. It had started its descent, but light remained in the summer day. The fields south of the farmhouse spread over a large set of round hills. All the way to the forest line, the pasture held a bright-green array of thick-seeded grass. The green tips of readied hay surrounded a patch of tilled vegetable gardens. Paths wove through a congregation of wooden huts a large stone chapel watched over. The chapel towered as the highest pillar in the area, standing completely untarnished. The remaining village structures bore the charred scars of a fiery battle. Blackened timbers jetted haphazardly into demolished piles where the homes of villagers once stood.

"How many days since the Norsemen came?" Hawk asked before Mòrag could get a question in.

"Three nights since and we are still picking up the pieces. They torched nine houses, took our granary stores, then torched the granary too. Lucky for us, the harvest is a few months away and stores were low. Not everyone was so lucky."

"How many killed?"

The baron coughed. "Only two, thank the Almighty. Brave souls, they were, took two of the bastards with them. It all happened so quick, I tell you. Some villagers made for the woods. Most hid in the chapel. But God protected them. By God, they did not touch the chapel. Too afraid of his wrath, no doubt."

"What else can you tell us?" Hawk continued, yearning to hear more.

He was so close, nearly salivating like a dog to a bone.

The baron, however, said nothing.

Hawk glanced back across the farmland. The sheep, no doubt frightened by the recent bouts of a brutal predator, huddled together in the pasture's corner. Baron Sinclair led the two down a dirt path toward an oak-timbered barn just before the village. Hawk's patience thinned at the lack of a response, but just before he repeated his inquiry, the baron finally spoke.

"Look at them," the baron said. "Terrified, they are. I haven't seen sheep so worked up in almost a decade, and I've been farming here my entire life. Some folk comes in, and they hear 'Baron' and think I'm some high-and-mighty lord. Could not be further from the truth." The baron stopped, halting their procession, and turned to face Hawk. "That was my father's way, and everyone hated him for it. I grew up watching the village spit at him behind his back. So I vowed to never be like him. I vowed to work harder than anyone else in these fields. I put my life into this estate. My people were attacked. Those sheep are family. Something is attacking my family. I must bring a stop to this. My people need stability—peace, not more terror. First, take care of the wolf, then ask me about that day." Baron Sinclair continued toward the barn.

Hawk closed his eyes and rubbed his hand through his spiked

hair. He thought of a hundred protests. He wanted to coerce every drop of information about the Norsemen from the baron, like a wrung-out shirt after the rain. But Hawk realized the baron spoke the truth. He should focus on the task ahead, finish the king's demand. Then he'd have plenty of time to ask about the Norse raiders and get back to the king for everything else.

The huntsman looked at Mòrag, and she raised a bemused eyebrow. She brushed her hair aside and trudged ahead of Hawk. The black hide of her mantle and the tartan wool cloth covered her back completely.

Hawk studied the ornamental designs etched into the bow strapped across her back. Celtic carvings adorned the yew wood end to end. Green-and-blue twine wrapped between the etchings of the bow. The sinew bowstring was pristine, save the middle portion where arrows gained their flight. How many would've found him before by the brook if Cursor hadn't fled?

Or should I ask how many it will take to bring down the monster? She could bark, yes, but can she bite?

They reached the plain wooden barn near the edge of the village. It, too, had survived the raid. Coarse yellow straw festooned the muddied entranceway. The pungent odor of necrotizing flesh wafted from inside the barn. No doubt the decay hastened from the heat of the summer's day.

The baron gestured toward the entrance, shaking his head. "I'll not see it again. There. The corpses are there. I hope to God they're the last."

"Thank you, Baron." Hawk grimaced. "We'll look. Oh, and remember—"

"Yes, yes, I'm going now. I shall tell the villagers to stay inside for the night. I'm aware. As if they needed reminding." The well-dressed man turned and headed down the path.

"I thought you had questions?" Hawk said to Mòrag, noticing she had remained silent on the walk.

"Ye asked too many. I didnae have a chance. Ye heard him. Now I want tae see what's in the barn."

Mòrag entered the barn, and Hawk followed. The smell led them. Hay had occupied each stall, save one. They walked to the last stall and opened the gate to find three piles of animals.

Hawk crouched at the first. A hound, it seemed, or rather what remained of one. Deep claw marks lacerated the neck and muzzle. It had fought its attacker head-on and lost. They had spread the rest of the dog in small sections of undesirable waste. Hawk examined the length and depth of the scars. They looked of equal size to the white stag's.

"The hounds stood their ground but were no doubt outmatched," Hawk said.

"The sheep's overgrown hooves and muddy front legs mean this lassie could barely walk. She had nae chance," added Mòrag, tossing a leg back onto the heap.

"One victim can't run, and the others stood and fought." Hawk nodded at the two dogs. "Prey without a chase. It makes sense. It's why the farmhand, Thomas, wasn't attacked. The beast was injured. I threw a blade into his collar."

"Did ye, aye?" Mòrag asked, amused.

She moved to examine the dogs.

"His recovery will keep him from traveling," Hawk went on. "He'll still be nearby, and he'll strike again. Tonight. This, I am sure. Set the trap, wait for darkness, and spring out when he reveals himself. Plan?"

Hawk looked at Mòrag for a reply and noticed her attention focused on the dog's lacerations. Mòrag bent down for a closer check.

"Tiree has a big bite. I've seen what he can do. But nae wolf could make a mark that big. Ye said ye saw it; ye hit it? Were yer eyes deceiving ye, or was it actually a bear?"

"It was indeed a wolf, but nothing like yours." Hawk's excitement of the hunt bubbled over. "It's a werewolf, and a grisly one at that," he explained, pointing to the marks on the hound.

"A werewolf? But . . . that's impossible . . . Are ye certain? Ye saw it?"

"I hit it."

"How?" she asked.

"I threw it end over end and—"

"Naw. How is there a werewolf? Here? Werewolves havnae been around for hundreds of years. They vanished with all the other beasts when magic left the land. They dinnae exist. Ye must be daft."

"What do you mean? I've seen plenty in my life," the huntsman said in astonishment.

"In Alba? I doubt it." She furrowed her brow, now a soft violet hue in the fading light. "They're just in stories, ye ken, like the ones my da told me of the past."

"Well, it doesn't matter. I swear to you, this one is indeed real. As you've never faced such a beast, I suggest you find the baron, stay put for the time. I'll find you when—"

"I'm coming with ye."

"I'll hunt better alone. You clearly don't know what you're dealing with," Hawk said, knowing she could just as easily be a distraction on the hunt. A liability.

"I'm coming with ye," Mòrag repeated, standing up and out of the dimming sunlight. For a moment, they stood and stared at one another, neither flinching. But Hawk knew the truth. Time grew short, and they still needed to prepare. Hawk caved in.

"Come, the sun is setting, and we must hide before he returns."

———

The orange light of the evening faded from the horizon. Hawk and the warrior sat with their backs against two large conifer trees at the edge of the pasture. He looked out over the field at the huddled woolen sheep, watching as the white disc of the full moon dominated the night sky. Clouds covered the stars in patches, both large and small. Their twinkling lights, like tiny freckles, flickered in and out of existence on a dark, distant complexion. The atmosphere glowed a midnight blue.

Hawk enjoyed the wait before the hunt. The thought of it sent icy spikes of anticipation down his arms to his fingertips. Long ago, his mentor told him to occupy that feeling with the weight of his weapon, and to stay ready. The huntsman spun his obsidian knife between his hands.

Hawk glanced at his companions as they, too, stared over the field. Mòrag laid her bow across her lap while Tiree sat next to her. She stroked the scruff of his neck. His eyes glowed a fierce, reflective green in the pale moonlight.

Tiree stood and stepped forward. He extended his entire body, lifting his head skyward. His ears flattened, and he let out a melodious, orchestral howl, which carried over the hills. Mòrag grabbed him and tried pulling him down, stopping the song abruptly.

"Tiree, ye bastard," she growled. "Pity's sake."

Hawk, coursing with adrenaline, had jumped up at Tiree's first motion and stared into the forest behind them. Across the pasture, beyond the line of trees at the edge of the farm, a harsh howl replied.

Mòrag released Tiree and grabbed the bow off her lap. She rose, looking toward the sound. Tiree walked a few paces. He lowered his stance, body homed in one direction. Hawk stepped behind him and followed the wolf's sightline.

A black figure shambled out of the woods and across the grass. It walked upright, stumbling before it fell on all fours and galloped. It didn't head for the sheep, but undeniably toward the calling challenger. Hawk slid the black blade into his belt and sighed at the changing plan.

Once, in Sunnmærafylki, on the western coast of the kingdom of Norway, Hawk spent a fortnight hunting a werewolf with Garrett. The werewolf had turned its taste to fat pigs. The local lord had quickly hired two experienced huntsmen, but seemed slightly more hesitant to allow them to use his large boar as bait. Garrett planned to tie the boar to a fence post on the edge of the woods and restrict its movement. The distressed pig would scream and call out, "Dinner is served," to the werewolf. It had worked flawlessly. The werewolf, though full from a previous night's dinner, wouldn't pass up the opportunity for an easy feast. It strolled out of the woods, straight to the crying pig. Before the beast could take a bite, the huntsmen launched their surprise attack.

Hawk, hoping to use a similar tactic, had haltered a growing lamb to a stake in the field. He hoped that when the monster showed, the flock would flee, and the lamb would be the obvious bait. Then, while the monster stood distracted, Mòrag and Hawk would spring out and overwhelm the beast. More than likely, it wouldn't touch the lamb, no innocent blood spilled. But hope could only get you so far.

Hawk hadn't expected Tiree. They set the challenge, but the surprise was on Hawk. He pulled the tomahawks from behind his back and swung them out, relaxing into their perfectly weighted balance and sleek blades. The black figure galloped closer. Hawk ran to meet it.

It's weak in the shoulder. Focus on the shoulder. Hawk fixed his eyes on the approaching creature. It dipped out of sight between the two hills. The huntsman increased his speed into the fight. The sheep, sensing the impending battle from all the commotion, flocked together. As one, they moved as far away as possible, all except for a single lamb. It remained bleating at its post alone.

The black figure emerged from the crest of the hill, close enough to reveal its wolven shape. Hawk slowed, his run becoming carefully calculated strides. A hiss passed over his right shoulder. Meticulous steps brought him into a honed hunter's rhythm, preparing his attack. Another hiss flew past his ear. An arrow from Mòrag, he assumed. She must've followed behind, soundless.

The beast bellowed and, rearing upright, halted its momentum. Hawk took the advantage. He sprinted forward. The werewolf spread out its arms to meet its attacker. The huntsman pressed on, about to crash into the monster's middle, when he dropped to his knees and slid on the lush grass. He swiped the tomahawks into his foe, slashing at its thighs and skidding between the beast's legs. He launched off the ground, spun 180 degrees, and landed on his back foot.

The monster cried out and spun to meet Hawk. In the moonlight, the huntsman noted the white fletching of an arrow in the beast's chest. Blood spurted from its legs.

The beast roared in fury and swiped its hands across its chest, snapping the arrow in two. It lunged at Hawk. The huntsman dodged the massive swiping paw and reset his position. A heartbeat later, the werewolf leaped off its hind limbs toward him. Hawk ducked, rolling out of the line of its charge. He scrambled up and steadied himself, carefully waiting for the right moment to counter.

The two stood face-to-face in a pivoting standoff. They walked around an invisible circle. Hawk stepped carefully, eyes locked on his prize. Left foot, then his right. It would soon be over. Blood dripped from the werewolf's thighs. Left foot, then right. Just where Hawk wanted the beast. Left and then . . . in an instant, he was falling. Foot caught in a rabbit hole, Hawk slammed to the ground, breath whooshing out a curse as he dropped one tomahawk. It flipped out of reach.

The werewolf didn't hesitate.

Twisting away from the ground, Hawk looked into glowing eyes. The werewolf let out a tremendous bark, revealing its fanged maw and salivating over its fallen prey. The creature's breath, stinking of rotten meat, huffed into his face. It dug its talons into the chain-mailed pads of Hawk's shoulder.

A shadow flew over Hawk's hair. It struck the werewolf in the torso, knocking it over in a tangle of fur and gnarled growls. The roaring, biting, and gnashing spared Hawk a moment to return to his feet. Tiree had jumped into the fray, but broke away from the beast quickly. Having gotten his bites in against his challenger, the wolf knew to step back when outmatched.

The monster shook. It stumbled, clutching its neck. It released a murderous snarl, thrashing about in the grass. Finally, it picked itself up and faced its new enemy. Tiree crouched low and growled, his glowing green eyes fixed on the bigger creature. Tiree retreated slowly as the monster approached.

Hawk, sensing an opportunity, sprinted toward the distracted foe. An arrow thunked into the beast's side a moment before he jumped onto the werewolf's back. Clutching the beast's fur like the mane of a horse, Hawk plunged his tomahawk into the creature's spine with his free hand and kicked the monster off. The huntsman crashed into the ground. Blood spurted, spraying the grass and Hawk's arm while the werewolf whimpered and fumbled at its back for the deep, embedded pain.

Thwack! A bow loosed an arrow into the beast. *Thwack!* Again, an arrow found its home in the beast's flesh, driving it off balance. Mòrag appeared out of the darkness, walking closer with her bow trained on her bleeding foe.

Hawk removed the knife from his belt. The werewolf staggered, still reaching for the unknown vice in its vertebrae. Without hesitating, the huntsman executed a swift pirouette and staked the black blade into the monster's heart. Blood oozed out from the gash. With a great quiver, the werewolf cried a final, desperate, and expiring howl.

Mòrag notched two arrows at once and, with a grunt, fired them into her target. Hawk licked his lips and, tasting sweat and blood, spat to the side. He reached for the tomahawk, wrenching it back and forth to dislodge it from the werewolf's flesh. The huntsman quickly hacked it into the underside of the creature's neck. The beast never stirred again.

"Ye were in my way!" Mòrag shouted, walking closer. "I could've brought him down from the edge of the woods if ye wasnae in my line of sight." She whistled and approached. Hawk glared at her, then turned to the sound of panting.

"Is he okay?" Hawk gasped, still catching his breath. Mòrag bent down, removed her gloves, and rubbed her hands quickly through Tiree's coat. Blood dripped from the wolf's muzzle but not Mòrag's hands.

"Ach, no blood from him. He'll be all right. He saved ye," she said, elated. "Right, boy?"

Hawk pulled the ax from the werewolf's neck and chopped off its head. The head rolled down to the ground, its once fiery eyes finally extinguished.

The huntsman dropped to one knee beside the fallen beast. He removed a small leather pouch from his belt and pulled out the dried leaves held inside. As his father had taught him over half a lifetime ago, he crumpled and sprinkled the dried leaves over the carcass.

"*Manto wikuw,*" Hawk whispered to no one and everyone.

"What's that? Ye praying?"

"Thanking. Thanking the Creator. And you for your help," Hawk said, putting his pouch away and offering his hand.

She reached out her ungloved hand and returned the grasp. "Are ye kidding? That was once in a lifetime!"

"Were it so easy."

Hawk had lost count of how many werewolves he had faced but still shared her excitement. He wrapped his hand around the gnarled fur of the severed head and snatched it off the soil. His shoulders strained as he held it outstretched to Mòrag, blood trickling from the neck.

"Come," Hawk said, "let's take this to the baron."

"Aye. I cannae believe it. Tae think, I've nae actually believed the stories. A real live werewolf. Do ye ken what this means?"

"What?"

"Magic has *returned*. The monsters of this land disappeared hundreds of years ago. When the kings of Alba conquered the Cruithnich, the Pechts, magic withered away with them. The Lady of Caledonia vanished and so, too, did the werewolves and all other sorts of creatures in this world."

Hawk had heard a similar sentiment from King David, that monsters were just fables from long ago. Hawk had lived most of his life in the kingdom of Norway, and they were very real to him. He never imagined a world where they didn't exist.

"That can't be right. As I already said, I've seen plenty of them in my life."

"Maybe where *yer* from. Maybe the continent. But, nae here, nae these lands. Unless . . . the Lady of Caledonia has returned . . ." she trailed off, staring at the head.

"Well, come on," Hawk managed, tiring of standing in the dark, "Magic or no magic, here's one now. Come, let's go to the baron."

"Aye. Let me talk tae the baron, eh?"

"Why?"

"I didnae get a chance before. Ye'll see, just . . . Just trust me. Please."

She hadn't seemed like one to plead. He eyed her, curious, and nodded. They set off. The lamb, still tied to the post in the middle of the field, cried out once more under the moonlight.

CHAPTER SIX

"My God, it's monstrous," cried Baron Sinclair. "It's positively monstrous."

The head of the werewolf rested on the wooden table as a grisly centerpiece, its jaws propped open with an arrow from Mòrag's quiver. Congealed blood gleamed in the fireplace's flickering light.

"This was what waited in the woods?" the baron marveled, prodding at the trophy with a dull knife. "Here, above the Rosslyn Glen? You mean right under our noses this entire time? And to think, I scolded Thomas's arse from the hay to his hearth for sleeping that night. By God, that's the first time I've heard of laziness saving a life. HA! Torpidity. Thank the Almighty. You hear that, Ida? Tomorrow we bake that boy a pie he'll never forget. Oh yes, a bloody good pie. God, that head is massive. What did you do with the body?"

"It's lying where it fell," Mòrag answered. "Ye should burn it. One less corpse for ye tae deal with." She sat at the table next to Hawk.

Hawk looked at Baron Sinclair and his wife, Ida, who slumped like she hadn't slept in weeks. The baron remained persistently bright, still dressed in his red doublet.

"Yes, good," he said with a nod. "Burn it, the cursed creature. Thank you, sirs. Erm, that is to say, my good huntsmen." The baron leaned back in his chair when he lit up with an idea. "Have a drink, the both of you. Ida, *uisge-beatha*. The whiskey . . . By the shelf . . . Damn it, woman. Not that one, the one on the right. On the right! Yes, finally, and the mugs, eh, please, Ida."

"Thanks," Hawk said as he grasped the fresh mug from Ida.

The malty aroma wafted from the glass as he took a sip. Hawk enjoyed the warmth of the taste spreading through his mouth, down to his belly. He watched, amused, as Mòrag took down the entire glass in one gulp. The baron, not as amused by the rapidity with which the girl drank, turned to Hawk.

"Eh, so, your reward, then. We haven't much silver. But Edinburgh's markets grow every day. We shall manage somehow. What'll it be?" the baron asked.

Hawk lifted his mug for another sip, and it was Mòrag who responded, "We dinnae come looking for any silver. We're looking for answers."

Hawk's eyebrows raised subtly, and he reflexively took another sip.

"Answers? To what questions?" the baron asked.

"The raid," Hawk blurted before Mòrag could respond. "Tell us about the raid. What happened? What were they after? Do you know who they were or where they headed?"

"I'd rather forget it."

"I know, my good man, but I promise you, it is important to us," Hawk said. "Please, help us understand what happened."

The baron sighed, his eyes darting side to side as if looking for a safe place to land amongst the terrifying memories. His voice was quiet as he began.

"They came upon us at first light, the Norsemen. Twenty or so, I'd wager. I had just finished my morning water near the glen's edge when I heard the shouting. At first, I thought it was one of the Gowens—big lads, strong in the field, and love to have a bit of fun, you know. Then I remembered the Gowen lads left with most of the able men a fortnight back. Of course, you must know of when King David called for men to serve in his army. I'm glad we sent them, or more might've died had they challenged the bastards through the village. I knew something was amiss when I heard a woman let out a long scream—Alice, I think. The kind of scream you never unhear, you know?"

The baron paused, taking a long swallow of whiskey. Hawk sat silent, not wishing to disturb the baron's tale.

"I rushed in, yelling for everyone to flee. Most ran for the trees or rushed into the church to pray. The raiders were running, snarling about like rabid dogs, I tell you, but soon realized there weren't any resistance. They began raising their shields, hooting and hollering. Never could speak Norse, the devilish tongue, but I know it when I hear it. 'Take what you need,' I pleaded with them. 'Take what you need and leave us be.' Well, it weren't long 'fore I realized they had surrounded me.

"One of them, a big brute, stepped forward. The leader, I suppose, I don't know. 'Food,' he says to me. Well, what was I to do? I pointed to the granary. He just laughed and pointed back at the church. 'Go. Pray,' he croaked. And so I did. But I'll tell you something, my good huntsmen, I've never been more afraid in my entire life. If only you'd seen his eyes. He had a dark squint to one, yes, but the other bore the color of snow or a cloud high in the blue sky. I shan't forget the sight of it, staring at me."

Hawk's mug clanked onto the table, and he slid to the edge of his seat. The baron continued.

"The way they chanted his name as I fled, 'Blow-Vice! Blow-Vice!' I thought it would be the end of me."

"What did you say?" Hawk rasped.

"I thought it would be the end of me. Luckily, it was not to be. They made off with a wagonload of our stored grain and a few items left in the dugout—"

"No," Hawk cut him off. "I mean the name they chanted. What was it you said?"

"Eh, 'BLOW-VICE,' " the baron said, louder, over-enunci-ating each syllable.

"Blåveis . . ." Hawk swallowed.

"Yes, yes, that's it."

"And those shields the raiders carried, the ones they held up, were they painted blue then, with a golden-winged lion?"

"Yes, that's right," replied the baron in tempered astonish-ment. "They did. To a man, they did. You know of them, eh, Huntsman?"

"Oh, I know of them. Your man Blåveis leads a Norse band from Tønsberg. They're raiders, pillagers, and worse."

Hawk paused, gritting his teeth at the memory of his mother's blood misting across his face. Warm and terrible. He took a moment to gather himself and continued, "They attacked in the morning, you say? Most likely, they meant to hide their travel inland from the sea under the cover of night, to slip in undetected so close to the castle. They're cunning. I traveled to Britannia on good word they'd come west to this land. That word, it seems, rang true." Hawk ran a hand through his spiked hair before asking, "Baron Sinclair, do you know where Blåveis and his men headed? Where were they going next?"

"Have you lost your senses? Do you think I stopped them for a chat? Asked them where they were off to, so I may send a letter of gratitude?"

"Well, no, I just thought—"

"No," the baron sighed, "I don't know where they went. They left as quick as they came, thank the Almighty. No doubt you're right: they were afraid of prowling so close to the castle and the king's men if they lingered too long. They stole the grain, a few horses, and what was left of the armory stores and set fire as they ran."

"The armory stores?" Mòrag interjected.

"Yes. Swords and shields for Rosslyn's defense," replied the baron. "What was left of it, anyway, after the lads went to help King David."

"I've been searching for a sword," Mòrag said.

"Well, hmm. I think, just now, swords are running low, m'lady."

"I'm nae looking for just any sword," Mòrag continued, looking into the tankard and placing it on the table, "The sword I'm after has a black leather hilt with a sapphire pommel. Inscribed on the blade is *Adharc bàis an tairbh*. Ye *ken* the sword I speak of."

So there was a reason for Mòrag to come to Rosslyn after all. Hawk smiled into his tankard.

"Well, no, I'm afraid I don't know of that sword. And I assure you there are no swords here with any inscriptions, sapphire pommels, or anything colorful of that nature. I'd sooner inscribe my shepherd's cane than waste the effort on steel. What makes you think I know of this sword?"

"My da's ancestors forged that sword for the sons and daughters of Clan MacTarbh. When King Alaxandair the Fierce asked for men to go south to the lands of Hawick, my da brought the sword with him. 'Smooth the transition of the prince of Cumbria,' they said. The battle was quick, but a knife found my da's gut, and he lost a great deal of blood. He lost consciousness too. He awoke in Edinburgh after almost a week had passed. The sword wasnae with him. Try as he might, naebody had seen it."

The baron grimaced and stood. He walked over to the hearth and warmed his back by the fire.

"I still don't see why you think I have it. I remember hearing of that campaign. But I wasn't at that battle. Nor were any of my sons."

Hawk listened attentively, forgetting his habit of fidgeting with the obsidian knife. The atmosphere in the room grew tighter.

"Well, it took some asking," Mòrag continued, "but I tracked the sword tae the mormaer of Menteith. The mormaer led the campaign south and found the sword on the battlefield. He brought it home on his return. Aye, Baron Sinclair, I do mean that mormaer. The same mormaer who yer son, Joseph, squired. He's returned home and brought with him this same sword. I ken he has it, 'cause he couldnae stop shite boasting about it in Falkirk. Everyone kens about the sword at the Fox Head Inn. He chopped the inn's signpost in two, from what I hear. I ken it followed him home. Where's Joseph?"

Mòrag stood behind Hawk and crossed her arms. Hawk shifted his feet beneath the table. He freed his hands, readying them. Rarely, in the huntsman's experience, did a person of nobility shrug off a threat easily. Hawk didn't know if he should help Mòrag or protect the baron. He braced for the baron's reply.

"The sins of the son now pass to the father?" the baron asked. "What a day. You know something? You're the second person who has come looking for Joseph today. The little shit. The scoundrel." He finished his drink. "My first two children were both lasses. Fine and beautiful daughters, they were. All the while, I prayed on my knees to God. 'Please, oh righteous God, bless me with a son.' For a son, I prayed. A son that would know the land and soil. A son that would love the steel of the scythe more than the steel of war. A son like his father. Instead, I get Joseph. He's spent his entire life expecting the name of Clan Sinclair, a baron's son, to bail him out. I'm sorry, my good huntsmen. I know you won't find Joseph here. He left, along with my second son, Edward, and most of the sons of Rosslyn. King David has called upon them for 'urgent need.' They left, as I have said, for Edinburgh. Ida, the cups are empty."

Hawk relaxed, lifting his mug, and politely let out a, "Thanks."

"Now that I think on it," the baron mused, scratching his chin, "he told me on his parting he was leaving his 'squire gifts' in the armory. Afraid they'd be stolen in the army camp. Two guesses where those gifts are now. Cursed irony."

"Stolen then, by the Norsemen?" Mòrag asked.

The baron nodded. Mòrag leaned her face up to the ceiling and ran a hand through her hair. She let out a long, heavy groan.

Only then did Hawk notice the day grew longer than he had expected.

"Baron Sinclair, who was the first person to ask about Joseph?" Hawk asked, taking over for a frustrated Mòrag.

"A lady from the Stirling court. Lady Phillipa, something or other. She had not mentioned a sword but said she had a message from the mormaer of Menteith. It's the only reason I know you must be speaking truly. I told her what I told you. He's not here."

The baron adjusted the top buttons of his doublet. He took his tankard from his wife and washed his drying throat.

"The lady is staying at the chapel in the village. I'll take you to her in the morning."

Hawk finished his drink, nodded to Ida, and stood next to Mòrag. His eyes found hers. She blinked forcefully, a pattern similar to when his frustration boiled over. He placed a hand on the black pelt on her shoulder. She didn't move. Hawk, not wanting the tension in the room to get out of control again, spoke once more.

"I think my friend would like to have a word with this lady now, if you don't mind. I don't believe either of us will sleep until we do."

"Err, right. Of course. Of course. As you wish. It's the least I can do for you helping me with that," the baron remarked, pointing to the decapitated centerpiece. "Grab your linens and come with me if you insist. Ida, please, go. Get some sleep. I'm just going to run them over and then I'll return."

They stepped into the brisk, dark night and headed for the village. Hawk looked across the field. He wondered if he could spot Tiree's glowing eyes, but the clouds had overtaken the light of the moon, leaving nothing else seen.

Blåveis came through here not three days past. So close, yet always trailing behind them. The king better make good on his promise of telling me where the Norsemen went. Hawk had done his part; it was only a matter of time.

Mòrag huffed. Hawk noticed she walked like a weight she

ignored earlier in the day now fell upon her. He wanted to pry. He wanted to ask her why she'd kept the sword a secret and why she hadn't mentioned it before the hunt. Hawk wanted to, but no one spoke on the way to the village.

The chapel, composed of rough chiseled granite stone and mortar, sat small, almost modest. A sconce holding a lit torch at the front façade of the chapel formed the base of a looming spire protruding unusually high for such a compact convent, or so Hawk thought. The brass bell at the top, barely visible in the baron's torchlight, flickered like a tallow candle in the dead of night, drawing Hawk's eyes.

The baron knocked once on the door, and the three of them entered. The chapel was a plain square. Stone walls gilded with a simple white paint dressed each side. A cross hung at the center of the back wall. Its shadow stretched across the chapel's walls. Blankets littered the corners of the room. Dirt and ashen-covered refugees occupied the woolen sheets. All appeared asleep, too exhausted to notice any disturbance, save one.

A woman sat at a dark oak desk in the room's corner. She faced the wall where the cross hung and didn't turn around.

"My lady? You're up at this hour?" the baron whispered from across the room.

"Tell me, how is one supposed to sleep in this village with all the howling outside?" asked the lady at the desk.

She stood, sliding the chair back across the hardwood floor. She glided over to meet the three intruders in the middle of the room. The green skirt of her layered tunic didn't waver as she moved.

"Excuse me. Where are my manners? My name is Lady Phillipa NicNeev. You must be the huntsmen I've heard talk of." She smiled, reaching a ringed hand toward Hawk.

"Indeed, my lady," the baron replied. "This here is—"

"Hawk, ma'am," the huntsman said, taking the lady's hand and nodding a bow. "Hawk the huntsman."

The lady smiled warmly, then turned to the girl.

"Mòrag. Also a huntsman," Mòrag said bluntly.

Hawk didn't shift his gaze to Mòrag, but he smiled at her newly claimed profession, knowing she only learned of it earlier that day. He noticed the lady didn't offer the girl a hand.

"They'll be staying here with you all tonight," the baron started. "If that pleases you, my lady? They wanted—"

"Enough, Peter," NicNeev cut in. "Thank you. We'll be fine from here. The hour is late, as you said."

The baron yawned, then smiled. "As you wish. Goodnight for now."

He turned and left the church, whistling as his melody faded into the night.

The three stood, locked in a mute stare. Lady NicNeev's bright appearance dimmed. She leaned on her hip. Her eyes studied Mòrag up and down.

"I thought you'd be taller," said Lady NicNeev. She smirked, reached for her collar, and adjusted its jutting angle. "Tell me, where's Tiree? And since when is Graeme MacTarbh's daughter a huntsman? Or rather huntswoman?"

"Wha-what?" Mòrag stuttered. "Who are ye? How do ye ken me?"

"Ah yes, of course. When would he ever have told you? Did you really think your father would trust you and only you for a task as important as returning Clan MacTarbh's sword, the great Claidheamh-mòr an Adhairc? Please, don't make me laugh."

Mòrag's face reminded Hawk of the dumbfounded expressions of a group of villagers when he informed them the reason their cows disappeared was an enormous troll patrolling the nearby forest. She grabbed a chair, turning it away from the altar, and plopped down. Hawk didn't miss Mòrag's shock, and his patience started to wear thin. Exhaustion set in.

He crossed his arms and spoke in a slow, deliberate voice as to not wake the guests. "Look, Lady NicNeev, who are you? How do you know about the sword?"

The lady returned to her desk, grabbed the candle, and

brought the light to the chairs. The candle accented raised cheek-bones and two creases giving an ever-present scowl found only in nobility. Her hair, tied tightly behind her head, shone golden in the flickering light.

"My name is indeed Phillipa NicNeev. I'm a healer from Forfarshire, simple medicine and a simple trade. However, my vocation allows me to be well-traveled, particularly to the courts of lords and ladies. Once, my work took me to Callander. It was there that I met Graeme and Fiona of Clan MacTarbh. Your father told me the fantastic tale of a sword, the battle of Hawick, and his unfortunate circumstances. He said he sent his daughter to recover what was lost. He told me about a wild, young warrior playing hero with her wolf pup, Tiree. I might not have recognized you all the way south here, except you have your mother's face, and you have her eyes. If only you had your father's talent. He said you'd try your best with your carved bow and wit, but . . ." NicNeev turned, looking into Mòrag's eyes and finishing, "he told me he didn't trust you to complete your task. He said you're too young and naïve. That you'd never manage on your own. You know the importance of that blade to your clan, do you not? You had to know others would help search. You can't blame him for rolling the dice twice instead of just once."

Mòrag looked like she could scream, a viciousness etching across her face like a savage bear. She shook her head, then rose and kicked the chair against the wall. The chair landed on its side with a crash. A few of the sleeping guests stirred from their slumber, but none paid much mind. Hawk looked at the floor in awkward silence, running a hand through his strip of hair.

"Of course, of course," Mòrag mumbled, her voice cracking under emotion. "Of course he'd never trust *me* with this." She paced through the chapel, her hands holding the back of her head.

"Don't be mad," Lady NicNeev said, changing her tone. "I want to see the sword returned as much as you do. It is a blessing that we have found each other. This means we're on the correct path. I'm not here to outdo you; I'm here to help."

Mòrag picked up the chair off the floor with a deep sigh. She brought it back into the circle of candlelight and sat.

"I can help you find it," Lady NicNeev added, placing a gentle hand on Mòrag's knee. "I assume you at least deduced the Norsemen stole the sword. Sinclair's son boasted to his neighbor that he left it in the armory and the Norsemen plundered it. We must find these Norsemen bandits, and to do that, we'll need to talk to those in the courts and castles. You'll find my charm valuable, I assure you, especially with your . . . wild appearance."

"What's that supposed to mean?" Mòrag asked, clearly offended.

"Eh, I think, what Lady NicNeev means," Hawk cut in, "is that there are different ways of persuasion with lords. Listen, I'm returning to see King David in Edinburgh tomorrow. I'm to collect my reward for the werewolf with him directly, and it just so happens I too wish to find these Norsemen bandits. Why not join me, just for tomorrow?"

He regretted it the moment it slipped from his mouth. How could he be so stupid? How could he not realize they'd only distract him before inevitably going their separate ways?

"Yes, that's perfect. Then it's settled. We shall come with you," NicNeev declared with delight, speaking for Mòrag. "Come, let us sleep and end this day."

She got up from their circle of chairs, hesitated a moment, and then blurted, "Wait a moment. Did you say werewolf?"

CHAPTER SEVEN

The boy opened his eyes. The boat rocked back and forth. The demons had stolen him from his village, and he sat in an unknown home.

Wooden walls creaked with every sway. Water crashed against them outside. Back and forth, the house swayed. His eyes adjusted to the morning light. No roof covered the house. He looked up at a sky of pure blue. A single cloud hung in the air. As his eyes focused, he saw it wasn't a cloud, but a giant woven cloth tied to the wooden post in the center of his home.

He licked his lips. A thick crust of salt coated them, but his tongue didn't have the moisture to soothe them. His lips ached. His tongue ached. Everything burned of salt. He reached a hand to his eyes and wiped the dried discharge. The metal shackles around his wrists clanged against their chain links. Where was he? How did he get there?

He sat up and rested his back against the wood behind him. To his left and right lay others. His tribe. His friends. His family. They all lay down or sat huddled in groups, connected together by the heavy chains he wore. Most were children, like him. Even his sister sat just past his reach. Some were old, the skin on their flesh hanging from their bones. Where was his mother? Where was his father?

He watched the pale demons walk about the wooden planks. They wore bear, elk, wolf, and beaver hides and carried shiny metal sticks and axes. They radiated hate.

Pain gripped his stomach. He couldn't remember the last time he'd eaten. He hungered for venison. He craved his mother's rabbit stew. What he wouldn't do for a creamy corn taste of *wiwáhcumsôp*.

He cried out his hunger, "*Nuyôtum! Nuyôtum!*" One of the demons slapped another on the shoulder and pointed at him. They boomed with laughter as they walked up to the boy and kicked his legs. He lowered his hands in a meager attempt at protection. He begged for them to stop. What did he do to deserve this punishment?

Days turned into weeks. The food was scarce. The shelter was none. His tribe slowly withered away. One by one, they wouldn't wake up in the morning. His last memories of them were their bodies being tossed into the sea.

His sister, normally a fiery beacon of energy and wisdom, struggled to smile. The once warm and embracing comfort extinguished beneath dull, tired eyes. His hope faded. He'd follow the others over the side soon enough, he knew.

Until, one day, he noticed the sail on the center wooden pole had gained another cloth. It was a dark blue square with a golden-winged cat breathing fire. He remembered the banner from the very first demon that grabbed him.

The noise around the house rose. The deck on which he lay came alive with activity. The pale, bearded demons hurried about the floor. They tugged on ropes and donned their metal skins.

One captor wrenched up the tribe's chains. The demon's singular pale eye frightened the boy beyond preservation. Blåveis, they called him. The captors forced the tribe to their feet, and he scrambled to stand. He wobbled, falling forward and bracing against the girl in front of him. The pale-eyed demon grabbed his shoulder and straightened him up. The monster yelled, screaming instructions in a tongue unknown to him. Blåveis pushed him forward, and they marched in a line. He lifted his head and looked over the side. The ocean washed up against a rocky coast mixed with dark, black sand.

The evil figures on the wooden ship threw a rope ladder down to the beach.

His toes gripped the smoothed, stony surfaces of the rocky beach. The remains of his kin marched in a haggard line. A girl collapsed on the shore, halting the procession. Her hands bound in chains, she couldn't break her fall, and her chin paid the toll. He knew that chin and that face: his sister, Ayaksak.

The demon with the pale eye approached the fallen girl. Blåveis kicked her side, but she didn't rise. The demon growled and, unshackling the girl, tossed her to the side. She didn't move. The boy screamed. Tears welled and trickled down the boy's wind-chaffed cheeks.

Blåveis turned his pale blue eye to him and barked again in the unfamiliar tongue. The demon held a long slender rope, tapered at one end. Blåveis snapped his wrist, and the rope lashed like a rattlesnake. It cracked like thunder above the boy's head. The line of tribesmen stepped back, then shuffled in the direction the demon pointed. They moved toward huts of stone lined up on the shore, smoke rising from a center fire. The boy in shackles entered a new world.

CHAPTER EIGHT

The streets of Edinburgh brimmed with life as traders and merchants moved about the cobbled Lawnmarket. Their stalls and carts bumped and prodded through the bustling square. The colorful market area called Hawk's attention as commerce moved this way and that. A girl corralled a gaggle of geese while shuffling past a man laden with wheels of white cheese on each shoulder, all delighting Hawk's appetite. The smell of freshly baked bread warmed his nose as bells rang and the townsfolk shouted their wares.

"Beer! Beer here. Whiskey, fresh from the barrel!" shouted a man from the side.

"Fruit here! Get your nice juicy apples. You've tasted nothing as sweet as these," said a vibrant woman seated on the back of a cart.

"Rye here. Bread straight from the fire!" yelled the baker, covered in flour and wearing a puffy gray hat.

"Soldier, hey! Please, try my salmon, fresh from the river. Caught only yesterday, you'll swear you are royalty with this quality!"

"No thanks, my good man," Hawk said, waving a dismissive hand.

He grabbed hold of the reins and continued onward. Lady NicNeev followed by his side. They rode atop two bay horses Baron Sinclair had happily lent them. The group set off from Rosslyn at first light and headed straight down the beaten road for Edinburgh. Mòrag, after careful council from Lady NicNeev and Hawk, agreed the castle of the king of Alba may not be ready for the warrior and her wolf. They would rejoin after the meeting.

Hawk and Lady NicNeev first searched Holyrood Abbey, where the king spent most of his time as of late. Upon recognizing Hawk from the previous hunting feast, the guard at the abbey told them the king was at the castle. They continued, riding up the Way of the King, the mile-long spine of the hill Hawk spotted from the Seat. It connected to the top of Castle Rock. The horses' hooves clopped along the cobblestone street all the way up the hill.

Hawk had only stayed in Edinburgh for a fortnight, but still witnessed the city grow every day. Stonemasons surveyed their constructions, barking orders to their indentured servant laborers. Pointed roofs practically sprouted up as Hawk rode on. Refined women, elegantly clad in dresses of exotic fabrics, waltzed down the hill on the arms of dapper men.

The huntsman never enjoyed cities. The smell of congregated piss and shit thrown into the muck of heavily trampled lanes repulsed him. It was the dreary melancholy grays and browns of the haphazard homes mixed with the unnatural presence of disease and death. Hawk hated the rats that crawled through the gullies and the verminous populace crowding the inns and taverns. No, as a rule, Hawk despised his time in cities.

Edinburgh, it seemed, existed as an exception to that rule. The church's orphaned youngsters swept the streets clean. Citizens tossed their waste over the craggy cliffs into the water north of the city, and it carried away to the ocean. A massive, sprawling oak halfway up the road, simply called "the Big Tree" by locals, helped to drown out the monotone of the stone. Yes, Hawk positively adored Edinburgh.

The huntsman and lady reached the castle's entrance. Hawk swung his foot over and climbed off his horse. While the baron's horse proved a sturdy, sufficient ride, the huntsman swallowed a pang of regret at not returning to the king with Cursor, the king's horse. He passed a hand through his hair and over the tomahawks adorning his back. Approaching the wrought-iron gate, Hawk noticed two guards on duty just behind the portcullis.

The pockmarked guard raised his eyes to meet the approaching huntsman. The second guard remained aloof. Hawk addressed whom he believed to be the most intelligent of the pair.

"Greetings, soldier. My name is Hawk. I am the huntsman who has business with King David."

"Aye, do ye? Business with the king, is it? I've nae heard of ye. Now, if ye dinnae mind, kindly piss off, ye foreigner," retorted the pockmarked guard.

"That wasn't very nice, now was it?" Hawk replied, not rising to agitation. "Perhaps if you asked the king if he was expecting a huntsman, we could clear this up."

"Why dinnae ye ask him yerself, freak?" laughed the guardsman and his buddy.

The green-cloaked lady placed a hand on Hawk's armored shoulder. He shifted to the side.

"Listen, sir," she said, adjusting her hood to reveal her elegant bun of golden hair. "I am Lady Phillipa NicNeev in the steward-ship of the mormaer of Menteith. You know, the Earl of Menteith? We've traveled all the way from Stirling Castle so my lord may speak with the king. I'm here to deliver a message to the king himself, personally." She slowly pulled a rolled parchment from her bodice. "His Grace would be very disappointed to know you kept me at the gate. Now, boys, let my friend and I through to see the king, and I'll let you hold the parchment."

The pockmarked guard licked his lips and looked at his nodding companion. "As you command, my lady. Open the gates!"

A guard jerked on a stocky horse's reins beyond the gate,

which lurched forward and tugged on an immense iron chain. The metal pulley system groaned as the sophisticated iron gate slotted up.

Hawk climbed back onto his mare. He returned Lady NicNeev's smile and signaled his horse forward under the castle's entrance.

Lady NicNeev reached down and handed the guardsman the rolled parchment as they passed by. "Take it. It's yours. I have another and know the message by heart," she said, winking at the guard and heading toward the main hall.

The guardsman smelled the parchment and paraded his prize in front of the other guard. He unfurled the paper. The message was easy to read, even for the most unlearned man. It was a simple, blank sheet.

———

The huntsman rummaged through the large sack, took out the rotting prize, and threw the werewolf's head at the foot of the king. King David made no attempt to move. He stared down at the monster's severed head for a long time, pressing his hand into his temples. The king's crown reflected the beast's grim expression.

They gathered in the throne room. White-crossed saltire banners, blazoned azure, hung from the rafters while sconces lined the stoned walls. The king stood on an elevated wooden altar, wearing regal blue robes, which matched his sapphire inlaid crown. An embroidered holy cross clung over his heart, bright and clear.

"It's done then?" David, king of Alba, finally broke the silence. "You killed the beast? God is good, my huntsman friend." He smiled at Hawk.

The king stepped over the decollated specimen, grasped the hand of the huntsman in respect, and turned to the lady beside Hawk.

"Your Grace," Hawk started, "allow me to introduce the Lady Phillipa NicNeev, the uhm . . ." He trailed off, not knowing exactly how she would wish to finish.

"Lady NicNeev will do just fine," she said, reaching out a hand to the king and curtseying.

"Greetings, my lady. It was my belief that Hawk worked alone. What magic have you cast that would allow him to bring you into his company? Besides your exquisite beauty, of course."

The king laughed. Lady NicNeev did too.

"Your Grace is too kind," the lady replied. "I am a messenger from the earl of Menteith's court. My lord has been troubled as of late, for a thief has stolen a precious item from him: a great sword with a sapphire pommel that was very dear to him. His squire, Joseph, son of the baron Sinclair, was thought to be in possession of it. I was at the baron's in Rosslyn pondering with him as to the sword's whereabouts. But the answer has become clear, Norsemen raiders took the sword."

"Did you help slay the werewolf?" the king asked in a polite bit of humor.

"I'm afraid I was not aware of the predicament. Only after the monster was no more did I meet Hawk. Though I heard the howling from Rosslyn's chapel. How could a lady such as myself help defeat a monster like that? I hear it was a tough battle. One for the ballads."

"Hawk also informed me that he was to meet with Your Grace again. Am I correct in saying Your Grace has news of a recent attack on the village of Rosslyn?"

The king smiled. "Come, walk with me."

The group exited the hall for the fortress's courtyard. Troops paraded around outside. Some moved in drill and others in preparation for unknown tasks, while some simply patrolled aimlessly. The king stopped one of his patrolling men, whispered inaudible instructions, and sent him fervently onward.

The king led them to the fortress's borders. Hawk climbed the steps of the outer wall behind the king's meandering stroll. King David leaned on the crenel of the wall.

"Do you know, Hawk," the king said, "when Cursor returned riderless, I thought that was the end of you, that the monster had annihilated you, just like that, and the only survivor was that damnable horse. I told myself, 'Just as soon as that farmer Sinclair sends word of more destroyed sheep, I'll have to rally my guard and bring it down myself.'" The king chuckled for a moment. "I'm glad I was wrong, Huntsman."

Hawk remained silent, staring resolutely over the battlements at the body of water stretched out across the north, the Forth River.

"I prayed for an end to the whole affair, there in the chapel, that you would slay the beast and that would be my last thought on it. And by God, my prayers were heard and—"

"Your Grace," Hawk interjected, "I helped you claim your white stag. I killed the werewolf as you asked, in replacement of the pelt. I made sure it would haunt you and your people no more. The proof was brought before your feet. Please, I want the information on the slavers as you promised." Hawk knew he sounded impatient, no doubt a first for the king of Alba.

The king stared at Hawk. For a moment, Hawk braced for a rebuke. Instead, a smile parted the king's face.

"Yes, yes, alright. You've earned it, Hawk. There can be no doubt of that." The king turned and walked down the battlement, Hawk and the lady close behind.

King David greeted the guards as they passed. He inspected the walls like he was a stonemason himself, running his hand over the mortar and rubbing the gray dust between his fingertips. He was stalling.

The king entered the castle bastion and finally came to a rest. He stared out at the northern expanse. A breeze shifted his dark mane beneath his crown.

A long sigh left the king before he said, "Look out to the north. What do you see?"

Hawk didn't answer.

The king continued, "No, you can't see it? Look south, look east, look west. You still don't see it? I'll tell you what I see. I see Highlands, islands, cities, clans, and everything of beauty in this world. And it's time someone brought it all together. One kingdom. One people. The time for unification is upon us, and through God, it will happen. I can promise you that. I will bring the Scoti people together, under a singular rule, through the word of God. As Christianity spreads over the land, so will the dominion of this kingdom."

"You think God will bring the people together?" Lady NicNeev cut in.

"It's the only way, the only way to cultivate the future," the king answered, turning to Lady NicNeev. "Alba will spread, grow, and blossom, and I'll be there to unite its leadership, one royal burgh at a time. Berwick, Roxburgh, Dunfermline, Perth, and Edinburgh all hold royal burgh charters. You walked through Edinburgh and have seen its beauty. Did you marvel at it? I've named Stirling a royal burgh, and now it, too, will shine with all of God's glory. Only when every city has become a royal burgh will this land truly be the kingdom of Alba. Most of the clans are already adjusting, like Sinclair, and soon we will bring the Highland clans into the fold with every new royal burgh and God. Until then, clans continue their petty squabbles with one another."

"I agree with you, Your Grace," the lady said. "The time for one kingdom is now. But do you really think religion bends all knees? That Christianity will bring unification just because of some royal township? There are clans out there as old as these hills. There are alliances of families older than the Roman forts. No charter or God will keep men from fighting their neighbors. Trust me on that." She scowled.

"If God wills it, so it shall be," the king said, a firm, authoritative tone building. "Wouldn't you agree, Huntsman?"

Hawk swallowed to clear his throat. King David's glare tore

into him. Lady NicNeev's smirk only doubled at his inability to escape the question.

"Yes," Hawk answered, wanting nothing more than the king's promised information.

"I guess time will tell all," Lady NicNeev said, her smile turning toward the king.

"Ha. I feel as though she's as likely to shoot me with an arrow as she is to dance with me at a banquet. It's good this one is in your company, Hawk. You're in good hands with her." The king smiled, turning his attention back out over the horizon. "I realize it won't be easy, and it won't happen overnight, but it will work. The kingdom of Alba is spreading already, which brings me to the solution to both your inquiries, I believe. I know where the Norsemen went. Several eyewitnesses reported an *unusual* vessel headed inward, up the river and toward Stirling. Do you know what they saw on the ship?"

"God?" Lady NicNeev mocked.

Hawk looked at the lady in surprise. She pushed her limits with the monarch. Lucky for her, the king ignored the jest.

"A band of raiders. A certain group of raiders flying a dark blue banner with a golden-winged lion breathing fire." King David looked at Hawk. "My scouts reported sightings just outside the burgh."

"So follow the shore to Stirling and we'll find the raiders?" Hawk asked.

He struggled to hide his excitement, a grin creeping along his face.

"Yes, follow the shore to Stirling," clarified the king. "Once there, seek out General Tylus. He oversees scouting reports. He'll direct you to those whom you seek. And, to see that you have no troubles on the road, I'll write a royal decree aiding you on your journey. And to deliver the decree, I'll send a knight in my service with you. I've asked the knight to meet you here at the bastion. You'll have no issues on the path, I'm sure of that. If you can track a werewolf, I have all faith you can track your raiders. Then, perhaps on your return, you can help me understand how it is a werewolf even came to be in Edinburgh."

"Thank you, Your Grace," Hawk said. "Truly, you don't know how much I appreciate this. Thank you."

"Well, you've seen what lengths I'd go to for my neighbor Sinclair, hiring a huntsman," the king laughed. "Imagine what I do for my friends."

Hawk processed the last word for a second. The king had always seemed on edge around the huntsman. He never considered their relationship as anything more than transactional. But kings see things differently than huntsmen, Hawk supposed. He reached out a hand in thanks. The king grasped his hand tight and placed a respectful hand on his shoulder.

"God will be with you out there," the king said. "Ah. Here he comes. One moment, as I have a word with him and let him know his task."

He relinquished his grip on Hawk to greet the approaching ornamented knight. The king's man wore a full chest plate and helm, a true knight errant. Atop the helm waved a blue feather.

"Your hands are shaking, Huntsman," Lady NicNeev noticed as she reached out and grabbed hold of Hawk's hands in her soft, pale ones. A purple-hued static shock arced between them. "Oh my . . . I can feel your excitement."

"You don't know how long I've waited for this moment," Hawk confessed, meeting her eyes. "How many years have I chased up their trail, this way and that? This is the closest lead I've had. I almost want to ride off after them right now."

"Who are these raiders?" asked Lady NicNeev.

"The only *monsters* I've ever feared," Hawk replied, watching the king and his knight return.

"Allow me to introduce Sir William Maurice of Holyrood. He's been in my service for many years now, and I've known him since before I took my oath as king. He's never failed me, and I trust him to see your purpose fulfilled."

The knight lowered to his knee, clanking against the stone.

"I cannot fathom why a lady of your stature travels these roads without an escort," King David said, "but my knight will see to your protection, my lady. Hawk, good luck, and may this bring some peace.

"Now, if you'll excuse me, I see I have duties to tend to with Commander Cormac. Huntsman. My lady." The king bowed and walked off to meet the waiting commander.

The knight removed his helm. Underneath was the dark face of a man that time served well. He was bald, to be sure, but handsome and not too aged. He wasted no time in greeting them.

"Good day to you both. I believe we've had the pleasure of meeting previously, Huntsman."

Hawk nodded. The annoyance of their previous visit vanished in the elation of the information received from the king.

The knight turned to Lady NicNeev. "However, I am embarrassingly unaware of your companion's name, my lady?"

"Lady NicNeev, in the service of the earl of Menteith." She gave him the courtesy of extending out her hand.

The knight kneeled and placed his lips against the back of her hand.

"My lady. Rest assured, we won't cease until we've found these treacherous foes," the knight said, rising and replacing his helm on his head. The feather moved to match the breeze's direction. "Come, I will guide you both to the royal livery."

———

The knight hadn't ceased talking since they departed Edinburgh Castle. Sir William of Holyrood was a man who spent a lifetime on silent guard. Whether on patrol of a city or protecting his lord, it seemed Sir William seldom had the chance to revel in conversation with companions.

He must've gone entire days without any genuine communication with others. Sir William made up for that lost time. He had already droned on about the chivalric duty and honor of knights and the practical applications of horseshoeing in everyday equine husbandry, even reciting by heart lines from his favorite French poem, "The Song of Roland."

Hawk enjoyed every minute. The huntsman rode with high spirits, knowing the raiders he sought remained close. Too long the slavers had haunted his dreams. Too long they had walked the earth without retribution. Too long.

Hawk, Lady NicNeev, and Sir William rode westerly, leaving the bustle of Edinburgh's city streets for the countryside. The road stretched wide, straight, and serene. Heather and hills followed the sides of the route as far as Hawk could see. An air of mystery hung along the road.

"The Roman military constructed and paved this road, Dere Street, long ago," Sir William explained. "It saw constant usage by the citizens of the Votadini. The Votadini used this road as the central passage west from the city of Din Eidyn before the Angles conquered all below the Firth. Many secrets still lie in the stones beneath our feet."

Further on down the road, they entered a grove of fir trees. Sir William, striding atop his dapper chestnut mare, insisted on being at the head of the pack. Hawk and Lady NicNeev, riding matching bay geldings, followed behind him, along with one lone gray horse. Fresh horses from the king. The gray horse, which carried their provisions, had its reins tied securely to Lady NicNeev's saddle.

"For you see," Sir William went on, "I've been in King David's service for many years now. When King Henry Beauclerc summoned him to England, I accompanied him southward. King Henry was to marry David's sister, Matilda. She was a beauty, I tell you."

"Truly, was she?" NicNeev humored blankly, having no doubt tuned out the knight's long-winded stories.

Hawk smiled as he reined in laughter. His gelding fell in line behind Lady NicNeev now.

"Yes, indeed," Sir William continued rambling, "and they

knighted me within a fortnight. So it was that *Sir* William Maurice was with David when he made a name for himself in the English courts. I was with David when he married Maud, Countess of Huntingdon, and I was with him when he reigned *Princeps Cumbrensis*, The prince of the Cumbrians. Which is why the king carries so much favor with the southern lords and clans."

"I don't recall seeing Maud at the feast in Holyrood Abbey," Hawk said.

"Aye, it is a poor shame, for you would've loved her spirit. I'm afraid she had affairs to address at her home in Huntingdon. Many affairs to settle these days. These clan quarrels really do occupy King David's time and resources. There are many clans throughout Alba. For centuries, they've led themselves with their own traditions and governance. But many heads lead to many arguments, and arguments have led to war."

Hawk's amusement with the knight's stories waned. They seemed to drone, and the riding pace hadn't increased since leaving the outskirts of Edinburgh. Hawk wanted to gallop but had to settle for barely a trot.

The knight went on. "As we're all members of King David's court, I feel that you're privy to the knowledge of the king's dream of bringing all clans under his fold with one governance. Truly a visionary. What a dream. Even now, there are soldiers somewhere on the move to carry out that dream. I believe, as David does, that the Highland clans, though many, will one day come together as one to see that dream."

As he spoke, Sir William's mount crested a hill on the route. Lady NicNeev slowed her horse. Hawk pulled up alongside her on the road.

"I can't listen anymore to that rabble," the lady said, rolling her eyes, shifting in her saddle, and drifting back behind Hawk.

Hawk let a small chuckle escape at Lady NicNeev's weariness. He urged his mount on, catching up to Sir William at the top of the hill. Sir William, however, halted. Hawk watched the knight draw his sword.

"By holy God!" hollered Sir William. "A most foul beast! What a monster to cross our path today. Huntsman, to arms! Lady NicNeev, guard yourself!"

CHAPTER NINE

"Wait! Sir William, STOP!" Hawk shouted. "Don't harm it!"

The huntsman raced toward Sir William's foul beast, hoping it wouldn't be slain. It was a large black wolf with green eyes. The knight, riding at a full canter with a raised sword, reached it quickly. The wolf didn't waver from the middle of the road. Hawk could only watch at what he thought was sure to be its end. But whether from hearing Hawk's words or from the wolf's show of courage, Sir William didn't strike Tiree. The wolf's eyes pivoted, following the mounted knight's missed charge.

Hawk climbed out of his saddle near the wolf and handed his reins to Lady NicNeev.

"Just when I thought things might be interesting," the lady said, her horse trotting lazily up behind.

"Mòrag, enough! Come out," Hawk yelled into the trees.

He studied the firs, looking behind him and all around.

Ah, the wolf will know, he thought. Hawk bent down to Tiree's eye level. The wolf's gaze fixed on one side of the road. The huntsman squinted. Mòrag sprung out of the bracken on the side of the road. She had her bow ready in her hands but no arrow drawn.

"What's with ye in trying tae kill Tiree?" Mòrag said with a short laugh. "That's twice in two days now!"

"I saved Tiree, if you were paying attention. The wolf and I are even," replied the huntsman.

Emboldened, he stroked the top of the wolf's head, saddened his glove robbed him of feeling Tiree's fur. Hawk and Mòrag grasped each other's forearm in greeting.

Lady NicNeev, in her hooded green tunic, nodded in acknowledgment at the warrior. The knight had finally rounded back to get a good look at the would-be attackers.

"Sir William, this is Mòrag of Clan MacTarbh," introduced Hawk. "She helped me slay the werewolf in Rosslyn and seeks the raiders as well. She's to aid the lady NicNeev and me on the trail, along with Tiree, her companion."

The knight removed his helm and held it at his waist. His face contorted in dissatisfaction.

"Now it's clear to me why we brought the gray mare with us. I thought it folly to bring so much for such a quick trip. Now I know why you insisted, Lord Huntsman."

"Are ye a laird now?" Mòrag asked in curiosity. "For killing the werewolf, aye?"

"No, I'm no lord. Sir William, it's just Huntsman. Please. Yes, I know. We told Mòrag to meet us on the Roman road. I didn't think she'd have Tiree meet us first. Luckily, Cursor reminded me to ask for horses not easily spooked. We've left that horse behind."

"That beast is no pet. It's a monster! This wasn't part of the king's plan," huffed Sir William.

"Tiree's nae beast. And who attacks a dug mindin' his own in the road, ye bastard? Be careful next time, aye?" Mòrag scowled at the knight.

"She's right, Sir William. That beast, as you say, saved my life in Rosslyn. He's coming with us. Now, come on. We must not waste any more time. We need to reach the ferry as soon as possible." Hawk grabbed the reins back from Lady NicNeev and climbed into the saddle. "The gray is yours."

"My own horse? Fancy that. Thank ye, my laird," Mòrag said, slinging the bow over her shoulder and grabbing hold of her mount.

Hawk shook his head, but a smile escaped despite his best efforts. Mòrag took off her bag, which hung over her hide mantle, and fixed it to her saddle. She clambered atop the horse, and they set off down the road once again.

Good to be on the move. He knew sending Mòrag to meet them west of Edinburgh would be tricky, but didn't know they'd be so close behind the Norsemen. Time pressed on the huntsman. It was the closest he'd come to catching the Norse raiders, and he didn't want the lead to slip away. Urgency was like a swift beat in his heart.

As long as we keep on moving, Hawk reassured himself, *we'll make it to Stirling by nightfall and—*

"What should I call her?" Mòrag butted into his thoughts.

"Uhm, 'the Gray One' worked for us," the huntsman managed, distracted.

"Nae, c'mon. The lass needs a real name. Every horse needs a name, somethin' that fills them with pride. What'd ye name yers?"

"I didn't," said Hawk. "Not every horse needs a name. These horses are from the king. They're not ours to name."

"Ah, that's pish. Ye can name a horse whatever ye like."

"Epona," Lady NicNeev interjected. "The goddess protector of mares."

"Epona? Epona. Aye, that's it," Mòrag said, brushing the mare's neck excitedly. "C'mon, Epona."

The huntsman and Mòrag soon drifted to the head of the four riders. Mòrag whispered the new name to the horse, hoping it would stick.

"You'll need a lifetime with the horse for that name to take hold," Hawk said.

"Give me a day, and this horse's head'll turn, aye," Mòrag assured him.

Hawk smiled. He hadn't expected their journey to continue

together past the werewolf but enjoyed her ability to brighten the long ride for now. He trotted ahead, watching as a flock of seagulls drifted high above in the distance. Relieved, Hawk knew they headed for the sea as he followed their cacophonous racket. One melodic chirping rang above, unlike any seagull Hawk had ever heard.

"That's a golden eagle," Mòrag said excitedly, no doubt referencing the unusual sound. She stared up at the sky, shouting above the growing rumble of ocean wind. "I havnae heard one call like that since I was a bairn. My friend Ulster and I had climbed near the edge of a bluff. We watched as the eagle swooped down on a wee rabbit. The eagle chirped just like that one. Ulster said they were messengers of the gods. That they could fly down with a flower and summon all the clans of Alba together. I dinnae ken that. This one here just lairds over the gulls, eh?"

The chirping and chattering of birds continued for some time as the band of riders continued toward their destination. They'd left the Roman road and gradually came down to a small coastal village. The wind picked up as they neared the Firth.

The band reached the Queensferry Crossing, hoping to use a ferryman to travel down the Firth of the Forth toward Stirling. Sir William reminded the group about his excellent decision to use the water to reach Stirling as quickly as possible. He regaled them with the history of the crossing.

"Well, Mòrag, the wife of King Màel Coluim III, Queen Margaret, set up a chapel along the crossing. And, in doing so, the crossing has forever become hers. For it was through King Màel Coluim's order that a permanent settlement for crossing was established . . ." the knight droned on again, all the way to shore.

A man on the shore stretched out his mesh hemp net. Gulls swarmed and dove in bunches, crying out in warbling shrieks. The man unwound the tangles of rope across the width of the beach. Hawk noted the man stood near a large sailing vessel.

The huntsman addressed the fisherman and asked for safe travel westward.

"Yer nae crossin' today, my lairds," explained the fisherman. "The wind is a whistlin' somethin' fierce. I'll nae take my ship on them seas. Ye folk should've come earlier. It wasnae like this afore."

The man glanced over his shoulders again at the crashing waves of the ocean. The water rose in peaks that clashed against each other and battered down against its current.

The huntsman gritted his teeth. He wasn't going to let some choppy water stop his progress.

"We rode with all haste from Edinburgh, and I doubt we would've outrun the wind."

"Aye, I ken that. Them horses be those oriental horses from the royal stock, King Alaxandair's imports, and nae others."

"Then you can see our travels are of grave importance, my good man. We don't mean to cross the river. Take us in with the waves. Ride the current inward up the Forth River, to Stirling."

"The current will do naught but smash us against the rocks, it would. There nae be any good in climbing aboard the vessel today, ye ken. The sea'll kill us all, and that's that." The fisherman spat, seemingly finding it troublesome to argue with four strangers over why he should save their lives.

Hawk heard the fisherman's message and knew no amount of persuasion would sway him. If the boat were destroyed, his livelihood would be too. Hawk knew no ships would enter the water with the day's wind. Without bidding them farewell, the fisherman retreated to his cabin.

Hawk kicked a stone into the water, the splash barely audible beneath the sounds of gusty winds and thrashing seawater. He wanted to curse. He wanted to fight the foe, with tomahawks in hand. But how can you fight the wind?

He took in a deep breath and let it out, clearing his head.

"We can't linger here," Hawk said, turning to his companions. "Sir William, do you think we could make for Stirling by land and be there before the break of dawn tomorrow?"

The knight stammered for a moment in thought. "Well, I . . . Hmm . . . I believe we . . ."

"Nonsense," Lady NicNeev interrupted. "Can you feel that? I believe the wind is shifting. Sir William, go retrieve the fisherman. Mòrag, run along and get Tiree. Huntsman, gather the horses. We'll be leaving on this boat soon enough."

Hawk stood for a moment, unsure what wind the lady felt shifting, then motioned for his company's horses. The others started their tasks.

Hawk held the reins of four horses, searching for a spot to tack them for a moment's rest. The lady moved toward the edge of the stony shore. She removed her green hood to better look at the waves. The lady gracefully bent down and grasped a piece of weathered driftwood. She spun the smooth surface of the branch in her hand and then violently plunged one end into the ocean.

The water rippled out from the branch. The ripples grew wider and wider, rushing out from wood and spreading out over the Firth. The malevolent waves crashed upon the ripples and vanished. The sea grew calmer and calmer until a chilling silence fell over the body of water. The ripples halted the might of the ocean waves and wind. Lady NicNeev let go of the branch, and it splashed into the sea to drift again.

Did that just happen? No, she couldn't have, Hawk thought. He seized the reins tight like he was about to float up into the sky. Ducking out of sight behind the horse's neck, he paused, fixated on the ground. He couldn't help but slink over. It couldn't have happened. Nobody could calm the sea like that—could they? He caught himself breathing unusually loud, almost panting.

"Everything okay?" Lady NicNeev asked, stepping around the horses in front of Hawk.

"Yes. Yes." Hawk said, pretending to scan the ground before him, "Thought I dropped oats from the saddlebag. But there's nothing."

"Good, it's high time we set sail."

—————

Hawk hated sailing. The huntsman clung to the starboard railing, looking toward the distant shores for earthen salvation. Although the boat sailed smoothly toward Stirling, Hawk still felt uneasy on its planks. He'd traveled by boat many times in his life, but never grew accustomed to their movements. It was the rhythmic sounds of creaking wood and the crying of seagulls in the gray sky. The swaying of the ship and the crashing of the bow against the current. It was the marine mist spraying up from the side of the vessel and into the air. Hawk licked his lips and tasted the salty residue covering them. No, Hawk didn't have a taste for sailing. He was, however, happy to sacrifice his comfort for the speed of reaching the slavers' trail.

A peculiar wind blew westerly, carrying them on their journey. They sailed aboard a small cog ship with a vast white sail harnessing the wind's momentum.

Hawk surveyed the ship's occupants. He could count the crew on one hand, but the ship moved with efficiency. The fisherman captain traveled the sea with his sons, each playing a crucial role in the cog's ability to stay afloat. Sir William occupied himself with comforting the tacked horses. The knight spoke to the chestnut mare softly, sneaking the horse an oatcake or two. Lady NicNeev remained at the stern, watching over the entire vessel. Hawk met her gaze.

What did she do by the water's edge? It wasn't pure luck that the waves stopped. She held command of them. When the lady had walked to get the others, he had stared in bewilderment at the sudden change of wind on the shore. Sir William had praised God, saying it was a miracle. Mòrag's elation swelled as she swore up and down that magic must've indeed returned to the kingdom. Hawk held more reservation. He knew the source of the wind's change. But Hawk cared little for how it happened, only that he kept on the course to meet the slavers.

Mòrag approached and put a hand on the huntsman's shoulder. "Amazing, eh?" she said, delighted. "I havnae been on a boat like this before. Naebody paddling with oars. I cannae believe it."

She loved every minute of the ferry. Mòrag gripped the side of the boat's bulwarks and leaned over the edge, embracing the salty air. She guffawed at every bump in the water, soaking up her time on the ship.

"Tiree loves it too," she said, pointing to the wolf, whose nose poked out of the side scupper. "Look how fast we're moving! We'll be there in nae time. Huh? What's wrong? Ye dinnae like the water?" Mòrag looked up, placing a hand on Hawk's shoulder.

He brushed it off almost immediately.

Hawk didn't mind the water, truly. As a boy, he floated across rivers hundreds of times with his tribe. They'd fish, hunt, and travel all from their *muhshoy*, their canoe. He even helped his father make a canoe, burning and scraping the wood until the day he could finally set it in the water. But one particular trip across open water changed all of that.

"I don't like big ships. I'd rather have my boots on the ground," Hawk answered.

"Are ye feeling sick?"

"No, it's not that. I . . ." He hesitated. She still didn't know about his past. "Ships like this bring back bad memories. Of Blåveis and the Norsemen. That's all. Ones I'd rather forget."

"So forget them. Here, I'll help. Look there, right there, the dark shadows in the water. See them?"

Mòrag pointed off the side of the ship into the deep blue. Shadows disappeared and reappeared along the water's surface. They moved at the pace of the ship. Suddenly, a shadow broke the surface. A large black fin crested toward the sky. A sharp blow of air and mist came from a black-colored shape before it dove back under the surface. Another appeared, blowing out its breath before inhaling. Mòrag cheered at every surface, smiling and laughing. A dozen of them surfaced around the ship before the pod went back to the shadows.

"Orcas. They're whales. They're so beautiful," she cried out.

The huntsman smiled at her excitement. The whales were quite a sight to the huntsman. He couldn't deny it. He remembered the sound of whales surfacing on journeys before but hadn't seen them with his own eyes.

The orcas danced like shadows in the water. The shadows eventually drifted toward the northern shore. Hawk only realized how much closer the vessel had come to the coast. Or rather, the coast had come to the ship. The Forth narrowed.

The sky shifted to a somber gray. Though no sign of the sun gleamed beneath the clouds, Hawk knew night slowly approached. They must be nearing the end of the voyage.

"Hey, Captain!" Hawk called out to the fisherman. "How goes our travel?"

"Seas are calmer than I've seen in my whole life. I dinnae ken the words ye spoke tae God, but he heard them." The fisherman stood holding a line from the canvas sail.

"We're making good time," Hawk replied.

"Aye. We sure are. Bit slower on the river, I'm afraid. But we'll get ye there soon enough. Ho, Hamish, grab that line. Tie it tae the cleat starboard side."

"Will we make it to Stirling before nightfall?" Lady NicNeev asked, stepping out from the rear of the ship.

"Nae, nae," the fisherman said, shaking his head. "We make for Alloa. On this vessel? I'll struggle tae turn any further in. Nae, I'll wrap around Alloa Inch, and I'll make for home. Ye'll have tae make yer way on foot from the shores there."

"Thanks, my good man," the huntsman said, and the ship continued the twisting journey through the Forth River.

Mòrag and Tiree moved to the opposite end of the vessel. Hawk's eyes followed their prance until his gaze fell on the encroaching Lady NicNeev.

"I see you're not one for sailing much. Your feet have stayed planted firmly at the rail," the lady said, releasing a long sigh. She brushed out a wrinkle on the shoulder of her tunic and flattened the collar of her hood.

"You could say that," Hawk replied, a slight clench to his words.

A silence fell between them. Finally, Hawk blurted what he could no longer contain: "How did you do it?"

"Do what?"

"Calm the wind and sea."

"I didn't do anything you couldn't have done yourself," she said with a laugh, glancing at him.

Hawk didn't return the smile. Her laugh cooled, and she grew calm once more.

"I felt the air changing, believe me. When you spend as many years as I have in this world, you get a sense of these sorts of things. I doubt we'll make it to Stirling tonight before nightfall."

The huntsman noticed she changed subjects with ease, but he didn't wish to push. Her confidence brokered trust, but her words told him a different story.

"The sun won't stay up forever, it's true," Hawk said.

"A shame," Lady NicNeev said. "I wished to stay in one of these *royal burghs* of King David's. Ha. Can you believe that nonsense about uniting the kingdom through God?"

Hawk didn't answer. Instead, he looked at the shore to steady his balance on the waves.

The lady continued, "He's a fool. You cannot tame the clans with rules and laws. This continental ideology will never take hold of the clans in Alba. Not while their leaders hold on to their family feuds. Certainly not through God, I assure you. But I suppose time will tell of his successes, will it not?" she asked, but must not have expected an answer.

Lady NicNeev had already turned away from Hawk. She walked from his side of the ship amidst sprays of salty ocean mists.

"Ho!" cried the fisherman. "There, up yonder. Starboard side."

"My word, it's a ship!" Sir William exclaimed.

"Grounded, from the look of the sail's tilt, I'd say," added the fisherman.

"Not just any ship." Hawk smiled, and reeled around to the others. "Come about, Captain. Set course for that ship."

"Whatever do you mean, Huntsman?" Sir William asked, puzzled. "We should head on for Alloa and on to Stirling."

"No," Hawk urged, turning back to the man at the helm. "Good fisherman, make for that shore. I know that vessel. It's a Norse longship."

CHAPTER TEN

The fire cracked and hissed. A cavalcade of sparks launched into the sky when the huntsman tossed on another log. The sun hadn't fully set, and an eerie glow hung in the air.

The band had made camp on the edge of the beached Norse longship. A large hole in the timbers listed the ship to one side. It certainly looked in need of repairs. They had searched the vessel for any signs of the Norsemen's return but found little evidence. Campsites, spread along the shore of the crash, held chilled charcoal. What little scraps of food speckled the camp showed the first signs of rot. The Norse had moved on, leaving their ship behind.

Hawk and the others had erected three small canvas tents. Sir William hadn't expected Mòrag's addition. It wasn't an issue, as the huntsman volunteered to sleep by the fire. He knew he'd be more comfortable in the elements than under a white sheet.

Sir William saw to the horses while Mòrag, Lady NicNeev, and Hawk stole warmth near the edge of the fire. The chance to dry his armor and woolen clothing elated Hawk. The pieces had soaked up much of the moisture in the ocean air. While the heat of the campfire warmed him and recharged his vitality, Hawk looked at the two women across the fire. Bound in search of

Mòrag's family sword, they had developed a silent truce with one another. They, too, seemed revived at the fire, stretching out their arms as though to grab the shimmering heat.

"I cannae believe how close we are tae the Norse and the sword. I can practically see Stirling from here," Mòrag said, taking off her boots and sticking her feet near the fire to dry.

"I still think we should've ridden the rest of the way. Even in the dark," Lady NicNeev added.

Her eagerness to return the sword to Mòrag's father as hired reminded Hawk of his own trade as a huntsman. Haste to complete a commission wasn't a new concept to Hawk. He'd certainly rushed a hunt or two in his life, but not at a moment like this.

"We're not as close as it seems," Hawk said. "Sir William said there's still a couple of hours of riding ahead of us before Stirling. And traveling in the dark isn't wise. You don't know what's lurking out there when the sun goes down, and you sure as hell can't see it. No. We'll camp here for the night, get some sleep, and leave at first light."

Sir William made his way to the campfire, having tied the horses together to prevent their escape. He sat down, removing his plated armor and exhaling a long, tired sigh.

He, too, needs time around the fire, thought Hawk.

"Why do ye wear so much metal if it exhausts ye like that?" Mòrag asked, slipping on her dry leather boots.

"A knight without armor is no knight at all," Sir William said, lifting his chin high before bringing it down to rest on his chest.

He stared into the fire.

"*All right* then." Mòrag rolled her eyes. "We're all tired. I'll see if Tiree and I cannae find something fresh tae snack on and be back in a wee bit."

She took the ornamented bow from around her back, whistled for Tiree, and rushed into the darkness that formed outside the ring of fire. Hawk flinched to call out, rolling his feet in to rise, but Mòrag had already disappeared. He hesitated. Had he not just warned them of the dangers of the wood after dark? To venture alone doubled that risk. But he supposed Tiree had Mòrag's back, and she proved her skill against the werewolf. Hawk sat back again and pushed the concern from his mind into the fire's heat.

"I think I'll retire for the night," Lady NicNeev said, yawning. She rose and stretched her arms, then made for one tent. "Wake me at first light if I'm not up. Good night, gentlemen. Tomorrow, we find our answers."

And with that, she disappeared into the tent.

Sir William and Hawk sat for a while, reticent and calm, Hawk absorbing the energy of the fire through his eyes. Time passed before Hawk realized Sir William stared at him. Hawk returned the gaze, and Sir William took it as an invitation. He stood, then sat next to the huntsman. When he spoke, he kept his voice low enough for only Hawk to hear.

"You were in the company of Lady NicNeev prior to meeting with the king, yes? Do you trust Lady NicNeev, Master Huntsman?"

Hawk raised an eyebrow at the knight, then looked toward the tents. Hawk spoke so no eavesdropper could listen in.

"Yes, I was. Although I don't know her well. Mòrag and the king both seem to trust her, and we both seek the same goal. What do you mean?"

"I mean today . . . the water . . . Miracles are few and far between. I didn't see how it happened, but I know our greed for haste led us to ignore the calming for sheer luck. Master Huntsman, we're both men of the world, and we know that was no luck. That was something else. She claimed to know the winds would change before they did. What happened? What did you see her do on the shore?" The knight seemed on edge as he picked up a stick and meddled aimlessly at the fire.

"You're right, Sir William. I thought I saw her touch the sea, but I don't know what I saw. It wasn't luck that calmed those waves. Though she claims it was." Hawk rubbed a hand through his strip of hair.

"She may have the trust of the king, but best to keep our wits about us."

"True. It reminds me of a city I saw in Norway, Jötnarborg, the castle of giants. They built it, magnificent and beautiful, into the side of a vast mountain. It was a marvel to behold, with its towers stretching along the crags. Its peaks stood adorned with bright red banners, and its stone was white as marble. Surrounded by rock on all three sides, it appeared impenetrable and formidable. I gazed upon its majesty but once in my travels with my fellow huntsman Garrett. He told me they built the castle not long before, seemingly overnight through the help of a powerful, I think he used the word, *sorceress*. The sorceress conjured the carved stone and assembled the castle within a season. It humbled me to see it with my eyes, but we didn't stay at Jötnarborg long.

"Years later, I heard the castle was destroyed. The lord of the castle had an affair with the sorceress. The lord's wife rallied the noblemen of the castle against the sorceress, accusing her of anti-Christian witchcraft, claiming she forced the affair with a spell. The wife eventually shot an arrow into the sorceress's heart, and the castle collapsed into ruin. Or so I heard . . ."

Sir William nodded and grunted. "A sorceress? Best be on our guards then."

Mòrag returned out of the darkness. She had a rabbit in her hands and plopped down near the fire. She tossed her dark hair out of her face and carved the skin off her kill with a knife.

"Two of ye are awfully close, eh?" Mòrag laughed. "Keeping warm?"

"Smoke, ma'am," Sir William answered quickly. "Smoke hounded me, so I moved. Your hunt was successful, I see."

"Aye, it was. I got two of the buggers but gave one tae Tiree tae stop him drooling over me."

"Well, it's always good to have two huntsmen with us; we'll not go hungry," the knight remarked.

Mòrag smiled at Hawk. "True, ye can nae have too many hunters."

Mòrag skewered the rabbit with a stick and held it above the hot coals. Her smile widened with satisfaction as it sizzled.

"So, Hawk, this other huntsman you spoke of, Garrett, was he as good a hunter as you? A werewolf slayer, as it was?" Sir William asked, sliding away from his seat next to Hawk and bringing balance to the circle around the fire.

"He was better. He was the greatest huntsman I've met. And I've met a few who call themselves by this trade."

"The greatest you ever met?"

"Yes."

"How did you meet then, if I may?" Sir William asked.

The knight stoked the embers with his stick once more.

Hawk leaned forward in his seat, his cheeks flushing with the whispering fire's heat. He always treated fire like a member of his tribe, his family. It cooked his food. It gave him shelter. Fire warmed like a mother's thick shawl, wrapping around him. Smoke rose from the fire into the heavens, carrying his words with it. His mother told him, long ago, that the elders who passed listened to those words with great anticipation. And they loved stories. Storytelling was sacred. The fire brought out the stories in Hawk.

"When I was a young boy, maybe seven, I got lost in Norway's wilderness. I lived as best as I could on what little food I found. I fashioned a bow, set some snares, and ate what came my way. One day, a man dressed in armor like I wear now came across my snares. I thought him a captor and shot at him with my bow. The huntsman deflected the arrow with a single swipe of his sword. He moved faster than any man I'd ever seen. He tried talking to me but quickly realized I couldn't understand. Gestures were the only way to speak to one another."

Hawk pointed to himself in an exaggerated motion. "Garrett, he called himself. He offered me food and water. Salted pork fat. Ha, I still remember. He showed me how to improve my snares and traps. And eventually, he geared himself to leave. I'd been alone in the woods. Hunger can motivate. I stalked behind Garrett for days as he traveled.

"I thought of myself as a clever lynx. Whenever I could, I stole from his saddle—a piece of dried meat here, two fingers' worth of bread there. I bribed his horse with grass pulled from meadows we passed so it wouldn't give me away in the night. Garrett would ride off in the morning, and I'd spend the day tracking his horse's prints to their camp. I thought I was so clever.

"Once, while gathering grass, I frightened a rabbit which tore through the meadow. A large, speckled raptor swooped down on it." Hawk spread out his arms before rapidly closing them in imitation. "The bird feasted on its kill. I watched for some time before I noticed Garrett next to me." Hawk extended his hand outward and then back to himself. "I pointed to my namesake—Hawk. Garrett told me he knew I was following the entire time. He told me I didn't need to steal anymore. He helped me hunt and taught me to track and survive. I learned to be a huntsman, and I am who I am today because of him," Hawk finished with a long sigh.

"Fascinating," the knight said, enjoying the huntsman's tale. "Raised in the wilderness, and now on a mission aided by the king of Alba. Ha. What a climb, Huntsman. What a climb."

"King David isn't the first king I've met, Sir William. I once met the king of Norway, Sigurd the Crusader. We hunted a vicious bear for the king. The bear terrorized a local village outside the capital of Konghelle. The king, Sigurd, sent for our services.

"We spent a week tracking the bear to a cave in a nearby wood. We set up a large snare trap on one of the bear's roaming paths. The bear walked right into it, tangling itself up in our web. I plunged the tomahawk into the bear's skull so deep that when I presented the animal's head to the king, the ax was still dug in."

Hawk swung his arm, demonstrating the deathly blow. He smiled, seeing the attentive faces around the fire.

"The king, so delighted by the end of the bear's reign,

presented me with enough gold to fund my travels for many years."

Hawk brandished the tomahawks that killed the bear from behind his back. He spun the black blades in the firelight so the others could see. The obsidian steel glistened.

"Truly incredible, Huntsman," the knight said. "They are fine instruments with which you paint your tapestry."

Indeed, they were. Passed down for generations in Hawk's tribe, a sacred gift given by the Creator, *Manto*, himself—or that's what his father told him. The tomahawks were always destined to be Hawk's. The slavers disrupted every aspect of that previous life when they captured him. Hawk's luck only turned the moment he recovered the tomahawks. He could still recall every detail of the night he broke into the slaver's hut and recovered the tomahawks before rushing into the wilderness. He wouldn't let the Norsemen take that from his tribe. From him.

"I'll say," Mòrag finally agreed, examining the seared flesh of the rabbit. "But what I dinnae get is why such a kingly gift? Why ye? Any hunter with skill could take down a bear. Why send for ye two? Ye're leaving out part of the story."

She took a bite of the rabbit, waiting for his reply.

Hawk chuckled. "You're right. It wasn't that simple." His laugh faded to a dryer, more serious note. "It never is. The bear wasn't actually a bear, but a berserker, a Norse warrior embedded with the power to morph into a bear in battle. What happens when the warrior enjoys the rush of blood too much? This *bear* was massive. It ripped the soldiers sent after it limb by limb. It grew to enjoy the taste of men. Too many died before the king finally asked for us. He simply wouldn't believe it was happening before it was too late. That's why he sent for us."

Mòrag watched him. She'd forgotten about her dinner for a moment. Sir William simply blinked, staring at the huntsman's story.

Hawk's eyes drifted out of focus, searching the embers of the fire for the memories. They scorched his heart as he unburied them.

"Even then, the fight proved a challenge. I fired a dozen arrows into the bear as it ate members of the king's knights in service. Birger Grey-Hand. Halvor Ironrock. Knights I'd spent a few weeks training and hunting with. Only after I mounted the monster and embedded my ax into its frontal sinus did it fall. That's why the reward was so large. Too much had been risked. I lost too much that day."

Tiree licked at the end of Mòrag's rabbit, her focus no longer concerned with her dinner.

"I see why ye wasnae afraid to charge at the werewolf," she said. "I thought ye're aff yer heid. But really, there's a lot hiding inside of ye."

"So there is," Sir William said, stoking the fire one last time before rising. "At least, every time you swing those axes on your back, you'll never forget that mighty battle of the berserker. Well, I'm afraid that's about all I can handle for one night."

Mòrag agreed and went to her tent. Tiree remained just outside, watching over his companion.

Sir William made his way to his tent and turned back to Hawk one last time. "I'll sleep soundly knowing you're here to watch my back from any bears, berserkers, or what-have-you . . ." The knight turned his head toward Lady NicNeev's tent, then finished, "'Til the morrow, Huntsman."

Hawk put another log on the fire. He grabbed a woolen sheet from his pack and laid it down in the warmth. Climbing onto the blanket, he stretched out and closed his eyes, trying to sleep. His mind took him back to the fight with the berserker. Visions of the blood that spurted from his ax in the bear flooded him; the blood that dripped from Garrett's arms after being ravaged by the monster's bite. The blood in Garrett's eyes as his life hung in jeopardy. He remembered Garrett walking away from Konghelle, alive but never the same. Soon after, Garrett left him on his own, alone in the world again. Abandoned.

No, Sir William, I'll never forget that fight for as long as I live.

Hawk reached underneath his shirt and took out a necklace decorated with beads of *wampum*. Beads the color of snow and profound purples melded to the thin strap around his neck. The wampum beads were one of his only possessions from his homeland. Garrett helped string the beads together in a necklace when he first found Hawk in the woods. Hawk rubbed their smooth exterior between his fingers and tried to forget those he'd left behind.

CHAPTER ELEVEN

The ground splashed mud up the boy's sinewy legs. His feet barely rose above the soaked, slopping embrace. The wet rope tied between his legs made his daily chores dreadfully difficult. He hobbled past the cattle pen with arms full. His arms burned with the weight of his labor while his back ached from the whip. But, at long last, he carried the final load of firewood to the warm stone house of his masters. He released the chopped wood under the shelter, brushing his tattered rags clean. He looked to the master under the shelter for his reward. The single best part of his day—food.

What did the day have in store? Only the bucket for collecting chicken eggs. More chores needed doing.

"Water, please," the boy pleaded.

Blåveis squinted the dark eye at the boy, but that one blue eye remained wide and menacing. The eye always made him cower in fear. But not that day. No fear showed on his face. He had no tears down his cheek. Nothing remained. It had all gone away.

The boy's sister, Ayaksak, had passed away one week ago. The loss crushed all the happiness that remained. He watched his sister smile one last time before she fell asleep forever. The sight of it racked his heart with grief, the smile of the sister he once knew long ago. The sister that would tease him for missing the target with an arrow. The sister who searched the forest for mysteries. The sister who helped clean his knee when he scraped it on the rock while climbing. The sister he loved.

He wore a necklace of wampum beads around his neck, her last gift to him.

He held his hands in the air, trying to demonstrate his thirst, but he only received a shove in response. As he fell, the Norseman wrenched at his necklace, snapping the sinewy string and scattering the beads on the ground. Blåveis laughed.

A lash and a sharp crack. A whip tore through his woolen rags and ripped at his back. Another bite of the whip. He covered his head with his arms until the thrashing ceased. Blåveis trudged back toward his stone house.

Blood and tears mixed into the mud. He righted himself and scanned the ground, frantic. The fresh lashes seared with pain. The whip's bites were a bobcat's claws, digging into his back with every movement. He collected the beads off the ground and, with his hands shaking nearly out of control, placed them in the pouch at his waist. He turned to gather the bucket for his chores, but he couldn't do it any longer. He couldn't bring himself to carry on the path as a slave.

He looked toward the hut where he'd normally eat, and an unusual sight in front of the cattle pen greeted him. A blue shield, decorated with a golden-winged cat breathing fire, and something he hadn't seen since his capture.

He hobbled to the shield, the movement like knives slicing across his back. He brushed the shield aside and gasped at the new prize. There were two of them. He bent over to seize them: the black tomahawks of his tribe.

His wrists strained at their weight, but his hands found a home in the axes' grip. The demons had brought them to the new land and left them where he could see. A mistake.

A shout roared from the stone house, directed at him. The

penned cattle shifted and stamped at the noise, but the fear never came. He was beyond fear.

He swung the tomahawk between his legs and cut the rope hobbling him. Blåveis ran at him, growling like a ferocious black bear. But the boy remained steady. Blåveis didn't stop. The boy swiped the tomahawk at his assailant, mimicking the steps of his father. His hands glowed red with fury. The blade found its mark, scraping down Blåveis's cheek. Surprised, the Norseman fell backward, grasping at his bloodied face. The man tried to rise but slipped on the mud-soaked ground.

The boy swiped the tomahawk at the rope holding the wooden gates of the cattle pen shut. The stamping cattle burst out of the pen, trampling the Norseman's feet as he tried to scuttle backward. Cries of pain rang out, but they didn't come from the boy.

He sprinted out of the compound, as fast as he could, away from the stone houses and into the woods. He leaped over a fallen log and tumbled under a low fir branch. Pushing back to his feet, he moved with speed he hadn't known in a long time. His legs carried him faster and faster. Nothing could stop him as he ran, tomahawks in each hand. Their weight didn't matter, for it seemed like the boy floated through the woods. Untethered, his legs begged for flight. He didn't know where he ran, but he seemed to soar.

Hawk was free.

CHAPTER TWELVE

"Get out of my way! Move, damn it! C'mon, sheep, move!" Mòrag bawled.

The road teemed with black-and-white-faced sheep parading about. They bleated, raising a cacophony of confused cries. Two walls of stone lined the road, trapping in the flock and the band of four riders.

"Epona, c'mon, ride through them."

A shepherd worked his cane at the back of the flock. He raised his arms, flailed them about, and cussed the creatures down the road. Hawk waited for the blockade to pass. Sir William, on the other hand, believed the farmers had a choice of routes and cursed them for taking up the king's road.

"They're moving as quickly as they can, Sir William," Lady NicNeev called out. "They will pass. Perhaps try speaking with the sheep themselves if you wish for the process to speed up." She smirked like a child, easily amused at her quip.

It would be a funny sight. Hawk imitated the sound of the bleating sheep, a mock attempt to communicate with the mass of wool.

Mòrag chortled. "Can ye tell them tae move, then? I dinnae think they ken my language. But yers sounds good. They'll listen to ye." Slowly the mass of wool, horns, fiber, and sheep moved behind them, down the road to Stirling.

The band had already visited Stirling that morning. It was a colossal waste of time. A plethora of tracks and evidence pointed the raiders north. But Lady NicNeev and Sir William insisted they enter Stirling, if only to resupply. They hadn't planned to journey north, and their supplies dwindled. Hawk and Mòrag might have been fine with roughing it, but the other two weren't.

Under the banner of King David, they consulted with General Tylus in Stirling. The general's words echoed in his mind.

"That contingent of Norsemen already left on foot along the north road—three days past. You ride mounted steeds. You'll catch them before long."

Hawk remained sure of that. A large group on foot moved slowly, and at least he could be sure someone had sighted them heading in the direction he traveled.

Once the riders navigated past the sheep, they continued north along the dirt road. It wasn't long before the group ventured into Glen Quaich. The rain had come out to play and showered the riders, although it did little to diminish their pace. They pushed on, over hills of jade and flaxen heather, and down into the valley of wild land. An ocean of grass covered the horizon. Tiree, having missed the excitement of the sheep, returned to the riders before fleeing again into the wild of the open grass. They trotted over stone and mud on the road and continued onward, hearing only the rain and hoofbeats.

The group stopped at the river in the glen's heart. Hawk dismounted and led his horse to drink from the moving water. Mòrag pulled Epona next to him and did the same. The horses gulped the refreshing water before moving to munch from the plentiful grass.

Earlier in the day, Hawk lamented the time lost traveling to Stirling. It was obvious they should follow along the raiders' tracks north. He hoped the new provisions would be worth the time lost. When they rejoined the road north, it eased some of his frustration. And, as Hawk walked around stretching his legs and groin, he was glad for a moment's respite from the rubbing leather saddle. He looked out over the glen at the rolling hills.

"We must be close. From the top of those hills there, we should be able tae see Loch Tay," Mòrag said to Hawk.

Hawk nodded. "Yes, I think you're right. We're close, at any rate." He reached into his bag and grabbed a bite of dried venison, fresh from Stirling's markets. "Think you could climb to the top of them hills? Without a horse?"

"Aye. That's barely a hill." She smirked. "That's a wee bump. My clan sits in the heart of the Highlands. I live in the mountains, and that's nae mountain."

"What do the mountains look like?" Hawk asked, amused.

"They're incredible! The bonnie Highlands spread out for miles tae see. And they climb up above the clouds. There's nae anything like them in the world. The tallest one is right near my village, Beinn Nibheis. When I was young, my da and I climbed tae the very top. Even in the middle of the summer, it snowed all around the peak. I remember it being so windy I nearly blew off the edge. But my da held on tae me tight. He'd pick me up and pretend I was an eagle. He'd spin me around, and I'd fly above the clouds, and he'd even pretend I was goin' tae fly off the side of the mountain. It was great. I loved it." She laughed, gazing off over the hills in memory of her time as a young eagle.

"Your mother must enjoy that story."

"Ha. C'mon, as if we'd tell her that. Nae, she worried a lot about me, I think 'cause I was her only child, maybe? I dinnae ken." She paused, staring at the ground beneath the huntsman's feet.

"You miss them, don't you? Your parents?" Hawk asked, trying to guess Mòrag's pondering hesitation.

"Aye, I do. I spent most of my life waiting tae get out and explore the rest of the world. Now that I've been away for so long, I cannae wait tae go back. Silly, right?"

"No, it's not."

"I've been away for months now. This will be the longest I've ever been away from my clan. It's nice, but it's different. Ye ken what I mean?"

"Yes. I understand." It was the huntsman's turn to pause in thought, lost in the mythical idea of a home.

It had been years since he had a place to call home. The very idea of a home had been stolen away, a forgotten wisp of a memory.

"If I can find the sword, then I can find my way back tae the clan," Mòrag said, brushing her hand over Epona's dark gray coat.

"This sword you're after must be important to you. Why? A sword can be reforged, a sapphire placed in a pommel. Why cross hundreds of leagues for the sentimentality of heirlooms?"

"It's nae about the sword, is it? It's my da trusting me in the world. It's proving that I'm more than the little lass he'd fly on top of the mountain. Tae prove I'm a warrior of Clan MacTarbh." Mòrag lifted her chin, daring Hawk to question her purpose again.

But he just nodded. "I understand."

She squinted her eyes. "Do ye?"

"You said you were the only child? You have no brothers? Then, I understand . . ."

Her gaze softened as she took in Hawk. "And ye? When were ye last home?"

Hawk paused, looking to the ground for inspiration for what to say, but found nothing. Being a huntsman made the road his home, it seemed, traveling from one village to the next. But it was the pursuit of the slavers that kept him moving most days. Still, he could never forget his first home.

"I haven't been home in some time," Hawk finally said, "but I can't seem to get it out of my head. It's been, perhaps, fifteen winters since I last saw it. We lived in a village on a large bluff, surrounded by forest. The forest made the village feel massive, like it was a part of our village itself. My sister and I played amidst trees. We'd always set out toward a long, tree-covered hill spattered with gray boulders. We loved to search for Makiawisug, the Little People. They were spirits that lived hidden in the shadows of the forest.

"They'd help our people where they could, in exchange for offerings of corn and berries. But they wanted to remain hidden. So naturally, my sister and I would go searching for them. At least that's what we told ourselves. I think we just really liked climbing the rocks together. We brought offerings of food in baskets to the rocks, then climbed around searching for them."

Hawk laughed, remembering how much fun it was to hide their reed baskets filled with colored corn, beans, and squash.

"Once," Hawk continued, "while on the rocks, one of the Makiawisug jumped out across the rock to retrieve the basket. The thing is, you're not supposed to stare at the Makiawisug, or they'll bring you misfortune. But I was a boy and couldn't help it —my first time seeing one. The Makiawisug turned, gave me quite the menacing glare, ran up to me, and grabbed my leg. I still remember that sharp, static shock of his touch. I stumbled back and slid down the face of the rock, scraping my knee up."

Hawk swallowed like he felt the scrape again. Despite the many years since, the incident never fleeted too far from his memory. A pang of regret always lingered in it. Did the Makiawisug curse him to this fate? Was he the cause of misfortune to his village?

"Was it a brownie?" Mòrag asked.

"A what?"

"A brownie, a small faerie creature that my da said used tae come out of the wood tae complete a task and ye had tae leave offerings for them."

"Maybe, although no one I knew called them anything but Makiawisug."

"What happened tae it?" Mòrag asked, her eyebrows raised.

"I lost track of it, I'm afraid. And learned my lesson not to stare. My sister came to my rescue, helping me clean my knee in a river. She even boasted about my brave chance encounter later in front of the village . . ." Hawk trailed off, the memory pulling at him like an eddy.

Somehow, Mòrag seemed to understand what that silence meant. "Ye miss yer sister, then?"

"Yes," Hawk said, "very much so. I've been seeing her again in dreams ever since the Norsemen's trail grew close. My family, my home, all of it. The dreams are just memories, over and over, every night. I know they're just a mob of raiders to you, but the Norsemen have felt like demons, haunting my nightmares."

Hawk clasped his hands together to cease the trembling.

Again, Mòrag seemed to understand. "Ye cannae go home until ye find these Norse yer after, is that right? Like the sword."

"Yes. Something of that sort." Hawk couldn't bring himself to explain that there wasn't a home to return to. That the Norse slavers had taken it from him. It was too much to share. Not yet. Mòrag didn't press for details, so he started again.

"We'll find that sword—"

"Ho there, Huntsman!" Sir William interrupted. "Lady NicNeev and I believe we're near Loch Tay. The ride is but over those hills. Let us tarry here no longer."

The knight and the lady stood waiting for Hawk and Mòrag.

"Agreed," Hawk answered. "Come, not far now."

Hawk led his horse up the road toward the northern horizon. They walked two by two. Lady NicNeev, still hooded in her green tunic, sat upon her saddle while the rest trudged on beside their mounts.

"Sir William, why do ye have that blue-and-white-striped scarf around your back? It's soaking, weighing ye down, naw?" Mòrag blurted, riled up, following behind the swaying blue cloth.

"My cloak? No, I shall not remove it. Never. It's a mark. A mark that I'm in service of the king. *The king.*"

Mòrag, unsatisfied, continued to pry, "Why the blue and white? Is that yer clan's colors?"

"No, it is the colors chosen by King David himself," Sir

William answered, shocked at the very notion that he'd choose to represent himself rather than his sovereign.

"Why does King David choose that for representation?" Hawk asked, *his* curiosity now piqued. "If I recall correctly, King David's heraldry is a golden dragon."

"The golden dragon is King David's, yes. But this cloak represents the kingdom of Alba. He chose it as a banner of peace and of a nation." Sir William flapped his cloak so they could see the full span of the white *X*.

"Why choose that, rather than a fierce dragon on yer back, Sir William?" Mòrag pressed, muddling up the knight.

"Well . . . You see . . . It's because . . ." Sir William stammered.

"You don't know?" Lady NicNeev probed, her voice higher pitched with a haughty air. "Ah, a first for the journey. Sir William knows not about the history of Alba, and I, Lady Phillipa NicNeev, do."

She let the taunt settle in for a moment before enlightening the group.

Clearing her voice, as though about to make a speech, she began.

"Óengus mac Fergusa, king of the Picts, led an army of Picts and Gaelic soldiers to war against the Angles. Óengus prayed to Saint Andrew. He begged on his knees for his blessing, asking for a sign of victory. On the battlefield the next day, Óengus witnessed a miracle, for the white clouds against the blue sky formed the cross of Saint Andrew. With Saint Andrew's blessing on his side, Óengus secured victory over the Angles. Óengus is said to have taken the blue sky and white cross as his banner. King David no doubt hopes to inspire the kingdom of Alba to rally behind the ancient, fabled banner."

"The king is a man of God," put forth the knight. "Doubtless, he'd choose to represent his kingdom with a symbol of the faith. I, for one, think it a grand gesture."

"If you ask me," NicNeev added, "David's golden dragon banner better represents the fiery nature of Alba's people."

"I agree," said Mòrag. She looked at the huntsman. "What about ye, Hawk? What do ye think?"

The huntsman didn't meet her eyes. "I don't have any problems with any of the king's banners."

"C'mon, ye must think something about it. Ye met the king after all."

Hawk shrugged. "He can wave whatever piece of cloth he wishes. Folks rarely choose whom to rally behind because of the animal or color of their banner. Rather, it's the man who leads the cause that the people follow. So, Mòrag, if the king wants to have a banner for peace, so be it. The golden dragon will soon be back, for if there's one truth that's certain in this world, it is that kingdoms wage war. The golden dragon will fly in the wind once again. No peace lingers for long."

Hawk gripped the reins of his horse tighter, surprised by his darker tone. There was one banner the huntsman despised, only one that would incite all Hawk's anger: a golden-winged lion upon a dark blue field. That was the one banner he'd rally against.

Hawk looked at Mòrag to see if it satisfied her curiosity. Her eyes had fallen on the ground in front of her feet as she walked alongside Epona. Hawk nearly explained his answer, worried he may have upset Mòrag, but there was no need. She had already moved on.

"How did ye become a knight, Sir William?" Mòrag asked, unaware that he had explained the very question in excruciating detail on the outskirts of Edinburgh. Hawk exhaled, and, placing his foot into the stirrups, climbed back into his saddle.

"I am glad you asked . . ." the knight began.

———

Sir William's story long past, the expedition fell back to the quiet reverence of the rain and their horses beneath them. The sun broke through the clouds on rare occasions to brighten the road, but the rain never faltered. The huntsman swayed in the saddle with every step. Lady NicNeev had stopped to relieve herself and insisted they ride on ahead. Meanwhile, Mòrag rode alongside Sir William, just ahead of Hawk.

Sir William perked up. He turned his head and made his best attempt at a dog raising its ear to disruption. In the distance, under the rain, voices carried toward the riders.

Around the bend of a jutting hill, a gathering of men surrounded a stuck cart heaped with stacked barrels and bushels of assorted vegetables and harvests, including a rather large yellow-and-green gourd. The abundance of marketable goods headed toward Stirling had weighed on the cart, sinking it into the wet mud of the washed-out path. A stout pony tied to the wagon gorged on the grass as the cart sat motionless. The men surrounding the cart cackled and hollered.

The huntsman rode his mount from behind Mòrag's, getting a better look at the commotion.

Four men surrounded a young girl whose back was pressed up against the cart. She stood soaked in dirtied woolen trousers and a frazzled black smock.

The huntsman squinted. Even in the rain, Hawk noticed the girl shook and cried. Only then did he notice that one of the four men held a knife to the cowering man beside him. There weren't four assailants but three. The man's face hung bloodied and purple, though Hawk didn't think the man's grimace came from his injuries.

Hawk, Mòrag, and Sir William approached softly on horseback. Whether from the drowning sound of rain or the preoccupation at hand, the trio of bandits around the cart didn't heed their approach.

"I'm first," snickered the bulky, bearded brute in the circle. "Best get under the wagon and out of the rain, eh?"

The man took a step forward and clutched at the lone lass. He flung her into the soft mud. She backpedaled defensively under the cart, trying to escape, but the brute proved more agile than he appeared. He clung to her trousers, seizing the girl as she writhed and kicked.

"Ho! Riders approaching. Shite!" shouted another of the gathered men, turning his attention from the day's entertainment to the approaching riders.

He kicked the brute on the ground. The man holding the hostage at knifepoint roughly moved his victim to the side. The bandits brandished steel.

"Halt at once!" roared Sir William

Not even taking the time to adorn his helm, the knight leaped from his mare. Like a flash of lightning, he unsheathed his sword. Sir William raised the hilt to his chest before readying himself.

"Get a look at this hero, eh," chortled a redheaded man in a brown gambeson. "Who'd you steal that plate from, eh?" Only then did Hawk notice their accent wasn't from Alba. Hawk's heart quickened.

"I am Sir William Maurice of Holyrood, a knight in service of King David. I command you, in the king's name, to cease your actions at once, bandits."

"You, a knight? A moor like you? I don't believe that, *oh, sir.*"

Sir William's voice shook with rage. "Lay down your arms at once." Then, with an unnerving calm, he said, "I won't warn you again."

"I know your bluff," said the man in the brown gambeson. "Let's see if you can dance as good as you dress. Then the lads and I will dance with your wench, eh? How's that sound?"

"Try it," Mòrag beckoned, nocking an arrow and raising her bow to aim at the brown gambeson.

"Oh, look here, lads," the man in the brown gambeson said, exaggeratedly licking his lips. "She means to put on a good row. But I'll work for it. We got ourselves a regular three-on-three scrap. I haven't had a good scrap in weeks. What do you say, lads, eh?"

The bearded brute nodded with a grin that rivaled a tusked boar.

"These must be some of the Norsemen we follow," Hawk said to his companions, searching for the rest of the mob. *Blåveis must be here, surely. There must be more.* His eyes darted around the area, but Hawk could only make out the three bandits there in front of them.

"There are too few of them," Hawk said, but no one listened.

Sir William's focus remained on the bandits ahead. Mòrag hopped down from her horse and grabbed the knight's reins. A scattered beam of sunlight broke through the clouds onto the riders, but the rain continued to fall.

The knight mocked the bandits. "The girl and the farmer there. It's clear bandit scum as yourselves prefer three against two. Not three against three. I am happy to give you that satisfaction, so my huntsman companion here will watch as justice is served." Sir William nodded with a proud grin.

"What?" Hawk asked, hesitating in the saddle as Mòrag shoved the horses' reins into his lap.

Before the huntsman could say anything more, events accelerated in front of him.

Sir William held his chin high, not wavering from the bandits cackling like hyenas. Without warning, he lunged. It was a feint, meant to draw an attack. It succeeded. The aged man on the end countered. He swung his club toward Sir William, who promptly parried and shoved the man over his feet and onto his back. The knight whirled, meeting the brutish man's attacking strike with a defensive horizontal swing of his blade. Their swords met with a resounding metallic clang before Sir William spun the blade, twisting the man's wrist until he released the blade with a cry.

Sir William leaped forward, this time without a feint, and plunged his steel blade into the brute's chest. A chilling gasp sounded as the brute's air escaped his lungs. Blood coughed from the wound and his mouth as he gargled uncontrollably, crashing into the mud.

Meanwhile, the man in the leather gambeson had thrown his knife at Mòrag. She sidestepped, pivoting her bow into the oncoming projectile and deflecting it. Mòrag's finger, slippery from the rain, slid from the string of her bow as she fired an arrow in response, which sailed straight into the side of the cart. Mòrag crouched instinctively, reaching into her quiver for another shaft. The man in the brown gambeson used the opportunity to sprint toward her, sword angled for a strike.

Hawk leaped out of his saddle toward Mòrag and the encroaching bandit, tomahawks already brandished. The bandit moved quickly—Hawk wouldn't reach Mòrag in time. He held an up ax, nearly glowing red with fury, and made ready to thrust it into the brown gambeson. But Hawk paused. The tomahawk took on a red luminosity.

Sir William appeared behind the Norseman and grasped his full mop of red hair. The bandit's head snapped back, and he spun around with the momentum. Wrapping a plated arm around the bandit's sword to prevent any swinging, Sir William drove his blade into the man's neck. The bandit coughed, blood spraying the muddy ground, before collapsing.

Hawk glanced back at the tomahawk. Its wet black steel no longer shined. *A trick of the sunlight in the rain.* The sunlight had vanished, leaving only a gray ceiling of clouds. Hawk moved over to the others.

Sir William helped Mòrag to her feet. They turned to face the first bandit Sir William had thrown to the ground, only to discover that he had dropped his club and fled.

"We must bring the king's justice," Sir William said quickly, voice vibrating with energy from the battle. "Quickly, Archeress, bring him down."

Mòrag swiveled the ornamented bow into position, knocked an arrow, and raised the angle of her bow in aim. She let go of the string, launching the shaft through the rainy sky. The man running across the deep heather dropped to the ground. He attempted to rise, but fell once more, then lay still against the wet earth.

"Excellent shot, my lady," Sir William crowed. "Upon my word, you are a fantastic archeress. Truly gifted. "

"Thank ye, sir," Mòrag replied. "And thank ye for back there. I . . ."

"Think nothing of it. It's but a duty of the service, my lady."

"What do you mean?" Hawk grumbled. "We should've interrogated them for information on the remaining Norsemen. We should've waited."

"Come now, Huntsman." Sir William laughed. "Do you really think those creatures wished to have a chat? There's no discussion to be had with men of that ilk."

"I would've tried," Hawk pressed, annoyance like an itch beneath his trousers.

He knew he should be grateful to his companions, but with the Norsemen, there was no room for brash action. If he wanted to bring them down, he needed to be at the top of his craft. He was too close to make foolish mistakes.

"Don't get in my way of finding the rest of them," he growled, "or I'll go it alone and leave you all behind."

"Come now," Sir William said. "They would've revealed nothing. It was my solemn duty as a knight. Now, let us help those in need."

Sir William made his way toward the cart. Mòrag lingered for a moment. She pursed her lips, cheeks drawing in as she considered Hawk. Part of him felt ashamed by what she must've seen in that stare. The desperation—and anger. They stood but feet from those demons, and yet Hawk learned nothing of Blåveis or the remaining Norsemen.

"We're all here tae help," she finally said quietly, lips parting to form a smile. "And that's three less Norsemen tae deal with— guaranteed. C'mon, let's see what we can learn." She turned and followed Sir William.

The rain dripped off the waxy resin in Hawk's hair as he stood unflinching in the mud. *Three less Norsemen tae deal with.* But was that the way he wanted them dealt with? Hawk had always imagined something more—something slower for Blåveis and the Norsemen. Perhaps a few bites with a whip or slow cuts with an ax—anything to give Blåveis a chance to regret what he'd done to Hawk's family. Yet Mòrag's words made him feel almost embarrassed at the thought. Would his family want that from Hawk? In the end, the huntsman sighed a brief respite. Mòrag's words rang true: that was three fewer Norsemen.

He hustled to catch the others. The wet soil squelched around Hawk's boots as he trudged behind her. He made his way toward the cart to see if they could do anything to help the terrorized woman and man. He passed the fallen Norsemen, checking with his boots to see if they still drew breath, hoping to question the position of the remaining slavers. None lived. It was clear; Hawk rode on the path that would lead to Blåveis and the rest of the Norsemen slavers. Something else was also clear to Hawk: Sir William knew how to dispense the king's justice.

CHAPTER THIRTEEN

"Ale, please, innkeeper," Hawk said, lifting his voice over the music swelling behind him. "Four, if you please."

The huntsman placed his silver pieces on the bar. The innkeeper, a portly old man, twisted the tap on the wooden keg and filled the tankards with the gilded beverage. He handed them to Hawk, ale brimming over and onto the counter.

The air swelled with merriment. The room rustled and bustled with the finest and destitute of Kenmore's village. Every citizen had a niche of joy inside Tatha Tavern's walls. Sorcha, daughter of Simidh, the cooper, piped an ethereal melody on her wooden flute. Mìcheil drummed a booming rhythm, much to the delight of the dancing patrons swirling and twirling around one another. Dàibhidh, the son of the village priest, strummed his lute in elegant harmony. Music swam through the air and mixed with laughter and shouting, creating a ringing chorus of happiness. The huntsman couldn't help but join in with the cheer.

Hawk and his companions had made it north to Kenmore before dusk. They sat at a table in a corner opposite the music. He sat on the bench, distributing ale to Mòrag, Lady NicNeev, and Sir William. They drank, quenching the thirst that had accumulated along the trail.

"If only it were wine," Lady NicNeev sighed.

She removed her green hood, revealing her delicate blonde bun.

"Ah, yes! If only it were wine from the grapes of the Loire in France. A delicacy!" the knight agreed, wiping the mustache of foam that hung from his lip.

Hawk disliked the sour vinegar taste of mediocre wine. And, in his experience, most wines tasted mediocre. But he withheld that opinion, occupying himself with the tankard. Hawk bobbed his head to the drumming beat.

"This place is great!" Mòrag burst out. "It's so full of energy. I dinnae see any Norsemen about though."

"I noticed no Norsemen too," the lady said as she scanned the room. "I believe the room has noticed us, however."

She wasn't mistaken. Stares and quizzical glances periodically fell on their table. It was clear the band of four riders from the south stood out. Every other patron wouldn't have been amiss in a farmer's field or kitchen with their rough woolen clothes.

"We must not make a scene," Lady NicNeev added. "We must blend in."

Sir William nodded. "Yes indeed, blend in for now. Ask about the bandits later."

Mòrag gulped down the rest of her ale, then stood and grabbed the huntsman's hand. "Here, I ken a way tae blend in. Hawk, c'mon, dance with me."

"I can't. No, wait—"

Despite his protests, Mòrag dragged him to the earthen floor of the dancing tavern-goers.

Hawk hesitantly stepped onto the floor, feeling awkward in his heavy leather armor. Mòrag twisted his arm toward the dancers. She gracefully fell into stride. Hawk clumsily attempted to follow Mòrag's lead. She clasped hands with the neighboring dancers, joining a circle of rhythm, spinning, and music. The huntsman's feet found their step. They flowed, encircled with the others, interlocking arms and moving in tempo to the musicians' art.

Mòrag's dark cascade of hair swayed with every twist and turn. Hawk met her eyes, vibrant and emerald, and fell further into the rhythm of the flute's trill. Mòrag's laughter, contagious, spread to the huntsman, first with a smile, then a breathless gasp of happiness. They danced until sweat dripped from their foreheads and thirst hung on their lips.

Hawk and Mòrag grabbed another round of ale and headed back to their table. The glee brimming in Hawk's chest might have lasted all night had he not seen the new guest on their bench. The man's chin sprouted a jolly beard. The lines on his face aged him older than most, but he hadn't lost the red of his hair. He welcomed Hawk and Mòrag back to the group as old friends.

"Greetings," said the new guest. "Sit down. Sit down. I hear you're the huntsman, Hawk. Good to meet you. And you, my lady Mòrag, good tidings to you. You are a grace to see dance, but I hear from the knight that you're also fierce with that decorated bow of yours," the man said, pointing to the weapon propped on the bench.

Mòrag nodded and affably asked, "Who might ye be?"

"Oh, aye, of course, I haven't introduced myself. My name is Magnus. I'm lord of Kenmore and these lands." He picked up his glass of wine for a sip.

"What's everyone celebrating tonight?" Hawk asked the lord, wiping the sweat off his forehead.

"A wedding," Magnus replied. "Anna and Lucas were married today. They've gone to bed, to be sure, but the celebration continues into the night. By God, did you miss a feast today. One to be remembered. We roasted a pig, an entire boar. Can you believe that?"

"A shame," Lady NicNeev remarked drily. "I can only imagine the spectacle of it all."

"You would've loved it, my lady. All of you would've—the

beauty of it. But now then . . . Where was it you said you were riding from?"

"We have traveled from Edinburgh, under the banner of King David," Sir William boasted, puffing up slightly.

"You don't look like King David's soldiers," the lord said matter-of-factly.

"So you've seen soldiers then? What about Norsemen?" NicNeev asked, turning her head in to better hear Magnus over the tavern's clatter.

"Yes, yes. They came in not more than two days ago. Fifty or so men there were."

"Fifty?" the lady asked, her eyes wide.

"Aye, fifty of the king's men and a dozen Norsemen in tow. The king's men told us they were on their way north and that we should give them a drink or they'd burn the village down. Well, they drank most of our ale and made off with a few of our cattle. But I suppose it could've been worse. No one was hurt, thankfully, or anything dreadful. Why do you ask?"

Interesting. Fifty of the king's men? They must have captured the Norsemen, Hawk thought while taking a sip of his tankard.

"My lord," Lady NicNeev said, assuming the responsibility of corresponding with Lord Magnus. "We traveled north to Kenmore following that regiment of troops. We travel with great haste, sent directly by the king."

Hawk listened and stared at NicNeev. She was not above using deceit to aid their efforts, he noted.

She continued, "We'd like to congress with the king's men. Where are they staying?"

"My lady, I apologize. Well, you see . . . they left. They took to the eastern road yesterday to Pitlochry. They wouldn't say where they were onto after that. *King's business*, you see." The lord gestured, showing what he thought of the *king's business*. "But from what I hear, they're towing along those Norsemen, and they make for Urquhart Castle, near Inverness. They'll be headed northward then, won't they?"

"It seems we're gaining on them, one step at a time," Sir William pointed out.

He rubbed his bald head with a piece of cloth and took another sip of ale.

"Those Norsemen were under the guard of the king's men? What else did you hear, my lord? If I may be so bold . . ." NicNeev said coquettishly, letting her eyes do the talking.

The lord blushed under the suggestion in her gaze and cleared his throat. "Well, they were heavily armored and heavily supplied. This wasn't a scouting party escorting those Norsemen. But, well . . . you know that as the king's messengers." He nodded to the gathered group.

Then his attention moved across the room. A pair of revelers climbed onto a bench and danced to the tune up high. Magnus huffed a laugh before turning his gaze back to Hawk's table.

"Well, I can see from your gloomy faces that you hoped for a bit more information. I'm afraid I don't know anymore. My concern is with my town and my people, and the men moved on, so I dug no deeper. But fret not, my new friends, for you are on horse and they're at the mercy of marching on foot. You shall catch them at Pitlochry. I'm sure of it."

"We've heard that before . . ." Hawk muttered.

He began thinking the Norsemen might be half horse with how swiftly they crossed the country. But if King David's troops captured them and escorted them north, tracking them would prove much easier. More soldiers meant more prints and a slower pace.

"Get some sleep here tonight. Your horses and yourselves could use a good rest. Then, on the morrow, you'll be on them in no time," Lord Magnus assured them. A crash shot up from the other side of the tavern. "Now, excuse me, sirs—my ladies. I must remind Pàdraig when enough is enough. Forgive me."

He got up from the table, leaving his drink behind, and cursed at the drunken man who had fallen to the floor.

"The Norsemen must've been captured, right?" Hawk said, hoping for reassurance to combat his creeping suspicions.

Sir William nodded fervently. "King David's troops would have come across the raiders and no doubt slapped them in irons. The king has no use for vile bandits of that sort."

Hawk could almost see it. Chained together in iron, Blåveis and the Norsemen were forced to march north under guard. Hawk wished for nothing more than to see them rotting in chains as he had. As his family had.

"We're one step behind," Mòrag said. "Captured too? We'll catch them, Hawk."

"I know. Yes. It's just taking longer than I thought," the huntsman replied with a weary sigh.

"Maybe it doesn't have to," Lady NicNeev pondered as if figuring out the winning maneuver in a tight battle. "These king's men will have left from here east to Pitlochry yesterday. By now, they've left Pitlochry and will be headed up northwest along the road."

She raised an eyebrow, anticipating her companions would gather her meaning. Hawk and the others disappointingly did not. He turned over what she said in his head, trying to figure it out.

Then it made sense. Hawk gathered what she hinted at and burst out, "Why are they headed east and then back west? Why not just head straight north?"

"Exactly, thank you. Someone is listening," she said with a smirk. "These raiders have taken the road around the forest that lies directly north. It's easier to travel on the road, that much is true. Riding after them around the forest would take us at the very least a day, mayhap two. However, cut through the forest, and we can catch them tomorrow as they move on the road toward Loch Ness and Urquhart Castle. We'll catch them in no time."

"A shortcut!" Mòrag chimed in excitedly.

"Must be an awfully large forest, to be worth going

around . . ." Hawk thought out loud. "Why else would the soldiers choose to march in the wrong direction? It would've been difficult to get supply wagons through a forest if it were large enough."

"It is large. Quite large indeed," NicNeev agreed.

"A large forest must have a name. Does it have a name, Lady NicNeev?" Mòrag asked in curious wonder.

Lady NicNeev drank the last sip of her ale, placing the tankard down hard on the table. She hesitated, as if afraid to give the answer. The huntsman cranked his head to the side, eager to hear the response.

"The Black Wood of Rannoch lies to the north of here . . ." answered Lady NicNeev.

"The Black Wood of Rannoch?" Mòrag's expression darkened. "We dinnae want tae go through there. Naw, better tae take the road with the raiders."

Hawk's curiosity grew. A moment ago, she was excited about a shortcut. What caused the turn of heart?

"Why not, Mòrag?" Hawk asked.

Mòrag's face paled, her voice growing quieter. "Even in the Highlands, I've heard of that forest. I told ye there's no magic in all of Alba. That it was gone from this land? Well, that wasnae entirely true. Magic remains in the dark corners of the land. That wood is one of those corners. They say a dark shroud hangs over it. An ancient evil lurks in that forest. We shouldnae go in there."

Mòrag's eyes were wide and earnest, almost pleading. Lady NicNeev tried taking a sip from her tankard but found it empty.

"If I may," Sir William said. "We have a duty to King David himself to follow the bandits. Following does not involve shortcuts through the woods. Our duty lies on the road to the east. Stay on the road, go through Pitlochry, and find the bandits on the path with those soldiers as planned. It's the easiest and safest plan. We know they took the bandits east, but we don't know where they will be if we cut through the forest."

Mòrag nodded in agreement while Lady NicNeev rolled her eyes.

The lady turned to Hawk. "What do you think, Huntsman? Shortcut through some woods, or saddle up and parade about the road again?"

The huntsman glanced around at his companions. Their eyes lingered on him, waiting for a response. He brushed his spiked raven hair with his hand, weighing his options. Risk their mission to save one day? Or take the easier, albeit longer, route to Blåveis and his raiders?

"I've never been afraid of any wood—ancient or otherwise," Hawk began. "It comes with being a huntsman. But Mòrag is from these lands, and I trust her instincts. If she thinks it is safer, or smarter, to go around, then I trust her judgment. We should head for Pitlochry first thing in the morning, then on the road northwest to this Urquhart Castle." Mòrag and Sir William smiled in approval. Lady NicNeev brought her tankard up, cursed its emptiness, and then slammed it down on the table.

"Fine," she said with a bit of ire. "Let's not dawdle. Get some rest. We ride hard tomorrow morning for these damn Norsemen." No one budged from their seats. "Suit yourselves. I'll see you all on the morrow." She pushed away and walked off toward the stairs where the rooms lay beyond.

Mòrag ran for another round of ale. The tavern grew loud, with chattering guests since the dancing stopped. The music had broken off for a moment. Even musicians needed an opportunity to drink. Mòrag returned and distributed the heavy tankards.

"Excellent sword work today, my friend," Hawk said to Sir William, raising his voice over the crowd and sipping the froth from his drink. "You made quite a show with your blade."

"I had a duty. Peace to uphold," the knight replied between gulps.

"Truly, Sir William," Mòrag said. "Thank ye. I slipped in that mud there and thought I was done for. Ye saved my arse. I'll nae forget that. Ye're a good man."

She raised her vessel toward the knight and huntsman. Hawk and Sir William followed the gesture.

"Tae good ale, with good company," she toasted.

As if on cue, the music fired up once again, and within moments, the floor flooded with the dancing and strutting of the merry tavern folk.

———

A thick slop of muck covered the street outside the Tatha Tavern stables from the previous day's unending rain. Hooves and feet splashed through a mess of puddles, shallow but slick. Hawk's onyx boots morphed into a dirty brown. He adjusted his buckskin kilt and grabbed the leather saddle off the post. He fixed the saddle atop his bay mare's rug, then fastened the girth around the horse and tightened the billets.

"Have ye thought of a name for him yet?" Mòrag asked, saddling Epona beside him.

Hawk hadn't given it any thought, for the horse was not his to name; it was the king's. "I don't know . . . The last horse I had from the king, the one Tiree scared off, was Cursor. Latin . . . So, maybe this is . . . Equus?"

"Equus? Aye, that sounds pretty," Mòrag said, nodding and murmuring the name as if to memorize it.

"I'll go with Equus then," Hawk said, bemused.

He fit the mare's bridle and secured it.

"Did ye dream again last night?" Mòrag asked quietly, as if not wanting to remind him of something unpleasant.

"Huh," Hawk said, realizing for the first time himself that his sleep hadn't fallen victim to the memories of the Norsemen.

Letting his guard down to blend in with the tavern guests, he allowed himself a moment of relaxation, and perhaps that helped. But Hawk didn't have an answer as to why no dreams plagued him.

"I guess I didn't. Maybe it was the ale." Hawk grinned, glancing over at Mòrag.

She met his smile with one of her own, then rolled her eyes back to the saddle.

Sunlight hadn't crested the tavern yet, and the riders remained in the shade, hidden from the morning rays. Sir William had already mounted his horse and sat in the saddle, ready to fulfill his duty. Lady NicNeev walked her tacked horse over to join the others. Her green tunic clung to her figure, shaded by the tavern. But her hair caught the first rays of sun billowing over the building and radiated in the golden light.

"We're late," the lady declared. "We should've been moving at dawn. Not once the sun was already in the sky."

"Come now. A good night's rest will make us swifter on the road," the knight countered.

His mount shifted in place, splashing muddy water over its fetlocks. The blue feather hanging on the knight's helm swished with every step.

"We're ready, I believe," Hawk said.

Mòrag grabbed Epona's leather reins and walked the gray mare in line with the others. With her out of the way, the huntsman could make out Lord Magnus approaching. He seemed in good spirits, pulling up the sides of his red beard with a toothy grin.

"Greetings, my friends!" the lord called out to them, arms wide in a humble gesture of welcoming. "Off so soon, are we? But you haven't even met Anna or Lucas. You danced at their festivities. At least come wish them good fortune."

"My lord, I'm afraid our king sends us with all haste," Lady NicNeev replied, stepping into the stirrup and launching onto her mount.

"Ah yes, *king's business*, as they say. Well, I wish you all good —" An earsplitting, horrible scream cut the lord off.

A woman ran down the adjacent street toward the tavern. She wailed a deep guttural sound that only came from pure terror. She stumbled, caught herself, and sprinted toward the line of horses. Falling into the mud on her knees, she grabbed the lord's robes and looked up with eyes rubbed raw and red. The stains of tears washed down from her pale face.

"What is this? What has happened, child?" Lord Magnus asked, reaching down and lifting the woman out of the muck by her arms.

"Th-th-the . . ." she stammered, unable to collect herself amidst her pool of tears.

"It's all right, child. Bless you. You're safe now. What has happened, Mhari? Speak. Help us understand."

"My daughter, Natalie . . ." the woman managed, sniffling through every breath. "She went out tae play at dawn, carrying that wooden sword of hers. She wanted tae pick flowers, the bluebells, at the wood's edge. Now I cannae find her. She went in tae the wood." She sobbed, twisting her whole body.

Hawk saw the look of concern wash over Mòrag's face. Mòrag glanced at him, then back at the woman.

"How long ago did you last see her?" Mòrag questioned.

"An hour, nae more," the woman cried, then fell to her knees once more, begging at the lord's feet. "Help me, please. Ye got tae do somethin' for my wee bairn."

Lord Magnus's voice was firm, a lord taking command of the situation. "Your other children, are they safe? Is it just the girl?"

"Aye," the woman managed, tears flowing down the curves of her lips.

Hawk was surely missing something. It didn't make sense to him.

"She's only been gone an hour? That's not that long . . . Surely she'll turn up. She must just be having fun in the woods."

Lord Magnus turned to Hawk, his jolly face transformed into scorn. "Little Natalie is only twelve years of age, sir. The Black Wood of Rannoch is no place for a girl that young. Grown men venture into the forest and don't return. You're not from this land, Huntsman. You're not in the south anymore. The wild is fierce here."

Hawk bit his cheek to stifle a rebuke. The lord squatted to eye level with Mhari, who was beside herself in the mud.

"Why did she go into the wood? Why didn't you tell her of the dangers?"

"I did. I have. She kens nae tae go in there. I dinnae ken why she did today. Help me. Please, ye got tae help me find my wee Talie!"

"What dangers lie in that wood?" Hawk demanded again.

"Bodach, it's said," the lord responded gravely, speaking a name Hawk hadn't heard before. "They say he walks these woods like a dark shadow. Talie isn't the first child to go missing in the wood, and I dare say she won't be the last."

"Bodach?" Hawk repeated.

"Aye, Bodach," the lord confirmed.

The woman shrieked. Lord Magnus picked Mhari up and helped her walk to the wooden railing of the tavern. They leaned against it, and the woman wailed once more. The lord spoke to her over the sound.

"Our fighting men are gone, Mhari . . . There's nothing I can do. It's out of my hands."

She responded like the words were a death sentence, collapsing against the large man's chest. His wool robes absorbed her cries.

Pieces shifted into place in Hawk's mind. The way drew clear now; an opportunity to catch those he chased bloomed before them. Something else bubbled and brewed as well. An urge. Hawk needed to see what danger grew too bold in the wood ahead of them.

Impulse erupted out of Hawk. "We should travel north then. A shortcut through the wood. Save us time catching up to the *soldiers* headed north."

Mòrag turned and looked directly into Hawk's eyes. Her face

was stony, but her eyes blazed with a piercing vibrant green. She spoke to Hawk in a soft, harsh tone, her words like a vow.

"Aye. We have tae go in tae the wood. We have tae find the girl."

Sir William protested, "What about Pitlochry? Those we follow? I am a knight, bound in honor to help those in need. But this would surely be folly. Our duties lie with the king's justice. We should follow the king's men. And," he added to Mòrag, "as you said yourself, avoid the Black Wood."

Mòrag's words snapped, "I ken what I said. But this is different. We have tae do somethin'. We have tae help her. We cannae just ride away and do nothin'."

Sir William shook his head in disapproval. Lady NicNeev only gave a wry smile.

"Hawk, you cannot mean this," the knight said, his last effort. "We shall surely lose our ground in the dark woods. Mark my words."

Mòrag clasped Hawk's hand in hers. "Ye said last night, ye trusted my instincts. Trust me now. We have tae help Talie," she pleaded.

She might even be bold enough to venture into the wood alone if I refuse. Something like pride lit Hawk's heart. But he wouldn't leave her alone. Their paths aligned once more.

"No, Sir William," Hawk said, "we shall go north. We can cut our travel time down and help find anyone lost on the way." He freed his hand and reflexively slid it over the tomahawks on his back.

Mòrag smiled, then spun and climbed into the saddle. "We'll do it!" she exclaimed to Lord Magnus. "We'll find the girl!"

CHAPTER FOURTEEN

The Black Wood of Rannoch grew in enormity with each step. Hawk's horse snorted in agitation, trundling over fallen logs. Vast shadows played across the forest's understory, their crepuscular shapes swiveled and twisted, a reflection of the canopy above.

Dark, ancient pines rose above the huntsman, their gnarled limbs zigzagging in a tangled mesh of wood, bark, and green needles. The darkness of the pine's bark was spared only by the lichen growths, which sprawled across the trunks of the towering timbers. Not to be outdone by the evergreen conifers, white birches sprung up sporadically, attempting to balance the dark wood.

There seemed to be no end to the forest. The huntsman and his companions had walked for some time with no signs of life. They had called out for little Talie, but received no answer. After a while, the thought of finding the girl through shouting slipped away, and they simply walked on. Hawk sensed unease resting on everyone's shoulders. No one spoke along their journey. Twice Hawk thought he noticed Lady NicNeev glance over her shoulder at what appeared to be nothing. But the most unsettling feeling to him was the utter silence the wood held. Whether it was the bracken and shrubbery absorbing their horses' hooves, or the complete absence of any breeze, an eerie chill hung about the forest.

"Nothing. Not a single squirrel or bird has crossed our paths," Sir William remarked.

Without wind to give it flight, his blue-and-white cloak draped the back of his horse as he rode. They rode in a single tight formation through the narrow wood. Tiree, having rejoined them, stalked just behind Mòrag's mount.

"Four riders and a wolf tracking through the wood can scare away any animal. It's not too surprising, sir," Hawk pointed out before taking a swig from his canteen.

"Yes, but I thought we would see some sign of life here. So far, the wolf in our company is the only life we have seen."

"Look around you," Hawk said. "There's life throughout. The trees and brush."

"I meant actual life," the knight huffed.

Hawk wanted to agree but kept his concerns to himself to preserve a good spirit in the others. He looked at Mòrag. The archeress pivoted her head from side to side, no doubt trying to find any sign of the missing girl. Mòrag hadn't lost hope, it would seem.

"Relax, Sir William," Lady NicNeev reassured. "While we may not find this girl, it won't be long until we're through this cursed forest."

She trotted ahead, the lead rider of the band. Mòrag scrunched her lips in a scowl.

"Why is it cursed? Why does everyone think it's so evil?" Hawk asked, trying to defuse the tension that rose amongst them.

"Bodach, the old man of the wood," Mòrag said.

"Who's that? Who is this Bodach?" Hawk asked.

"He was Cailleach's husband."

"And who is that?"

Mòrag, now perturbed, ranted at Hawk, "Do ye ken anything? Cailleach was a powerful goddess from the ancient otherworld, Tìr nan Òg. Her husband was Bodach, and together they lived in this very glen: Glen Lyon. They lived and thrived with their bonnie bairns. They say that for generations upon generations, she brought the land a mighty harvest. She'd bless the area with bountiful, fertile soil tae cultivate the people's crops. It was a blessing only a true mother could give tae her people. And so those people worshipped her. They gave thanks every year for the blessing she laid upon them. Everyone kens the generosity of the goddess Cailleach.

"That worship, though, drove her husband Bodach tae jealousy. For, ye see, naebody worshipped or prayed at his feet. The jealousy festered and brewed until one day he couldnae stand it anymore. He cursed Cailleach and turned their bairns tae stone out of spite. Cailleach, enraged as only a mother could be, banished Bodach tae the Black Wood of Rannoch, never tae be seen again. Cailleach, in grief, asked her followers tae carry her stone bairns tae the glen once a year, so they may bring the bountiful harvests again. They must also, it's said, carry the stones inside their homes for winter. Every year they must do this, so Cailleach's blessing continues. Cailleach, however, stricken with grief, roamed the land and seas, never tae be seen again. I imagine if we searched the glen tae the west right this very moment, we would find the stones of her bairns."

Hawk stared ahead, soaking in every detail. "I see. This Bodach doesn't seem like the right kind to upset," he finally said.

While rumors and legends grow a tale, at its core, there's a foundational truth to respect.

Lady NicNeev seemed unimpressed. "What? Mòrag, who told you all that? What I mean is, that's not how I remember it. Cailleach was the goddess of winter. She loved the chill of the winter air. People said she was an artist, painting each snowflake as it fell to the ground. She was radiant and beautiful. It was Bodach who was the monster. He was charming at first, good-looking of course, but deceptively cunning. Cailleach was innocent, wonderful, and thus fell for his ruse completely. He preyed on her, making her feel like she wasn't good enough. That she'd never be good enough. They had children, it's true, but no matter how hard Cailleach tried, she never could obtain Bodach's approval.

"One day, Bodach turned his sights to another. It was Cailleach's sister. The sister, however, didn't fall for Bodach's charms and deflected them. But the damage was done. Cailleach was scorned, pushed too far. She was hurt and betrayed, like only a woman who spent a lifetime in misery could be. She cursed all those she loved. Her children turned to stone. Cailleach cast the sister back to the land of Tìr nan Òg. And Bodach . . . Bodach was cursed to live out the rest of his days as the monster he truly is. She banished him to the Black Wood of Rannoch for all of eternity."

"What happened to Cailleach?" Hawk asked.

"Cailleach was utterly alone afterward. She aged into an old woman, as if the years of ethereal existence finally took their toll. She spends her time in hiding, emerging only to ravage the sea or flood a valley with her tears and sorrow."

Mòrag blinked. "And the bairns? What of the stone children?"

"The stones get carried out for summer and in for winter out of remembrance of the love Cailleach once bore her children. How did you phrase it? Like only a true mother could?" Lady NicNeev smiled at Mòrag, who hesitated a moment as if unsure, then returned in kind.

The reassurance seemed to help, as Mòrag and the group relaxed for a short while.

Finally, Mòrag signaled the group to halt. She climbed down off Epona, her ornamental bow strapped tight to her back.

"Everything as it should be?" Sir William probed.

"I have tae piss. Give me a moment," Mòrag retorted, unfastening her belt and breeches beneath her black hide skirt.

She went behind a pine. Sir William took a few steps ahead to maintain his honor.

The huntsman turned away and took a moment to stroke his

horse's mane. "Equus. Equus," he mumbled, only audible to the horse and himself. The huntsman reached for his saddle, unstrapped his canteen, and took another sip.

He strapped the canteen to his saddle again when he saw Mòrag climb back onto Epona out of the corner of his eye.

Except it wasn't Mòrag. It was far too short to be Mòrag. He whirled around to get a better look. A small creature with unruly hair covering its body sat atop the horse. Its pointed ears, broad nose, and long limbs stretched its features in an ungodly shape. It most certainly was not Mòrag.

Epona reared, frightening Hawk's mount and shifting the huntsman off balance. Epona darted off to the right.

"Hey! Wha—" Mòrag shouted from behind the pine, scrambling to tie her breeches.

"C'mon!" Hawk reached out a hand, wrenching Mòrag onto his mount. Before Sir William and Lady NicNeev could turn around to see what happened, Hawk raced after Epona.

They galloped, weaving through the ancient pines like a roaring wind. Hawk leaned forward in the saddle, trying to edge as much speed as possible. Mòrag clung to his armor, gripping at whatever handhold she could manage.

"Hold on!" the huntsman yelled, pulling in his elbows against her grip. "Hold on!"

The air rushed past them as they galloped this way and that. Hawk stayed fixed on the trail behind Epona, following the phantom rider.

They rode further into the wood. Pines, oaks, birches, and beeches flew past them, wooden spectators, each unable to reach out and stop the stolen horse. The huntsman drove his horse harder and faster.

They drew closer. The gasping snorts of Epona grew louder with every stride. They crisscrossed in synchrony, dipping and diving past branches and logs. The dark gray of Epona didn't falter. Hawk was close enough to make out the rider's ghoulish shape. The beast gripped the leather reins with its hairy paws. It never looked back, never taking its eyes off the forest ahead.

"Your hands! Take the reins," Hawk commanded, grabbing Mòrag's hands and shoving the reins into them. Mòrag gripped them around the huntsman's waist. Hawk gauged his horse's movements, taking in the pace of its gait. They neared Epona, the gap between them diminishing as they came alongside. Hawk pressed out of the stirrups and crouched on top of the saddle like a lion. Then, at the right moment, he sprung toward the creature on Epona's back. The huntsman tackled the rider, wrapping his arms around the hairy ghoul and tumbling into the bracken below. He thumped against the ground, his shoulder taking the brunt of the force, but with a practiced roll, he softened the fall.

The creature wriggled and writhed. Hawk grunted and squeezed his arms tighter. It flailed, squealing like a greased pig finally caught. Facing away from him, its arms twisted and raked at Hawk's armor. But its efforts proved futile, and the huntsman's grip grew stronger. Pinning it to the ground with his body, Hawk pressed a hand on its head, then reached one hand back and pulled out the obsidian knife.

"Stop wiggling, or I'll finish you here!" Hawk barked.

He ratcheted the ghoul's head back, holding the knife up against its thick neck. It stopped struggling, flopping limply with a sigh of defeat. Hawk adjusted his position and studied the foul creature before him.

It was small. Brown fur grew from its every feature. Its fore-limbs were unusually long and clawed for any creature Hawk had ever seen. Its two legs, stubbed and short like a badger's, sapped away any height. It resembled a disproportioned form of an ape Hawk had seen in Konghelle with distant traders.

Tiree romped from behind the brush toward Hawk and his captive. The wolf seemed blissfully unaware of why the pursuit took place. Hawk heard Mòrag's owl hoot from his right. The wolf, snapping out of its playful pant, hunched and growled at the new creature. The monster immediately startled, and, seeking shelter, curled up against the huntsman.

"Please. Please. Leave me at ease!" the creature begged, cowering further beneath Hawk.

Tiree didn't relent, moving closer, snarling and snapping. The creature reached its long arms up and began to climb the huntsman. Hawk grasped the creature and threw it back to the ground, putting a boot on its neck. It kicked at the leaves and needles under its feet. Its long nose exhaled in exaggerated puffs. Its large blue eyes looked only at the snarling wolf.

Mòrag appeared from Hawk's periphery. She sharply whistled, and Tiree relaxed. Her curved bow drawn and ready, the warrior approached.

"Stop struggling. It's over," Mòrag said.

"You're trapped, you little shit," Hawk spat.

The creature finally looked over at the huntsman.

Hawk continued, "So you must be Bodach. Tell us where the girl is and I might stop my friend from putting an arrow between your eyes." Hawk flexed the knife in his hand, making his threat plain.

"I'm . . . I'm . . . I'm nae . . ." the creature croaked. Its eyes darted back and forth between the three attackers. It wretched a throaty giggle. "I'm . . . nae . . . him . . ."

Hawk didn't flinch, unconvinced by the pleading monster. In his vast experience as a huntsman, Hawk had learned that if it looked like a monster, then it was indeed a monster.

Mòrag, too, did not relinquish her aim. "What's yer name? Tell us, and tell us quickly, or my wolf will have ye for supper," she commanded, her voice infused with a rigidity brought about by the aggravating day.

"Benji! Ben-ji, they calls me. Please, sirs. Have a cares." It clasped its arms together, begging at Hawk's heels. "I ask ye, please, on my knees."

The huntsman removed his foot from the creature. It scurried against him, cowering from the wolf and sheltering beneath its long arms. Pine needles clung to its brown coat.

"I ken what ye are. Small, hairy creature of the wood? A goblin, no doubt," Mòrag said.

"Goblin yerself!" it snapped.

"Don't make this any harder on yourself," Hawk said, sliding his knife between the monster's arms to uncover its face.

"Fine. Fine. Benji be good. Just like I should. Bauchan do well, and all is swell," it muttered in an odd melodic voice. Hawk and Mòrag peered at one another, each a mirror of bewilderment.

Mòrag pressed the creature, "Bauchan? A hobgoblin? What were ye doing with my horse? Careful now, my arm's starting tae get tired. I wouldnae want it tae slip if I was ye."

"The horse? That horse?" the bauchan pointed to Epona tied up against a tree. "Of course. Only a bit of fun. Now I'm done."

"Fun?"

"Fun. Aye, fun. I see horse. No one on, of course. Horse mine now. Sit on like a sow. Ride far away. No friends for ye. Ha! Fun," it chortled.

"That's yer idea of fun, ye wee shite."

"Aye, fun for the raveled. Nae fun for traveled."

"Have you seen a girl? A wee girl?" Mòrag asked, pressing the arrow closer to the hobgoblin's eye. The metal tip caught its attention in a flash.

"G-g-girl?" it stuttered, fear creeping back into his voice.

"The girl. Where's the little girl?" Hawk asked, putting a hand on Mòrag's bow and crouching down to the bauchan. "She came into the wood this morning, alone and unarmed. She never came home, so we know she's here. Someone such as you must know of all creatures of the wood. So tell us, have you seen the little girl? Do you know where she is?"

It relaxed, opening its wide blue eyes to gaze at the huntsman. It answered, "She is with . . . him."

"Him?"

"Bodach," it rasped, as if the name itself cursed the air.

It shrank against the huntsman once more. Hawk's heart sank. Everyone's fears rang true, it seemed. Bodach was some devil.

This creature trembles at the very name of it, Hawk thought. But then, the bauchan also shriveled at the sight of a wolf, a large dog. *Can you judge one monster from another's fright?*

Mòrag crouched next to the huntsman, her normally playful smile replaced with a stern look of determination across her face.

She whispered to the bauchan, "Can ye take us tae him? Can ye take us tae Bodach?"

"Take ye there? I ken his lair." It turned its head in a puzzled bemusement.

"We're going tae find the girl, Talie. Will ye help us?"

"Aye." The hobgoblin scrambled up onto its stumpy legs. "If ye dinnae eat me, Benji show ye and wolfie." He waddled away.

"Hey, wait!" Mòrag shouted, jogging after the bauchan.

Hawk darted for the horses, untying them and leading them after Mòrag, Tiree, and Benji. The horses were soaked in sweat from the chase. The huntsman caught up and gave Epona's reins to Mòrag.

"The others?" She looked at Hawk.

"Nae time. Nae time. Must go now. Very close," the waddling bauchan interposed. He walked with his arms swinging from side to side, an unnatural attempt to balance on his tiny legs. It wouldn't be hard to chase the small creature anymore.

"C'mon, we'll find them later," Hawk said as they followed the creature farther into the wood.

They passed through the stretching pine timbers and the dense underbrush. The forest remained in its eerie silence. No birds chirped. The wind didn't whisper. But one creature broke the quiet and sang on its journey:

Through the trees,
On stubbled knees,

We carry forth,
Tae his house north,
I help them find,
One of their kind,
A lost wee bairn,
So I can earn,
My life so sweet,
Not eat my meat,
Nae ask me thrice,
Benji is nice.

Hawk smirked at the scratchy baritone voice. The odd melody was clearly a favorite of Benji's. The bauchan continued to hum his tune, wading through the sea of bracken. Mòrag didn't share Hawk's grin.

"That voice. The way he speaks and all, how do ye ken we can trust him?" she asked Hawk, leaning over toward him and adjusting the bow across her back.

"I don't. But he's too happy to be leading us to betrayal."

"He is weirdly happy, the wee devil," she paused, stepping Epona over a large moss-eaten pine. "What about the others?"

"Don't worry. Remember what Lady NicNeev said when we first entered the wood. If we get separated, head north. We'll meet on the north road." Hawk placed a calm, reassuring hand on Mòrag's shoulder. "Don't worry. We'll find the girl, meet up with them, and place Talie with a safe escort home along the road from Pitlochry."

Mòrag relented, smiling and nodding in satisfaction. They marched on, trundling through the brush behind the bauchan. His tune carried up into the pines.

We're full of glee,
    It's me Benji,

Through the brush,
We're in a rush,
Let's go and walk
Tae the loch,
They no eat me,
The vicious three,
Big scary dug,
Squash me like a bug,
I sing my song,
As we carry on.

They wandered down a large hill. The air grew thicker as water hung in the wood. Hawk recognized a cloud moving through the forest. The mist dulled the way ahead. The sunlight that once penetrated the gaps of the pine and birch leaves faded into a gray haze. The huntsman grew wary, stepping lighter and sweeping his eyes across the forest. He led his horse onward as Benji continued to hum his melody.

They pushed on down the slope when Hawk noticed the trees parted into a gray void. The hobgoblin continued past the trees and through the void. The fog began to clear, and the world revealed itself once more. Hawk's mouth opened in awe.

Chapter Fifteen

A loch extended across the horizon. It shimmered, cobalt and still against the gray ceiling. The cloud of fog rolling through the valley carried over the loch and against the wooded banks. The mist encapsulated the area.

They stood at the edge of the water, the shore crumbling cascades of clay into the murky depths beneath their boots. Hawk glanced at the loch, flat and still. The water seemed to absorb the surrounding sound, leaving only an endless black abyss.

"Loch Rannoch," the bauchan proclaimed, stretching his long arms out to the loch like a child impressed with their own handiwork.

"We asked you to take us to Bodach, not the loch," Hawk growled. "Where is Bodach?"

Benji sneered. "I did help thee. Turn and see." He shifted, gesturing to their right.

Hawk followed the creature's hand. Across the way, in the depths of the loch, sprouted a single towering structure. It floated above the water on four massive timbers. The thatched, round wooden tower rose into the heavens. The same mist that veiled the loch shrouded the tower's crown, giving it the appearance of infinitude. Hawk bristled with a haunting chill.

"Bodach's crannog," Benji yelped, squirming at the name. "Now we run?"

"Naw," Mòrag said, stepping onto the shore and pointing. "Look. There, connecting the crannog tae the shore. It's a bridge or pier or something. We can use that tae reach the tower. C'mon." Mòrag started toward the tower, and Tiree followed.

The huntsman hesitated, looking up at the immensity of the peculiar tower. Something was off. The air hung cold and deadly silent. Hawk nearly agreed with Benji about turning to flee. Nearly. Mòrag's determination helped Hawk onward.

"Benji, let's go," the huntsman said, using his foot to push the bauchan along.

They walked along the clay shore. The forest stretched out toward the loch, narrowing the path and pressing them into single file. Hawk led his horse carefully, avoiding a misplacement of his foot that would plunge him into the loch. If he fell in, Hawk suspected he may never surface.

The tower loomed ever higher. Even Hawk's horse Equus, chosen for its inability to spook, stirred, exaggerating its steps with unease. Hawk rubbed a soothing hand along the horse's neck.

A terrible, shrieking scream pierced the silence from the peak of the wooden crannog. The screech dug into Hawk's ears like a rusty nail against slate. It filled the valley and beyond—the unmistakable cry of a twelve-year-old girl.

"Talie's alive," Mòrag called out. "Hurry, we can still help her!"

Mòrag glared at Hawk with the whites of her eyes. The huntsman wasted no time.

"Give me those," he said, reaching for Mòrag's reins. "I'll tie the horses to that tree."

Hawk quickly fastened the horses around the nearest sturdy pine with a highwayman's hitch. He looked back at Mòrag. She motioned to the bauchan. Benji's eyes were glued to the tower since the shriek, his face a frozen slate. Even in a creature such as Benji, Hawk recognized the universal expression of fear.

"Tiree. Guard," Mòrag commanded, pointing at Epona. "I'll nae lose a horse again."

Ever obedient, Tiree walked to the horses' sides and sat. The wolf's green eyes and stoic expression looked at Mòrag for approval.

Hawk rubbed a finger over the tomahawks sheathed in an *X* along his back. He cleared his mind with a deep sigh.

"C'mon, let's find the girl."

They rushed along the shore. The fog grew denser as they approached, the tower sinking into the pall. They trekked along the bank to the pier's edge. Hawk stood at the threshold, staring over the water on the other side. The wooden planks, soaked from forgotten rain, extended into the mist. The cloud completely enveloped the crannog.

Benji made a break for it. He scurried and leaped to the nearest tree, ascending its trunk into the low branches. The bauchan used its long arms to swing from branch to branch. It sung in the same offbeat melodious croak as before.

The deed is done,
  This nae fun,
  Time tae flee,
  Save only me.

The bauchan's voice faded into the dark wood. And, once again, silence fell over Loch Rannoch.

Then, for a second time, a screech emanated from beyond the pier. The high-pitched shrill rang through Hawk's body. He gritted his teeth and, reaching over his back, whipped out his black steel tomahawks. Mòrag swung out her recurve bow, an arrow ready in her other hand.

"Focus, Mòrag. Don't let it get a jump on us," Hawk said,

stepping onto the planks. "Can you think of anything else about Bodach that might help us?"

"Me putting as many arrows as I can in tae Bodach, the bastard."

Hawk rushed his words. "We grab the girl and get out as soon as we can. Head for the horses and ride north. If something happens to me, get Talie and yourself away; don't look back."

"I'm nae leaving ye behind," she growled.

Hawk said nothing. He only moved forward, the wood groaning beneath his feet. They trod cautiously on the balls of their feet into the empty gray void. Hawk swiveled his head around—no more landmarks. With only a few steps onto the pier, the shore, too, faded into the waste. A thick fog surrounded them. Hawk's heartbeat quickened. Every step took them further out. Every tentative step brought them closer to the ghastly tower.

Mòrag halted. Hawk squinted into the mist, straining to see what caused the standstill. Then it came forth. An impending shadow appeared from out of the gray. It was a ghost, a malevolent silhouette looming above the huntsman. But as the apparition drifted toward him, it took shape. It condensed, shrinking and shrinking to the height of the huntsman, growing smaller until it morphed into the shape of a little girl.

The girl tottered along the pier. Her footsteps seemed quiet, not carrying enough weight to stress the wooden planks. She wore a ragged, woolen smock stained in the shore's clay. Bright red curls flowed down her shoulders. She held her hand across her chest, a small bouquet of bluebells clutched in it, their violet petals bent and cupped.

Something wasn't right. Hawk could feel it. *A girl doesn't scream and then walk out holding flowers.*

Mòrag slung her bow back over her shoulder.

"Talie," she exhaled, racing toward the girl.

"Wait. No, Mòrag, stop!" Hawk yelled too late.

As Mòrag approached the girl, it happened. Little Talie morphed, burgeoning and snaking, into a faceless hood, which soared in height. Her spindly arms peeled into pine bark and sprouted long branches of thick wood. The figure grew taller than any man or bear Hawk had seen. Dark, dusty, and tattered robes clung to its shape.

Its thorny twig fingers removed its hood, revealing a bleached elk skull. Broad, flat antlers budded from its peak in a prominent display of might and wickedness. It could only be Bodach.

Hawk watched as the shock and surprise overwhelmed Mòrag. She stumbled, falling forward against the planks. Bodach loomed over her. Hawk ran, sprinting at the specter with a ferocity he'd never felt before. He cried out, releasing a brutal bellow. Anything to grab Bodach's attention.

It wasn't enough. The monster swiped its branched arms at Mòrag. She rolled, dodging at the last moment while Bodach's limb crashed down, shattering the planks.

The huntsman saw an opportunity. He sprinted under the monster, swiping his ax at the arm stuck in the pier. The bark crunched, releasing a satisfying snap as the ax busted through the limb. Hawk carried his momentum past the monster to its rear. Mòrag crawled beneath its legs next to Hawk. The huntsman quickly bent, grasped her black hide mantle, and helped her to her feet.

Bodach roared at his severed arm. Hawk gathered himself, dropping his stance and readying to make another blow. The monster raised its broken arm into the gray mist. Hawk couldn't believe his eyes. The splintered end grew, twisting and spurting into a new limb, just like the first. Hawk paused in disbelief.

What kind of cursed monster is this? Hawk swore. Werewolves fought savagely, but predictably. *How can I predict this monster's intentions?*

An arrow hissed and stuck beneath Bodach's robes. *Thwack!* Another landed. Hawk shook off his hesitation and dashed for a strike. He swiped his tomahawks at Bodach's thick, muscular leg. They found their mark, carving into a leg built like a thick tree trunk. He ran beneath Bodach, then spun to face his attacker's back again. The huntsman spared a moment to look at his blades. Shredded slivers of wood covered the edges. But not blood.

The distraction cost him. The monster swiped, catching the huntsman in his chest and launching him into the air. He tumbled, end over end, and slammed into the pier on his back, air gushing from his lungs. His head smacked against the wood. The blinding pain battering his skull was nothing compared to the terrifying fit of compression clamping his lungs closed. He desperately tried to take a breath, wheezing against it, but couldn't. Bodach loomed over him, the menacing skull peering into Hawk's chest as though it could see his heart beating wildly.

Mòrag stepped over Hawk, putting herself between him and Bodach. She fired an arrow straight into the monster's chest. Reaching into her quiver, she grabbed another, nocked, and loosed. The shaft drilled into its mark.

Enraged, Bodach swept his long arms toward Mòrag, but she leaped out of the way. The swipe came down, brushing through Hawk's spiked hair. His breath hadn't returned. He gasped, unable to take in the air he needed. The monster twisted around and prepared for another crushing blow to Hawk's skull.

It was the end. Helpless, he couldn't escape. Bodach's branched limbs accelerated. In an instant, it would be over for Hawk, and he could finally see his mother again. He could finally rest. He could finally join them at the fire, dancing to the heart of the drum.

The arm grew closer. Hawk could almost see the flames of the fire and his mother's face sitting next to him on the log.

Bodach's blow missed.

Stumbling forward, it whirled around to reveal Mòrag hanging on to a dagger plunged into Bodach's back.

"Get up!" she cried, letting go of the dagger's handle and falling on top of the huntsman.

He cushioned her fall.

"C'mon!" she said again.

Time slowed for Hawk. Mòrag's emerald eyes bore into his

soul. He could see every delicate fiber of green and blue coiling in her corneas. Her soft, thread-like waves of dark brown hair cascaded toward his face. No. Not just brown, but streaks of auburn too. He hadn't noticed them before.

Mòrag sprung to her feet, grabbing Hawk's hand and yanking him up. Quickly, he took in a deep breath, his diaphragm having corrected itself. The air rushed into his drained lungs. His mind fell back to the moment at hand.

"NOW! Do something!" Mòrag yelled, reaching into her quiver for one of her last three arrows.

The huntsman grabbed his ax from the pier and spun it in his hand, finding the familiar grip. He turned to face the monster.

Bodach boomed a thunderous challenge, an attempt to scare off the foes. But the huntsman didn't back away. Instead, he threw the tomahawk, end over end, straight into the monster's chest—where the heart should be. Bodach collapsed to one knee.

The huntsman darted forward and removed the ax from the monster. He swung his hips, collecting all his power and force, before releasing that strength into a single, upper-cutting strike to Bodach's antler.

It split off, cracking under the might of Hawk's swing. The huntsman followed the swing back across the opposite side of the skull, shattering the other broad antler. Hawk unsheathed his obsidian knife. He placed the blade against the ax and, with a shearing swipe, launched a shower of sparks at Bodach.

Bodach reeled, flapping its arms where the antlers once sat. Hawk did it again, showering the monster in sparks from his blades. Again, the steel brushed the rock and sparked Bodach. The ax illuminated a fiery red with every brush of the knife.

It worked. The dust on the monster's tattered robe ignited, sending a surge of fire across the fabric. Bursting into a howl of flames, Bodach stood upright. The monster flailed, swinging its wooden arms in a panicked fury. It thrashed, stamping its feet against the pier. Arms moved violently through the air as it tried to put out the flames on its torso.

Bodach's wooden limb swung down and grasped the huntsman in its clutches. Hawk lurched off the ground as it tightened and squeezed around his belly. Hawk feared he would burst. Once more, he could barely breathe. The flames climbed over the beast. A little too close for comfort. The yellow-and-orange flashes danced over Hawk's boots. Heat snapped at the huntsman like an angry viper.

At once, the flames shifted into a violet hue. They coursed over Bodach's wooden flesh. Hawk fell, landing on the wooden pier in a hump. Bodach riled in agony as the sweltering violet flames tormented it. Hawk held a hand over his eyes, shielding himself from the blistering heat. Another ball of flames struck Bodach. Hawk looked for the source.

Lady NicNeev glided down the pier, arms raised above her head. Her green tunic was still, motionless as she stepped over the hole in the dock from where the monster's arm had gotten caught. She strolled up alongside Hawk lying on the pier, her arms and eyes fixed ahead. The ambient purple embers of the fiery Bodach tinged the lady's golden head of hair.

Violet sparks emanated from Lady NicNeev's fingers. They dove into the loch. A woman rose from the sparks and out of the water. She climbed onto the pier beside Lady NicNeev. The woman stood pale, almost ethereal, in the violet light. She was beautiful, with a full black mane and, surprisingly, without clothes.

The woman nodded at Lady NicNeev, then turned toward a swatting Bodach. She leaped into the air and morphed into a magnificent black horse. She landed on all fours, steadying herself with a few quick steps. Her beauty wasn't lost, even as a massive horse. She strode out toward Bodach, a marvelous specimen. Her black mane danced from the rush of the violet flames. The horse seemed undeterred by the flaming beast.

Hawk could only watch in awe as the horse reared on its hind legs and crashed down on Bodach's shoulders. The horse's hooves trampled the monster into the pier, shaking the wood beneath

Hawk. Bodach screeched in agony as the black horse stomped on him. The horse swiveled, bucked its back legs, and kicked the monster. Bodach flew, singed cloak flaring, up and over the sides of the dock.

A gigantic splash resounded over the loch. Water washed over the monster, but the flames weren't doused. The violet blaze boiled the water around Bodach. The bubbling and brewing produced a spectacular hiss and gurgle. Bodach crumbled. His skull head turned to ash, floating away with the bubbling heat and flame. Beneath, the face an old man wailed into the gray mist, crackling like charcoal, disintegrating until the violet flames vanished. Their fuel diminished, no longer present to burn. Bodach was gone. And, once again, a silence fell over Loch Rannoch.

"*Manto wikuw,*" Hawked gasped, taking out the wampum necklace from under his armor and rubbing his finger along the polished lavender beads. Mòrag approached the huntsman, panting with exhaustion. She reached out her hand. Hawk grabbed hold, and she lifted him to his feet.

Hawk stood stunned. He couldn't think of anything to say. He didn't want to say anything. Mòrag wiped at a spot of blood on his bronze cheek. He nodded at her, then turned to look at NicNeev.

Lady NicNeev let loose a devilish smirk. Hawk didn't mind. He was happy to have help at the moment. She reached out a hand and placed it on his shoulder pad.

"Ah, Kelpie," Lady NicNeev said, breaking the calm and moving toward the black horse on the pier. "How can I thank you for your help?"

In an instant, the horse morphed back into the woman, splashing a wave of water out from her body in all directions. She stood on the pier, her pale human figure returned.

"It was nothing, truly," the woman said.

"You have my thanks for now. Until the next time, Kelpie," NicNeev said, bowing her head in appreciation.

The pale woman smiled, then turned to the edge of the pier and dove. She stretched her arms out in front of herself, her hands breaking the water as she pierced its surface. The splash rippled out from where she landed, skimming across the entire loch. She disappeared into the black abyss. Hawk didn't see the woman reemerge.

"It's done," Lady NicNeev said. "Bodach is no more. My word, he truly was a monster."

Hawk met her gaze. "You're a sorceress."

"Figured that out, did you?"

"Of course yer a sorceress," Mòrag exclaimed. "I've heard stories of sorceresses. Magic returns and sorceresses with it! Wait . . . Was it ye? Did ye calm the Forth River? I thought it might have been a miracle of a coincidence, but naw, it was some kind of witchcraft."

"That was quite the feat, wasn't it? What you didn't know was how much energy that took. I spent most of yesterday recovering. Magic is exhausting."

"How? How do ye do it?" Mòrag asked.

Hawk pondered the same thing. He was no stranger to the products of magic: creatures, ghouls, monsters, and even curses. But true magical beings, sorceresses, they were always more myth than reality. Until now.

"Talent honed through experience," Lady NicNeev said, brushing a fleck of ash from her tunic. "Magic is an exceptionally rare gift. One you're born with, I'm afraid. A gift I cannot share."

"Are there others like yerself?"

"Of course. Ask him," the lady said, pivoting to face Hawk.

The wry smile on her face burned as brightly as her violet flames had.

Hawk squinted, not catching her meaning. He hadn't come across any sorceresses in his travels as a huntsman. Stories, of course, but nothing more. Unless she meant something else? Him? But the huntsman only fought with strength and steel. That wasn't magic.

"I don't know what you mean? I've only ever heard stories of sorceresses. I've never met—"

"What else can ye do?" Mòrag cut in.

"Nothing at this moment. I'll faint if I even try. Now come along. I've wasted enough time scouring the Black Wood for you two. It's time to keep moving and find our way out of the forest." Lady NicNeev brushed her green bodice to ensure it was pristine, then said, "One more point of note. Say nothing to the knight. I don't think Sir William's holy, chivalric duty could comprehend what occurred."

"I don't think even I know what just occurred," Hawk added.

Lady NicNeev raised her eyebrows, lingered for a moment, and turned to walk down the pier.

Was she about to tell me something?

"Wait," Mòrag blurted. "The girl. The scream. She must be at the top of the tower." She looked at the huntsman.

"You're right," Hawk said. "We should check the tower. We'll hurry." He grabbed his tomahawks from the pier and slid them into their sheaths across his back. "Our horses are along the shore—"

"I know," Lady NicNeev said. "Sir William and I saw them tied to a pine, valiantly guarded by a black wolf. He wouldn't even let us approach them. Can you believe that?"

"Good boy," Mòrag laughed.

"I'll rejoin Sir William and meet you two along the shore then. Be quick about it," Lady NicNeev finished and turned toward the gray mist of the shore.

"Let's go," Hawk said, and they jogged in the opposite direction.

The mist remained heavy, the fog still shrouding the crannog. But soon it came into focus. A lone entranceway stood at the thatched, round tower's base along the dock.

The huntsman and warrior made for the door. Hawk ignored the pain shooting through his back and the stitch forming in his

abdomen. The collateral aches of battle could wait. They needed
to find Talie.

Mòrag reached the entrance and opened it. Riveted just inside
the entranceway was a sconce. Hawk stole its lit torch and held it
up for better light. Inside the crannog was a single circular room.
Cobwebs and dust draped every surface and space. The thick,
musty smell of aged death hung in the air. A plain straw bed sat
against the wall. In the center of the room was a table and three
chairs. Hawk walked over to the table. Scattered across its surface
were a single clay bowl and one wooden spoon. Dried, decaying
leaves sprinkled the tabletop. Though gone, Bodach's perturbing
presence lingered.

"Hawk, look here," Mòrag called. He moved the torch to see
what caught her interest. She stood at the base of what appeared
to be a spiraling staircase. It traveled up along the edge of the
tower wall into the darkness. At the very top of the stair, a faint
glow of firelight.

"Look," Mòrag said again, clutching an object to her chest.
Hawk moved closer to examine it in the torchlight. Mòrag held
three flowers, their purple petals drooping to brush her hand.
They were bluebells. The bluebells that grew at the wood's edge.

The girl is here. She must be.

"The torchlight at the top of the stairs," Hawk said.
"Let's go!"

Mòrag took the lead, hurrying up the endless steps. They
spiraled along the tower's wall. Hawk lapped around the crannog,
going up and up. The climb seemed never-ending. Hawk's leg
burned with every step, his lungs aching and laboring from their
recent bout. He wanted a rest, but he couldn't bring himself to
stop. They approached the light. It wasn't the orange blaze of
torchlight, but the white glow from the sun.

They reached the crannog's ceiling and followed the staircase
to a wooden landing atop the tower. It was a pavilion, looking
over the valley.

Mòrag leaned over the side railing and pointed. "We're above the fog. The cloud is moving off the loch, anyway."

Hawk glanced over the side. The gray mist indeed dissipated. The black shimmer of the water glistened below. He followed the sunlight, then looked north.

"The Black Wood ends up ahead. You can see the grass from the hill just there. We'll be out and on the road in no time."

Finally, he breathed a sigh of relief. Excitement ignited a smile on the huntsman's face. The end was in sight. He bent down and massaged his legs under his buckskin kilt. Then, thinking it strange, Hawk noticed Mòrag hadn't moved, hadn't said anything.

He looked up at her. Mòrag froze, her mouth agape, her face in utter incomprehension. She stared across the tower's pavilion. He spun around.

Sat against the railing was the little redheaded, twelve-year-old girl. Her wooden sword hugged against her, unbent and unbroken. She sat, watching her two rescuers. Her eyes were glazed, her skin shriveled and shrunken against her bones, her jaw hung down unnaturally. The little girl sat there, desiccated and withered. She was gone from the world. Talie rested in absolute silence, Bodach's last victim.

CHAPTER SIXTEEN

The sun beat overhead, its golden rays caressing the majestic highland hills. The stony slopes glistened amongst the gentle valleys of purple-flowered heather and grassy meadows. The world beamed bright, the weather exuberantly summer. Clear, blue skies sheltered the band of four riders the rest of the day.

The riders traveled in a dull haze, however. They spoke not a word between them since they departed the forest. In fact, the huntsman hadn't uttered a single word since he walked down the spiral steps of the crannog with Talie swaddled in his arms. He didn't speak while Mòrag tossed the torch onto the straw bed inside and made no sound watching the thatched wooden tower ignite. Hawk and Mòrag stood on the pier in somberness as the walls of the round tower blackened and blazed. Even after reuniting with the others and setting off, the kind, noble-hearted Sir William knew no words would ease their anguish.

Hawk buried the girl just out of the wood. Silent prayers guided Talie to her rest. He marked the site with a circle of earth-covered rocks. Then they rode on.

The huntsman sat in the saddle, swaying in cadence with his horse's stride. Mòrag trotted along, exceptionally quiet. Her eyes fell on the path directly in front of Epona's feet. Behind Mòrag, strapped to her saddle, was Talie's wooden sword.

In her daze, Mòrag missed the white hare that sprang up on the side of the road and darted through the grass on her right. Tiree didn't miss it and gave chase, running over the shoulder of the hill. Tiree disappeared from the riders' sight. But Mòrag didn't seem to care.

The road circumnavigated Loch Ericht, and they reached the eastern shore. The loch formed inside a sizeable mountainous valley.

It felt like a particularly long ride to Hawk. They trotted most of the twenty miles outside the forest, slowing only to walk up the hills, of which many loomed before them. It had only been a few hours, but for Hawk, it was one of the longest rides of his life.

Hawk couldn't shake the feeling of Talie in his arms. Her shriveled, bony skin left a mark deeper than any wound from a hunt. His sister would've been just older than Talie when she died. Was Ayaksak that bony and frail when she passed? The memory of her lifeless frame flashed into his mind. He'd purposively forgotten that image, but it weaseled back into his vision help-lessly. Hawk wished he could've carried Ayaksak from Blåveis's camp the way he'd done for Talie. The thought welled in Hawk's throat like a vice, and he shook his head, forcing himself to think of anything else.

Tiree dashed back down the hill. His long face dripped with the remnants of the white hare. His eyes made for Mòrag's, but she didn't return the gesture. It was more than the huntsman could bear. They needed a change of pace. It was time to take a break.

Hawk coughed, clearing his voice, and called to his companions, "We should stop soon. We should set up camp when we can."

"Here's as good a place as any," Sir William agreed.

He stopped his horse along with Lady NicNeev.

"We should set up camp just there," Hawk said, pointing to

a nearby hill whose steep slopes formed a perfect inlet. "The stone face will shelter us from the northerly winds, and the slope will keep us dry. We should make camp now, give the horses a rest."

"Well thought, Huntsman," Sir William said, dismounting his mare.

Lady NicNeev guided her horse over to the campsite, a quiet peace in her posture.

Hawk climbed down from his saddle and shifted to head toward the camp, but stopped. Sir William maneuvered in front of him, leaning his head in to look at the huntsman with dark pupils.

"What happened in the wood?" the knight asked Hawk. "Was it Lady NicNeev? Is she a sorceress?"

Hawk cleared his throat. "It doesn't matter," he said. "She saved my life, Sir William. Were it not for her, I surely would've perished. If she wished to do us harm, the opportunity has passed. We can rest easy."

Sir William looked toward the loch and the sun above before nodding at Hawk. "Perhaps you're right. I have the kindling; I'll see to the fire."

The knight turned his horse and walked on toward the inlet.

Hawk started behind Sir William. He looked for Mòrag but noticed she hadn't gone to the campsite.

Mòrag had headed to the shore of the loch. She let go of Epona's reins near the edge of the water. The huntsman followed, walking Equus to the stony shore and releasing him. Mòrag plopped down on the stony beach against a fallen log and wrapped her arms around her knees. Tiree lay down next to Mòrag, nudging his dark head to rest in her lap.

Hawk sat on the driftwood next to Mòrag. Tears streamed down her cheek. She sniffled, rubbing her face clean against the wolf's soft fur. Hawk turned his gaze out over the loch. They sat there for some time. Hawk wasn't sure what to say, or if there was anything to say at all.

Mòrag broke the calm. "It hurts," she said, groggy and strained.

"I know it does," was the only thing he could think to say.

"Why am I the only one crying then? Some warrior, huh?"

Hawk took her in. Her fierce green eyes blazed equally with sorrow and passion. A thin layer of silver glassed their surfaces in the sunlight.

"Everyone hurts, but not everyone has the strength to show it," he said.

With a whine, Tiree lifted his head, extending his neck to lick the tears from Mòrag's face as they formed.

"I thought . . . I thought we'd save her," she wept.

"Talie, the girl?"

"Aye."

"So did I."

"I thought fate had brought us there at that very moment, when her mum, the woman, ran up tae us. I thought it was destiny. We'd surely find the lass." Mòrag rubbed her eyes with her sleeve.

"Fate is cruel," replied Hawk bitterly.

If there's one thing I know, it's that.

"Miserable even," Mòrag agreed.

Epona nickered, biting at Equus, sending them both into a splashing frenzy before stepping back onto the grass of the shore and stooping to eat.

"That mother. Her sorrow—" Mòrag choked on the words. "I ken we had tae help her because . . . 'cause . . . 'cause I couldnae see naught but my mum in her face. My mum greetin', crying. . ." she trailed off, unable to bring out the words.

Something in Hawk's chest cracked.

"Over little Mòrag, lost in the woods . . ." Hawk said.

"Fighting with her wooden sword," she finished. "That could've been me. That *was* me. That's why I wanted tae find her so badly. I wish . . . I wish I had never seen her at the top of the crannog. I wish I had never seen her face. I'll nae forget it, Hawk."

"I know exactly what you mean. It hurts," Hawk said, peering over the mountains across the loch.

Hawk wouldn't forget it either. He wished he could've protected Mòrag from that moment when her hope turned rotten, that moment she'd never unsee. He knew how deep some scars etched once they took hold. This would be one for them both.

The mountains still shone bright with sun, despite the shade that began to set in the heart of the valley. The sun meandered down the horizon, leisurely and peaceful.

"How can the world be filled with such misery?" Mòrag asked.

And something about the way she said it, the pain heavy in her voice, had Hawk saying, "Did I ever tell you why I'm here?"

She swallowed. "Ye mean Blåveis? The raiders with that winged-lion banner?"

He knew there wasn't much he could offer her in the moment, except a bit of truth, a piece of himself only one other person held.

"No, I mean here, on this side of the world. Look at this."

Hawk gently took her hand and held it up to his face. His bronze complexion contrasted with her whitened skin, like white clouds against a setting sun.

"I'm no Norseman, and I'm certainly not a Scoti. I lived far away, across the ocean to the west. In a village in the forest with a family, a tribe, my own community of love and happiness."

Hawk swallowed, the memory still hard to voice. But for her, this warrior with tear-stained cheeks, he managed.

"One night, Blåveis and the lot came into my village and murdered my family. He killed my mother in front of me. These demons captured me, chained me, and sailed me to the Isle of Ice and the kingdom of Norway, never to see those I loved ever again."

He blew out a breath, dropping her hand. "I've had my fair share of misery. But I escaped. Broke free of their chains and moved forward. I learned that the world is full of misery. But misery doesn't have to fill us. We can choose to fall victim to it. We can wallow in misery, sink to incredible fathoms of pain and grief. Or we can embrace the misery, absorb all it has to teach us, then rise above it. We don't have to choose to fill ourselves with misery. We can choose better. We can choose to move forward."

Hawk looked at Mòrag, wondering what he'd find in her eyes. She merely brushed her fingers through Tiree's charcoal coat, considering. Tiree rolled over, flipping to peer over the loch.

"And ye?" Mòrag finally asked. "Ye havnae moved on. Why are ye still chasing these slavers?"

She stabbed at the heart of it. It had been so long since he started pursuing the Norsemen, the reasons often pushed to the back of his memories. It was a habit, a ritual even. Following Blåveis, who stole his life away, became life itself for Hawk.

"They are something more to me," was all Hawk could say.

"They sound miserable tae me. Why dinnae ye move on yerself?"

Hawk gritted his teeth, clenching back the words he wished to say or even to shout about how much pain they caused him.

"What of the woman's misery?" Mòrag pushed. "Talie's mum, how is she tae choose? She will be without Talie forevermore."

Hawk calmed for a moment, trying to think through his own emotions and imagine what it must be like for the mother. "You're right. It's hard to move on from that. She had other children, did she not?"

"Aye."

"Well, because of Talie, and because of you, we ventured into the Black Wood. And now, Bodach is no more. Never again will he torment the children of Kenmore. Her brothers will grow old and live happy lives, thanks to Talie. Her mother can grieve, yes. But she can live on knowing the world is a safer place."

Ignorant of their conversation, the wolf rose. He sauntered

down to the water's edge and bowed his head, drinking from the loch's tiny rippling waves.

"It still hurts, though, ye ken?" Mòrag said.

"Of course it does, Mòrag. Mo, misery will always hurt . . ." The huntsman smiled tentatively. "It will always hurt, but we can learn from it and move on with our lives."

"Mo?" Mòrag asked, raising her brow.

She lifted her tartan scarf and dried the last of her tears. Placing a hand on the ground, the warrior rolled onto her feet. Mòrag walked over to Epona, brushing the mare's neck as the horse ate. The small wooden sword hung from her saddle's strap slid out easily into her hand. She returned to the loch's edge and drove the blade into the stones. It fixed into the beach upright, the wood hilt and crossguard prominent against the loch's darkening blue.

Mòrag fell to her knees in front of the sword. Her mouth moved in a hushed whisper.

She's praying for the girl, he realized. Mòrag then reached into the pouch on her belt and removed a blue flower, the bluebell from the stairs. She placed it on the ground next to the sword, then rose. A faint smile crossed her face as she sat on the log beside him and leaned against him, putting her head on his shoulder.

"We'll send word tae the next farmer headed south? Tae tell Mhari in Kenmore of Talie?" Mòrag asked, her emerald eyes now dry.

"Of course," Hawk said, wrapping an arm around her. His hand brushed against her soft skin stretched over defined muscle. "We're on the road. No one will pass through without our notice."

"We must be at Dalwhinnie by now. I saw the bogs from the hilltop. I thought we would've seen someone by now."

"The fresh wagon tracks we've been following are undoubtedly the soldiers and their prisoners. But the cattle tracks in the other direction mean someone will pass through," the huntsman said with certainty. Mòrag's hair tickled Hawk's cheek, and he instinctively lightened his breath, afraid any motion may disturb her.

"Good, I hope they do. Thank ye," she said, looking over the loch at the setting sun.

Hawk knew the sight in front of them held irresistible beauty, but found he couldn't take his eyes off the warrior next to him.

They remained there on the driftwood together. The sun painted the clouds beautiful shades of fluorescent orange and magnificent lavender as it dipped behind the valley. The stars winked on, one by one, in the night sky. Firelight from the camp behind them crept along the shore's edge. They heard Sir William's clanking steps before he spoke.

"I'm not sure what happened in the Black Wood. No one has spoken of it, and I dare not ask." He crept closer. "Archeress, I have seen your troubles these past few hours, and it pains me. I pray, take these." He revealed a hand, which he'd held tucked behind his back. Wrapped in the center of his palm was an elegant bouquet of petals. But Hawk could see in the dim light that they weren't the petals of flowers.

"These are fletchings from King David's royal armory," the knight explained. "The finest feathers in Alba. An archeress like you should have them in my stead, for I'll have no need for them in your company."

Mòrag cleared her throat of emotion before replying, "Thank ye, pal. Yer too kind tae me."

"We're all in this world together. Come now, the stew has begun to simmer. We shall eat. Fill our bellies with hot food and some ale and end this day."

———

"You've seen them then? The soldiers, that is?" Lady NicNeev asked a handsome cattle farmer.

The farmer removed his hat and held it across his plain shirt.

"Aye," the man replied to her horse, unable to grace Lady NicNeev with his gaze.

"They headed north then? To the castle?"

"Naw, my lady. East it be, ye ken?"

"North. East. Northeast. Up along the shore of Loch Ness?"

"Forsooth," he nodded, pleased at the understanding.

Hawk's mare sniffed the ground. The band of riders had traveled all day along the Highland road. They slogged through the bogs, then over the stony passes of the Grampian Mountains. Hawk spent most of the day in the saddle, taking in the stunning vistas and the crisp air only elevation could bring. He saw a wildcat hiss in her cubs' defense against the curious, abominable Tiree. Hawk witnessed a heavily antlered red stag tangle with a rather formidable Highland cow. He even saw an osprey fetch a salmon while crossing a river on a ramshackle stone bridge. It would've been a tremendous ride if the huntsman hadn't remained vigilant of the tracks they followed and the time they spent while chasing the Norsemen.

Although the huntsman saw many sights along the way, he kept one eye on Lady NicNeev. She had saved his life, and he was grateful the band of four had become closer. Yet she was an anomaly, a sorceress, something he hadn't encountered before. A character in a tale he might've heard around a campfire from a passing storyteller. However, that character had come to life, and although it took him a while to process, he was finally aware. It shouldn't have been a surprise to the huntsman, for he knew all too well the hearty truth in tales and legends.

I hope she recovered well from the previous day's encounter.

Hawk wanted to ask Lady NicNeev, but knowing her steadfast attitude, he didn't pry. He also wished to ask her about what she said on the pier, about him knowing sorcerers. Were there other sorcerers he'd known from Norway? And if she hadn't meant that, could she have meant him? That seemed impossible. Hawk was simply a huntsman.

They had arrived at the shores of Loch Ness late in the

evening and crossed the cattle bridge near the mouth of the Oich River into the village Cille Chuimein. The farmer Lady NicNeev engaged with had likely never seen a sight like the four riders before him: a knight, a lady, a warrior, a huntsman, and a black wolf.

"By God! That's nae dug, that is!" the farmer cried, finally seeing Tiree hiding behind the many pairs of horse legs.

"Thank you, Taog," Lady NicNeev said, ignoring the man's justifiably concerned comment. "How far to Urquhart Castle from here?"

"Well . . . with them steeds? It nae be long for ye. Those horses look fitter than any I ever saw. Fit for a king, I'd wager."

"You wouldn't believe," NicNeev said with a smirk. She spun her horse toward the loch. "Come, we should be off."

Wordlessly, the band of riders trotted on toward the northern shore of Loch Ness. The road from the village swerved around a large oak tree before clinging to the coastline, toward Urquhart Castle.

It was difficult for Hawk to imagine that, since leaving Edinburgh four days prior, they hadn't caught the Norsemen. Blåveis had an almost three days' head start, but it seemed Hawk and his band were always one step behind.

Hawk pondered the notion to his companions out loud. "The Norse slavers and King David's soldiers move extraordinarily quick. I was certain we'd catch them before they reached their end journey."

Lady NicNeev seemed to agree. "Are these not the fastest soldiers in the history of mankind? I am serious; it's ludicrous. Watch out, my companions. King David's troops know the true meaning of haste."

"They're motivated by their cause," Sir William said, offering his opinion. "King David inspires them to travel swiftly. I'm proud of their work, protecting the lands from villainous bandits. The lord of the castle will see to the king's justice."

That justice better include mine as well, Hawk thought. The image of Blåveis and the Norsemen in chains drifted back into Hawk's mind.

"Think we'll reach them before Urquhart Castle?" Mòrag asked.

Lady NicNeev quickly answered, "Knowing our luck, I wouldn't count on it. But we probably should have asked that Taog how long ago he saw those soldiers. That might have helped. Although he was not the brightest, that man . . ." She laughed, then added, "Well, it doesn't matter now. We have followed them this far, and we know where they're headed. Come on, we'll find them soon."

Mòrag still had concerns. "What's our plan? When we find the Norsemen, ye ken? My family's sword should be with the Norsemen who stole it from Rosslyn. Or at the very least with the king's soldiers if they took it off them. How are we planning tae get it back?"

It was Sir William who put forth the idea. "I'll call on the lord of the castle. I've been privy to King David's commands to take this castle and know he sent Lord Gospatric there. I'll show them my decree, of course." He puffed up his chest, as if to further his reassurance.

"Aye, but will that even help?"

"It's sealed by King David himself, ordering the return of the sword, Claidheamh-mòr an Adhairc. As simple as that, Mòrag MacTarbh. I assure you."

"Aye, but . . . ye ken Norsemen are nae knights, Sir William. I havnae met anyone as chivalric and kind as ye, either."

A rare smile split the knight's face. Mòrag continued, "What happens when the soldiers take the sword and tell ye to get tae—"

"That, my dear," interjected Lady NicNeev, "is precisely why I've traveled all this way to help you. If the royal decree doesn't persuade the lord, I will. And *I assure you*, I am very persuasive. Why else would your father have hired me?"

"Aye, but . . ."

"We will get the sword back, that I am sure."

"Aye. Thanks. I appreciate your help," Mòrag said, nodding at Lady NicNeev with a forced smile.

Lady NicNeev raised a hand and adjusted the yellow bun atop her head. When she perfected it, she lifted the green hood of her tunic over her head, concealing the golden hair beneath. She turned and looked at Hawk, raising her eyebrow.

"What I'm interested in knowing is what our huntsman's plan is," Lady NicNeev pondered. "What will you do when our search leads you to them?"

The huntsman looked at the others. Their eyes all fell on him. Hawk hadn't really planned out what he'd do when he finally reached the Norsemen. Sure, he wanted the visceral relief of unleashing a knout on Blåveis's back as he did to his family. He imagined Blåveis crying out in anguish as Hawk had as a child. Shackled together, the Norsemen would beg for mercy as Hawk's family had. He desperately wanted to finish the tomahawk swipe on Blåveis's cheek from years before. But the more Hawk thought about it, the more he just wanted to know why. Why his tribe? Why did he survive? Why did they trap him across the ocean from his people? And that was if the Norsemen were even at Urquhart.

If they weren't there, Hawk would have to begin his search all over. It was the closest he'd come to catching them, yet it felt like they could still slip through his fingers.

She's right. What will I do? It was a dream, a goal so inconceivably unobtainable that he hadn't thought of the end. Hawk couldn't demand an apology. He'd confront them, yes, but then what? He was a huntsman, but they weren't creatures he could simply lure into a trap.

"I don't know," Hawk finally said. "I don't have a plan. I've never hunted monsters like them before. I guess we'll see soon enough."

"We shall indeed," said Lady NicNeev.

"Well," said Sir William, "you can count on my support against the bandits. I'll help you bring them to the king's justice."

"Thank you, Sir William."

"Ye ken I'll help, Hawk," Mòrag added.

"Thank you. And Tiree? Will he also pledge to support me?" Hawk asked, chuckling to himself, even as something squeezed in his chest to hear their proclamations of support.

Like his fight was also theirs.

"Aye, ye can count on him. But he'll nae be coming in tae Urquhart. Castles dinnae enjoy the sight of wolves, do they, boy?" she asked, watching Tiree as he trotted along with the band. "He'll have tae wait out and away."

"Wise," Lady NicNeev smiled. "Now, come, let's see what these horses are made of. The sun will be down soon enough, and I wish to sleep in a bed under a roof, not a tent and stars."

Together, they set off along the coast, cantering with the sun at their backs.

CHAPTER SEVENTEEN

The riders reached the campfires in the growing dusk. Smoke rose in swirls, vanishing into the dark blue sky as they headed through the orderly filing of military tents. The white canvas structures had the weathered appearance of prolonged use: stained, filthy, and above all, occupied. Soldiers paraded amidst the smell of ale, sweat, and smoke wafting through the makeshift housing. Gamblers rolled away their savings for a chance meeting with lady luck. Men with tankards boozed and boasted of times long ago. A particular cluster of troops formed a circle around two burley hooligans, expressing their pent-up energy through their fists.

Hawk enjoyed watching the soldiers turn their heads in baffled surprise at the sight of Sir William. They nodded in acknowledgment of the unknown knight. The knight, in plate armor and a blue-feathered helm, was a perfect contrast to their shirtless frivolity. Even Lady NicNeev's olive-green tunic and pristine yellow braided bun drew the soldiers' eyes. Mòrag didn't bring any attention.

In fact, Mòrag wasn't even with the three riders. She had, as they planned earlier, gone over the hill to find a spot where Tiree could hide.

"Any wandering guardsmen would think him a hero for shooting such a beast," Sir William had remarked.

Mòrag agreed and searched for a safe place to stay. She would join them shortly.

The rest of the band marched past the tents into the full view of Urquhart Castle.

Situated an outcropping of land, it jutted out into Loch Ness atop a motte. The castle stood as a beautiful amalgamation of stone and wood. The soldiers' campfires dazzled the castle's surfaces. Two square stone towers stood within a high stone wall. A wooden hoarding bridged the two towers along the wall's battlements.

Something dark dangled from the window of one hoarding. Hawk squinted, then his eyes widened. His mouth dropped slightly and his brow furrowed. The charred remains of a person hung from a window, bringing the foul stench of burnt flesh with it. The body's leg had fallen off, while its face listed, unrecognizable and distorted. But it was once a person, that the huntsman knew. Sir William and Lady NicNeev didn't seem to notice the charred body.

The huntsman rode beneath the imposing castle gate.

Two guards moved in front and blocked their entrance. "Halt. State yer business," the taller one commanded.

"We're here to see Lord Gospatric III of Dunbar," Sir William boomed, taking off his helm to project his voice. "By order of the king."

Sir William placed a hand on his cloak and flapped the blue-and-white cloth to the side of his mount, as if it weren't already abundantly clear that he was a knight in King David's service.

"Sir William Maurice of Holyrood!" a voice cried from inside the castle courtyard.

A man wearing the same plate and cloak as Sir William strolled up to the gate. Without a doubt, the man pledged his service to King David. Unlike Sir William, however, he sported a full head of brown hair.

"Welcome! Welcome, old friend," the man said, grabbing hold of Sir William's horse as he dismounted.

They embraced as though their kinship hadn't wavered over time and distance.

"Gospatric, you old fool. It's truly good to see you again. I see your hair hasn't grayed yet."

"And I see you left yours behind," Lord Gospatric laughed, leaning in and landing a friendly jab at Sir William.

"I'm afraid I left it behind years ago," Sir William smiled. "Makes it easier to wear the helm."

"I was under the impression the helm made it easier for us to look at you. I'm sure of it."

Everyone joined in on the laughter.

"But as pleasing as it is to see you, all the way at the north of the world, why are you here, my friend?"

"King David himself sent us on a mission," Sir William said.

"A mission?" the lord asked, perplexed. "Come now."

"I wouldn't have left the king's side if it weren't true."

"I see. Well now, that I can believe." Lord Gospatric smiled. "Guardian of the king, William. How is that old chap, my cousin David?"

"Very well, still youthful," Sir William said.

"Unlike us, no doubt. And Maud, is she well?"

"She's more beautiful than you could ever imagine."

"Wonderful. Speaking of beauty, William . . . who do I have the pleasure of standing before here?" Lord Gospatric asked, turning to bow to Lady NicNeev.

Sir William cleared his throat and adopted a heraldic manner. "Allow me to introduce the Lady Phillipa NicNeev, in the service of the mormaer of Menteith."

"Thomas? The mormaer of Menteith? How fairs he?" Lord Gospatric asked, proffering his hand to Lady NicNeev so she could climb down off her stirrups.

"Well indeed, my lord, though my travels have kept me from the court for some time now. May we come inside?"

"Yes, yes," the lord said, his face turning red. "Forgive my manners. My chambers are in the eastern tower. Come inside. You, take their mounts to the stables," he said, pointing to one of the gate guards.

Hawk appreciated not having to suffer through his own introduction. Everyone realized he was different, an outsider, a foreigner. He didn't enjoy greeting strangers because, unlike Sir William, he didn't have the king's cloak or helm to hide his story.

They entered the castle walls and walked toward the formidable stone tower. The structures inside stood constructed of timber and earth. A chapel, kitchen, barracks, and main hall all squeezed together around the central courtyard. A handful of soldiers laid down arms on a wooden table, and at its end, a blacksmith sharpened the blades on a wheeled grindstone. The clanging and scraping of metal filled the walls with sound. Hawk, distracted by the smith's performance, narrowly avoided walking into a boy with what could only have been a wooden pot of excrement. The vulgar smell turned Hawk's nose up.

"Idiot boy," Lord Gospatric muttered, then more clearly said, "This way, in here."

They entered the square tower through a thick wooden door. Hawk moved past the thin staircase and entered the ground floor's main chamber—a large but utterly dull room. There being no possessions or furniture, save for a single desk and straw bed, made the room larger still. The desk's candle lit up the workspace. Parchments, maps, and letters littered the desk's surface, with a single wooden chair pushed beneath. The man was either a person of few items, or one who took his work seriously.

Lord Gospatric sat behind the desk. "Forgive me. I'm afraid it's not often I have guests in my room." It was more of a statement than an apology.

"We've been sitting in a saddle all day," Lady NicNeev said. "We're happy to stand." She walked with Sir William up to the desk.

"Squire!" Lord Gospatric barked.

There was rustling, then a boy of fifteen with a blonde mop of hair ran in from behind the huntsman. He'd evidently been eavesdropping behind the door.

"Bring us some chairs and then wine. The blue keg, boy."

The squire's eyes widened. "The good stock, my lord?" he asked, clarifying before accidentally opening the castle's rare supplies.

"Yes, my boy. Be quick."

The boy exited rapidly, slamming the door behind him. The occupants of the room jolted slightly, then calmed once more.

Gospatric continued, "It's been a while since I've treated with guests of your class, my lady. But now is as good a time as any to drink the finer wines."

"The lads outside, they seem eager for a fight," Sir William commented, rubbing a hand over his dark temple.

"That they are, my friend. I always enjoy bringing the sons of enlightened southern families north to teach these Highlanders the meaning of being civilized. Fresh recruits just arrived today; mixed with the rest of the boys smoothly. It's good to have fresh recruits and supplies. Gives the soldiers something to occupy their minds. King David sent us up here to take the castle in early summer. Easy enough campaign. There were few occupying the castle, maybe a couple of families. They yielded quickly and quite easily. One tried to assassinate me during the negotiations, but we dealt with them. It was all too easy. I think that's why the men are so eager. They came expecting a fight and didn't have one."

"Easy victory," agreed Sir William.

"Truly, it was. Nothing compares to it. King David was happy to compensate the clan leader's family too. 'God's charitable gift!' he told me. Civilized members of King David's army reclaimed this castle, so some of the gift went to us. We gave the Highland clans a minuscule portion. *My charitable gift,*" Lord Gospatric said, turning a wry smile.

Sir William, for the first time, didn't join in his friend's revelry. Lord Gospatric shifted in his chair. Hawk enjoyed the awkward silence permeating the room.

It only lasted a moment as the squire returned, setting down two wooden chairs opposite Lord Gospatric. The squire quickly darted out of the room once more. Sir William offered Lady NicNeev the first choice of a seat. He then turned to Hawk. Hawk closed his eyes for a moment, shook his head in a gesture of no thanks, and stood behind the chairs.

"Who is your escort, William?" the lord asked, formalities forgotten as he acknowledged the huntsman for the first time. Hawk swallowed, preparing for his answer.

The lord turned to Hawk. "What's your name, lad?"

"Hawk," said Hawk.

"Hawk?" the lord repeated.

"Yes."

"Not a very godly name," the lord said, his accusation like a prodding knife. "Where's this one from Will—"

"He's a huntsman," Sir William cut the lord off, "in service of King David. He has the king's trust."

"Well, your word shall suffice. Greetings, Hawk. I am Lord Gospatric III of Dunbar, as William has already mentioned. Well. Now that we're all properly introduced, please tell me, what do a knight, a lady, and a huntsman have in common service of my cousin, King David? Especially here, on the edge of the kingdom of Alba."

"My friend, we've ridden with haste from Edinburgh on a mission from the king of direct importance," Sir William said, leaning in so only the members of the room could hear him.

"I gathered that, William."

Sir William went on, "Soldiers, some of your new recruits, it sounds, brought with them a party of Norsemen. It's our understanding that these Norsemen possess something our king would have returned with us back to Edinburgh." Sir William leaned back in his chair, giving time for Lord Gospatric to process.

"They've stolen from the king?" Gospatric asked slowly, a

shocked expression hanging on his face. "Someone here in my castle?"

"No, my lord," Sir William clarified, "not from the king directly, but a subject dear to King David."

"Oh. Thank God. I thought for a moment I had someone who committed high treason within my ranks." The lord sighed.

Hawk twitched at the lord's exaggerated look of relief upon clearing up exactly who was stolen from, as if that changed the very act of stealing.

Sir William rummaged in his pouch, then pulled out a rolled piece of parchment. He held it in the desk's candlelight to show Lord Gospatric.

"We carry with us a royal decree," Sir William said, spinning it to reveal every aspect of the letter. A black wax circle stamped the letter shut. "Sealed by the king's seal."

"Yes, yes." The lord waved in dismissal. "I trust your word if it's from the king. You are a knight of honor, *Sir* William. Do you know—" the lord turned to the other two gathered "—that this man once refused the advances of a certain Amelia 'La Beauté,' eldest daughter of Lord Greenhollow, simply because King David asked him to keep an eye on Maud's whelping bitch? He could've succumbed to her will and to the night of his life. What did I tell you again? Oh yes, I said to him that dogs have been whelping for thousands of years. They can survive one night without your help. But no, not *Sir* William. Instead of watching Amelia, he watched a dog sleep all night, if I recall correctly. The bitch didn't whelp for two more days."

The room filled with laughter. Everyone save Hawk. He smiled reflexively but became increasingly distracted by Mòrag's prolonged absence. He thought she would've arrived already.

"Indeed . . . Amelia . . ." Sir William said, delving deep into his memory at the mention of the name. "I'd forgotten 'La Beauté.' She was beautiful, to be true. I wonder what she's up to now."

"Sadly, she passed away more than a few years ago. Giving

birth to twins, I hear. The girls survived, but Amelia did not." The laughter faded.

"A shame . . ." Sir William frowned.

The squire burst open the door again and walked in with a handful of tankards. Dark liquid tipped over the cups as he carefully brought them to Lord Gospatric and his guests.

"Squire, send for Lieutenant Marc. Hurry now."

The boy exited the room once more.

The lord raised his tankard and gave a half-hearted toast, "To Amelia 'La Beauté.'"

Hawk raised his tankard in salute and then drank the wine. It tasted of sour strawberries and summer fruits. The huntsman scrunched his face after every sip.

The lord tasted a mouthful of his tankard and then said, "The world was a duller place when I heard of her passing. But you, Lady NicNeev, have brightened it again. Let me see this decree."

Sir William handed him the roll. The lord snapped open the wax seal.

He read aloud, "'By order of King David, ruler of the kingdom of Alba, it is decreed . . .'" He paused, scanning the document and mouthing the words to himself as he read. "'The safe return of the mormaer of Menteith's sword by the knight, Sir William Maurice of Holyrood, in possession of this decree . . . Currently in unlawful possession by the bandits of Rosslyn . . .' Well, it would appear that I have a common thief amongst my men, does it not?"

"Yes, it would seem," Sir William agreed, taking a drink from his tankard.

"Did the king have a method for suggested punishment?" Lord Gospatric asked.

"No," chimed in Lady NicNeev. "However, as representative of the mormaer's interest, I would imagine whatever you felt was necessary would be sufficient, my lord. We wouldn't want to tread on your military command," she added with a wink.

Hawk grew anxious. He couldn't believe it. Blåveis was near.

But where? A dungeon of sorts? And where was Mòrag? She should've arrived already, or at least be yelling from inside the courtyard. The lord and lady giggled in their cups again.

I wish Mòrag at least could be here to give her opinion or say in the matter of the sword, Hawk thought. *She's missing the whole conversation.* Luckily for her, Lady NicNeev and Hawk had her best interest at heart. Another laugh rang out from the desk, followed by the thunk of drained tankards. Hawk could only hope Mòrag was well and that nothing befell her or Tiree.

The lord slammed his cup onto the desk. "Well, you can be sure we'll fix this problem straight away, my lady."

"Thank you, my lord," Lady NicNeev said with a bow of her head.

"Yes, thank you, Gospatric," Sir William added.

Lord Gospatric turned to lean in toward the knight, a sign that the matters to be spoken about were only for the room.

The lord started, "William, I don't believe it's a secret to you, privy to the king as you are, that the troops stationed here will be a staging area for further eastern conquests, yes? We're to tame the unruly clans to the east and unite under one leadership. Might I convince you to stay and help lead my troops? I could use a man of your caliber and experience."

Sir William's chivalric bravado elevated. "I'm afraid my duties lie with the king, Gospatric."

"My cousin is lucky to have a knight such as yourself by his side."

Hawk couldn't hold back any longer. The demon of his nightmare was close. He had to ask. He had to know.

"The raiders brought with your new recruits," Hawk asked, "where are they? Why were they brought so far north?"

"Yes, Huntsman?" the lord asked. "What raiders?"

"The Norsemen raiders who stole this sword before being brought here by your soldiers. *The* raiders. They'd be flying the banner of a winged lion—"

"On a midnight-blue field?" the lord finished.

He tilted his head in curiosity. The casual movement annoyed Hawk.

"Well, do you know about them?"

"Of course I do, the miserable lot," the lord said with fervor. "We only heard of them the other day. Marc and his men brought them under escort here for God's retribution, eh? Hearty bunch of barbarians. But they're here, alright."

"We would like to speak with them if we could, my friend," Sir William asked.

"Certainly. How is your Norse, William?"

"Not as good as my French, I'm afraid. But my companion, no doubt, speaks well enough for all."

Hawk nodded, ready to demonstrate when the door flung open again, nearly off its hinges. The room jumped once more. A man with a grizzled appearance marched in and stood at the edge of the room.

"My lord?" the man said in question.

"Ah, Lieutenant Marc." The lord stood in welcome, introducing the room. "This is Sir William Maurice of Holyrood, a dear friend of mine. This is the lovely Lady NicNeev and the king's own personal huntsman, Hawk, all of whom are in the service of our gracious King David."

The lieutenant nodded in acknowledgment.

Gospatric continued, "You'll treat them with the utmost respect. Now, Lieutenant, I want you to listen to me carefully. The king has made a royal decree that a soldier in your unit is in unlawful possession of a sword belonging to the mormaer of Menteith." Hawk grew frustrated at the lord's confusion.

Hawk tried to correct him, "No, the sword was in the Norsemen's possession."

"Right. He has the truth of it. The king *and myself* would like to see it returned to its proper owner. Sir William will handle carrying the sword. I leave you all with Lieutenant Marc. When you've settled your business, the lieutenant will have someone escort you to the guest suite and bring food from the kitchen. You must be starved."

"Many thanks, my lord. You are too kind," Lady NicNeev cooed.

She played the part of the lady of the court well.

"Truly, my friend," Sir William said in earnest.

"Now, if you'll excuse me, I have matters to see to." Lord Gospatric bowed and marched out of the door.

"Follow me," the lieutenant said, making for the exit.

Sir William followed in tow. Lady NicNeev made for the door, but Hawk reached out and grabbed at her sleeve.

She whirled in surprise. "Yes?"

"Wait, slow down. Why aren't we waiting for Mòrag? She'd want to be here," Hawk said with force.

"The sword is the priority. The sooner we get our hands on the blade, the better. Sir William has *popped* the royal decree. If word gets around why we're here, where we're from, or even what path we took to get here, someone will realize the sword's worth, and it will disappear from our grasp and sight. We must keep going on Mòrag's behalf."

Hawk scowled and closed his eyes with a sigh. She had the truth of it. They had to keep moving, for the wheels had already rolled downhill.

"She's fine, trust me," Lady NicNeev said, sensing the huntsman's worry. "She's perfectly capable on her own. She'll join us shortly."

Hawk nodded in agreement. Hearing someone say it aloud helped alleviate his mood. She smiled at him in comfort, and they moved for the exit.

Chapter Eighteen

Hawk walked through the castle courtyard with the others once more. Night had fully set in. The sky darkened, but the castle was bright with torch-light. Lieutenant Marc and Sir William seemed to be discussing the finer points of castle upkeep when the two stragglers caught up. As they walked toward the barracks, Hawk scanned the courtyard for any clues of the Norse raiders—no torn banners or signs of them. They likely would've burned all banners and placed the men in the dungeon or stockade. He couldn't wait to confront them. His excitement built.

A shout from Lord Gospatric carried through the open gate. He yelled at his men in an indiscernible rant. The men weren't receiving praise, that much was clear. Hawk hoped they weren't shouting about a lone warrior woman approaching on a horse. He had expected to see her standing in the courtyard but was disappointed.

That's okay, he thought. *Find the sword, deal with the raiders, and then find Mòrag.*

Lieutenant Marc barked at three armed soldiers outside the barracks to follow them. He led the party around the back of the barracks, away from the courtyard and the torchlight. He brought them along the outer wall, past the western tower.

"Follow me."

The lieutenant guided them in the dark. He knocked his hand along the stone wall as they walked, searching for something hidden. Finally, he found it along the western edge. It was the knock of three conspicuous wooden planks. Lieutenant Marc grabbed the wooden planks and moved them aside. Even in the dark, the lieutenant's grin shone when he said, "Shortcut."

Hawk could only suspect it led to the dungeon. They ducked into the tunnel, leading under the wall. The lieutenant moved the next set of planks, covering the thin exit. Hawk stepped through.

They stood on the top edge of the motte outside the castle walls. Confused where the lieutenant was leading them, Hawk walked along the side of the wall toward the loch's shore.

A large campfire stood along the beachhead, lighting a new group of bearded men. The bearded men laughed and relaxed, not unlike the soldiers seen outside the castle's front gate. That's when Hawk saw it. It waved in the light of the fire, what he searched for those long, hard years—a golden-winged lion breathing flame, dancing on a blue banner.

The Norse raiders had set up camp, laughing freely in the open.

"They're not prisoners?" Hawk blurted, befuddled.

"Who? Them? Of course not," the lieutenant said matter-of-factly.

Hawk's hands shook. "Those men are raiders. They've committed horrendous crimes. Raided villages. Lord Gospatric said you escorted them north, did you not?"

"We don't punish good men for getting hungry," Marc snorted dismissively.

Hawk's blood boiled. He couldn't believe what he had witnessed.

"What?" the huntsman said, jaw clenched.

How are they not rotting in a dungeon cell at a castle run by

King David's men?

"Well, they're barbarians, to be sure, but they've been conscripted into service. They're in the king's army now. Come on, then."

"How . . ." Hawk couldn't move, his eyes fixed on the slavers, the demons of his nightmares. They camped right there, down the hill, on the water's edge—laughing, smiling, and drinking. He couldn't make sense of it.

Marc saw his expression and explained, "We met with them on our way to Urquhart Castle, up from Stirling. Near Loch Tay, was it? Just about, anyway. We were marching north and plowed into them all lost. Three of them fled at the mere sight of us. The other fifteen looked at the big bloke—Blåveis or something."

Hawk's gut twisted at the name.

"He knew he was outmatched. Said his ship ran aground. I knew Lord Gospatric and that he was looking for fighting men. Lord Gospatric likes fighters. I made Blåveis the offer of the king's service. Fight with us, and we'd get him that ship he wanted. Told him we were headed to the northern sea. Think he liked the sound of that. 'You pay us ship to fight in battles?' he said. Simple." The lieutenant guffawed at his mock accent.

"But they were under guard?" Hawk pushed. "Escorted?"

"Aye, they were under guard. How often do you see Norsemen walking down the road? We kept a close eye on them to make sure they weren't seen as the bandits people might have suspected. We escorted them under our protection."

"Protection!" the huntsman spat.

"Aye . . ." the lieutenant said, turning to study Hawk. "When you have a mad hound on the loose, you don't just kill it, you use it. Grab the dog by the collar and train it to bite your enemy rather than bite you. The king requested more soldiers in his army. Lord Gospatric decreed to do whatever we can to defend these lands."

"You cannot be seri—" Hawk began, but was stopped.

Something grabbed the huntsman's sleeve. He whirled

around and met Lady NicNeev's insistent glare.

"Well," Sir William said a little too casually, "let us continue, Lieutenant. I shall wish to have this sword in our possession, then have a strong word with our lord, I think."

Sir William pushed on, his metallic armor vibrating with his every step. The lieutenant agreed and followed, his three soldiers as close as shadows.

Lady NicNeev thrust Hawk toward the beachhead. He stumbled, catching his footing down the motte. Hawk's adrenaline spiked. His heart pounded under his armor as they advanced on the demons of his nightmares.

"Ho, Blåveis," Lieutenant Marc shouted with authority.

Around the campfire, a burly hulk of a man rose, wearing nothing but hair above his waist. The man spun like a heavy barrel. He reached down and grabbed a sword off the bench and raised it into the air. Even in the dim backlight of the campfire, the hulking man's singular blue eye penetrated Hawk's every piece of armor. The huntsman wove to the front and stood with his feet apart, ready to spring at any chance.

Blåveis still appeared as the demon Hawk remembered. Even the scar down the man's cheek curved exactly how Hawk saw it in his nightmares. Just as he did before countless hunts in his life, the huntsman spun the obsidian knife in his hand.

The lieutenant's shrewd confidence didn't falter. "Evening, gentlemen."

Blåveis barked, and immediately two other bearded Norsemen sided up alongside him. The lieutenant snickered.

"Ah, tsk, tsk. Settle down. Settle down."

Blåveis pivoted and looked at Hawk. The huntsman spun the blade again, catching the handle on every spin. The brute of a Norseman squinted, the blue eye dominating Hawk's attention. He spun the blade once more. Blåveis took one step forward. Quicker than a flash of lightning, Hawk's blade flipped into his hand, raising it to throw it at the Norseman. Blåveis recoiled, then revealed a jagged tooth grin.

"*A Vinland slave*," Blåveis said in Norse.

Hawk twitched at the deep, hoarse voice. It was the voice that laughed at the deaths of family and friends, the voice that lashed at his sister collapsed on the ground. The rush of pain ignited by the sound of that voice was too much.

The huntsman threw the knife purposively at the ground beneath Blåveis's feet. Hawk brandished the black tomahawks from their sheathes as the Norsemen stepped out of the way.

"*Do you remember?*" Hawk began, switching to his Norse tongue. "*All those years ago, the boy who gave you that scar on your cheek. I bet you do. I bet you remember these too.*" Hawk—methodically and calmly—spun the tomahawks with his wrists in a full circle.

They whirled around a second time.

Everyone stared in surprise, unsure of what the huntsman might do. Even the lieutenant froze in awe. The tomahawks started a third spin when Hawk lunged. He swung, as quick as a viper, bringing the blade of the ax to meet the sword.

Catching the sword in the ax's curve, he torqued it from Blåveis's grip, tossing the sword to the ground at Sir William's feet. Blåveis was defenseless and without armor. Hawk moved in to strike him down. The naked flesh of the Norseman's torso begged to be cut through. Hawk would shred that skin just like the slaver's whip had cut him.

But Blåveis didn't need a sword.

Hawk rushed his swing. Blåveis stepped forward to meet him, shortening Hawk's attack. Massive bear-like paws came down on Hawk. One grabbed his wrist like a vice while the other grabbed the top of the other ax's handle. They locked together, arms wide. Blåveis snarled, peppering Hawk with spit. Shouts rose around them.

Soon, Blåveis overpowered Hawk. He flexed the huntsman's arms in, pulling Hawk into a tight squeeze before thrusting his head forward and crashing it into Hawk's forehead. Hawk's vision blackened for a moment as Blåveis released him. Hawk shuffled backward before shifting his stance, readying for retaliation. Every man drew their sword. For a moment, chaos yearned to erupt like the wind before a storm.

"Stand down!" Lieutenant Marc barked, jumping between Hawk and Blåveis. "Stand down. Don't make me cut you down, both of you."

He turned to the Norsemen and attempted to make peace over their hooting and growling. "Back up. Back up."

Sir William moved in front of Hawk, steel at the ready. Lieutenant Marc shouted over the Norsemen, "Hey, listen. Listen! The ship, damn it! Do you want the ship or not? We gave you the boats now as a gift. But if you want the ship like we said, you need to calm down, okay? Okay? Stand down. Now! And you—" he whirled around to Hawk "—I don't know who the blazes you think you are, but pull that kind of shite again and I'll kill you myself."

Hawk's eyes didn't waver from Blåveis. Blåveis, unperturbed, laughed at him.

"*You're still weak, boy. Brave, but weak*," Blåveis said.

"Shut it, you dog," Lieutenant Marc snapped. Sir William picked up Hawk's knife and backpedaled into the huntsman. He pushed Hawk further away from the Norseman. Hawk's hands shakily found the tomahawks' sheathes. He patted his forehead at the point of contact. A small trickle of blood oozed across his temple. Hawk swiped it away.

Lieutenant Marc pointed a sword at Blåveis. "I'd take one step back. There's a good lad." He turned to Sir William and, gesturing to Blåveis's sword in the dirt with his head, asked, "Is that the sword? Right." Turning back to the Norseman, he continued. "My compatriots have lost something—something dear to them. And they'd like it back. Your new pretty sword? Course it is. I've seen you brushing it for three days, like it was your own manhood."

The other king's men laughed. Hawk did not.

"Lieutenant," Sir William spoke up, "the sword is here. Let us stay no more. I have need of words with Lord Gospatric. We must go."

"Right then." The lieutenant straightened up.

A firm hand dragged Hawk away from the Norse campfire by the shoulder pad. His feet moved, though his mind didn't want them to. Pain shot through his head, but it didn't compare to the unfinished hunt. Hawk's body still trembled from the adrenaline. He'd found them, finally. The Norsemen were there.

"Come," Lady NicNeev pleaded quietly. "Focus. There will be time enough for *that* later." She walked next to the huntsman, guiding him back up the motte.

Hawk struggled to comprehend how Lord Gospatric protected the Norsemen, even though it all made sense. They never saw or heard about the raiders pillaging on the road from Edinburgh, because they were bought. They were bought and paid for, in the service of Lord Gospatric—of King David's own men.

They shuffled to the postern once more and ducked into the castle walls. The lieutenant led them behind the barracks to the western tower. Hawk breathed through his nose heavily. He fumed. Those raiders stood there at the foot of the castle, and Hawk couldn't do anything. At least not without setting the king's men against him and betraying the king. How could the soldiers be so trusting? How could the Norsemen stand around the fire, unchallenged for their many crimes? They were slavers!

Hawk took in a deep breath and exhaled through his nose. He couldn't do anything yet, not even run back and fight them. There were too many, and all in service of the castle. Fighting them would turn him against Lord Gospatric and the crown. It had to be, as Lady NicNeev said, *time enough for that later.*

Lieutenant Marc led them to the torchlight outside the western tower. Sir William approached the tower's torch to view the new sword more clearly. It shined in the light, a perfect reflection of the flames.

"Is this it?" the knight asked.

Lady NicNeev walked over to the sconce and removed the torch. She held it over the sword. She studied it, first the steel blade, carved and etched with slanted lines of Gaelic runes, then the leather hilt, black and worn. A sapphire gem embedded in the sword's pommel glowed.

"Yes, that's it," she whispered, her eyes widening with a smile.

Sir William held the sword up to examine it himself, from end to end. He seemed to search for a secret. The knight had traveled the entire journey for a simple sword. He let out a deep, rumbling laugh.

"All for simple steel," the knight said. "Fine steel, but steel no different from my own. Lieutenant, I believe you, and I should have a word with Lord Gospatric, shall we?"

The lieutenant nodded and started toward the courtyard. Sir William turned and spoke directly to Hawk.

"I leave you with the sword. See to its safety. It'll be easier for all if you remain here. I'll join you when I learn the whole truth. Then we shall see what can be done."

He handed Hawk his knife, then the sword, hilt first, and sauntered on. Hawk thought about protesting, wanting to be a part of the conversation, but decided Sir William was right. Hawk needed to reel himself in first.

The huntsman grasped the sword with his gloved hand and held it up, testing the blade's weight. It was light in his hands. He gave the sword a test swing, then brought it up to Lady NicNeev's torchlight.

Hawk took off his glove to feel the cold of the steel. It was as sharp as a razor and polished smooth. The Gaelic etchings burned a crimson glow under his fingertips. Or was it the light of the flame?

The huntsman flipped the sword, tip downward, to carry it.

Where is Mòrag? I can't believe she's missed this moment. She must've waited months for this, and now her absence will rob her of the joy.

"Can you believe we finally have it?" asked Lady NicNeev, her sky-blue eyes happier than the huntsman had ever seen. A quiver wobbled her voice in a strange lust. "How many miles? How many hours in that saddle? Oh, Claidheamh-mòr an Adhairc."

"It's great . . ." Hawk said with a hint of distraction.

It was time to find Mòrag.

"Mind on the raiders?" the lady asked, perhaps hearing the hesitation in his voice.

"Yes. Well, no." Both were true. His mind was full of too many things, close to bursting, including a hovering worry—" Mòrag. Where is she?"

"She's fine. You worry too much."

The answer brought no ease. Hawk found it odd that Lady NicNeev could be bound with Mòrag for the entire journey, sharing the same goal of returning the sword to her father, and yet at the moment of its seizure, care not of Mòrag's whereabouts.

"We should try to find her," Hawk said. "Patrols outside the castle must've stopped her. Let's take the sword to her."

"Yes, we should. Do you mind if I hold it? I'd very much like to see if these inscriptions match what her father told me." Lady NicNeev held out the torch.

"Here, take it." Hawk swapped the sword for the torch and held it up so she might read it. She placed her hands on the blade, and Hawk noticed the inscriptions glow with her touch. They shone a ferocious violet. He was right, then. It hadn't been a trick of the light.

"Mmm, yes," she whispered. She looked around to see if anyone eavesdropped on them, then continued in a hushed murmur, "I can tell this is the one. The inscription is clear: *Adharc bàis an tairbh.* It glows to the touch. Did I see it glow for your touch too?"

"Yes," Hawk whispered back, matching her secretive tone.

"Interesting. Very interesting. You know what that means, of course?"

"In truth, no. I haven't the faintest idea," Hawk replied.

Then it struck him like a galloping horse. As if he forgot with whom he spoke.

"The sword, it's magic?"

She nodded. "Yes. Only those imbibed with the source of the ethereal world would reveal that glow. Not Blåveis. Not Sir William. It would seem just myself and—"

"Me? H-how can that be?" Hawk stammered.

"Does it matter how? I've searched all of Alba for this sword. The magic of the world, its magic, has led us here—now. *This* is the time, Huntsman," she said, extending a hand toward him in a humble offering. "Join me, Hawk. I know who you are. I know your past. We both saw what happened when you touched the sword, Claidheamh-mòr an Adhairc. The illumination. Only those blessed with magic can bring such a reaction. There's great magic in you. Can you not feel it?" She inhaled, as if sensing something. "Ah, yes, even now it surrounds you. But without me, it will remain dormant. Join me, and I will unlock that power."

Hawk wasn't sure if he should laugh or feel terrified. "Power? What are you talking about? I have no magic."

"Can you truly be so naïve to it?" she asked, a sinister lash to her words.

"Naïve?" Hawk asked, stepping back from Lady NicNeev's leer.

He strangely thought of the bandits Sir William fought on the road, remembering his tomahawk.

Hawk shook his head at the thoughts. "What do you even mean, join you?"

"The king is a fool. He cares not that his men hired those slavers." She pointed to the western wall with her hand wildly. "You have traveled far hoping to destroy them, but there they sit, being fed by King David's own soldiers. Blåveis is protected. The king will bring war and ruin to this land. Join me," she said, holding her hand out to him once more, "and together we'll destroy the Norsemen. Together, we can bring peace to Alba."

"*Bring peace?* Slow down a moment. We should find Mòrag

and show her the sword. It's her family's heirloom. What are you getting at?"

"She's distracted you, Huntsman," she said, rolling her eyes. "Forget about her. Only I can bring you what you desire most. The end of the Norsemen. The end of those nightmares." She ran her tongue against the front of her teeth.

Cold snaked down Hawk's spine. "How do you know of that?"

"If you haven't gathered that, then you truly are naïve." Lady NicNeev shook her head at the huntsman. She raised her chin like a disappointed parent. "The time will come when what lies dormant inside will burst from you—a power greater than you've known. You'll never control it without help though." She chuckled and then promptly tightened her mouth. "You would do best to remember that *only I* can help you wield it. Only I can help you master your power. Only I can help you bring an end to Blåveis. Remember that, Huntsman, for when that time comes, you shall seek my help."

She brought the sword to her chest, sighed, and looked around like that settled matters. "Hmm, well. Now it's time I thanked you, Hawk. Thank you for your help in finding this. For everything, truly. And when you find Mòrag, tell her I'm very sorry." She winked.

Hawk twisted his face in puzzlement. "Sorry? For what? Give me the sword."

Lady NicNeev laughed. "No. I'll return it to where it belongs. To Clan MacTarbh." Hawk expected venom to drool from her smirk.

He repeated his words, "Give me the sword—"

A roar of violent violet flames rose from Lady NicNeev's feet. They rapidly engulfed her, consuming every inch of her and the sword. Hawk stepped back in surprise, avoiding the heat. The flames crested her golden head of hair. And as quickly as the flames appeared, they died away. Lady NicNeev vanished beneath them.

CHAPTER NINETEEN

Equus cantered past the white canvas tents in front of the castle. The faces, which had glued their eyes to the huntsman's companions on their way in, took no notice of Hawk's fleeing horse. The smell of ale proved inescapable. The troops' cacophony of drunken revelry combined with their competitive masculinity created a muffled rumble over the field in front of Urquhart.

Hawk clenched his fists around Equus's leather reins. He shivered in the saddle, though the night's summer air was warm. His heart raced faster than the horse's feet. He cursed under his breath as he rode away, distancing himself from the castle. How could Lady NicNeev be there one second and gone the next?

The violet flames hung in his mind, seared into his memory. He remembered standing there after she vanished, waiting for her to reappear or tell him it was all a game. But if it was a game, he wasn't sure of the rules. He had simply remained, his mouth hung open in disbelief.

For a while, the only thing the huntsman could do was listen to the hum of the castle. He stared at his own hands. They made the sword glow, and she called him magic. They seemed unrecognizable, yet he felt no different. How could that be? Nothing had burst out of him. He couldn't think of anything magic he'd done. He fought monsters, sure. But so had Garrett, and he never used magic. Hawk hadn't either. He simply was a huntsman.

Eventually, it grated on him. Hawk forced himself to move into the dark alley. He made his way out from behind the barracks to find Sir William. Hawk stopped and turned back to look once more at where he'd last seen Lady NicNeev, then back toward the courtyard. With his mind preoccupied, his feet moved awkwardly and out of stride. Sweat trickled across his palms. What could he do? How could he just march into the eastern tower with Sir William and Lord Gospatric and tell them Lady NicNeev had . . . disappeared? As if anyone could believe that. Hell, he still didn't believe it.

No, they'd think I harmed her. A simple noblewoman, he conceded. Sir William might believe him, but disappearing in flames would be hard to fully convince anyone. And there was the sword. The sorceress took Mòrag's family sword. It was the reason the band of four had set out from Edinburgh. *Now, it's gone.*

There was only one option for Hawk. He needed to discover what delayed Mòrag's return to the castle and tell her about the sword. The only spot of luck so far for Hawk was that the stables sat unguarded and Equus remained saddled.

The huntsman reached the edge of the soldiers' tents. The light from their campfires faded from his path, and Hawk's eyes slowly adjusted. He had to guide himself with the moon's light, its large, circular shape reflecting off the loch. Brilliant stars above blurred into one swirling sparkle as his eyes welled with tears. He told himself the rush of wind from riding wet his vision, but his trembling hands said otherwise.

Equus pulled up on the path, slowing to a walk, then halting altogether. Hawk took his eyes off the stars. He wiped them on his sleeve to see what lay in front of him. Two reflective, glowing orbs floated in the way. His mind jolted clear, and Hawk's hands found his tomahawks behind his head in a flash. He leaped from his perch, his body moving in habitual rhythm from years of experience. A predator lay in his path. He approached the reflective orbs. They looked like the tapetal reflection of eyes he knew, but of whose?

A voice called out from behind him, "When will ye ken nae tae fall for the wolf?" asked the familiar voice.

He nearly dropped his ax at the sound. He wiped his eyes once more and turned around slowly. Mòrag stood next to Equus, her bow out and ready. Hawk squinted in the moonlight. Two other people moved out of the darkness, shadows surrounding Mòrag.

"Mo!" Hawk said with a smile.

"Hawk," she responded in kind.

"Mo. I . . . I . . ." Hawk stuttered, his mind moving faster than his tongue could follow.

His throat grew tight. It wouldn't work. Hawk mulled over what he wanted to say.

"What? What is it?" Mòrag asked, sensing his hesitation. "What happened tae yer head? I thought I'd have more time tae meet ye."

"What happened to you? You never came to the castle?" Hawk finally spoke.

"Aye, I meant tae. It's just . . . I went tae find a spot for Tiree and went over the hill. When I did, I found them." Mòrag flicked a thumb at the new shadows. "The Moravians."

"The what?" Hawk asked, bewildered.

"The Moravians, those from the land of Moray. This is Ulster of Clan Sruidh, actually. Ye remember I mentioned him?"

The left shadow moved forward and raised a hand in greeting. Hawk looked up to meet the man's eyes, but found his eyes hadn't fully adjusted to the dark yet.

Mòrag continued, "And this is Ceitidh of Moray." The second shadow didn't move from her spot, only nodding.

"So . . ." Hawk said.

"So, my da and Ulster's da were best mates. My da loved telling me stories of their fighting together, and we even hosted Ulster's family at our home a few summers ago."

"So you had a chat?" Hawk said a bit too harshly.

The smile on the huntsman's face faded.

"Ach, I'm nae finished. Ulster told me there was tae be a raid on the castle. A retaliation for stealing their homeland and castle. And it's tonight!" Mòrag said with enthusiasm, like it was the most surprising thing that had occurred that night.

Hawk took a moment, returning his tomahawks to their sheathes.

Then he asked, "You abandoned the rest of us to the fate of the castle?"

"Naw. Why do ye think I'm bloody here? I was goin' tae ride in myself asking for Sir William, as we planned. Then I was goin' tae warn ye all. That reminds me, where are the other two? Wait . . . Why are *ye* even here?"

"I . . . I . . ." Hawk stammered, surprised. "I rode out here looking for you. You never arrived. Events moved so quickly there . . . I thought we'd have more time, but . . ." Hawk cut himself off.

He stepped up and grabbed Mòrag's hand, pulling her away from her two shadows.

She leaned in as Hawk spoke. "We found Blåveis. We found your family's sword."

"Aye?" she whispered, her eyes growing as wide as the moon. "Is it safe? Does Lady NicNeev have it, then?"

"Yes, she does."

"Good. Let's get her out of there," Mòrag said, turning away.

The huntsman pulled her back. "No, wait, listen. She . . ." Hawk again fought to find the words.

"What is it? Spit out already. What's wrong?" Mòrag asked.

Despite her blunt tone, she leaned in, as if to ease the words out of Hawk. It must've helped, as the huntsman finally got it all out. He told her of the castle visit. He didn't spare any of the details—all except his touch of the sword and Lady NicNeev's offer.

"What?" Mòrag blurted out, causing the huntsman to recoil slightly.

"She vanished. Those violet flames engulfed her. You know what I mean. The same violet flames we saw in Rannoch. It was some kind of magic. There was nothing I could do. She's gone, and she's taken the sword with her."

"I dinnae believe ye," she said, taking a step back.

"Why would I lie? She was a sorceress. You know that. You know the violet flames I speak of. I'm telling you, she vanished."

"And she dinnae tell ye where she was goin'?" Mòrag asked. "This must have been part of the plan or something."

"Part of *her* plan, yes. But it wasn't part of ours." Hawk kicked his heel into the dirt, digging a divot below his boot and scraping along the ground. He couldn't believe Lady NicNeev's betrayal and that she placed him in the position of explaining it all to Mòrag. "She's gone, Mòrag."

"Then where's Sir William?" Mòrag countered, her voice quavering slightly.

"He'd gone to the lord of the castle to talk about the Norsemen."

Ceitidh stepped out from the shadows next to Mòrag and Hawk.

She looked to the huntsman and asked, "I couldnae hear ye clearly, but did ye say ye have seen inside the castle?"

"Yes, I did," replied Hawk tightly.

"How many men were in there?" Ceitidh asked, who must have thought it the right time to ask questions the huntsman had no interest in answering.

"I don't know for sure. Hundreds, but—" Hawk started.

Ceitidh cut in. "Mòrag, we attack tonight. If ye want yer friends out of Urquhart, ye have tae go in there now."

"I was goin' tae come and get all of ye . . ." Mòrag exhaled. "Yer here, Lady NicNeev is gone, and Sir William?"

"Sir William won't leave. The lord of the castle is his close friend. Sir William doesn't know about Lady NicNeev at Rannoch. He doesn't know about her now. He doesn't even know I've left," Hawk said.

Although it sat wrong with him, he shook his head in a glum recognition of fate.

"Ye dinnae ken if we could convince him tae go?" Mòrag asked, arching her eyebrows in slow realization.

"How? What would you say?"

"Try to convince him tae leave," Mòrag said. "Tell him the castle is about tae be under attack."

"Tell him that his friend and the countrymen he's loyal to are about to be attacked?" Hawk asked, taking his time so Mòrag would understand his message. "There's nothing we could say to stop him from raising the alarm, surely. Then we wouldn't be able to leave. We'd be forced into defending the castle, or marked as traitors, cowards, or treasonous."

"What if ye lied? Trick him tae come out of the castle?"

"Maybe . . . But any suspicion we raise will make it obvious that something has happened to Lady NicNeev. He thinks she serves the mormaer of Menteith, remember? Not your father. Sir William would blame me, or you, or both of us for her disappearance."

"Ye really think so?" Mòrag asked, defeat creeping into her voice.

The huntsman shuffled his feet. He couldn't bring himself to look at Mòrag's reaction. He whispered, "I was the last to see her. We were alone together and . . . Now I've been gone a suspiciously long time. I'm sorry, Mòrag. If your friend's army is about to attack the castle, I don't think there's anything we can do to help Sir William out of there."

Mòrag cursed under her breath. Hawk repeated the curse for emphasis.

"So are we goin' in tae the castle now or naw?" Ceitidh asked.

Mòrag stared into Hawk's eyes. The tremble of her jaw as they stood there could've cut Hawk to his knees if it carried on any longer. She broke the silence.

"Naw," Mòrag answered.

"No," answered Hawk.

CHAPTER TWENTY

The huntsman spread his feet and crossed his arms over his chest. He stood at the peak of a tall hill overlooking Urquhart Castle. The loch below glistened brightly under the moon and stars. The castle seemed strange from the top of the hill. It felt to Hawk like he stared into a princess's playroom with tiny, armored dolls walking along the walls and courtyard. Fewer soldiers ventured out and about the castle than had earlier. The dim glow of campfires near the tents illuminated the castle, like tiny sparks floating from a hall's fireplace.

Hawk stood apart from the Moravian warriors. He had walked in and amongst them, with Mòrag and her two shadows. It was clear the warriors seldom saw any outsiders given the stares from the quiet, hardened faces. Hawk had quickly pushed past them to the hill's edge.

Rubbing a hand through his spiked hair, he tapped the welt Blåveis gave him. Hawk looked down, ignoring the mark. Mòrag bumped elbows with him on the right. They gazed at Urquhart together in silence. The silence was expected. They overlooked the castle from a hostile position. But Hawk hadn't talked during their walk through the Moravian camp. An unusual weight bore down on him as he climbed the hill. A burden he hadn't felt in a long time pressed down on him with reckless enormity—guilt.

Hawk shifted his gaze to the stars, away from the castle, as if he could find answers in their vastness.

What did the lady mean, I'm imbibed with the source? I don't feel any magic inside me. Surely it was a trick. And what about the sword? Why hadn't he kept the blade in his safekeeping? Why did he hand the sword to Lady NicNeev? Hawk had let Blåveis distract him. Or had Mòrag been the distraction the whole time? Alone, his search for the Norsemen never faltered, but the moment he allowed someone inside his head, everything slipped through his grasp. The huntsman cursed himself again for not getting the sword, even as conciliation. Hawk glanced at Mòrag. She, too, was quiet.

She's no doubt frustrated with my blunders, he thought. She hadn't taken her eyes off Urquhart since they reached the crest. Hawk couldn't imagine the regret she felt for not having seen to the sword herself. Or perhaps her only concern was for their remaining companion, Sir William.

Reminded of the knight, Hawk winced. Why didn't he run for Sir William the moment Lady NicNeev vanished instead of waiting around like an imbecile?

You fool. You've doomed Sir William to the castle's fate.

Mòrag finally took her eyes off the castle to look over Hawk's shoulder. She gestured behind the huntsman. On his left, an intricately armored man approached. The man nodded to Hawk and Mòrag in greeting, then joined their watch over the castle below.

The man had a solemn presence, reminding Hawk of his tribal village elders. Despite the presence, he couldn't have been older than Hawk, only just a man. He recognized the man based on a brief story Ceitidh mentioned on their way to the Moravians' camp: Lulach. He wore a thick set of brown leather armor across his torso. Elegant, curved depictions and designs pressed into the leather's surface. Lulach's stoic aura, coupled with his elegant red-

and-yellow cloak, left little doubt that he was the Moravians' clan chief.

Ceitidh had told Hawk and Mòrag that the army currently inhabiting the hills behind Hawk chose Lulach as clan chief. The huntsman sized up the lad next to him. He certainly looked the part of clan chief; armor from head to toe, his biceps exposed. But Hawk knew the clan chief was chosen by birthright and spirit, not by seasoned experience.

The clan chief broke the silent watch.

"So I hear ye have been inside the castle. Ye ken how many soldiers are in there?" Lulach asked in a hushed tone, as not to project his voice down the hill.

"There aren't as many as yours," Hawk answered. He kept his arms crossed and his eyes fixed on the castle below. "Their garrison was maybe a few hundred."

"That's good tae hear. I take it ye ken who I am?" the chief wondered aloud.

"I've guessed."

"Lulach of Moray, clan chief of the Moravians. Those Moravians," he gestured behind him.

Hawk nodded, as if Lulach needed approval. The huntsman wasn't in the mood for a conversation, particularly with the leader of the army outside the castle Sir William occupied.

"Hawk, is it?" Lulach asked.

The huntsman saw the clan chief shift position out of his periphery.

Lulach changed his tactics. "A huntsman, right?"

"Yes."

"What does that involve, exactly?"

"I hunt," Hawk said succinctly.

Lulach wore a puzzled expression. Rather than let it linger, the huntsman explained, "You want an elk delivered to your feet? You want someone to take care of the wolf eating your sheep? Is there something even *more* vile hunting in your woods? You call me."

"I see . . . Did ye get a good look at Urquhart's food supply? Do ye think they'd need tae hire a huntsman like yerself?"

The huntsman clenched his jaw. "You could just ask if I think they'd survive a siege." Hawk grew tired of the grating conversation.

"Do ye?"

"I don't know. I never saw the food supply."

"That's too bad, Huntsman," Lulach replied.

He unsheathed his longsword and checked the blade's edge. The moon's light reflected across its cold polished steel.

"It's a siege, then? Is that what you are after?" the huntsman blurted out.

Hawk's blood boiled. It had been a long day, and it was getting longer. He made to raise his voice again, when a hand grasped his wrist—a gentle grasp. It was Mòrag. She gave a half smile and barely, almost imperceptibly, shook her head. He let out a long exhale and dropped his shoulders. Hawk turned back to Lulach, who politely waited. Lulach looked toward Urquhart.

"I'm looking tae take back what's mine by rights. I am Lulach, son of Óengus of Moray, son of Lulach, the former king of Alba. My father held the title mormaer of Moray. He decided tae progress his own authority and crowned himself king of Moray.

"He allied with Máel Coluim, the eldest son of King Alaxandair. A bastard tae be sure, but the rightful heir tae the throne of Alba. My father, Óengus of Moray, and his new ally marched south nae long ago, taking five thousand Moravian warriors with them. He met King David's army, which was led by the cunning Edward Siwardsson in the fields of Brechin.

"They fought. They battled. And my father was slain, along with four thousand Moravians. Máel Coluim slipped away, and King David's army marched north. The southern leaders placed Uilleam MacDonnchada in my father's role of mormaer of Moray. My father's remaining troops disbanded and were forced tae run. I brought them back together, and the remnants of my father's forces stand behind us."

"That's a lot of names—" Hawk said.

"Aye, it's a lot of names because I have a lot of names tae remember. Names I will nae let myself forget. Names I will nae let others soon forget. I bet, Huntsman, ye have names such as that too. Names ye will nae forget."

Lulach spoke truly, for there were many names Hawk could never forget. The huntsman felt the wampum necklace under his armor. Their faces floated back with each bead his fingers caressed. There was his brother, Piwáhcuk Aniks. Hawk could still see him leaping from the tallest tree into the lake near his village. They were so young then. And of course Hawk couldn't forget his cousin, Nis Áhsitash. Tall and devilishly funny. No matter what, he'd always bring Hawk to tears laughing. He last saw his cousin on the ship, wasted away in chains. He could even recall his mother's name, Yôpôwi Pupiqáwôk: Morning Music. She was the light of all that's good in the world, and yet they took her.

The memories of their names boiled and raged in Hawk. His sister's face, Ayaksak, her cheek bruised and lifeless on the stony shores so long ago. He could never forget it.

Even his own name—the one given to him by the elders of his tribe—was stolen by Blåveis and the Norsemen. The name, Hawk, came from a need to translate—for the new world to understand him, to connect with him. He adored the name Hawk, harnessed it to his new life, but it would never be the name his mother called him, Musqayanuk.

It became too much. Hawk rubbed a hand over his aching temple and turned away from the hill. He started walking away from Lulach and Mòrag—away from everything.

Lulach grabbed Hawk's elbow, and the huntsman reflexively swung his arm up from the clan chief.

"Wait," Lulach said.

Hawk froze and exhaled.

"I want to show you something." Lulach pointed toward the castle, using his sword as an extension of his arm. "Look down there, on the wall. Do you see that body hung there? Just over there, tae the left of the gate."

"I saw it when I entered the castle," the huntsman replied.

A sour taste returned, remembering the charred remains hanging from the hoarding.

"That's my brother. He was Óengus II, named after our father. He was fourteen. My people tell me he ran at the lord of the castle with his fists. They tell me the lord had defiled the steward's wife in front of him tae provoke him. He was a lad. A foolish lad, but just a wee lad. And now my sister and I must look at him there. I've come to make sure the men who did that suffer through God's retribution." Lulach jabbed with his sword, punctuating the end of his words.

"God's retribution?"

"Aye."

The huntsman twisted his lips and spun to face the clan chief. It grew too much for Hawk. He couldn't hold back any longer. He scowled, keeping his tone hushed and precise.

"Around the back of the castle, guarding those boats, is a group of Norse slavers. Raiders. Monsters. Demons. I came to the castle expecting to find the slavers in the dungeon. The lord of the castle was well aware of who and what they were. And do you know what Lord Gospatric told me he was going to do? Show them God's retribution.

"'God's retribution' for him and his king was to pay the slavers and to conscript them into King David's army to attack the likes of you. Forgive me, my lord, but God's retribution means shit all. You think God's retribution is to siege the castle? Starve them out? Or storm its walls and slay its occupants, all because of your brother's murder? Don't claim to have a moral high ground with God's retribution. At least have the decency to call it what it is. Or else, I'm afraid all you lords will sound the same."

"What's it called then, Huntsman?" the chief asked, carefully threading out his words.

"Revenge. Yours. Your father's. It doesn't matter. You want revenge." Hawk spat down the hill toward the castle.

Lulach shrugged noncommittally. "That is true. I want revenge. I want it more than anything, and I'd do anything tae have it. When ye came tae the castle tae find the slavers, tell me, what did ye want?"

"Revenge," Hawk acknowledged.

The word felt right rolling off his tongue. He had never admitted it to himself or out loud, but it was true. That's what he wanted: revenge. In his months and years of searching, he wanted to confront them, but what he longed for, what he traveled hundreds of miles for, what he spent long hours into the night thinking about and imagining, was revenge.

"Then it seems tonight, we shall both have our revenge." Lulach grinned like a boy who had hit a target with an arrow for the first time.

Hawk fixed his eyes on the orange glow of the castle. Hawk repeated Lulach's words in his head over again. *Both have our revenge.* Is that how he wanted his revenge? By attacking the castle he had left? It seemed odd to him. The entire night rang odd. But the chance of fulfilling the revenge he set out for all that time ago stood right in front of him. It had an allure, a taste he couldn't resist. The temptation rested just below the hill, and Lulach held out the opportunity to take it. Hawk wanted to reach out and take a bite.

Mòrag stepped around to face them both. "Ye'll nae have any revenge tonight, if yer planning a siege. That could take weeks. Months."

"Eh, true," Lulach said, his smile defeated. "We have the numbers tae storm the walls tae be sure, but at what costs? Yer right, my people dinnae deserve that fate."

"You don't need to throw your men at the walls," the huntsman mused.

"What do ye suggest?" the clan chief asked, raising one eyebrow.

"A deal. You want the castle and I know its secret. I want the raiders by the boat taken down, and you can help me do that. Help me, and I'll help you."

"This I can do," Lulach replied, clasping Hawk's shoulder. "Tell me the secret."

"Behind the western tower, hidden by wooden debris, is a rear postern. It goes underneath the wall. It's hidden and unguarded tonight. I know because I went through it earlier today." Hawk smiled as Lulach had, his arrow on the target.

Lulach looked stunned. "Is this the truth? How have I nae heard of this?"

Hawk shrugged. "I imagine none know of it. It lies hidden for that very reason; for you not to know of it. They've buried it behind a false wooden wall. Distract the castle at the front with your host. Send fifteen swift warriors through the postern. They'll rush into the castle and open the gates. You can then move your army in through the front and on to victory. Their stone walls will mean very little with you inside. You'll overwhelm their numbers and they'll be defenseless."

"Revenge," Lulach said with light laughter.

Hawk brightened with a smile, but it quickly dimmed. He remembered once more that his friend Sir William resided inside the castle.

Lulach pressed Hawk. "Will ye show these men the way tae the postern and gate?"

Hawk shook his head. "I told you I'd tell you the castle's secret. I can't go in there again. My friend is in that castle."

"So are the Norse slavers," Lulach countered. "Help me and I'll help ye, remember? I swear it."

He threw his sword down, the tip piercing into the ground, and reached out a hand toward Hawk. The huntsman hesitated. He looked at Mòrag. Her face appeared emotionless, indifferent, offering the huntsman no help or guidance. Lulach sensed his uncertainty.

"We can get yer friend out of there safely. I'll give ye a moment while I inform my commanders.

Lulach marched toward the group of Moravian warriors behind them, leaving Mòrag and Hawk. Hawk looked back at the castle. Mòrag's eyes never left the huntsman.

"Are ye stupid?" she finally asked. "Ye'll risk yer life for all that? Ye cannae run in tae the castle, open the gates, and expect tae come out alive. Sir William is in there. Are ye planning on fighting him too?"

"No, but I have to try. I've come too far to walk away from this chance," Hawk said, a slight quaver in his now subdued tone.

"Revenge? Is it worth the chance of dying?"

"Yes," he answered without hesitation. "I'm not asking you to come with me."

"Oh, aye? Of course. I'll just sit here and watch then. Watch everything from atop this hill."

Hawk glanced back at the group of warriors, then to Mòrag. "Would you help them?"

Mòrag removed one of her gloves. She ran a hand through her hair and repositioned her tartan sash.

"This is all so much," she said. "I came here for my family's sword. But this . . . When I saw Ulster, it made me think of my family and . . . so much is happening so quickly, I just . . ."

"I know exactly what you mean," replied the huntsman.

The Norsemen, NicNeev's betrayal, his own abandoning of Sir William, and the gathering group behind him—it was too much to process.

"If I do naught, I'll be lost. The only way I can ever go back tae my da is if I ken, for certain, that the sword is nae in that castle. That Lady NicNeev is nae hiding in the tops of those towers. I need tae go in tae that castle."

Hawk hedged, "It's possible, but—"

"I'm nae afraid tae fight. Are ye?"

Hawk looked away from the castle and met Mòrag's eyes. They blazed with the impending battle.

"I'm a huntsman, not a soldier. But I must take care of Blåveis. I have to finish what I started." He talked it through out loud. "And I suppose . . . if I do nothing, Sir William is doomed. If I help Lulach, there's a chance I may spare Sir William and help him escape." He glanced behind them again warily. He whispered, "Are you sure you want to help them?"

Mòrag, however, seemed resolute. "When I talked tae Ulster, he told me his clan, Clan Sruidh, was starving. They've had tae live in the wild because of the men at the castle. This laird drove them from their homes and villages. They stole cattle and sheep tae feed the soldiers, stolen from the mouths of Clan Sruidh children. I ken some of these children. I cannae leave them tae starve. And summer is for growing crops. They willnae have anything come winter.

"I cannae stand by and do naught. I have tae help the clans of the Highlands. This could be my clan. I need tae help as if it were my own. And if it gives me a chance tae find my clan's sword inside, then I must. I certainly cannae leave ye tae do it alone."

Hawk warmed with a forgotten sensation. He took off his gloves and stuffed them into his belt.

"Then we shall surely succeed if you're with us, Mo."

Hawk gently laced his fingers around the soft backs of her hands. His fingertips touched her callused palms. Mòrag's lips curved upward, and her eyes, emerald even in the dark, seemed to brighten on the hilltop.

"I like Mo," she whispered.

"Me too," said Hawk.

Footsteps approached from behind them. Hawk released his grip and turned to meet Lulach, returning from his walk. Lulach grasped the sword out from the ground.

"My people are ready. I have the fifteen insurgents. Ceitidh is my second in command. She'll join ye under yer lead. Are ye ready? Will ye help my people?" Lulach's voice rang with renewed command.

"I'm in," Hawk said, nodding and sliding a finger over the tomahawks fastened across his back. "I can show them the way."

"So will I," Mòrag added, putting on her gloves and grabbing her bow to examine the string.

Lulach beamed. "Good, ye shall nae regret this. Both of ye."

"What's your plan then?" the huntsman asked, placing his hands on his hips.

"I'll cause chaos and distract from the north at the main gate. Ye will lead my warriors tae the postern on the west and in tae open the gates. Then, guard yerself. We'll rush in and, how did ye phrase it? 'Overwhelm their numbers.' They'll have most of their men stationed on the wall and hoarding, and hopefully, their attention will be on us. Ye shall nae have much trouble."

"How will you distract them?" Hawk asked.

Lulach smiled. "My brother there . . . It seems the laird of Urquhart Castle likes tae play with fire. Well, if he likes fire, we'll give him some. Ye'll ken when tae come out and strike."

CHAPTER TWENTY-ONE

A shroud of darkness swallowed the huntsman. Hawk hunkered down outside Urquhart castle. He ducked out of the way of a coniferous juniper branch. He hoped to steal one more glance up the motte to the castle. The shrubs' tendrils coiled around him into the ground. The junipers' roots dug into the soil, protecting the hill from the abuse of erosion. Their needle-like leaves protected Lulach's team from the eyes of the castle's watch.

They laid in ambush, the huntsman, Mòrag, and the Moravians. Hawk listened to the loch's rippling water and the faint shift of leaves in the breeze. He could hardly make out the soft whisper of anxious breath from the party behind him.

Hawk turned to glance at those following him. Ceitidh and Liùsaidh were up front. Ellar and Pòl were just behind them, and others further back. Even Mòrag's friend, Ulster, joined them. Fifteen in total and their faces proved all stone, chiseled in the art form of battle and war—cold, calculated, ready for a fight. Before they left Lulach's camp on the hill for the cover of the juniper, the Moravians had decorated their faces with blue woad dye. It blackened in the darkness like the stripes of a wildcat. They had the visual silence of camouflage. It seemed to Hawk that they were ready to die for their clan chief and his plight.

Hawk took out his obsidian knife and flipped it in his hands. The simple trick calmed his mind. He waited for the signal. But the waiting made him think about the plan. The insurgent team relied on him, but he didn't feel like a battle commander. What did Hawk know about leading troops? How would he know what to do once they accomplished their task, or if something went wrong? And a lot could go wrong. He tossed the knife again, hand to hand, spinning the blade in a circle and catching the handle once more.

Mòrag squatted next to Hawk. She held her ornamented bow in front of her and already nocked an arrow at the sinew string. Dark woad dye covered her face. She painted herself with dark raven wings out from her eyes, stretching over her cheeks and to her ears. It reminded Hawk of the warriors from his tribe, how they'd decorate themselves before the battle. She would've fit right in.

Hawk stopped flipping the blade and returned it to its sheath. Still crouched, he leaned over and gently bumped Mòrag. She rolled her eyes at him. A faint twist at the end of her mouth appeared, and a slight smile rose. The huntsman returned the smile. Her color depleted in the night air, surrounded by the dark woad paint. Mòrag's eyes proved no less brilliant in the moonlight.

Suddenly, her eyes brightened. They replenished their green color as a thousand tiny sparks lit up across them. Her mouth fell open, her face taking on a bright blaze.

Hawk spun, turning to identify the light's origin. Fire rained down from the hill above Urquhart. Flaming projectiles lit the sky in a fiery burst of radiance. It poured from the heavens onto the white tents in front of the castle.

Shouts from in front of the castle rose. "Wake up!" voices yelled. "We're under attack!"

Hawk and his band shuffled to see through the shrubs. They

wanted to glimpse the chaos that consumed the camp in front. Flaming arrows fell as soldiers, drunk from their festivities, scrambled around in confusion. A steady rumble of fear and pandemonium erupted.

This is it, Hawk thought. *This is the signal.*

"Now," Hawk whispered hoarsely.

He grabbed the leather straps of a wooden shield at his feet, and, like a lion sprung from hiding, ran for the castle walls. The band of fifteen broke from the cover of the brush. Hawk rushed toward the castle motte.

Frantically glancing over the battlements, he scanned about to make sure the castle guards didn't see them. He didn't notice any torches or wandering eyes. It could've been a stroke of luck, perhaps, or just a thorough distraction? Either way, he made it to the western wall of the castle. He leaned against the rough stone and took in a few heavy breaths. He watched as the fifteen trekked quickly up the slope and filed alongside him, their faces still hard as stone.

Hawk rushed to the wooden debris blocking the secret entrance Lieutenant Marc revealed just hours before. He swiftly moved it aside quietly, not wanting to ruin their entrance with a clatter. Then Hawk darted into the black postern and out the other side. He entered the dark alleyway behind the barracks, still swathed in shadow. Mòrag appeared next. The other Moravian warriors followed close behind.

The huntsman crept toward the corner of the barracks and the western tower. A man, armored as a soldier in King David's army, ran out from the tower's entrance. Hawk stopped and spread out his arms to halt the insurgent band. The soldier, wrapped in his own panic, took no notice of Hawk or his team and jogged toward his destination in the castle courtyard. Hawk clenched his jaw.

This isn't good, he thought, listening to the sounds of the castle. The castle was waking quicker than Hawk had expected. He had hoped to reach the gates before soldiers mobilized in the courtyard. The clatter of metal on wood and stone signified the soldiers clambering and scuffling to their battle-ready positions. The castle bristled to life, and soldiers moved to defend from the hoarding of the front castle wall to the north. At the center of the north wall, in the middle of the castle courtyard, stood the main gate—the insurgents' target.

Hawk waited a moment, trying to determine when to run for the gate. Shouts rang out for archers. The soldiers meant to defend against the Moravians outside.

Steps approached from the western tower. Another soldier rushed out of the tower's entrance. That time, however, the soldier saw the insurgents. His eyes widened at the unknown warriors inside the castle walls. The soldier's mouth opened, about to yell, scream, or even laugh. No one would ever know. An arrow sprouted out of his neck, as if from nowhere. Mòrag nocked another arrow to her bow and made to shoot again. But the soldier had already fallen to his knees, slumping to the ground in a spreading pool of blood.

Hawk's heart pounded in his chest. That was far too close. He reached behind him, taking a black tomahawk from its sheath and fixing it in his right hand. He raised the plain wooden shield in his left. The leather straps felt loose. He wished he'd taken the time to tighten them. But no time remained. It was now or never.

"Shields up," Hawk barked.

The fifteen warriors raised their shields in near unison. Ordinarily, Hawk wasn't a proponent of shields. They felt cumbersome, heavy, and slowed his movement in his line of work. Most of Hawk's hunts involved a target that required speed and precision. A huntsman needed to jump out of the way of a charging beast, or spring out in an ambush.

A shield couldn't do much against a bear's biting jaws, and it would slow him in a dodge from a swiping claw. There was, however, one good reason to have a shield in Hawk's eyes: arrows. That's why he suggested it when discussing the plan with the Moravian warriors. They'd use their shields to guard against arrow attacks on the wall as they ran toward the main gates. Once underneath the castle hoarding at the main entranceway, they'd be safe from the archers. They'd open the gates, and their reinforcements could enter.

A simple plan, Hawk thought anxiously, *just waiting to fall apart.*

A howling wave of shouts and screams rose over the wall. The Moravians outside must've charged the flaming camp. Lord Gospatric's men's attention would be trained entirely outside the castle walls. Now was their chance.

Hawk peered around the corner of the barracks toward the castle's courtyard. The path lay clear ahead. He ran for it, digging his toes into the hard ground. Hawk sprinted with every muscle of his body, swinging his tomahawk with every stride. His shield remained steady on his left side, protecting his face and torso. Hawk made no war cry. He didn't yell in a fit of rage or to intimidate the soldiers in the courtyard. All his energy focused on sprinting to the gates. Hawk dug his toes into his boots with every stride, grasping the dirt underneath their leather soles.

The huntsman neared the main gate. Two soldiers stood watching the battle beyond the walls through arrow slits on the side of the large wooden gate. Hawk aimed his charge at the further, larger guard. Five strides away. He readied his shield. Two strides away. SMASH! Hawk crashed into the guard, slamming the shield into the back of the soldier's helmet, flattening his face against the thick gate's wooden surface. Hawk whirled around to confront the other guard, but he had no need. The others crushed the second guard against the gate and tossed him to the side.

The huntsman scanned the doors for an opening mechanism. A drawbar held the doors locked shut. Hawk scrambled to raise it. But the thick timber proved too much while holding his tomahawk.

Then Ulster moved Hawk out of the way. A great brute of a man, he bellowed with the fury of a large bull and swung a war hammer at the bottom of the beam. It thundered with a rumbling clunk. The drawbar popped up and off, clattering against the cobbled stone and on top of the fallen guardsmen.

Mòrag, Hawk, and Ulster pressed their weight into the doors. The hinges groaned, but the doors proved no match for the insurgents' efforts. The wooden planks swung open. Hawk spared a glance through the crack and beyond the doors.

Warriors clad in woad face paint clashed with the king's soldiers. Fire danced along the white tent tops in a wild inferno. Screams and grunts mixed with the clash of steel on steel outside Urquhart's walls.

But he didn't have time to stare. Hawk turned back to the castle courtyard. He saw what he expected. The Moravian insurgents formed a semi-circle, defending the gate. What he didn't expect, however, was the absolute shock on the faces of the enemy soldiers making their way into the courtyard. Two scores of them stood wearing the same crooked expression of disbelief. They had no notion of whether Hawk's company stood there as enemies or as part of the castle's defense. The insurgents' surprise attack had worked.

A grizzled Lieutenant Marc entered the courtyard, skin mottled purple with rage. Sweat poured from his disheveled brow.

"What in God's name are you all doing?" he barked at the soldiers. The man unsheathed his sword, brandished it in the air, and cried, "Attack, you mongrels! Kill the bastards!"

None other than the man who enabled the attack, Lieutenant Marc, strutted forward, sword in hand. The lieutenant charged at the fifteen, and the remaining king's soldiers in the courtyard followed his valiant lead.

Hawk joined the Moravians' formation. He whipped his shield around and braced for the incoming charge. A thin, wiry lad approached him first, carrying his sword over his head. Hawk stood his ground and braced for the impact. It came at him screaming, but just before the clash, the huntsman ducked and pushed forward. The wiry soldier tripped onto Hawk's shield and was promptly tossed over Hawk's head. The huntsman whirled and threw his shield at the next soldier's open-faced helm, flinging him off his feet. Hawk ripped the second tomahawk from behind his back with his free hand, and the fighting commenced.

The fifteen held their arched formation. But the enemy's charge proved unrelenting. Hawk slashed at a burly swordsman, cutting him down at the neck. The huntsman spun, burying his second ax into the next victim. He kicked away from the first to land another blow at a third. He swiveled, maneuvering out of the way of the impending swipes before slicing into more exposed flesh.

The insurgents moved like a ferocious pack of animals. Ulster, as mighty as any bear, swung his hammer at the enemy. Blow after blow, swing after swing, his hammer came down with crushing force. Ceitidh, like a wildcat, pounced on a bearded guardsman. She slashed him to bits and jumped on the other attackers, one by one, with her steel blade. Mòrag, like a wolf, gnawed at opponents with her arrows, driving her fangs into Lieutenant Marc's neck before aiming for the rest. There was Gormelin, the bull, and Gordon, the rugged boar. One after another, the charging enemy soldiers fell before the animals.

Lord Gospatric's men crashed upon the fifteen like waves of a hurricane against a rocky shore. Hawk fought, dancing around his opponents. The enemy swords had reach, but Hawk had swiftness, dodging a slash, pulling the soldier off-balance, and finishing them with a traumatic blow. But, like any bad storm, the waves kept crashing against the fifteen.

Soldiers retreating from outside the castle to the gates fought them on the other side. Gordon fell after taking five with him. Ellar, separated from the fifteen, was overwhelmed. The insurgent Moravians circled around in defense. But they couldn't hold out much longer. The welt on Hawk's head pounded with every thrust of his arm, a constant reminder of why he fought, renewing his strength. But strength mattered in numbers too. More of the king's soldiers arrived from outside the castle. The insurgents needed to get out of the storm.

"Break right!" Hawk cried out, shouting over the noise of clattering steel. "Push back to the postern!"

Ulster rang out with a tremendous bellow. He swung his hammer horizontally, dispersing the attacking soldiers. Lord Gospatric's men stumbled back, out of the way of the immense swings. Hawk scrambled, returning an ax to its home on his back. He grabbed a shield off the ground and made for Ulster. Mòrag fired another arrow before throwing the bow over her back. Hawk charged into the breaking crowd. He wasn't alone. An arm thrust against his back, forcing him forward as they pierced the courtyard's soldiers. Hawk collided and pushed through armor, helm, sword, and anything in his way, moving toward the postern. Within moments, they passed through the army and into the other side of the courtyard.

Hawk made for the alleyway behind the barracks. The huntsman peered over his shoulder to see who followed him. Mòrag, Gormelin, Ceitidh, and the rest shadowed Hawk. It was too difficult to count. He could just see the tail of the group, Ulster, still swinging his hammer at any soldier foolish enough to approach.

Hawk rounded the corner of the barracks, expecting to slip into darkness. He'd make for the postern and run out the same way they came in. But no darkness shaded the back of the barracks. He skidded to a halt in the alleyway in front of the postern exit. Standing there, holding a torch behind his head, stood a knight in the armored plate of the king's service. The knight's face loomed in shadow, but Hawk knew precisely who it was.

"Sir William!" Hawk called in surprise.

The man took a step and maneuvered the torch's light.

"Hawk? Mòrag? What are you . . ." A trembling shock rippled through the knight's voice. "By all that is holy . . . It cannot be."

Mòrag burst in. "Sir William, there's nae time. We must flee. C'mon, through the postern. The castle is breached. It will soon be overrun with Moravians. Save yerself. Leave with us and ye will be spared. I swear it."

Sir William, now calm, almost distant, replied, "What happened to you? To Hawk and Lady NicNeev?"

"I can explain everything!" Hawk shouted. "We came inside the castle looking for you. Come with us through the postern. There's no time." He gestured to the tunnel holding their salvation.

But no one moved, not even a flinch. The knight remained unwavering.

The fight inside the castle rounded the barracks and reached the remnants of the fifteen. Hawk heard the last of the insurgents holding off the soldiers. The groans of anguish and effort from those Hawk was supposed to lead rose in a cacophony of blood and steel. And yet he couldn't bring himself to look back at them. He couldn't move his eyes from Sir William. The light of the torch altered to illuminate Sir William's face. Hawk hardly recognized his once jovial companion. The knight's face tightened with icy contempt. The weight of it beat down on the huntsman. The wooden shield, once light and nimble, grew too much for his grasp. It slipped from his hand, sliding to the ground and rolling away into the darkness.

"We have tae go!" Ceitidh snarled from behind Mòrag and Hawk. "We cannae hold out over here!"

Mòrag moved for the postern, but the knight unsheathed his longsword. He took one giant step into her path to block the exit way.

Mòrag stopped in her tracks. "Sir William, please!" she pleaded.

"I spoke to Lord Gospatric about the Norsemen. While I don't agree with his methods, those men are under the service of King David. I vowed to defend the king's justice. I also vowed not to let a single soul through that path." His head tipped back slightly, indicating the postern. "I mean to keep *all* my vows."

The words were steady. Determined.

"Dinnae do this, Sir William," Mòrag said in exasperation.

She opened her arms wide, beckoning the knight to put an end to it.

"It's my duty for the kingdom of Alba," Sir William began, his chivalric tone returning. "A knight swears to defend that duty. No matter the cost." He raised his sword into the night sky, bringing the hilt to the bridge of his nose before striking toward the dirt.

"William . . . My friend . . . Please . . ." Hawk called out, his voice cracking.

"I wish you good fortune, Huntsman. I hope you find the peace you're looking for."

The knight donned his plated helmet. Firelight danced across its steel face. A feather sitting atop the helm, as blue as the summer sky, danced in the night's breeze. The knight spun, the torch in his hand cascading shadows and firelight around the surrounding stone walls. Sir William spread his stance wide and took a step toward Mòrag. She remained rooted in the spot, not heeding the knight's advancement.

Hawk's adrenaline peaked. He jumped forward, reaching out and grabbing the black fur of Mòrag's mantle. He yanked Mòrag of the way of Sir William's trajectory. Hawk met the whites of Sir William's eyes. The knight held the torch to the side as his sword raised into the air. Hawk removed the obsidian knife from his belt and braced to parry.

Sir William's sword arched back, drawing power for a strike. Out of the darkness behind the knight, a giant battle-ax swiped into the exposed area of Sir William's sword arm. It severed completely. The knight's arm, still in possession of the sword, careened into the shadows. The knight fell to his knees, screaming in agony. The torch bounced upon the dirt. Blood flowed from where his limb once was. A second swipe of the phantom battle-ax came at Sir William and swiped at the knight's helm. The plate metal crushed in, and his body flung to the side.

"No!" Hawk screamed, his gut twisting and wrenching.

He stumbled backward.

A bulky demon approached from the shadowed corridor of the postern. The demon showed its fangs in a cruel twist of a grin.

Hawk, all too familiar with Norse, heard the man exclaim, *"The knight befriended the enemies!"*

Another demon emerged behind the first, and then . . . Blåveis. He wore thick metal scales, but his armor seemed far different from the swordsmen of the castle courtyard. The nightmare he hunted materialized before him. The Norse raiders had joined the fray.

"You!" Blåveis yelled.

Hawk's shock boiled over. A tumultuous fury boomed inside of him. Every muscle in his body came alive as he launched up to his feet. Hawk wouldn't let Sir William's assault go without reprisal.

I won't turn around this time. I won't walk away.

The Norsemen readied their swords, the steel talons of Hawk's demons. The huntsman took a step, pivoted his hips, and, swinging his arm with every fiber of ferocity, fired his tomahawk at the first demon. It spun, end over end, until it stuck with a satisfying thump into the first Norseman's mouth. An arrow pierced the shining white of the Norseman's eye with a thwak!

"Bastards!" Mòrag spat.

The Norsemen flinched at the sight of their fallen comrade. Mòrag loaded a second arrow. Then, without warning, a resounding chant rose from the courtyard. Hawk heard his insurgents—Ceitidh, Gormelin, and the others—joining in.

"Moray! Moray! Moray!" they cried.

Blåveis looked at the other Norse raiders and shouted, *"To the boats!"*

They reversed, darting into the corridor and vanishing beneath the castle's wall.

The chants from the courtyard grew louder.

"Moray! Moray!"

Hawk broke his attention from the Norsemen. His friend lay there on the ground.

"William . . ." Hawk exhaled.

He slid on the dirt to the knight's fallen body. Mòrag rushed to his other side. Her hands went to Sir William's remaining hand and brought it to her chest. Sir William's breathing was labored, his pulse a weak flutter in his neck. Hawk had seen the signs of death many times before. The knight, Sir William Maurice of Holyrood, soon would be no more. Sir William's eyes peered straight at the heavens, looking millions of miles away.

Through mangled teeth, the knight muttered, "Don't forget the dream. Don't forget the dream. Don't forget . . ."

Hawk listened, but the knight's breathing hushed. An anguished sob burst from Mòrag.

"Don't forget the dream?" Hawk repeated. His fury rose as the revelation came to him. "I won't let the Norsemen escape! I must stop Blåveis. I must stop this nightmare. Come on!"

Hawk stood, beckoning Mòrag to follow. She rubbed her eyes against her woolen sleeves, streaking the wet woad dye. Hawk extended his hand, grabbing Mòrag's and whisking her onto her feet. The huntsman retrieved his thrown tomahawk from the Norseman. Together, they hurried through the postern gate.

The huntsman ran, ripping along the outside of the castle walls. He headed straight to the loch where he'd seen the Norse boats.

They're just around the last edge of the wall here. The time he spent on the road chasing the vile creatures had come to a point. The moment was now. It was the end. Hawk rounded the last edge.

The boats had vanished. At least they didn't sit on the shore. Three boats had made it into the loch, each one sprawling with men shouting and cursing.

Hawk kept going, his boots racing to the edge of the water. He'd come so far; he wasn't going to let them get away. The boat closest to the shore held a banner, curiously upright on such a packed and chaotic vessel. It shone blue, and upon it flew a winged lion breathing fire. The Norse raiders had escaped.

The huntsman waded into the loch's tide. The water lapped at his ankles, then his knees—the smooth stones under his boots made for tricky footing. Hawk's foot twisted, and he lost his footing, plunging his waist below the loch's surface. The huntsman stopped, trying to gather his feet under him again. The first two boats floated mere yards away.

Should I swim? Could I swim? he asked himself, knowing full well he'd never catch their oars. Hawk cursed at them as loud as he could manage.

Thwack! An arrow lodged into the nearest raider in the first boat. A howl of pain rose from the vessel. Hawk whirled around. Mòrag stood, bow in hand, on the shore. She reached behind her for her quiver but came around empty-handed. She'd sent her last arrow.

The man on the boat continued screaming in agony before being pushed off the boat. He landed in the water with an enormous splash. The man surfaced, thrashing in the water, screaming and bleeding in his last moments before sinking beneath the depths.

"Row, you dogs! Faster!" a man from the furthest vessel shouted. "Row like your lives depend on it, men!"

Hawk identified that the distinguishing shouts came from none other than Lord Gospatric himself. Trying to escape defeat, he must've sprung onto the boats first, leading the retreat. And there, amidst the chaos, Blåveis stood on the boat, laughing at the shore.

Hawk raised his tomahawk over his head with a furious rage he didn't recognize. Everything—all the tracking and pursuing— led to that moment, and it had slipped past him. With a single, vicious swipe, he plunged the tomahawk into the waves. A red pulse of light rippled out from the swipe like a crimson lightning bolt and dissipated beneath the water.

The first rays of light from the east began illuminating the night sky. The boats rowed on toward the rising sun. Loch Ness, which was a black abyss earlier in the night, brightened.

Suddenly, the boat closest to Hawk shot out of the water at an alarming speed. The vessel flung into the air, catapulting its crew like an overturned basket of fruit.

A black serpentine creature rose from the water beneath the boat. It soared into the sky, as large as a castle tower. The creature caught the vessel in its lengthy jaws, revealing a plethora of razor-sharp teeth before splintering the boat into a thousand shards.

The serpentine monster arched over the loch before plummeting to the water's surface. One by one, the crew of the boat crashed into the water.

The Norsemen in the water frantically shouted. They screamed in terror, but a new sound muffled their cries. A guttural warble emanated from the murky depths. The massive, monstrous creature glided out of the waves and pulled the raiders below the surface.

The second boat of rowing Norsemen raced in the opposite direction of their rowing oars. Something was carrying them, Hawk realized. The men inside gripped the edge of the vessel before it was pulled underneath the frenzied waves.

Hysteria gripped the swimming men. Men sunk in their heavy armor. Others latched onto their crewmates, scrambling to get on top of them and out of the monster's path. But it was no use. The monster rippled in and out of the water, pulling the stragglers down one by one, feasting on the fallen.

Hawk backed out of the water, his interest in pursuing the boats replaced with the fierce priority of his own safety. The huntsman gave thanks as he did, for no other person made it out of the water to the shores of Urquhart Castle that night. The raiders from the capsized boat swam toward the coast, but none succeeded. Tears welled in his eyes, the product of exhaustion. He couldn't make out if any Norsemen made it to the distant shores. The sounds of their attempts rang over the loch but then, like the sounds of battle in the castle, faded into the calm of the rising sun.

CHAPTER TWENTY-TWO

S unlight crawled along the shore outside Urquhart Castle. Stones, smoothed through generations of turbulence and polish, warmed as they soaked up the rays. A great spotted woodpecker, disheveled from the previous night's disturbances, called out, hoping to begin its day with no further disruptions. A light breeze, cooled from the night, swirled over the waves and stony beaches. Smoke, drifting from the castle, became trapped in the breeze's clutches. It spread across the sunlight in a cascade of diffusion and brought the foul odor of death and destruction with it.

The huntsman sat on the stones of the shore with his arms wrapped tightly around his bent knees. He was a peculiar sight on Urquhart Castle's beach. Not because he wore onyx leather boots and onyx leather armor over his gambeson. Nor because he had almost no hair on his head, save for a long strip of jagged raven hair. Not even because of the two curious axes set in an X-shape sheath on his back.

What made the huntsman on the shore look peculiar was the tears streaming down his reddened cheeks. They jotted a course of least resistance down his face before plunging to the ground. His face didn't twist in a grimace, nor did he make a sound as he sat there with tears in his eyes. The huntsman remained utterly silent —frozen in an endless stare with the loch and the tide. The tide, it seemed, tried to mock the huntsman. It lapped at the shore, and with it, the bodies from the loch came too.

Death rolled onto the shores of Urquhart Castle in front of the huntsman. He didn't look away. He couldn't. The demons that haunted him most of his life lay around the edge of the water, their faces bloated and ghastly white. Some, split from the jaws of the black monster, had no faces at all. But even those brought the sight and utter stench of death. It singed and burned through the huntsman's nose, and for a moment, he thanked the tears obscuring his vision of the immediate shore in front of him.

A warrior plopped beside the huntsman, crashing against him before regaining control and sitting upright. She sat by his side, their shoulder's pressed against one another as they stared into the loch. She hawked and spat into the tide. Wiping her forehead, she brushed away her disheveled hair and left a mud-colored streak in its wake. Haphazard blemishes of blood, sweat, and tears streaked her face, once decorated with the proud woad wings of battle.

The two sat there in silence, looking out at the rising sun. Time passed and the sun ascended, but the huntsman and the warrior didn't move or rise. They didn't speak. They melded together, two cold statues along the shore. The silence, however, didn't carry into the huntsman's head.

Hawk wallowed in sadness. The Norse raiders had perished, and with them, Blåveis. Surely he should feel nothing but joy. Yet sadness dug deep. One boat had slipped into the night unharmed, but from what he could tell, it carried mostly Lord Gospatric's men.

I wanted that revenge. I waited so long for it, and now it's gone, forever out of my reach. Stolen from me.

The huntsman felt his heart dropping into the chasm of his chest. Even concentrating on his heart made it race all the harder, out of his control and further into despair. Pangs of nausea and regret ripped through his veins and into his stomach. He might be sick. He would've been happy with the release of vomit if it meant an end to the nightmare of misery he faced. That nightmare would stretch on, however, daunting and toying with him. Again and again, it would repeat as he chased the Norsemen. His misery would continue. It already continued.

"Sir William . . ." Hawk muttered aloud, breaking the chilling hush of the sunrise.

"Aye." The word cracked from Mòrag, her voice no doubt garbled from the prolonged inactivity.

"I tried to . . . I . . ." Hawk broke off.

His larynx tightened fiercely with grief, stopping the words from leaving his lips.

Mòrag cleared her throat. "Aye. I thought we could . . ." But she, too, couldn't finish.

"I know," the huntsman answered, knowing all too well what she meant to say.

Hawk wanted to scream. He wanted to run back to the castle and save the knight. He wanted to help Sir William off the ground and tell him it was all a misunderstanding. Hawk wanted to, but nothing could be done. He reached over, sliding his fingers through Mòrag's black fur mantle before squeezing her shoulder closer. Mòrag leaned her head into the huntsman and sobbed. She shook with every sniffle, her tears mixing with snot and spit, but she didn't wipe them away. It took everything in the huntsman's will to not weep himself.

For a while, they sat there, merged as one, sharing their grief and sorrow. The tide rolled endlessly onto the shore. A blue ribbon shifted and swayed with the waves in the black depths. It glowed beneath the water, floating toward the surface, and, with a gentle surge of the loch, glided onto the rocks of the shore.

The ribbon was a banner. The blue knitted canvas swelled with water, melded to the smooth oval rocks, resisting the temptation to drift back into the loch. On the banner, rumpled and distorted, rippled the fire springing from the winged lion's mouth. The lion, emblazoned on the canvas, stared menacingly into the eyes of the huntsman—taunting him. The nightmare dared to continue, but Hawk didn't have to let it.

He broke from his silent inaction and rose. Mòrag flinched in surprise, but Hawk made no apology. The huntsman marched over to the banner and bent to pick it up. It proved heavier than expected with the absorbed remnants of the loch. Hawk folded the banner over once, splitting the lion in half and removing the eyes from sight. Grasping the canvas at both ends, he wrung out the water with all his might.

The huntsman turned and walked toward the former Norse camp. In the center stood a fire pit encircled with rocks, over which rested a square iron spit. He tossed the banner at the foot of the circle of rocks and kneeled on it, pressing his knees into the canvas. Leaning over the lingering coals, the heat of the white ash warmed his face. The fire, which raged throughout the night, glowed with the white light of the sun.

Hawk leaned to one side and, opening his lungs with what remained of his energy, took in a deep breath. He blew on the fire, took in a large breath, then blew again. With a third breath, he blew as hard as he could on the embers. Ash and dust flew into the air, dancing into the breeze. And with their dance, flames joined in a prance, rising from the coals. Hawk grabbed the kindling alongside the circle of rocks and fed the reignited flare of heat. Around it, he placed large, sturdier logs in a pyramid of support. The heat lapped at the wood and took hold.

The huntsman retrieved the blue banner from the dirt. He shook it out to one side, flinging it open into the breeze. He placed the spread banner over the iron spit above the fire pit.

Within moments, steam rose from the lion on the canvas. It sizzled with the heat. Hawk stared into the lion's eyes once more. Not blinking, his eyes watered from the rising smoke. The smell gripped him and whisked him deep inside his mind. The fire's heat carried him. Drums echoed in his mind. He could see himself dancing with the flames as his mother moved around him, laughing and swaying. Hawk felt his family's warmth surround him and the dance. He felt no fear, only love. He wanted to reach out to his mother, but the eyes of the lion wrenched him back. Their cruelty bore into his very soul.

Hawk flung a fist into the steaming banner, pressing it into the revitalized blaze. Thick gray smoke rose from the canvas, billowing into the blue sky. The lion breathed genuine flames. The banner curled and shriveled helplessly in the unrelenting heat of the inferno. The flames consumed the winged cat, morphing the lion, first black, then finally into faint wisps of fabric. The fibers glowed a brilliant orange before lifting off into the air and fading away into the sunlit sky. The banner soon vanished without a trace.

"Huntsman? Eh, is that ye?" a voice called out from a distance.

Hawk couldn't pry his eyes from the burning coals. He couldn't lift his gaze to find the voice.

They shouted again. "Hey, Huntsman! It is ye, thank God. We've been looking everywhere for ye. Yer alive, both of ye! Thank God twice over. What a triumph. Are ye listening?"

The huntsman still hadn't turned to meet the voice. It sounded friendly and jovial, and yet at the moment, it completely repulsed the huntsman. The sound grew closer.

"Hiya! Are ye alive? Did ye hear me? We were victorious, Huntsman."

The sound of the voice finally brought recognition. Its approach made it easier to discern Ceitidh's lilting cadence. She was Lulach's second in command and someone he knew, yet he couldn't look away from the embers before him. They paralyzed him, mesmerizing him in their fiery splendor. He couldn't look away. His muscles ached. His grief was too much to move.

"How are ye, lass?" Ceitidh said behind Hawk. "Can ye stand? C'mon, that's it. Here, let me help ye. God, ye two must've taken a beaten out here. Huntsman, are ye—"

"Hawk?" Mòrag interrupted.

Her voice trembled in a desperate plea. The huntsman

wavered and slowly turned to face Mòrag. Supporting beneath her
arm, Ceitidh helped Mòrag to her feet. They walked toward the
fire. Hawk's cheeks lifted, and his lips spread together in an
exhausted, faux smile. Mòrag returned in kind.

"Do ye have any wounds? Either of ye?" Ceitidh asked, no
doubt concerned by their slow, defeated looks.

"Nae," Mòrag replied. "Just aches. Just . . . scars."

"Aye. Nae bother," Ceitidh said, excitement breaking through
her concern. "We should head tae the castle, then. Time tae
revel."

"Ye won?" Mòrag asked, still subdued.

"Aye. Course we have. Or ye and I wouldnae be here. The
castle is ours. The plan worked, it would seem. Yer plan worked!"
The last part, she said to Hawk, beaming.

Hawk couldn't find it in himself to return the gesture.

Mòrag moved out from Ceitidh's support and placed a hand
on Hawk's shoulder. "How?" she asked.

"What do ye mean, how?"

"I mean, how did ye win?" Mòrag reiterated, stretching down
and grabbing another birch log to toss onto the fire.

"We've taken the castle, of course," Ceitidh began eagerly, flipping her dark braided hair to her other shoulder.

Hawk knew she wanted to jump into the story, not realizing
her companions had no interest in hearing it. At least, not yet. But
Ceitidh continued.

"That Laird Patric, or what have ye, tucked tail and ran as
soon as he seen Lulach and the men running in through the main
gate. He was so afeared, Lulach says he jumped from the east
tower in tae the loch. Course that cannae be entirely true. But
how would I ken? We fought for our lives in that alleyway. If it
wasnae for Lulach, we'd be lying there still."

Hawk winced, remembering who lay in that alleyway. Sir
William waited there, cut down at the foot of the postern. Hawk
looked at the castle. Only then did he notice the dull roar of
revelry from within the castle walls.

Ceitidh, following the huntsman's gaze, said, "C'mon, ye two. We should celebrate with everyone else. We're missing it."

Mòrag looked at Hawk. He nodded and gestured toward the castle. They walked toward the western walls, with Ceitidh leading the way. She moved bright and alert, almost like she'd break into a run at any point, just to get back inside the castle walls.

"Did Lulach talk about the rest of the battle?" Mòrag asked, her curiosity no doubt growing.

"Aye, course he did. He seemed . . ." Ceitidh hesitated, seeming to search for the correct word ". . . grateful. From what I hear, they started by expending most of the arrows down in tae the camp from the hill—firing the arrows high, so they came near straight down on tae the tents. And the flames, well . . . I dinnae have tae tell ye. We saw the flames. Aye. By the time the king's southern soldiers finished wiping the shit from their breeches, Lulach's men descended—a triumphant victory. We had few casualties in the battle on our side. They had archers on the wall tae be sure, but by the time we opened the gates, the castle garrison didnae ken where tae turn their attention. We plundered them. The fools . . . Showing ye the postern? A victory for the Moravians! A victory for the Highland clans! Lulach has done well. He took a swipe of a sword tae his left arm. But, well, scars befit the clan chief, eh?"

"He's okay though?" Mòrag asked concernedly. They moved around as if to walk to the main front gate of the castle. "Wait, stop!" Mòrag blurted. "Can we please go through the postern once more? I wish tae see the other side."

"Aye. Suits me all the same. I only seem tae enter this gate anyway." Ceitidh laughed, amused by her jest. She spoke on, "Of course Lulach is fine, aye. It was only a scratch. He's in the courtyard, drinking the laird's fancy wine I bet. They've started plundering already."

Hawk ducked his head as he went through the dark corridor of the postern again.

Too many times, he thought. The light from the other side brought with it the sight of death. The Norse raiders, cut down by Hawk and Mòrag, lay at the foot of the postern entrance.

A man lay on the ground next to them. He rested, adorned with a shimmering steel breastplate armor. His crushed helmet reflected the searing bright sun. The huntsman put up a hand to block the glare and saw the vividly blue feather atop the helm.

Hawk walked over to the knight on the ground. Mòrag kneeled at Sir William's side and grasped his hand. Hawk knew no life pulsed there, that the skin would be cold. Mòrag gently placed it on top of the knight's chest. Her eyes welled once again.

"Fancy armor. Dinnae save him, though, did it? Think it would fit ye, Huntsman?" Ceitidh snorted with laughter.

"No," Hawk retorted with a stern, cold voice.

"Oh." Ceitidh's voice was quietly apologetic.

"He was our companion," Mòrag said. Her glare could have scorched.

"I'm sorry. I didnae ken."

"He was our friend," Mòrag repeated, turning back to the knight. "Naebody should touch him."

"Aye. I'll be sure of it."

Hawk kneeled next to Sir William. He reached for the knight's long blue cloak and unclasped the fasteners that held it to Sir William's armor. Then he slid the cloak out from underneath the knight. He tugged at the cloth pinned beneath the metallic plate until it finally shifted and freed. Hawk snapped his wrists, opening the cloak up to its full breadth. Mòrag, anticipating the huntsman, stood up and grabbed the other end of the cloak. They spread it out, revealing the bright blue and white of a knight in the service of King David of Alba. Together, they laid the cloak over Sir William, covering him completely.

Still, not all was as it should be. Hawk grimaced as he noticed a long, steel-plated arm next to Sir William. The huntsman placed his boot against the arm and pushed it with a brisk roll, covering it with the grace of the knight's cloak.

"Was he on our side?" Ceitidh asked, breaking Mòrag's attention away from Sir William.

"Our side?" Mòrag replied in a sharp, puzzled retort.

"I dinnae remember any knight on our side."

"What side is that, exactly?" Mòrag turned to face Ceitidh more fully. "The side that wanted tae live? Aye, he was on that side. Or was he on the side with the soldiers following their leader's mission with devout faith? Aye, he was on that side too. Or was he following Lulach in tae battle? Nae. He wasnae on that side, but that doesnae make him less of a loyal man, less of a knight, or less of a kind soul. He saved my life once."

"Aye . . . W-well . . . Is that true, then?" Ceitidh stammered, her eyes racing between Mòrag and Hawk, looking for an escape from her ill-formed question. Mòrag offered little chance of that escape. She stood firm to the ground, her hands clenched into fists.

"Perhaps some time?" Ceitidh said quickly. "Do ye want some time? Alone, that is, tae mourn. I ken Lulach wishes to speak with ye, but he could wait. Ye could have a moment or two?"

In truth, Hawk had only barely known the knight. They had shared a single journey across towns and wilderness together. He had grown to like the knight and knew Mòrag had even more so. But the huntsman gave Ceitidh the escape she was after.

"No," he said, putting a hand on Mòrag's shoulder, alleviating the rising tension in her posture. "Thank you, Ceitidh. Let's go on to Lulach. There will be time to mourn after."

"Aye, come on, together," Ceitidh said, her voice finding its confidence again and turning toward the path to the courtyard.

Mòrag's chin lowered to her chest, staring at the ground in front of her. Hawk looked at Mòrag to see if she was all right, but she didn't return his gaze.

"Are you okay?" Hawk asked in a hushed tone only Mòrag would hear.

"I'm fine. I was just being stupid. C'mon." She quickened her pace to join Ceitidh once more. "Ye never actually said why Lulach wanted tae see us so bad, Ceitidh."

Ceitidh laughed through her nose. "Tae see if ye were alive, for one. He kept asking about Mòrag and the huntsman. Where's Mòrag and the huntsman? As soon as the battle ended, he did. It wasnae until I finally spoke with him that someone who kent where ye were could get tae ye. I saw ye run out after them. I couldnae follow 'cause . . . Well . . ."

"'Cause of what happened tae Ulster?" Mòrag asked, her previously sharp tone wholly abandoned. "I saw him tangle up last night."

"Aye . . ."

"What happened to Ulster?" Hawk asked.

"Well," Ceitidh began, halting to better tell the news. "Ye see, they slashed his leg something fierce. Ye saw him, big bear and all. Well, the big bear makes for a big target."

"Is he alright?" Mòrag asked with genuine concern, raising an eyebrow.

Ceitidh raised her reddened cheeks, attempting to smile. It failed. "I helped him tae the courtyard. We were goin' tae try tae carry him back up tae the hill, me and another lad. We wanted tae get him up the hill, tae those that could heal, but with the rest of Lulach and his men chanting victory, Ulster begged tae stay. He wrapped a belt and bandage over his leg and joined the rest in celebration. I watched him collapse as he tried tae drink with them. They swarmed him up in tae their arms and took him tae the healers. That's when Lulach found me."

"Sounds tae me like he's in good hands," Mòrag said in reassurance.

"Aye. I hope so. He's either with the rest, drinking himself sick. Or . . . Or he's in the pile of bodies . . ."

"Bollocks." Mòrag laughed. "C'mon, we'll look for him."

She gestured to the courtyard, and the trio marched on. They turned the corner of the barracks only to greet an ugly sight.

"So many dead," Mòrag exclaimed, placing a hand over her

mouth and nose for a moment before submitting to the rising stench of death. "So many of that laird's men fallen all around here."

"Aye. They had us good and trapped, remember? I'm thankful for the shields and those at my side here. And Ulster. I wouldnae be here without them."

"Neither would we," the huntsman added, surveying the fallen soldiers in front of them.

Their bodies clustered just around the corner of the barracks, laid out like a child's doll collection. Swords and shields were strewn across the packed dirt haphazardly, their owners flinging them down in their final breaths. The metal and blood of death painted the path to the courtyard.

Ahead of the huntsman, a group of women rummaged over the fallen. They dressed unlike any of the women Hawk had seen in the company of Lulach. They wore dull, ragged sheets down the length of their bodies. A piece of bright red cloth covered the ladies' faces, shielding their noses and mouths. Unlike Mòrag and Ceitidh, they had their hair tied tightly above their head, so it wouldn't drop below their shoulders.

"Hey there, Lily!" Ceitidh called to the group.

The shorter lady of the group looked over. She stood soaked in blood from her waist down. She seemed frantic, grasping at the side of a downed soldier and tossing aside his metal greaves.

"Lily, may I have a word?"

"I'm busy here, ye ken?" said Lily, her words audibly muffled behind the red cloth. "What do ye need, m'lady?"

Her eyes fell back to the man in front of her. Only then did Hawk notice him twitch.

Is the man alive? The huntsman couldn't believe it.

Hawk followed Ceitidh and Mòrag as they made their way over to Lily. Lily took out a stained strip of cloth. She lifted the man's arm, wrapping the fabric quickly and tightly around his elbow. Blood seeped from the end of his arm. Where a hand once was, only twitching tendons and muscle remained.

"That man is dead, Lily," Ceitidh said, putting a hand on Lily's shoulder. "Ye cannae save him. Look in his eyes." Lily readjusted the man, grasping his hair and pulling his head to face her.

"Ach. Waste a whiskey, pouring it on him." Lily stood up, brushing the dirt off her soiled garments.

She pulled down her cloth mask to reveal a soft, pale expression. Lily looked up at the sky and muttered indistinctly, then refocused her attention back on Ceitidh.

"Ye needed a word, m'lady?"

"Aye. How goes it? I mean, look at ye, yer covered in blood from yer boots tae yer brow, Lily. How many have you saved?"

"Saved?" the woman snorted. "One, maybe two tae be fair. Aided on their way tae death? Maybe two scores. Rabbie's seein' tae our lads and lassies . . ." Lily scoffed again, looking behind her toward the courtyard. Three young boys ran over to Lily. They wore excited expressions only innocent youth could when surrounded by so much death. They descended on the fallen man.

Lily continued, "The priests are tending tae those who cannae rise. The courtyard is already empty, m'lady. These crows here have been following me tae pick and clean what can be. Aye ye, ye wee crow." She rustled the fair hair of a boy at her waist.

The boy shimmied the boots off the man Lily had placed the tourniquet on. Gripping his new prize, the boy bolted toward the courtyard.

Ceitidh nodded, then said, "There's a knight over there. Nae, there, where my finger is pointing. Aye. He's covered with a blue cloak over him. He's nae tae be touched or tampered with, ye hear me?"

"He's nae alive, is he?" Lily asked, curious concern in her voice.

"Eh, nae. Naebody is tae touch him though. Except one of us three." Ceitidh gestured to herself, Hawk, and Mòrag. "Is that understood?"

"Aye, m'lady. As ye wish." Lily moved the bright cloth over

the bridge of her nose once more and made to move on. She stopped at Ceitidh's grasp.

"Lily, did ye . . . Did Ulster get . . ."

"Aye. He's fine, Ceitidh." Lily returned Ceitidh's grasp, embracing her hand with a kind touch. "He's with Rabbie. Or was, at least. He's fine. Dinnae worry. It's hard tae fell a mighty oak with a little sword, eh?"

Ceitidh smiled. "Thank ye," she said, choking back her words. Her eyes welled with tears. Lily simply nodded and moved to check on the next soldier.

"Wait. Lily, right?" Mòrag cut in, stopping the lady from continuing her work. "Please, could I ask ye a favor?"

"Of course, m'lady."

Mòrag moved over to Lily, and they shuffled out of earshot.

What's that about? Hawk spun around to see if Ceitidh knew anything, but she hadn't seemed to notice.

Her eyes looked elsewhere, following another woman moving about the corpses. Ceitidh swiveled her jaw around before biting her lip. The huntsman grunted a faint cough to break her stare. She wiped at her eyes, as if embarrassed to remember Hawk was there. Streaks of wet created tracks down her dirt-covered cheeks.

"Sorry," Ceitidh mumbled.

"You don't have to be."

"I ken. It's just that . . . Ulster is a kind man. Big and strong, aye. But kind too. We're close. Not that close . . . But I . . . Well . . . Ye ken how these things can be."

"I do."

"I was just so worried when I saw what happened. I wanted tae make sure those who ken how tae deal with wounds saw tae him."

Hawk, for some reason unknown to him, could only think of what he'd do if Mòrag were in Ulster's place and the concern that would swarm him. He wanted to ease Ceitidh's woes.

"If he's already walking about as she says, then I'm sure Ulster will be fine. You have no need to worry."

"I hope so, truly. The last words Ulster's father said tae me were, 'Ye better look after 'em. He's a wee lad, and he needs yer help.' His father took me in when my da died fighting years ago. My mum died at birth, so all I had was Ulster's family for most of my life. We grew up together, ye ken? Did everything together."

"Now you fight together," Hawk added.

"Aye, so it would seem."

"What are you doing here, then? Go look for him. C'mon, get on. It'll set your mind at ease."

"No. No," she replied hastily. "I cannae leave ye two."

"I know where the courtyard is. Go," Hawk encouraged again.

She hummed, pondering her options. Hawk knew she was only half present anyway. Any moment away from Ulster would be agony for her, casting doubts into her head about his health. The mind preyed on someone's fears until they saw reality with their own eyes. Hawk's words were gentle.

"I'll wait for Mòrag. I know what Lulach looks like. I'm sure I'll find him. Go. I don't mind."

"No, I cannae do that. I said I'd bring the huntsman, and that's what I'll do."

She nodded, reassuring herself more than the huntsman. He knew when the issue was settled. Nothing he could say would change her mind.

"If you insist. Here, Mòrag is returning anyway."

"Right. Sorry," Mòrag apologized. "Let's get out from behind the barracks."

They set off toward Urquhart Castle's courtyard.

Hawk, still curious, leaned over to Mòrag and asked quietly, "What was that?"

"Nothing," Mòrag replied with a blunt air to end the discussion. "Dinnae worry."

"Sir William?" he couldn't help but ask.

Mòrag nodded without any further word on the matter. The huntsman wouldn't pry.

The three of them rounded the end of the barracks and entered the castle's open courtyard. The castle grew louder. On the far end, near Lord Gospatric's eastern tower, an ample band of Moravians mobbed the tower's entrance. They shouted in unison. Not shouted, Hawk realized, but sang a gruff melody of victory. The smell of ale and whiskey rapidly overtook the scent of death and fire. Every soldier held a cup, flask, or horn to drink. Their Gaelic chant rose into the sky.

No bodies scattered the courtyard. The battle Hawk took part in the night before, the bodies he no doubt laid down himself, had disappeared. It surprised him that the victors took little time to make themselves at home.

I suppose it was their home before it was the king's soldiers'.

A young man dashed with a wooden cask across the court-yard to join the mob, passing in front of the huntsman. The lad moved his legs quicker than his arms could keep up. The cask slipped from his grasp and fell to the ground with a resounding CRACK! A deep burgundy liquid gushed from the damaged barrel. The fruity aroma of it wafted high over the mob of Moravians.

"Wine for all, lads!" the young man yelled. "Get it. Quick, before it goes!"

The crowd roared in excitement as the Moravians swooped in to grab up the wooden cask. They poured the contents of the barrel into their drinks for another round.

Hawk and Mòrag followed Ceitidh. The crowd parted as they approached. The men and women nodded in courtesy toward Ceitidh.

They continued when, as if from heaven above, a voice roared from the castle walls.

"Moravians!" it cried out.

Silence immediately fell over the mob. Heads turned upward.

"The man of the night has returned," the voice went on.

Hawk looked up to find its maker. Dressed in all the splendor of clan chief was Lulach. A fresh splatter of blood painted his armor. They bandaged his arm tight to his chest, but his voice didn't quaver.

"Leading the assault. Charging through tae the gate!" Lulach waved his free hand to Hawk. "The huntsman!"

The eyes of the mob turned to Hawk.

A roar surged through the crowd. A chant rose all around. "Hunts-man! Hunts-man! Hunts-man!" Hands reached from every direction, clutching at Hawk's armor. They rambunctiously pushed him back and forth in revelry. He couldn't help but smirk.

"Mòrag!" Lulach called again from above.

The soldiers shifted and spread their cheer to Mòrag. They chanted her name as she laughed. She waved a hand in appreciation.

"Ceitidh!" Lulach bellowed.

The last name dug into the heart of every soldier. The last name meant something to some of them, most of them, and all of them. She was one of their own, a true Moravian. She was there through the months of hunger, displacement, and uncertainty—right alongside them.

The mob swallowed Ceitidh with their celebration until she disappeared beneath them. Ceitidh then flew above the crowd, hoisted onto the shoulders of a soldier. It was none other than Ulster.

The crowd continued chanting, "Ceitidh! Ceitidh!" Ulster danced about with Ceitidh atop his massive paws. He didn't grimace in the slightest. Ceitidh laughed heartily, swinging her arms to grab any passing hand. Someone handed her a bull's horn. She drank the contents of the cup, then dumped the empty horn over. The crowd was in love.

Mòrag backed into Hawk. She spun to apologize and then, seeing the huntsman, burst into laughter, pointing to Ceitidh. And for the first time since setting off from Edinburgh, Hawk stood surrounded by pure bliss.

CHAPTER TWENTY-THREE

Hawk walked along Urquhart Castle's eastern wall. A cool breeze drifted across the top of his head as he strolled toward the southern end. He left the scent of ale and wine behind until it faded into the harsh odor of the loch and smoke. The huntsman followed the now ruler of Urquhart Castle, Lulach, clan chief of the Moravians.

During the celebration, Lulach had sent a younger sister into the mob to seize Hawk and Mòrag from its midst. She darted away to explore the castle while Lulach beckoned them from the crowd to the wall along the edge of the battlements.

Hawk kept one hand on the wall as the other side of the walkway led to a steep fall into the courtyard below. Mòrag, seemingly unperturbed by the height, moved with ease.

A turret stood at the intersection of the southern and eastern walls of the castle. Guarded by two men, the turret cast a broad view of Loch Ness and the beachhead where Mòrag and Hawk spent most of the morning.

"Leave us, please," Lulach commanded.

The guardsmen grabbed their bows and, before hurrying away to likely sneak a draught of ale, nodded to Lulach, Mòrag, and finally the huntsman.

Lulach leaned over the edge of the battlement. He snorted, gathering phlegm, then spat off the castle. Hawk watched as the wind carried it straight against the wall they stood on. The huntsman allowed himself a single snort of amusement.

"I'm sorry I pulled ye away from the fun, Huntsman, but there will be time enough tae celebrate. All day, in fact, for both of ye."

"It's fine, really," Hawk assured him.

"Aye," Mòrag nodded.

"I wanted tae take a moment and thank ye both." Lulach spun, meeting them face to face. "I wouldnae be standing here without yer help. Ye handed me the castle. Ye saved a lot of death and destruction. Ye saved a lot of suffering."

"Not all of it," the huntsman added, recalling the screams of battle the night before.

"Aye, there'll always be suffering with war. We can only do our part tae make the journey better. Ye helped me. I'm in yer debt. Now, allow me the honor of paying that debt."

Hawk glanced at Mòrag. She raised her eyebrows at the huntsman and then shrugged.

"What do ye mean?" Mòrag asked. "What do ye propose?"

"I thought I'd leave that up tae ye. There must be something I could help ye with."

"Aye," Mòrag burst in, seizing an opportunity before Hawk even had time to process the question. "There was a lady in the castle. She was older. A proper lady, ye ken? She wouldnae be confused with a common servant or maid, nae even a warrior. Did ye see anyone in the castle like that today?"

"Nae, lass. I dinnae ken anyone in the castle with that description. I'm afraid I have nae help with that."

"She was wearing a green tunic," Mòrag tried again. "Hair as golden as the sun, a highborn lady she was."

"This is yer friend ye mentioned from last night?"

"Yes," Hawk cut in with the lie before Mòrag could answer. "Yes, it is."

"I'm afraid I cannae help ye. We searched the halls as soon as we gained victory. Some searched the granary and kitchens, others the barracks and main hall. Myself, the eastern tower tae find the laird of the castle. I saw him flee. But nae lady as ye spoke of was here. There were nae highborn ladies here at all. Disappointing because their ransom could've proved useful. Nae bother though. I'm sorry. I think she must've fled before the battle was over."

"Aye, figured as much," Mòrag said in disappointment, looking over at Hawk.

She wanted his help. He saw her mind searching, and then it must have come to her.

"The sword. She had a sword."

"Yes, she carried the sword on her," Hawk said.

"Aye, one dear tae my clan and me. The blade was engraved, and the pommel decorated with a prized sapphire."

The etching burned again in Hawk's mind. He saw the glowing glyphs on the sword and the bright flash of violet flames erupting around Lady NicNeev.

"It sounds beautiful, truly, but I'm afraid again I'm of nae use. The armory will be emptied. Ye may examine every sword ye wish. Ye may have any of them, I swear it." Lulach spread his one stable arm out in good faith but winced at his gesture.

"She wouldn't have left the sword in the armory like some kind of trinket blade," the huntsman said, addressing Mòrag. "It wasn't a common piece of steel, and she knew that. She wouldn't have left it. If she's not here, the sword is not as well."

"We could still search the castle," Mòrag said in desperation.

"We should," Hawk replied, "but I saw her holding the sword. I saw the look in her eyes when she knew it was truly in her possession. She wouldn't have abandoned it. She's gone, Mòrag. And the sword is too."

"Damn it! I was so close. I dinnae understand it. How can she just disappear like that?"

"I'm sorry, Mo," Hawk said as if offering a condolence.

"I have tae keep searching," Mòrag said, choking on the last syllable.

She stared at the huntsman, placing both her hands behind her head. She screwed her chin up in disgust and paced along the turret's edge. Hawk stood in stony silence.

The clan chief attempted to diffuse the situation. "I see this friend and sword mean a great deal tae ye. I wish there was more tae do, or even tae say . . ." He broke off. Someone approached, grabbing Lulach's attention. "Ah, Ceitidh, ye've made it. Thank ye for joining us."

"Greetings, again," Ceitidh said to the huntsman.

She looked to Mòrag but found no response. Mòrag had turned away to stare over the castle walls at Loch Ness.

"Everything all right?" Ceitidh asked Hawk.

"It will be in time. How is he?"

"Ulster? He's good. He'll be okay, thankfully," she said in delight.

Hawk grinned in approval.

"Good, I'm glad," Mòrag said, finally joining the group again.

Mòrag nodded to Ceitidh, and she returned in kind. For a moment, an awkward silence fell over the group. Lulach broke it first.

"Ye three really made this happen. This castle. This view. Come look."

They moved to the southern edge of the turret. Hawk put his hand on the granite and gazed at the hills on the distant shores. Then back at the beach. He could still make out the fire he had started earlier that day.

Lulach continued, "Look at everything of beauty in this world. Have you ever seen anything like it? The hills, the loch, the beaches."

"There are bodies on that shore . . ." Hawk replied with a cold edge, looking over the battlements.

Lulach squinted below, then flinched in surprise, as if

noticing the carnage that lay outside the castle walls for the first time.

"Oh, God . . . Well, I meant out, over the loch with the sun rising in tae the clouds. But, aye, I see what ye mean. Thank ye, Hawk, Mòrag. I heard ye pursued my enemies tae their boats, threatening them with death even as they fled in terror. Tell me truly, how did ye destroy those boats? Were they sabotaged before ye entered the castle?"

"No, my lord. Err . . . Your Grace?" Hawk stammered, unsure of how to address the new lord of the castle.

"Just Lulach, please."

"No, Lulach. We didn't sabotage any boats. Something else attacked the boats. Something bigger. It was some sort of creature or other, from the deep of the loch."

"Come now, Huntsman," Lulach scoffed. "I am tae believe a monster swam out and attacked those men?"

"Yes. It was incredible, in fact. Look at that half of the boat, the one just there, near the brush. The jaws of some beast in the water split it. Look at it. That's not sabotage."

"What could do that?" Lulach asked, the slightest pang of fear crawling into his voice.

"Damned if I know. I'm a huntsman. Not a fisherman."

Hawk stared into the water, envisioning the red bolt of light that pierced the water before the monster's rise. It shot out from his tomahawk. Lady NicNeev had summoned a Kelpie from the water with a spark of magic. Could he have summoned the monster? The harder he tried to focus on the bolt of light, the more it faded away.

Lulach looked between Hawk and Mòrag, his face completely screwed up in disbelief. "The scouts told me this morning of three boats escaping into the darkness. Yet here I see half of just one. Am I tae understand the others got consumed?"

"The monster pulled another under the water. The other boat rowed on," Mòrag answered. She pointed to the eastern sky. "It went east along the loch until they dipped out of our sight. They were spared, as far as I could tell."

"A creature, though, truly?" Lulach asked in stunned perplexity.

Hawk had seen that shock repeatedly. Folks rarely believed a monster could exist until they attacked. Kings and clan chiefs were no exception.

The huntsman looked at the gnawed edge of the wooden boat down below. "I've been told," Hawk said, turning back to glance at Mòrag, "that magic has finally returned to your land. Lulach, the monster, was violent, black, but quick. If you weren't on the shore, I'm not surprised you couldn't see it."

"Why aren't there more bodies washed up on the shore then, Huntsman?"

Hawk paused, then said ominously, "Why do you think?"

"Oh, God . . ." Lulach gasped.

A long silence fell over the group. The clan chief gripped the edge of the wall. He scraped the side of the stone with his gloved hands and, as if to clean the mess he made, brushed off the dusty grit of the stone. Finally, Lulach looked down into his hands and spoke.

"Magic, huh? There were stories when I was younger. An old gran from my village would come in tae help change my sheets and tidy my mum and da's home. She'd sometimes tell me stories about a great monster that lived in the loch. It was a giant serpent-headed beast that slithered through the water." Lulach moved along the wall as if needing a better look into the loch.

The clan chief went on, "She spoke of a time when a great missionary, Calum Cille, traveled with his apostles tae a loch in the north. For the life of me now, I cannae recall which loch she said. But perhaps it was this very one.

"She spoke of Calum Cille and his apostles attempting tae cross a loch. Calum Cille watched from the shores as a monster feasted on a man in the water. When the monster had eaten its fill, it turned tae Calum Cille's apostle, Lugne. They sent Lugne tae swim across the shore tae retrieve a boat moored on the opposite bank. The water beast set upon Lugne, and all in witness cried in terror. Calum Cille, however, raised a hand and shouted, 'Ye will go nae further and willnae touch the man. Go back at once.' And the beast fled. I dinnae do the story justice as gran would. But it was a chilling story. Or I thought it was just a story."

Hawk shifted to lean against the battlement before saying, "It seems there may have been an element of truth to it."

Lulach shook his head slowly. "I cannae decide what's more frightening, Huntsman. When she first told me the story, or seeing that boat down there in the brush torn asunder."

Although the monster frightened Hawk, too, he'd seen his fair share of monsters.

"The scariest stories are always the ones based on the truth. Nothing is more frightening than reality, Lulach. Even the darkest story you can create pales in comparison to the truth. It makes no matter whether it's a werewolf terrorizing a village's sheep, a trio of thugs about to attack a farmer's daughter, or even a monster who towers from the water to devour your boat. The world, it seems, is miserable with fear."

Hawk's entire life seemed to prove that true. The fear drained him. Fear that no home could ever be safe or that everyone you hold close could be taken away. Fear grows like fire and can dominate every aspect of your being.

Quiet fell over the group on the turret. Hawk looked along the shore to the bodies floating and crashing along the edge of the water.

"How do we move on from this?" Lulach asked finally. It was unclear if he was referencing the beast or the larger darkness in the world. "The world cannae be so bad."

"You're right," Hawk agreed. "There's another critical part of the story, the best part of any story: the end. Calum Cille raises his hand and expels the watery beast."

"The werewolf is killed," Mòrag added.

"The castle is taken back from the captors," Lulach put in.

"Exactly," Hawk went on. "Your story has its end. And now, another story begins."

Lulach smiled, turning to face Hawk once again. "Yer right, Huntsman."

"I wanted the ending to my story, Lulach," Hawk said. "The men in the boats, the Norsemen I pursued, were mine to finish. My *revenge*, remember? The monster stopped the boats, to be sure, but they were mine to finish. I waited years for that moment, and it flashed before me. The ending to my story is something I need. I must go east to find the last boat."

"There is naught else on this loch but the city that lies at the eastern mouth tae the ocean—Inverness."

"Whatever it's called. So be it then. Help me, Lulach. Lord Gospatric escaped with them. I heard his voice on the boats last night. I'm sure of it."

"He was on the boat?" Lulach asked, glaring at Hawk in surprise. "I'd seen him jump off the battlements. I thought the fall might've killed him, but I was disappointed when my soldiers returned empty-handed."

"Yes, I'm certain he was on the boat. Help me follow the few remaining Norse before they escape our grasp."

It will be simple. They'd ride into Inverness and stop Lord Gospatric's men before he could rally. The remaining Norsemen would be in disarray and no match for Hawk and the Highland clansmen.

"They're already out of yer grasp," Lulach said, looking up at the still-rising sun.

"I'm a huntsman," Hawk stated, placing a fist over his chest. "I can track a patrol. They'll make to regroup there. Don't give them that chance."

"Ye mean stamp them out, once and for all?"

"Yes." Hawk nodded, knowing the opportunity would entice the clan chief.

Lulach rubbed his injured arm. The bandage, stained a dark,

dry red, slipped down his arm. He adjusted it back into its original position.

"I cannae go just now." Lulach's words cut into Hawk like a spear. "We, too, must regroup. Inverness will be stationed with many soldiers, many *fresh* soldiers in the service of King David, who are nae tired from travel or war. My people must rest first, a few days at least, tae gather their strength back."

"You can't be serious. A few days and Inverness will be fortified for war," Hawk replied, grinding his jaw in frustration.

"They already fortified Inverness for war. My scouts have told me so. I cannae rush off in tae battle for yer 'end.' I'm afraid we must regroup first."

Hawk grunted. He took off his glove and rubbed his fingers through his stiff hair. "Then I'll go myself. Tonight. I'll find my ending."

"I'll help ye as much as I can, Huntsman. Food, supplies, whatever I can manage."

"My thanks, Lulach," Hawk said, his tone colder than before.

He spun to ask Mòrag if she'd come with him, when he noticed Ceitidh and Mòrag's eyes fixed on the air. Hawk followed their gaze. He put a hand over his brow to help shield the light from the sun. He saw the blue hue of the sky, some harmless clouds, and maybe a circling bird. A rather enormous bird, to be fair, but not something to stare at. Although, the more Hawk looked at the bird, the more interesting it became. From that height in the sky, it would almost certainly be the largest bird he had ever seen.

"An eagle," Hawk said to clarify before anyone asked.

"Magnificent creature," Mòrag added. The eagle swooped down from its lofty flight and dove toward the loch.

"Look, there, between its talons," Lulach exclaimed. "It's got something gripped in its talons. A snake?"

"I think it's a branch," Mòrag pondered, moving along the turret to get a better look.

Ceitidh followed close behind and excitedly added, "It's going tae miss the loch. In fact . . . It's going right over our heads. Look out!"

Mòrag and Ceitidh ducked behind the stony wall. But there was no need. The eagle, having spread its brilliant wings out, slowed its descent near instantly before landing on the edge of the castle's battlement. It stood on the side, wings splayed in splendid majesty. Golden in the sun's light, its wings stretched larger than any grown man Hawk had ever seen. For a moment, the eagle stood frozen.

Finally, it brought its wings to rest at its sides. Only then did Hawk notice that clutched in its great yellow talons was a long, green stem. The tip of the green stem sprouted a thorny bud, which blossomed into a dazzling, lavishly purple flower.

The eagle shifted, turning its head to one side, and with its one visible eye peered at each of them. Hawk saw no malice in that eye, nor innocence. Its eye was cunning, scrutinizing, and magisterial, as if it was aware of its exalted status. That eye found Lulach.

The eagle opened its wings once more and, balancing on one talon, extended its foot toward Lulach. Lulach took a step toward the eagle.

Hawk's face stretched in a dumbfounded expression.

Is this his bird? A pet? Hawk had seen hunters with trained falcons before, but an eagle? And why did Lulach look like a child discovering his first bow and arrow?

"Lulach . . ." Ceitidh whispered under her breath.

Lulach inched closer to the bird. He reached out, cautiously and meticulously, using every muscle fiber he had functioning to steady his trembling hand. Lulach took the flower from the bird's talon and brought the flower up to his nose. His eyes reflexively closed as he inhaled, lost in the sweet aroma of the petals. The clan chief's mouth dropped open, then suddenly, violently, he thrust the flower into the air as high as he could manage.

"It cannae be . . ." Ceitidh stammered, moving closer to have a better look.

"The thistle . . ." Mòrag gasped.

"I've never seen anything like that," admitted the huntsman.

"Naebody has. None alive, that is," Lulach said, clutching the flower with wonder.

The eagle chirped, loudly and shrilly. The bird extended its neck, stretching as far as it could, and chirped again.

Lulach addressed the eagle's shouts, "Thank ye, truly. Our clan will come."

The bird relaxed its neck; then, as gracefully and abruptly as it landed, it fluttered up and away. It soared, climbing into the sky with unnatural speed. Hawk—no, everybody on the turret—watched in awe as the eagle disappeared into the horizon.

Lulach, remembering what he had held, turned to Ceitidh. "Do ye ken what this means?"

"Aye," Ceitidh answered.

"Aye," Mòrag replied, also understanding the situation it would seem.

The huntsman, however, felt completely lost. He looked around at the excited faces.

"What? What just happened? You all seem to know that was planned?"

"Nae planned, Huntsman," corrected Lulach.

"What was that then?"

"We're summoned, it would seem," Lulach said, caressing the edge of the thistle petal. "Another one of old gran's stories, I'm afraid. The legend tells of a golden eagle flying tae every clan chief in Alba, bringing them a single thistle bloom. Every clan chief would then bring themselves and their finest representatives tae the summoning stones. It was a must."

"The what?"

"The summoning stones, lad. From what I remember, this hasnae happened in about a hundred years."

"Three hundred at least," Ceitidh corrected. "Well, from what I remember, anyway."

Mòrag, too, knew of the ritual. "Aye, it's as I've been telling,

Hawk. Magic has returned. It hasnae happened since before the conquering of the Cruithnich. My clan, MacTarbh, lives near the summoning stones. I grew up hearing tales from my da. Stories from his da and his da."

"Hawk talked of magic's return," Lulach said. "What did the stories say?"

"Nothing really," Mòrag answered. "Just like ye said. That a great eagle would summon the leaders of every clan. They'd send a host and meet at the summoning stones. There they'd meet in peace, feast, and celebrate. They were there tae choose the direction of the kingdom. Sometimes it was a new king or religious leader or the likes. Sometimes it was whether tae go tae war. It was a way tae set guidance for all clans."

"Aye," Lulach confirmed.

"Aye," Ceitidh seconded. "That's what I remember as well. We must go, Lulach."

"We shall. Although, I dinnae ken where the summoning stones be. I'll have tae ask the elders, unless . . ." Lulach glanced curiously over at Mòrag. She shrugged, but the movement was more excited than casual.

"It's like I said. I live near them. The summoning stones are near Glenfinnan, of course."

"Of course . . ." Lulach repeated quietly to himself. Then he squared himself to the group. "Good. Ceitidh, come, we must prepare."

Lulach and Ceitidh made for a quick exit. Lulach hesitated and turned around to look at Mòrag and Hawk. His stare asked for support. Hawk couldn't believe the haste that came over the clan chief.

A moment before he talked of resting. Now he mobilized?

Mòrag spoke for them both, "Aye, we must."

"Good, prepare yerselves. We'll make tae leave at dawn on the morrow." And with that, Lulach and Ceitidh disappeared into the castle.

Hawk's mouth still hadn't closed. Finally, he swallowed hard and tried to figure out what he had missed.

"Can ye believe it?" Mòrag asked in delight.

"What? What's going on here? What just happened?"

"That eagle flew directly to Lulach and handed him the thistle, a thistle from the clutches of a golden eagle. How are ye the only one who hasnae heard of this story? I ken I told ye this, the legendary summoning method tae travel tae the summoning stones at Glenfinnan. Eagles are the messengers of the gods."

"I gathered that. But so what? That's it? Just like that, you're going to drop everything and go to these summoning stones?"

"Aye. Ye heard what I said? This hasnae happened in three hundred years. All the clan leaders are going tae be there . . ." She shook her head, emphasizing her last point.

"So that's it, then. Just abandon your search for your sword and run to this . . . this summoning?"

"Are ye listening? *All* the clan leaders will be there. My da will be there as clan chief of the MacTarbhs. He'll bring a small host with him. He'll want me there. I have tae be there."

Hawk stood in silence. Frustrated, he played what she said over in his head. He hadn't thought about the fact that Mòrag's father was also a clan chief.

Damn it, he cursed himself. *She's right.* The huntsman grew afraid to speak.

It all had crumbled so quickly. The years of searching for the Norse had built up to tremendous proportions, only to end in an instant over the loch. No revenge. No retribution. Hawk wanted to follow the last boat to Inverness in the vain hope that there might be any surviving Norse he could confront. But, deep down, he knew the truth of the matter.

It is over, he cursed to himself. *So why do I still feel such misery? And now this eagle and its thistle.* How could a flower pull Mòrag away so easily? How could Lulach become so invested in traveling. Hawk felt sick, like a hot ember ignited in the pit of his stomach. He leaned his shoulder against the battlement and slid down with a crash. He was helpless to the weight of it all. Hawk stared at the stone beneath him.

Mòrag squatted and sat next to him. And for a second time that day, they simply sat next to one another, without speaking. That is, until Hawk finally managed to.

"We were so close. Your best lead at finding the sword is at the end of this loch."

"Naw. That's nae true. Lady NicNeev has traveled with the sword back tae my da."

She was right. Her father had hired Lady NicNeev. Hawk struggled to think of a good reason for the lady to be in Inverness. He'd made the thought that she would be out of desperation. But Lady NicNeev told him she went back to Clan MacTarbh.

The sickness that brought him to sit on the wall festered. Hawk looked up at the sky, unable to face Mòrag, as if that would deepen his shame. His jaw trembled as he collected himself for one more effort.

"Please, don't leave me. Come with me to Inverness."

"The only people hiding in Inverness are that cowardly laird and a few other survivors. The sword is gone. The Norse are gone. The sooner we realize that, the better."

Mòrag's words pummeled Hawk worse than any monster. As in any battle, he instinctively protected himself.

"Fine then. I guess I'll go there alone. I don't need your help. I don't need Lulach or the Moravians. I don't need anyone's help. Before I came to Alba, I was perfectly fine tracking the Norsemen. I can track the survivors myself. I know where they are, and I know where they're going; I mean to follow them."

Hawk put his hands against the wall and launched himself up. His face flushed, and he nearly keeled back over with a head rush. He wanted to scream, to howl, retch, slam his fist into the nearest wall, but he couldn't. He couldn't do anything. Forged with anger, the huntsman fled.

Chapter Twenty-Four

Hawk stormed through the castle's courtyard. He trudged through the spilled wine sullying the ground. Clumps of wet dirt clung to his boots, shedding as he made his way past the Highlanders' celebration. Hawk didn't waste energy looking in their direction. The thought of them offering him a drink soured his mouth. He made for the castle's main gate.

Hawk needed to find Equus. All his belongings would be saddled and packed from the night before. Find the horse and he could start for Inverness. It was time he left the castle and didn't look back.

Approaching the threshold of the castle's gate, a dark stain across the ground caught Hawk's eyes. It didn't glisten with moisture like wine. It simply sat there like a forgotten brush stroke of paint. The huntsman examined it. Countless times he tracked animals and monsters with that paint: blood. The spot of blood lay where he held the gate with the others. Was it the blood of the king's men who fell to his ax? Hawk supposed it didn't matter. The king. The Highland clans. They didn't care about him, so why should he care about them? Hawk kicked dirt over the bloodstain to cover it.

"Watch it," a voice cried in front of him, muffled by a red piece of cloth.

Moving her mask down, Lily revealed her face.

"Sorry," Hawk said, a croak to his words. He coughed to clear his throat and repeated it, "Sorry."

"It's alright," Lily said. She moved to walk past Hawk, then stopped and brightened.

"Hey, it's ye. Eh, can ye tell yer friend I did what she asked? He's just over there on a wagon."

Lily gestured to one side. Hawk didn't understand. Who was she talking about?

She stared at Hawk, but her eyes moved past him. "Nae mind. I'll tell her myself."

Hawk whirled around. Mòrag stood, arms crossed, a few paces behind them. She had followed him from the battlements. Brown eyebrows glowered at him. Hawk wanted to turn and walk away, but once again, he couldn't leave his position at Urquhart's gate.

Lily walked over and spoke to Mòrag in a hushed tone. They embraced before Lily went on her way. Mòrag approached the huntsman.

"Help me," Mòrag said, still burrowing into Hawk with her scowl. "Before ye run off, at least help me bury Sir William. I dinnae ken if I can manage on my own."

Hawk thought of what would happen if he said no. He thought about it but couldn't bring himself to say it. He owed it to Sir William to help, and he couldn't refuse her.

"Fine," was all Hawk could manage.

They walked around the castle and down the motte in silence. A two-wheeled cart tipped its pulling bars into the air at the grassy basin, holding an unusually bright-blue-and-white-draped shape. Hawk approached the cart and grabbed a spade next to it.

"Over by the juniper bushes?" Mòrag asked.

Hawk nodded in agreement. Mòrag placed her spade back against the cart.

"I just need tae do something first. I'll be right back."

Hawk couldn't hide his displeasure at her wanting to leave. She was the one who asked him to come with her. Mòrag answered as if reading his mind.

"Tiree is guarding our horses up that hill. I'll fetch them all here. Just gi'e us a minute." She started off toward the hilltop.

Hawk walked on to the junipers, dragging the spade behind him. He made it to the edge of the bushes and grasped the spade's handle.

Hawk cut into the thick mat of grass with the spade's blade. Outlining the edge of the site, he dug into the earth, forcing his weight onto the spade with every stroke. He tried to recall if he'd ever buried someone. Of course, there was Talie just days earlier, the sting of it still lingering. And certainly Garrett came close. The blood lost from the bear's attack was enough for any man to die. Garrett had withered and paled, but eventually the warmth returned. He'd seen others die, though none who Hawk had the chance to mourn.

Hawk thrust the spade into the dirt, pushing with his boot against the root cluster. The rusting metal spade severed the ties of the plant root to earth before he tossed the grass bundles over to one side. Leaning on the handle for a moment, Hawk caught his breath. He hadn't slept since the shore of Loch Ericht, and after the night's battle, exhaustion had set in. Fatigue would inevitably prevent him from finishing Sir William's grave; he was sure of it. Hawk never had the chance to bury his family either. Blåveis had taken that away from him.

Determined to fight off the fatigue, he started again, gouging out the clumps of grass under the junipers. What would his sister, Ayaksak, think of him for taking the time to bury Sir William but not her? To bury Talie but not her? Hawk kicked a small stone out of the dirt and thrust the spade in again. Long ago, Hawk watched an elder in his tribe laid to rest. Crouched in a sit, they wrapped the old woman in blankets of white-tailed deer and soft, velvet fox.

Is that what you would've wanted, Ayaksak? He knew the answer already. Her love of tribe and tradition fueled his own. He'd hunt a thousand deer to make just one blanket to wrap around her. But Blåveis made sure that would never happen.

That's why Hawk had to go to Inverness. He'd follow the loch's edge until he spotted the moored boat. From there, the huntsman would follow the Norsemen's footsteps, and if they scattered in the city, he'd simply ask around like he had in the past.

*Until someone turned me into the guard, or someone recognized me from the castle figh*t, Hawk thought. If they caught him, who would bury him?

Horse hooves clapped in dull thumps against the tufts of grass near the wooden cart. Mòrag approached on Epona with Equus in close tow. Tiree scampered out from behind the horses and made for Hawk. Hawk brushed a hand along the wolf's black fur, watching the wolf rush through into the junipers. The huntsman leaned on his spade once more.

"He sat next tae the horses all night," Mòrag said, stepping onto the dirt site with the second spade in hand. "He's probably thirsty and headed tae the loch."

Hawk nodded and slammed his spade's metal blade into the dirt. He heaved the contents to the side.

"How far should we dig?" Mòrag asked.

Hawk didn't look her way. How should he know? He'd only done this once, and she was there. The huntsman shrugged and took another scoop of earth.

"Hawk, dinnae do this."

"Do what?" he grunted through gritted teeth.

"This," Mòrag said, opening her palm up and raising it to the huntsman. "This silence."

Hawk couldn't reply. He could barely think. He clenched the spade handle tighter and thrust it into the last patch of grass in his outline. The white tendrils of knotted roots split under his weight behind the spade.

"Will ye talk tae me?" Mòrag asked in a gentler tone. "Please, Hawk, just talk tae me."

She walked up and put a hand on the huntsman's arm. He didn't flinch. He didn't move. Hawk barely mustered a defeated reply.

"What do you want me to say?"

"I just want ye tae talk tae me. What are ye goin' tae do when ye get there? Seriously, Hawk! Think about it. The slavers are dead. Ye've won. Ye've done what ye set off tae do."

"I've spent half my life now thinking of how I'd confront those demons. Kill them. Make them pay for what they did to my family. What they're still doing to me. Tell me, if I've won, then why do I still feel so miserable?"

He lifted the final clump of grass and tossed it away. Hawk wiped the sweat from his head and threw the spade down into the dirt.

"Ye've lost something that's a part of ye. Half yer life? It'll take a while to move past it then."

"I'm going to Inverness to avenge Sir William then."

"Ye think Sir William would've wanted ye tae throw yer life away?"

Hawk doubted the knight would appreciate any further acts of aggression toward the king's men. He stared at the roots exposed on the edge of the outline he made, slithering in tangles from the sides.

"Then, just for me. What makes you think I can't do it? I need to do this."

"Nae, ye dinnae need tae do it at all," Mòrag spat.

She moved in front of the huntsman. He looked up from the ground into her eyes—her emerald eyes. They swelled with tears.

"Come with us tae the summoning, Hawk," she pleaded. "Dinnae leave us on some suicidal revenge."

"Revenge?"

"That's what ye called it, isn't it? Ye said it last night yerself. But ye also said that we should move on with our lives. Ye said that the world is full of misery, that misery would always hurt, but that we can learn from it and move on. It's time ye listened to yerself; it's time tae move on, Hawk."

She slid her hands under his arms and swiftly pulled him into her embrace. Hawk stayed rigid, caught between impulses. He wanted to run, jump on his horse, and ride toward the eastern horizon. He wanted to, but he couldn't move.

Mòrag was right. His own words cut to the core. What would his sister think if he was killed, alone in Inverness? What revenge would that be? Hawk always wished better for his sister and his family. Wouldn't Ayaksak want better for him the same way? She would have wished for something more.

Hawk felt the weight of the world pressing down on him. He slowly collapsed into Mòrag. His head slumped onto Mòrag's black hide mantle. He finally returned Mòrag's embrace, squeezing around her tightly. His chin rested on her shoulder and the burning sensation of tears formed. But he blinked them away.

"We both ken Lady NicNeev didnae get on that boat," Mòrag said. "I need tae accept ye were right. She's gone. She's brought the sword back tae my da like she wanted. He would've offered a handsome reward for the sword tae her. What I would do for honor, she did for gold. I'm nae surprised, really. But I'm moving on. Move on with me."

Hawk embraced tighter at her words. He swallowed the knot forming in his throat.

Mòrag tempered the vibration in her voice with a cough and spoke on. "This could be a once-in-a-lifetime ceremony. Ye can meet Clan MacTarbh at the summoning and be there when I tell my da about Lady NicNeev stealing the sword from us. I need someone tae help back my side of the story."

"Seriously—" the huntsman laughed through the burn in his eyes "—who would believe it?"

He wiped at his face, yearning to see the warrior's smile as if it would make everything clear. Mòrag's face, soiled in the woad and stresses of the last day, brightened Hawk with her expression. The huntsman's eyes gazed at the auburn glimmer of her dark hair in the sun, lingering for a moment.

"Aye. So ye'll come then with me?"

"Yes," he said, releasing his hold and nodding. "You're right. It's time to move on. And I'd like to talk to Lady NicNeev again. I want to know why she betrayed you. Betrayed us."

Hawk also thought about what Lady NicNeev told him in the castle. She told him a time would come when what lies dormant inside would burst forth from him. Once more, the red flash of light in the loch seared into his memory. There was plenty to ask Lady NicNeev once Hawk found her.

"I . . ." Hawk started.

Mòrag, before Hawk could finish, replied, "Good. C'mon then. Let's finish this for Sir William."

Hawk smiled, grabbing the spade from the soft dirt, and dug again. They spent most of the day digging that hole. Deep and wide, they shoveled for hours. Exhausted, they slept in shifts, taking turns shoveling the earth and gathering stones. By nightfall, they buried Sir William. Lily had made the knight whole again. They lowered him in his full helm and plate. A knight of honor must need his armor for duty in the next life. They piled stones over the burial site and placed a lonesome cross on top. Sir William was gone, and the huntsman had to make peace with that.

Hawk distributed his ceremonial dried herbs from his pouch and gave thanks to the Creator for everything the knight sacrificed for him.

They buried him away from the castle and the common rabble. Lulach had ordered his people to strip the supplies from the other soldiers and bury them in mass. Hawk and Mòrag saved Sir William from that fate.

Despite having stayed up the previous night in battle, Hawk watched Lulach excitedly directing his troops through recovering the castle. A lot of cleanup remained. Stocks of supplies needed counting and a new system of order had to be established. And, after the adrenaline of battle waned, Lulach's arm finally started antagonizing him. The clan chief could barely raise a mug of ale, let alone a sword.

Exuding so much effort in the restorations, Lulach agreed to let Ceitidh ride ahead with much of the host toward the summoning stones. They planned for Lulach to follow a few days later when the work settled at Urquhart.

Hawk headed out with the company of Moravians toward Glenfinnan, and while looking back at the castle a final time, he wondered if he would ever see Lulach again.

Chapter Twenty-Five

"We'll set up camp, here, on the edge of the others. Gormelin, get a fire going. Raonaid, roast those rabbits from the trail. Frang, tie up the horses. And this time, make sure the trees are actually rooted. I swear by all that's holy, if I have tae chase a horse tonight, ye'll walk tae the stones tomorrow, ye hear me?" Ceitidh pointed a finger accusingly.

Hawk snickered at the jest, walking Equus toward Mòrag.

"Ack, Ceitidh, it was one time, lass," said Frang, a stout, balding man in the company of the Moravians.

"One time too many," Ceitidh retorted. She spun around to address the group again. "Remember, this is Sàmchair, so keep tae yerself. Mind yer own damn business. And dinnae start any fights with the MacDòmhnalls." A rumble of snickers and snorts moved through the Moravians.

They parted, dispersing to carry out the menial tasks needed to erect their make-shift camp. And Ceitidh made sure they completed them.

Ceitidh did well in absorbing her temporary position as leader of the host for the journey. She had kept spirits high while heading south through the Great Glen. She had even prevented violence when the retinue merged with other clans along the way. Hawk wasn't sure why he didn't expect the merging to happen, but it seemed inevitable. The golden eagle had also summoned the other clans to the stones. But that didn't mean old feuds didn't flare up. Ceitidh kept the amity, however, and she'd keep that amity as they set up camp.

They finally arrived in Sàmchair after a long, hard ride from Urquhart Castle. Too long, it seemed to Hawk, even if it was only one day. He chafed with saddle sores near the end of the journey, choosing to jog alongside the retinue rather than ride. Mòrag had laughed. She continued to laugh.

"Do ye want tae sit down near the fire for a rest?" she asked with a sardonic sneer. Tiree zoomed between her legs, and she bent over to pet him. "Or can ye nae sit down, eh?"

"It's not that bad," Hawk brushed her off. "I'll be fine. But I'd rather not sit yet. C'mon, I'll walk the horses to drink from the river. They're probably thirstier than me after that ride. Epona and Equus will need a week off after this."

Ceitidh seemed surprised. "Why nae the loch? It's closer."

"They'll need longer off than that if ye lead them that way," Mòrag said. "Dinnae take them tae the loch."

"Why not?" Ceitidh asked.

Mòrag laughed again. "That's Loch Eil. It's salted. The loch goes out into the sea."

"That loch is connected to the sea?" Ceitidh asked, dumbfounded.

"Yes," Hawk said, shaking his head, just as dumbfounded by Ceitidh's inability to recognize a salted loch. "Can't you smell it?"

"But we're miles from the sea," Ceitidh said. "I don't smell the sea."

"Are ye sure about that?" he asked, smirking and shaking his head once again.

She sniffed like a hound. Hawk surmised that between the dung and campfire smoke, she missed the salty crispness of the loch's breeze when they arrived.

"You're right," she admitted.

"So . . . Dinnae let them drink that water, eh, Huntsman?" Mòrag said.

"Can you imagine?" Hawk said, laughing with Mòrag. "The river it shall be."

Hawk led Epona and Equus toward Sàmchair's center and the lonely fort. The fort sat dull and uninspiring. Its wooden palisade walls were ramshackle and strewn about in a hurry many years prior, only to sit and weather in the rain. A passing army must have constructed the fort in a single summer month. Having sat abandoned by its military makers, locals took over the fort and left it in disrepair. Some timbers had fallen to the side or, in some cases, were missing altogether. The roof of the main hall had collapsed, and a few buildings in the fort remained. No, the Sàmchair fort hadn't stood the test of time.

It wasn't a true city. No houses and no proper buildings existed in the structure, save the fort. It was well traveled and heavily trafficked, but no one lived in Sàmchair.

"My da used tae take me here in the late summer," Mòrag had said when they first rode past the fort. "We'd bring our sheep and sell them there near the water's edge. People from all over the Highlands would come here for a few weeks a year tae trade. After that, most folks would disperse back tae their homes for the winter."

"Who runs the fort?" Hawk had asked.

"Naebody. That fort protects those who stay here from the wild more than passing armies. This place is called Sàmchair. It means silence. There's nae ruler. Nae clans. Just peace and silence."

Peaceful was the word for it. The markets of Edinburgh proved too boisterous. In Sàmchair, no markets sprouted. No vendors or bakers shouted from the streets or fort—only silence.

There were, however, a plethora of tents outside the fort's walls. They spaced themselves randomly, their campfires sporadic. No resemblance existed between the fort and Urquhart's ordered

military camps. It was a conglomeration of travelers all inter-
secting at one point. They all gathered in one valley for one
reason: it was the last shelter before Glenfinnan, where the
summons was called.

*This is the first day in hundreds that I haven't thought about
tracking down those raiders,* Hawk realized. The misery that
smothered him the day before had evaporated during the long
ride south. Although physically sore, the tethers that once
surrounded his mind unleashed him.

Hawk walked through the alleys to the river with a strange
new freedom. The horses gulped as much water as they could
from the cold, flowing river. It was peaceful, the last remaining
sunlight dipping behind the Great Glen's hills. Peace was restored.

––––

"And so, we went up tae Ol' Sinclair and dropped the head right
on his dining table," Mòrag exclaimed to reverential expressions
around the campfire.

Hawk and company had finished their supper. There was only
one thing to do after eating dinner around a fire. They partici-
pated in the age-old tradition of all campfires: storytelling.

"Just ye and the huntsman?" asked a shocked Ceitidh.
"Taking down the werewolf all by yerselves?"

"Aye, well, and Tiree, of course." Mòrag smiled, both
eyebrows raised.

She rubbed a hand through the shaggy beast's fur. Hawk
noticed a few around the fire remained unsettled by the wolf's
presence. But it wasn't simply the wolf that made them anxious.

Everyone gathered in Sàmchair for the summoning. Yet no
one alive had been to one. They hung on the rumors and specula-
tion about what might occur. Hawk didn't fancy guessing, but he
knew something big was occurring. The gathering of the clans,
the nervous storytelling around the fire, it reminded him of his
tribe just before war. When Hawk had but six summers to his

name, they called a great war party. Tribes from all over the region gathered in his tribal village. They met with his tribe, shared their stories, danced, and finally they left for war. Hawk shifted in his seat, hoping their gathering proved different.

"Yer lucky tae be alive. Them's magic beasts," a young lass said before taking a bite of the remaining spoonful of rabbit stew.

"I'll say," Ceitidh added. "I thought the eagles might be a fluke, but if ye're seeing werewolves, then it's true. Magic is back. Yer lucky tae be alive. Damn right. I would've tucked tail and run. A bloody werewolf? Foul creatures. Devil's spawn, they be. Do ye remember, Frang, the wolf beast haunting Elgin all those years ago? I was a bairn. Maybe ten winters tae my name."

"Aye," said Frang. He sipped from his goatskin flask to wash his throat. "Aye, the beast were enormous. Head thicker than an ox, it were, and spotted as a fawn. It appeared the first night and ravaged those two poor weans. The town and I thought it might have been wild dogs. They get in tae those packs sometimes and get brave and all. Certainly, it hadnae occurred tae anyone it could be something else. But then, the next night, it came tae the town looking for more. It grabbed a guardsman and . . . well . . . there were nae much left of him the next day. People were frightened then. If an armed man couldnae stop the monster, who could?"

"A huntsman," Hawk whispered to Mòrag, quiet enough to not disturb the circle.

She nearly giggled, but shook her head instead.

"That's what I remember," Ceitidh said, stoking the fire with a long pointed stick. "The utter fear of it. My da wouldnae leave the house. I could barely leave my bed 'cause of it. Everyone's lives just stopped."

Fear dominates people's memories. Hawk wasn't surprised Ceitidh only remembered the fear. He knew perfectly well how much it grabbed hold in the face of a monster.

"Aye, so it were," Frang said. "Eventually, Óengus, Lulach's father, got word of it and ordered the townsfolk tae rise together at once. Sure enough, one week later, the monster showed itself.

Nearly pissed myself when I saw it. Wide jaws like a lion, it had. Well, the beast were mighty, but so are a score of flaming arrows. He didnae get a chance tae fight us. We poured tar on it and set it ablaze. I can still hear it laughing."

Frang took another sip of the goatskin and let out a contented sigh. Hawk squinted, trying to picture what kind of monster laughed. Frang went on.

"We tossed most of the beast's bones into the sea. People were afeared of keeping them in Elgin."

"I remember that," Ceitidh said. "By the ocean, they pushed that canoe out and set it ablaze so it would burn at sea. My da brought me down tae watch it happen, so I wasnae tae be afraid anymore."

"Laughing, did you say?" Hawk said, looking at the old man. "Spotted wolf beast? Sounds as though you had a hyena lose."

"Aye, a *heenar*. Although . . ." Frang paused, looking around the campfire at all in attendance. "It wasnae the worst sight."

"Oh?" Mòrag remarked. "How so?"

"A *heenar* only be scary cause of its size or its freakish strength. But other creatures in this world are fouler. There are other monsters whose terrible deeds dinnae involve mighty jaws and fangs. Ain't that right, Huntsman?"

"That's true," Hawk said.

He closed his eyes for the briefest moments, and the chilling flash of Bodach returned, the elk skull forever etched in his recesses. The huntsman opened his eyes again and formed a closed, tight-lipped smile.

"The hyena and werewolf are predictable, understandable," Hawk said. "But some monsters are quite the opposite."

"That's true . . ." Mòrag agreed, somber and distant.

"What d'ye mean? What could be scarier than a *heenar* or a werewolf?" Ceitidh asked, the unmistakable quiver of fear creeping into her voice.

"Well . . ." Frang and Hawk replied simultaneously.

Hawk, not eager to play storyteller, gestured for Frang to speak. "Go on, good man. What keeps you up at night?"

"Glaistig," Frang said with a sharp shudder.

"What?" Mòrag asked, sliding off the log she sat on to get closer to the warm fire.

"The glaistig. It was a creature fouler than ever. Even now, I shudder at the name."

"What's the glaistig?" Ceitidh asked, already enraptured by the name. "What happened that frightened ye?"

Frang took another sip from his goatskin. It was clear to Hawk that the story might need the rest of its contents. He hadn't heard of the glaistig, but knew a few creatures whose name alone invoked fear in those who dealt with it. Toskur, the monstrously horned boar in Rygjafylki, or Blóta Nepja, a wolverine whose bite left its victims drained of blood in Gunnarskog. Bodach was a perfect example. Talie's mother wailed at the very name. Hawk shivered at the memory of her scream. No matter how long he worked as a huntsman, Hawk would never be immune to that kind of raw reaction from people.

Frang started, "I went on a hunting party a while back, me and the lads, ye see. In tae the forest of Glen Affric, we were. Elk in them woods, tae be sure, but deep in the wood. Deep, where magic had nae left this world, but that's where we needed tae go.

"The forest grew dark. Days blended quickly, and our way was soon shrouded. We got lost, and anytime yer lost, tensions grow tight. Maybe cause of fear, or maybe cause of hunger. I dinnae ken. But I tried tae lead us out. East and out, surely. While making our way, we found elk tracks. Scraping on trees, prints in the mud, ye ken, that sort of thing. It were close, surely.

"We followed the tracks through a meadow when, from the forest edge, came a woman. She were bonnie. More bonnie than anything I'd ever seen. And she were completely nude, like the day she were born. We all froze. Why in the world would a nymph beauty be in this dark forest?

"She approached us slowly and calmly, with nae a care in the world. 'Uaine's my name,' she told us. 'Are ye lost?' Some lads said aye, but I told her nae, we's tracking the elk, we's nae lost. She offered tae take us tae her house. Give us food and shelter for a while, then show us out of the wood. Well . . . the lads were beaming. Ecstatic. I were a bit flapped. We were so close tae the elk, I said. We should keep tracking, I said.

"We decided tae send Calum and Eònan tae go with her. They started tae look sick from no food and could use the rest. Then we'd find them later. She seemed happy tae help, so the two lads left with her tae her home. We tracked the elk for another hour and eventually came tae a cave in a hillside.

"Tall it were. High cliff edges. The elk must've taken shelter in a cave. One lad, Bran, makes a torch and we go in. Well . . . what we found inside still haunts me tae this day . . ."

Ceitidh gulped, though not imperceptibly enough to go unnoticed by Hawk.

"What?" she asked. "What was inside? The glaistig?"

"Aye . . ." Frang continued. "Well . . . we saw a beast, alright. Its legs were hooved like a goat's were and it were bent over and . . . Well . . . it were eating Calum. His face—his look of terror . . . Bran screamed. The beast rose. It were hideous. A right horned and toothed creature. It were the devil incarnate. It shifted before our eyes, changing in tae the girl from the meadows. Still bonnie, but covered in blood. She spoke in an eerie booming voice, 'I am Glaistig Uaine,' she said. 'Welcome tae my home for tea.' The horns grew. I ran. I didnae say anything, I just ran. I heard Bran scream, and I saw the torch go out, but I kept running out of that cave. We all did. We made it into the forest, and a loud booming shrill echoed from the cave. It were the glaistig's laughter. What kind of monster could do that? What kind of monster can do that and laugh? By God, I'll tell ye, I can still hear that laugh now."

"How did ye make it out of the forest?" Mòrag asked.

"We ran. We didnae stop. Everyone sprinted in a single direction. Eventually, we broke free in tae the eastern valley."

"Did everyone else make it?" Ceitidh asked, eyes wide.

"I never saw Calum, Eònan, or Bran ever again. The rest of us made it, aye. But I'll tell ye this, we nae spoke of it again. Calum and Eònan had nae family. But Bran . . . well . . . we told his family he'd gotten ill, and while ill, he fell from a great bluff and plummeted tae his end. His family grieved at the story of our lie. But the truth would've brought even more grief. So we kept the truth tae ourselves."

Frang finished and sipped from his goatskin once more, tipping the end up with his second hand and emptying the contents.

"Sometimes that's all you can do," Hawk acknowledged, knowing how lies and half truths could be blessings. "So they may heal."

He lowered his head and gazed into the fire, wishing he had Ceitidh's stick to move a log, which had rolled out of the blaze.

"I'll nae heal. I'll hear that laugh till the day I die, I fear," Frang muttered.

A quiet air hung around the campfire as everyone seemed preoccupied with their thoughts. Sparks popped and whizzed from the center of the flames. Frang cast the empty goatskin aside and seemed befuddled with what his hands ought to do.

Hawk glanced at Mòrag. She, too, watched Frang. Then, like she sensed his gaze, Mòrag turned to him and smiled before her eyes drifted back to the fire.

She's been through a lot recently, and tomorrow will bring more unknowns.

"Well," Ceitidh broke the silence. "I'm exhausted. Tae bed, I think. I'll see ye all at first light. At dawn, we make for Glenfinnan."

She rose, stretching her back and arms with a throaty yawn, then disappeared into the cluster of tents. The others moved, following Ceitidh's example.

"Hawk, care for a walk with me?" Mòrag asked in the shuffle.

"Sure," he replied without a second thought.

Hawk was exhausted, but talking to Mòrag about tomorrow proved too enticing.

"On the morrow then, lads," Mòrag said, departing with Tiree toward the loch.

———

Innumerous tumbled stones dotted the shoreline of Loch Eil. The water was nearly pure black, its depth absorbing all the light. The huntsman couldn't see out over the loch, for a deep blue haze of clouds obscured the moon.

Having left the fire, Hawk's aching muscles from the day's ride caught up to him. He hadn't slept the night of the battle at Urquhart, and even with a full night's rest last night, he was sore and heavy with exhaustion. Every muscle shouted at him as it learned how to move again, requiring extra concentration to trudge about.

He walked on. Even though his fatigue nearly overwhelmed him, his desire to spend time with Mòrag was greater. A natural kinship he had never experienced. Her spirit brought tranquility. The threat of the Norse raiders, which loomed over him for so many years, disappeared more by the hour, thanks to Mòrag of Clan MacTarbh.

Tiree glided alongside the pair. Hawk leaned over to brush a hand under the wolf's chin, scratching up to his ear. Tiree curled toward the scratching hand before breaking away. He sniffed at the water's edge but didn't drink from it.

"I wouldnae believed that story of the glaistig," Mòrag said in a somber hushed tone, "if it was told tae me a week ago. But, after Rannoch . . ."

"Perceptions change, I guess," Hawk replied.

He had encountered plenty of people who didn't believe in the monsters he killed for a living. It was different after someone saw it before their eyes—what they previously thought didn't exist. It would frighten them. Once one monster was proven real, it left the door open for all the others. Hawk bent down, searching the stones for a flat one.

"I wonder if they did anything about the glaistig?" Mòrag asked.

"It didn't sound like it to me. He kept the truth to himself."

"A pity tae live with that."

"Indeed," Hawk said, picking up a split piece of slate from the ground.

He spun the rock in his hand, then turned to the loch. Placing his bare finger around the curve of the stone, he tossed the rock into the loch, spinning it on its axis with the tip of his finger. The stone grazed the surface of the loch, launching itself again. It bounced a second time, then a third, before dipping into the black abyss. Mòrag gasped, looking over the rippling surface of the loch.

"Excited to return to your family?" the huntsman asked, smiling, pleased with himself for skipping the rock.

"Aye. Although, my da might nae be happy tae see me."

Upon situating themselves in Sàmchair, Mòrag had searched for Clan MacTarbh and her father, only to learn they'd already reached Glenfinnan. Mòrag would have to wait until tomorrow. Hawk knew when they reunited with her father, they'd confront Lady NicNeev too.

"Speaking of your father," Hawk started, "are you still thinking about what you'll say to him?"

"Of course I am. It's all I can bloody think about. All day. It's just lingering there—what do I say?"

"What will you say?"

Mòrag shrugged. "I dinnae ken. Should I curse him for hiring some sorceress behind my back? Some magician hag who stole my right tae the sword, my right tae bring the family's blade back. How could he do that tae me? How could he think I wouldnae be good enough tae get the task done? All these years, he's treated me like a wee bairn. 'Mòrag, be careful. Mòrag, ye cannae do that. Mòrag, yer nae as strong as the boys, be careful.' I cannae stand it."

She crouched, grasping a stone, and, in her best imitation of Hawk, cast the rock into the water. It didn't skip. Mòrag released a long exhale.

"It wasn't your fault. How could you know what would happen? How could anyone have known?"

"I should've guessed. That's why I'm nae sure if I should just drop tae my knees and ask for forgiveness for failing tae accomplish what I set out tae do. I promised I wouldnae let him down. I swore I would come back with the sword in my hands. And I failed."

We both failed. They had set out on their own journeys. They intertwined, supporting one another along the way, yet they still failed their tasks. But Hawk felt no sense of failure standing on the shore. Circumstances had changed.

"You didn't fail. He hired another to beat you to it, and a cunning sorceress at that."

"What if that was part of the test? I'm sure he didnae ken she was a sorceress, but what if he saw Lady NicNeev as a way tae motivate me tae succeed and I wasnae able tae rise tae the challenge?"

Hawk picked up another rock and, upon further inspection, handed it to Mòrag. "Here, try this one."

She took it and, throwing the rock from her side, skipped the piece of slate once across the surface. Mòrag smiled excitedly, turning to Hawk. He relished that smile and nodded in approval.

"I wasn't there when you set out for the sword, but it sounds like you set this challenge yourself. You chose to search for it. Why would he try to make it harder for you?"

"Maybe it's because he believed I'd give up. That I wouldnae be capable of doing it on my own. He hired her tae help me, but Lady NicNeev only cares about the money he offered."

"Maybe. So what will you say then?"

Mòrag smirked and shook her head. "If only I had that answer."

Tiree, who ran back to greet Mòrag, emitted a low whine. His eyes fixed over the loch.

Odd, Hawk thought. The huntsman glanced in the same direction—nothing.

It started as a whisper, low and hushed. A sharp tone rose over the loch. Hawk couldn't figure it out.

"Do you hear that?" Hawk asked Mòrag, his eyes searching for the source.

"Aye. It sounds familiar," Mòrag mentioned as they approached the edge, scuffing through the stones.

Mòrag recognized it first.

"It's crying. I ken that sound. It's crying. It's coming from the middle of the loch."

Hawk struggled to make it out. It came and went, a faint whimpering. He couldn't pinpoint its origin.

Could someone be drowning in the loch? Did they dip in and out of the water?

"I can't see anything out there," Hawk said, squinting in the dim light. "No splashing or anything."

The whimpering grew louder. It shrieked a vile wail, the sound boring into Hawk's ear, penetrating the canal and digging into his mind. He wanted to fall to his knees and beg the sound to stop. Fighting the urge to cover his ears, the huntsman's hands went to his back and the tomahawks.

"There!" Mòrag shouted in frantic surprise. "Standing on the water. A lass. She's standing on the water!"

"Where? I don't see anything out there."

"She's there. Right there," Mòrag pointed, leaning over and extending her arm. It was in vain, however, as Hawk saw nothing. The whimpering ceased. And for a moment the world grew quiet. But only for a moment.

A groan echoed across the water. A hoarse, fierce voice rose from the depths.

"Destined for war," it lamented.

Where's that coming from, damn it? He reached for the tomahawk, but Mòrag stopped him, pulling his hand toward her side and holding on.

"Who is?" Mòrag asked, her voice quivering. "Tell us." Her hand trembled in his.

The lass's voice croaked again. "Destined for war is the kingdom of Alba. Dark are they who wear the crown of gold. They sit at the seat of rule, a sovereign destined to unite Alba, but it will only bring death. War brings only death. Death. You'll know death as it comes to you. Death. Death. Death!"

Tiree raised his head to the night sky and howled a long note. Hawk jolted at the sound, nearly leaping out of his boots. Mòrag squeezed his hand, then looked around in panic.

"What the—? She's gone. The lass is gone," Mòrag muttered.

"I saw no girl. But I heard her. She can't be gone," Hawk said.

"It was Caoineag . . ." Mòrag said in a whisper. "The weeping angel. She's gone, Hawk, if she was even there . . ."

"What?" Hawk stammered.

"She wouldnae attack. She only weeps in warning."

"Warning? A ruler destined to unite Alba brings war and death?"

"King David?" Mòrag suggested.

"It must be. Sits at the seat of rule in Edinburgh. He even told me before I left; his goal was to unite Alba, a land of the Scots."

"Caoineag is a weeping angel of death," Mòrag explained further. She continued quickly, her voice rising with concern. "I saw her. She was out there, above the water. I saw her and heard her speak. War is coming. Death too."

"I heard it," Hawk said, unable to think of a calming response. He, too, was shaken.

"Do ye think it means my death?" Mòrag asked.

"I doubt it."

"Yers?"

"I doubt that even more," Hawk said. "We control our fates. Come on, we should head to the tents. We shouldn't linger."

He started walking, but Mòrag didn't move.

"What we should do is heed that warning," Mòrag said, her feet firmly in place. "We shouldnae go tomorrow. What if something terrible lies in wait? What if death is waiting for us? We shouldnae go tomorrow."

"Where should we go then?"

"Anywhere, just nae there."

The huntsman looked over the loch. In that instance, the moon burst through its cloud cover over the water, illuminating the rolling waves. No girl walked on the water.

"Mòrag, we traveled all day to get here. My arse is sore from the saddle, all so I could help you reach the summoning and help tell your father your side of the tale. I've come seeking Lady NicNeev. She owes us answers. I've come for something bigger than myself. We can't run away now."

Mòrag stood, rooted in the spot. Tiree brushed against Mòrag. She bit her lip, then spoke.

"But my father. Caoineag. I'm . . . I'm scared of what tomorrow brings."

"So is everyone in this mass of camps," the huntsman began. "Everyone is nervous about what tomorrow brings. What will happen at the summoning, what will be decided, what will happen to their clan, their family? The shepherd wonders if his lambs will make it through the stormy winter night. He wonders what price he'll get for his lambs and if it'll be enough to feed his children. The soldier wonders if he'll be given the order to march on his neighbor tomorrow because his neighbor didn't have enough for the lord's tax. We're all nervous about what tomorrow brings. But we must keep moving. We must move on with our lives and embrace what's to come. We must take things day by day."

Mòrag shook her head. She looked at the sky. Her eyes reflected the white-hot glow of the moon. They turned to Hawk, and she nodded in agreement.

She spoke in a whisper. "Tomorrow is just like any other day?"

"Yes, the sun will rise and set, just like any other day, and you'll survive. I'll make sure of it," he promised.

"Hawk?"

"Mo?"

"Stay with me tonight," Mòrag said, grabbing Hawk's hand. "I dinnae want tae be alone in case death is waiting for me. Please."

"I can," Hawk replied, and they walked toward the light of the campfires and tents.

———

He delicately placed the gambeson on the ground next to his armor. His fingers worked at the shirt's lacing, untying the sinew strings fastening his collar. The tallow candlelight flickered a cavalcade of shadows across the ivory canvas tent. Hawk removed his shirt and tossed it on his armor.

A hand slithered up his back. It was a gentle touch, dancing up and down in an unknown pattern. The archeress grazed her callused fingertips across his skin. The hair on Hawk's arms prickled. The finger hovered on three jagged lines etched into the huntsman's back.

"How did ye get this one?" Mòrag asked, tracing the gnarled scar.

"A bear swiped me while I spun away from it. The bear was quicker."

"It must've hurt something awful."

"It did," Hawk admitted, remembering the weeks of bandaging required for the wound to heal.

Mòrag swayed her fingers across his back, jumping from one to the next like a constellation in a starry sky.

"And this one?" she asked, pointing to a thick blot of fibrous skin just above his left hip.

"An arrow. A centaur fired one through my side as a warning for getting too close to his foals, err, children."

Mòrag's hands went up, reaching his shoulders and sliding across from one side to the other. Her fingertips bounced across multiple lines of striped scars like a musician playing the harp.

"And these? What monster could make these?" She laughed.

"A lash from a whip. I asked my captors, Blåveis, for water. I got those instead."

Mòrag snatched her hand back like she was scorched. "Oh. I'm sorry . . ."

"It's okay. That's in the past now," Hawk reassured her.

"I dinnae have scars like yers."

He turned and faced Mòrag. "Let's see," he said in quiet curiosity.

Mòrag smiled, delicately unlacing her boots before kicking them to the corner. She slid her hands underneath the black fur mantle on her shoulders, lifting it over her head before tossing it to the ground. She carefully undid the leather fasteners holding her tartan up. Her hands betrayed a faint tremble, which Hawk knew came from a racing heart. She removed the tartan, and then, sliding it off her shoulders, it too fell to the ground. Mòrag pulled her arms into her woolen shirt—first one arm, then the other. The huntsman watched as she raised the shirt over her head. The collar caught her dark cascade of hair and tugged it to the side before releasing its grip, and the shirt floated to the tent's floor.

Mòrag flashed her eyes at the huntsman, emerald fires dancing in the candlelight. Hawk moved down from her eyes. She wore a band of soft, white cloth, bound tightly around her chest and back. But even the white cloth stood in contrast to her bright, pale skin. Standing next to him, she was like fresh spring snow, unblemished. He wondered how long it had been since the sun touched her skin. He wondered many things.

"I don't see any marks. Turn around," Hawk directed gently.

She responded. Hawk's hand reached out, a rough and stark

difference to Mòrag's smooth complexion. His hands explored, sneaking carefully over every inch.

"Perfect," he whispered.

Hawk, strangely, oddly, felt the urge to put his lips to her shoulder. But he didn't, pulling away from Mòrag and dropping to the bed beside their feet. Hawk lifted his deer-hide sheets and slipped beneath them.

Mòrag turned around and, gracefully sliding in next to him, joined Hawk. He leaned his head against the rolled woolen pillow, placing one arm behind his head. Mòrag swung her hair out of her face and brought her head to rest against Hawk's muscled chest. Her skin warmed against his. The huntsman wrapped his arm around her, pulling her in close.

"Perfect," she whispered. And for a long while, they lay there together, frozen in time. Even after their eyelids shut, having given in to the heavy burden of remaining open—even after the tallow of the candle exhausted and the light vanished—they remained, together, the huntsman and the warrior.

CHAPTER TWENTY-SIX

There existed one sound in the entire world that the huntsman would never understand. A sound both menacing and beautiful, both illustrative and ear-splitting. Every time it rang out, he couldn't help but smile while simultaneously wanting to cover his ears. The sheer audacity of it puzzled him. But Hawk still loved the bagpipe's sound. And that day, their sound echoed over the Highlands of Glenfinnan.

"This way, c'mon," Mòrag barked, riding her mare between the darting and shuffling wayward crowd. "Tiree, *trobhad*! C'mon, Hawk, quit yer gawking; they're just pipes. My clan was this way. Mind yerself!"

A dark-haired man bumped into Mòrag's horse. He spun a full circle on his boot, laughing before he drank from his horn, and continued on like nothing had happened.

"This is incredible," Hawk called. "Pandemonium. How are there so many people here, in one place?"

"Glenfinnan is wide. Every clan has been summoned. They've all sent a host. For some, it seems . . ." she paused, tugging on Epona's reins and maneuvering around four children tossing a rock between them in a circle ". . . it seems the entire clan has come."

Hawk passed the children and swept the area. It was a veritable cacophonous jumble of people. It seemed the entire isle had sent representatives and made their way to the glen. Hundreds, if not thousands, swarmed the valley.

Tents of all colors dotted the landscape. Fires spread along the path, and the feasts that fed the clans came with them. Roasted venison and charred goose. Turnips and onions. The smells wafted directly into the huntsman's stomach. He wished for nothing more than to jump off his horse and join the celebration. For it was a celebration.

Clans from all over joined the mass, each bringing a unique culture. But there, in the gathering, they were one. A shared goal united them, and thus, they seemed free to share their mutton, whiskey, and merriment. Cheers sprung up all around as he rode, laughter chorusing throughout. And the bagpipes blasted. They'd blare in musical delirium for brief moments during their ride through the crowd. Hawk enjoyed every minute as they sought after Clan MacTarbh.

Ahead of Hawk, Mòrag reined in her horse. She stopped next to a long wooden caber, a long ribbon of tartan waving at the top. The same blue-and-green tartan Mòrag wore.

Hawk rode up beside her. She swung her leg over the saddle and jumped down.

"Wait. Lochlann?" Mòrag shouted, already knowing the answer to her question.

"Wee Mòrag? By God, it is ye!" a large boulder of a man hollered.

He grabbed Mòrag by both arms, squeezing her tight like a bundle of sticks, and spun her around in a circle. Mòrag gasped with laughter.

"How are ye?" she managed after the man set her on the ground.

"Still going, aye. But how are ye?" Lochlann asked, dragging out the last word in an exaggerated question. The man's eyes darted away from Mòrag to Epona. "My word. This is an amazing horse. Magnificent. How did ye get a hold of such a horse? Did ye steal it?"

"Nae, c'mon." Mòrag chuckled.

"Are ye in debt? Tae this man?" he asked, pointing a finger at Hawk.

Hawk smirked at the jest.

"Ach, c'mon. I'm in nae debt, Lochlann."

"Where did ye get them then?" Lochlann persisted.

"Ye wouldnae believe me if I told ye."

"Alright then, keep yer secrets. Who's yer pal?"

"This is Hawk," Mòrag said, introducing the huntsman.

"Greetings." Hawk nodded.

Lochlann made no gesture in return. His jovial nature with Mòrag was replaced by the stern, stony face of mistrust.

"What clan be ye from?" Lochlann asked, measuring up the huntsman.

"I'm from no clan, my good man. None from here anyway," Hawk answered.

"God, and that accent. Mòrag, where did ye find this tanned one?"

Lochlann's face betrayed no amusement.

"I served as a huntsman to the king of Alba. I met Mòrag along the way on the road."

"He's since left that service," Mòrag quickly pointed out.

"Aye?" Lochlann nodded his balding head slowly.

Then the smile on his face broke free again, and he bellowed with glee, patting Hawk on the mailed shoulder. It had been a ruse. Hawk couldn't help but laugh.

Lochlann went on. "Yer full of surprises, Mòrag. But I'm glad yer here. Yer da will be too."

"Where is he?" she asked. "I must speak with him."

Lochlann scrunched up his face, then shrugged. "He's around. He met with other clan chiefs earlier, but he'll be back any moment. Come, eat while we wait. Lad!" A young boy, the spitting image of Lochlann, appeared from behind the tent. "Take the horses and feed them. Guard them, too, ye wee shite. I'll nae have the Sruidh clan walking away with these prized ones."

The huntsman took Equus's reins and handed them to the disappointed boy. He didn't doubt the lad hoped to join the others in celebrating, not be on guard duty.

Hawk followed Mòrag and Lochlann as they walked around a large tent. Behind it sat a small campfire surrounded by four makeshift benches. The huntsman looked for any sign of Lady NicNeev, but disappointedly found none. Instead, two men sat opposite one another, similarly clad as Lochlann. Their faces were wrinkled and leathered, while dark patches of fur peppered their silver beards. Hawk could hardly tell them apart. They both lit up with excitement at the sight of Mòrag.

"Wee Mòrag?" asked the man on the right. He stood at once and jumped to embrace her.

"Artair," Mòrag yelped, "good tae see ye."

The other man, not missing a beat, also stood and wrapped Mòrag up just as the first.

"Bhaltair, ye as well."

"Aye, what's it been? Three months now?" asked Bhaltair, letting Mòrag go and gesturing for them to sit.

"Aye, something close to that. I set off in the spring, anyway."

"What was it ye traveled for again?" asked Bhaltair.

"Oh—" Mòrag hesitated "—it wasnae for anything really . . ."

"Oh aye, that's right," Bhaltair remembered, scratching at his muzzle. "It was tae find yer da's sword, eh? Claidheamh-mòr an Adhairc? Did ye find it?"

"Aye, well, nae exactly," Mòrag said ashamedly, shrinking as she shrugged.

Hawk fought the urge to reach out and take her hand.

"Ach, a shame . . ." Bhaltair said, dropping his eyes toward the fire.

"Bugger it," roared Artair. "That sword was lost long ago. It nae be yer problem, lass. That's for certain."

Lochlann approached from the back of the tent. He brought

a precious gift: food. Notably, he brought tender venison roast and onion soup. Lochlann gave Mòrag a bowl, then Hawk.

"Thank you," the huntsman said on reflex.

"Dinnae thank him just yet," Mòrag said sardonically, loud enough for the circle to hear. "Ye havnae tasted it first. Tastes like poison."

"Only yers does," Lochlann returned the jest. "I made that bowl for ye in particular. The huntsman's is safe."

"A huntsman?" Artair asked in astonishment. "A hunter for hire?"

"Yes. More or less." Hawk gobbled down a spoonful of aromatic broth.

"Right, this is Hawk. Hawk, Artair and Bhaltair, a pair of dolts who call my da their mate."

"Good tae meet ye, lad," saluted Artair. "Ye here for the summoning then too?"

"Yes, though I'm afraid I don't know much about it."

Artair smiled. "Course ye dinnae ken. No one alive does. There hasnae been a summoning in nearly three hundred years. The entire camp is alive and wondering what will happen today."

Mòrag wiped the soup dripping down her chin and asked, "It's definitely today then? The summoning, that is."

"Aye, it's definitely today. Sure as rain in the spring."

Hawk chewed a chunk of meat. He savored the flavor as long as he could before swallowing.

With his mouth still full, he looked at Artair and asked, "What do you think will happen at the summoning?"

"Well, I believe yer da, Mòrag, will be summoned tae the stones with the other chiefs at Eilean Na Mòine. Graeme already met with the other clan leaders. That's what he's doing now, meeting with them and all. But other than that, I dinnae ken what will happen."

"I hear the king of England has died," guessed Bhaltair. "I think we're here tae decide tae go tae war with England."

Artair had other ideas. "Poppycock, the Lady of Caledonia

has returned. She's returned and heralded this summoning tae bless us with her grace."

Hawk, having finished the venison chunks, spoke more clearly. "The Lady of Caledonia? Forgive me, but who is she again?"

"She's the Lady of Caledonia," Artair stated, like it was obvious. "Graced by the gods herself, she's a beautiful young maiden who is summoned tae earth tae help us in our time of need. None live who have seen her walk these lands, but tales of her ethereal power still exist. There are even whispers that magic has returned tae Alba. But they're just tales, lad."

"Aye, but they're nae tales," Mòrag chimed in. "I've seen the magic with my own eyes. I ken magic is back."

"Did ye, aye?" Bhaltair laughed.

"Aye, Mòrag must be speaking true," Artair continued, "for the Lady of Caledonia has returned. They say she's a comely young lass who comes in times of great need. They say . . ."

Bhaltair cut him off. "Ye sound like yer in love."

"Aye, course I'd be. She is a goddess incarnate. If ever I could love someone, it would be her. The blacksmith of Clan MacFhionghuin said he saw her by the loch in the wee hours of the morning. Said she strolled along the shore toward the stones."

Bhaltair coughed his disbelief. "He saw her? The Lady?"

"Aye. And he's nae a man that would lie."

"She was young, you say?" Hawk asked in interest.

"Aye, a maiden fair, young, and as beautiful as wee Mòrag, if ye believe the blacksmith. And I do."

"Nevertheless," Hawk said, wanting to know more, "what will happen at the summoning?"

"Who's tae say, Huntsman?" Bhaltair laughed.

"He can," shouted Artair, looking over Hawk's shoulder. "Graeme, look who's here."

Mòrag spun around in her seat as quick as lightning before launching to her feet.

"Da!" she cried.

"Mòrag!" shouted the sturdy, chiseled newcomer, grasping Mòrag in a tight hug. He held her outstretched in his long arms and spoke in a deep, bullish manner. "Yer safe and well, look at ye. And Tiree? Oh, over there, eh? Lazy pup, always lounging by the food, eh?"

"How are ye, Da?"

"Good, now that I ken yer okay. How was everything?"

"Good, aye. It was good. Da, this is Hawk. He helped me on my travels."

"A huntsman," Artair added.

Graeme nodded at Hawk with a hearty smile. "Hawk, good tae meet ye."

The huntsman shot him a studying glance. Graeme stood tall, a brute of a man, bearded and wild. He dressed down in everyday woolen clothing and what seemed like a shared MacTarbh tartan. Hawk wouldn't have guessed him the leader of any clan. However, the huntsman's eyes didn't miss what adorned his right hip—a large claymore sword. Fixed into the pommel of the sword was a cold, blue stone. Mòrag's sword, it would seem, had found its way home. Lady NicNeev must be close.

"The feeling is mutual, my lord." Hawk nodded in kind.

"Oh . . ." Lochlann laughed. "My laird, eh?" The entire circle laughed, save for Hawk.

Graeme chuckled then, composing himself, and said, "No lairds here, lad. Just a man chosen tae lead shites like these three."

"Aye, he's right," Bhaltair said, still snorting in amusement. "We are shites."

"So, Graeme, cut with the niceties," Artair barked. "What's the bloody word? What's happening today? We're all dying tae find out."

Graeme coughed and cleared his throat. "Aye, yer right. Mòrag, it's good yer here. Ye should hear this too." He leaned closer to the fire.

They all mirrored the action, dying to know what secrets lay ahead. Hawk nearly fell off his bench.

"Well, it's simpler than we had thought. Nearly every clan that's supposed tae be here is. MacTarbhs, Sruidhs, MacTamhais. Ye name it, they're here. Clan MacDonnchada and King David—naw, but that's tae be expected, I suppose. Anyway, Clan Ghriogair has been tae the stones. Those of the stones who have summoned us passed on that each clan will send five representatives tae the stones at Eilean Na Mòine, one hour from now, when the sun reaches its highest peak. The stones are west, so we'll need tae leave soon."

"Who then?" asked Artair, his eyes wide. "Who summoned us tae the stones?"

Mòrag's father hesitated, looking down at his boots. "I . . ."

Bhaltair couldn't believe it. "Ye did ask, though, right?"

"I did. But I cannae say, lads. I'm sworn tae secrecy."

"Ahhhh," everyone moaned in near unison.

"That's bollocks," Artair said, casting a hand in Graeme's direction.

"What bloody shite," Lochlann added.

"I cannae say, lads. I'm sorry. Now quit yer greetin', ye wee bairns. I cannae say, and that's that."

"Who are the five, then?" Mòrag asked, her eyes sweeping the circle and returning to her father. "Ye said ye needed five representatives." All eyes fell on the clan leader of MacTarbh. He rubbed his bearded chin and weighed his words.

"Well . . . I hadn't considered Mòrag's return. This changes matters, aye. Well, it would have tae be myself, Lochlann, Wee Lochlann, Artair, and now . . . Mòrag."

"But . . ." interjected Bhaltair.

"Sorry, pal. I ken what ye mean and all. Yer frustrated. But Mòrag is here. Mòrag is my own flesh and blood, the heart of Clan MacTarbh. And since she's returned from her journey, she'll take her true place at my side," stated Graeme, rubbing Mòrag's head and ruffling her dark hair.

Her face lit up, blushing a harsh crimson.

Bhaltair sat back in a blank stare, flummoxed at his predicament. Hawk let out an amused snort, pitying the man's misfortune thanks to Mòrag's arrival. But Hawk wasn't going to miss the summoning. He didn't need to be chosen as Clan MacTarbh's representative to see the ceremony, or any clan. He'd be present on his own accord.

Bhaltair leaned over to Hawk and whispered, "What did we ride all this way for?"

The clan leader heard the whisper.

"'Cause I commanded ye tae," Graeme shouted with mocking authority. "'Cause the summoning asked for a host. 'Cause if this council breaks in tae war, ye'll be ready. 'Cause if this council demands strength, ye'll be ready. Ye certainly didnae come tae represent Clan MacTarbh's good looks, ye ugly stump."

"Ye are fairly ugly, Bhaltair," Artair added, as if it settled the matter.

The campfire snickered, including Bhaltair.

"Da, may I have a word with ye? Away from here?" Mòrag asked, pulling her father's woolen shirt.

"Huh, what? Oh, aye. Of course, my child." Graeme removed Mòrag's hand from his shirt and led her around to the opposite side of the tent.

Mòrag glanced hurriedly at Hawk, gesturing for him to follow. He obeyed immediately. The time drew near. They'd confront her father and Lady NicNeev. Hawk had questioned what Mòrag might ask her father when they reconnected. But there, faced with the eminent chance to question Lady NicNeev, he, too, came up empty.

They walked until they approached two large makeshift hitching posts recently hammered into existence. A dozen horses and one rather large goat stood tied to the posts.

Thick-necked with powerful, muscular legs, the cob horses proved experts in the harsh conditions of the Highland mountains. The horses looked of hearty northern stock, except two. Sleek, slender, and athletic, the oriental mounts stood out among the rest. Beautifully elegant, they towered over their sturdy neighbors.

"Lochlann, lad, go tae yer da," Graeme barked. "We'll be heading out soon."

"Headed where?" asked the boy guarding the menagerie of horses and one goat.

"Tae the stones, lad. Away with ye and get ye ready. Ye are coming with us tae the council. Yer da will tell ye the rest and help ye get settled. Go now." The boy's delight lit his face, and then, suppressing that elation, he nodded and ran off.

"Wait a minute . . ." Graeme stammered, his voice elevating. "Whose bloody horses are these? Lad?" But Lochlann, son of Lochlann, had already disappeared.

Fortunately, Mòrag had the answer he sought. "Those horses are ours, Da. This is Hawk's horse Equus, and this is mine, Epona." The horse's head moved up to the name.

"We-he-hell . . . A couple of fancy horses? Aye. Seems ye did well for yerself on this journey, eh, Mòrag? How did ye come by them? Hawk, are they yers, perhaps? Quite the—"

"Da, listen," Mòrag interrupted him. "Listen, I wanted tae talk tae ye about my journey. About the sword. *Our* sword."

"Aye, of course. I want tae hear all about yer travels. Do ye have the sword with ye? Nae on yer hip, I see."

"Aye, well of course it isnae," Mòrag said, confused. "I dinnae have it. I would've thought ye did?" She pointed to his hip, and the sword hilted to his side.

"Oh, this? Nae, this is the same sword ye saw when ye left. Inspired by all the tales I told ye, I went tae the blacksmith and had tempered glass put in tae the pommel. It looks good, but it's nae sapphire."

Hawk agreed the sword looked good. So good, in fact, that he would have sworn the pommel held a sapphire. But once known, he could now see the slight discoloration, the imperfections in the glass. Indeed, it wasn't the sapphire blade from Urquhart.

"Ye dinnae have it?" Mòrag asked, unable to comprehend.

"Why would I have it?" he asked, unsure of the game Mòrag played. "Ye went after the sword, nae me."

"But Lady NicNeev?"

"Who? What do ye mean?"

Mòrag took in a deep breath, closing her eyes. "Ye hired Lady Phillipa NicNeev to get the sword as well, right?"

"I did nae such thing." Graeme laughed. "Who is Lady NicNeev? What are ye on about? Why would I hire someone else? C'mon, did ye have trouble finding it? Did ye start at Hawick?"

He doesn't know what we're talking about, Hawk thought, catching on. His gut twisted. Maybe the stew made him ill, but he didn't quite believe that.

"Aye, I did. Ye didnae hire anyone else tae help me find it? A lady, older and more noble? She was a—"

Hawk butted in before Mòrag could finish the thought. "A friend of ours. She said she was an acquaintance of yours as well."

"C'mon now, what are ye playing at, Mòrag. What lady? I didnae tell a soul about the sword. It's been lost for so long, and ye seemed so happy tae retrieve it. It was yer own journey. What are ye on about a lady?"

"Lady NicNeev," Mòrag said, her voice quivering in a desperate realization.

Her chin dropped further toward her chest. Hawk tried to think of something to say, anything to offer comfort as the truth fully set it. But he, too, reeled at the notion that Lady NicNeev had lied again—her biggest lie yet—and was gone, the sword with her.

"Dinnae worry, lass," Mòrag's father said, reaching a hand under Mòrag's chin and lifting it. "That sword was gone ages before ye set out. It's nae yer fault. I'm nae surprised ye didnae manage tae find it."

"I've failed ye, Da. The sword's lost," Mòrag said, unable to meet his eyes.

Hawk, too, lowered his eyes to the ground. He held the sword at one point. His eyes gazed at the Gaelic etchings and the magisterial glistening of the pommel sapphire. Mòrag didn't lose the sword—he did.

"What?" he gasped. "Ye didnae fail anyone, lass. I'm happy ye took on the responsibility. I'm ecstatic ye went out in tae the world. Ye saw it, experienced it, and learned from it. I cannae teach ye that from our village. Now look at ye: stronger than ever, a noble horse tae boot, a mighty-looking friend, and another summer under yer belt."

"I thought ye wanted the sword. Ye were so happy tae hear I was goin' tae look for it. Ye told me where tae look and helped me prepare. I thought it was important. I thought it meant something to ye."

"It did. It does. I maybe went a bit overboard with the excitement, true. All I wanted was for ye tae take that motivation with ye. But why would I be mad at ye for nae finding what I lost years ago? Come now, Mòrag. What's for ye'll nae go past ye. Ye're here, and that's all that matters tae me. Now, c'mon and get ready, or we'll be late tae the ceremony. The council will meet at the summoning stones soon. Here comes Artair, Lochlann, and Wee Lochlann." The others approached, carrying their daypacks to be strapped to their mounts.

"Now let's go. We must ride."

CHAPTER TWENTY-SEVEN

Clouds covered the horizon in a white blanket, blemished only by the streaks of gray accumulations. It wouldn't rain, the huntsman felt sure, but the clouds certainly tried their best to impose. He never liked overcast days, for who likes a clouded sky? But in particular, Hawk disliked any day where the sun's precise direction and location couldn't be ascertained. On those days, time lost all meaning, and the day would often get the better of him.

This isn't one of those days, however.

Directly above them hung a curious circular break in the clouds. Like an eye in the mist, a magnificent ball of light revealed the heavenly blue shimmer of the sky above. It was only just past midday, the perfect time for the council to meet at the summoning stones.

They gathered together, all of the clans, at the stones Hawk had heard about so much. Each clan sent their five representatives to the council, making for quite the crowd. Along the way, Hawk overheard the number of clans reached nearly three score, which meant a significant number of bodies on the shore near the isle of Eilean Na Mòine.

The stones extended out of the isle in the loch, just offshore.

The isle grew tall, rising out of the dark depths of the water like the shell of an enormous turtle. Tall fir trees flourished on that shell, stretching up toward the blue circle of sky. And the reason they all gathered: six tall stones. The stones' arrangement served a purpose, but what that purpose was, he couldn't make out from the shore of the loch.

The huntsman had separated himself. His disappointment at the lack of Lady NicNeev's presence hadn't waned. He wished to remain on the outskirts of the congregation and not sully the ceremony, rather than with Mòrag and Clan MacTarbh, among the others. But mostly, Hawk knew it was Mòrag's moment, not his, and he didn't wish to interrupt. He stood in the soggy grass of the shore, water soaking his boots. It wouldn't be long before they soaked all the way through. He hoped the ceremony would start soon.

A man Hawk didn't recognize paced in front of the gathering. He wore pure white robes. From his distance, Hawk struggled to discern if the color showed his common status or his genuine purity. It meant little, for what mainly caught Hawk's eyes moved next to the robed man.

A young woman glided across the grass in splendor and majesty. Her dress, a brilliant sea foam, fluttered and twisted behind her in an ethereal flow, dancing as if caught in an ever-blowing breeze. But no wind blew along the shore. Her golden yellow hair looked transcendent, almost glowing in the bright rays of the sun. Her presence alone silenced the hundreds of people gathered and left little doubt about whom Hawk stood before—the Lady of Caledonia.

Everyone's excited eyes locked onto the Lady of Caledonia. Indeed, what they all hoped to see walked in front of them.

The man in the white robe raised his arms to the sky, gesturing to all that he meant to speak. He didn't disappoint. The man shouted in a booming heraldic baritone.

"Thank you all for gathering here before Eilean Na Mòine. And

my thanks again for your haste." He paused, pacing across the shoreline before bellowing again. "I am Fionn, the fount keeper of this
place. There hasn't been a gathering here at the sacred summoning
stones since the times of old. I'm glad to see so many new faces here.
I've spoken with the Lady of Caledonia. We will begin. She's asked
to select individuals who will partake in the sacred ritual for us all.
She'll walk among you, and with her grace and touch, you'll come
forward and take part in the noble ceremony. To take part is a great
honor. Be not afraid. The purpose of this summoning and the
council will be made clear once the ritual is complete."

The Lady of Caledonia moved along the front row of those
gathered, walking barefoot among soggy grass and weeds. She
scanned the crowd with a blissful innocence. She stopped and,
reaching between two men, grabbed a lad from two rows back.
The boy stepped forward and walked toward the man in white.

The lady drifted on, gracing another with her selection, a wiry
redheaded girl. The girl beamed, trotting over to join the first
selected. The Lady of Caledonia didn't stop, choosing two more
young lads to participate in the ritual. And then, to Hawk's
surprise, the Lady tapped Mòrag. Hawk watched in delight as
Mòrag stepped out of the crowd, her face aglow with curiosity
and wonder.

She deserves that honor, that happiness. The huntsman
thought he could see her look his way. He almost missed that the
Lady of Caledonia reached his end of the shore and stood in front
of him.

She had only selected youthful representatives for the ritual,
and Hawk looked around to see which youthful neighbor would
be chosen. It stunned him when he finally looked back, and the
lady's eyes fell on him. Her young, pale beauty and fluorescent
blue eyes froze Hawk in place.

This can't be. I'm young, but I'm not from Alba.

The lady of Caledonia took one step toward him. The two
men in front of Hawk parted at her approach. She reached and

brushed his armored shoulder. Abruptly turning, she walked back toward the man in white.

"I'm not in a clan, my lady," Hawk confessed, still rooted in his spot. "You want someone else, I'm afraid."

She turned, and, for the first time, a smile parted her lips. She raised her hand and beckoned him.

"I don't thin—" Hawk began, but stopped, having been thrust forward by those around him.

"C'mon, lad. Get on," called someone behind him.

The huntsman looked back at them. They wore expressions of jealousy and scorn at Hawk hesitating in that sacred moment. But why wouldn't he? He wasn't from Alba. Why should he take part in their sacred rituals? It didn't feel right to him. Nor did taking any bit of Mòrag's moment away from her by being there. She seemed so happy, but would she still be when he came forward?

The Lady of Caledonia walked in front of the huntsman. He followed, his eyes watching her bare feet navigate the grass. They approached the white-robed man. Mòrag stared at Hawk, eyebrows raised in surprise. She didn't, however, show any malice. In fact, she moved closer to Hawk and bumped him, subtly but deliberately, in gentle acknowledgment. Hawk smiled and watched the Lady of Caledonia move to the edge of the water.

Where the white-robed man and the lady once stood alone, six awaited their instructions with bated breath. The water below the bank in front of them slumbered, dark and shimmering. Even with the light of the sun directly above, no light penetrated the loch's midnight-blue water. Although only a good stone's throw away, Hawk didn't look forward to swimming across to the isle, if that's what the ritual called for. He could almost feel the cold water from the shore. There'd be no swimming to the isle, however. The Lady of Caledonia reached the shore's edge and gracefully dipped a bare foot into the water.

Logs, as if from ghostly timbers, erupted from the water and grew into fir trees, branches sprouting out to the other trunks.

The branches weaved and tangled in a magical tapestry of wood and plant. Before Hawk could even recognize what had occurred, a living bridge formed from the shore to the isle. He wouldn't have to swim.

The others seemed overwhelmed, in near ecstasy at their first taste of magic. Even Mòrag appeared pleasantly surprised by the living bridge as she moved to get a better look. Hawk clenched his teeth, less assured. He wouldn't be the first to cross that bridge.

"Welcome, everyone," boomed the man in white.

Hawk tried to decipher the man's role in this ceremony, admitting that he possessed a gift for projection.

"Will the leaders of each clan here today please step forward and lead your people from the front of the council? You must bear witness and mark your role in this ritual. You must witness history."

An excited shuffle broke out among those gathered as the chiefs of each clan made their way to the front. Ornamented and decorated, they strutted about, waiting for their turn to partici-pate. Hawk even noticed Ceitidh push a member aside as she emerged from the congregated clansman.

Mòrag tugged Hawk's hand, and he turned his attention back to the Lady of Caledonia. She was crossing the bridge. The other four crossed the bridge in tow, and finally, Mòrag and Hawk. The white-robed man stayed behind, halting any who attempted to follow.

Hawk stepped gingerly across the branches. They bent, absorbing his weight under his boots like he walked amongst actual trees. Even the sound of his heel striking the planks rang as if against actual wood. But Hawk knew they couldn't be real. Or at least he thought so.

As he continued marching, his adrenaline got the better of him, his excitement growing. He wished their crossing was met with music or drums or cheering, but tried to ignore the eerie silence that befell the air.

Hawk stepped onto the island. The spongy ground beneath

his feet gave an absorbing elastic spring with every step, owing to the plethora of fallen fir branches and needles littering the soil.

Only then did the huntsman notice three hooded figures standing at the edge of the isle. Adorned in dark red robes, Hawk could only imagine the role they shared in the ceremony.

They made their way to the center of the small island where, decorated in two unnatural concentric rings, stood six great gray granite menhirs. Erected taller than two men stacked on top of one another, the stones stood weather-beaten, scarred, and solemn. Smaller stones formed two perfect circles between the menhirs. Directly at the center of the circles was a large fir stump. Its position in the middle of the rings wasn't an accident—that much Hawk knew.

The Lady of Caledonia extended her hand, gesturing at the selected participants, then to their corresponding stones. Hawk approached the monolith furthest away from the shore of on-looking clansmen. He was glad to be at the opposite end of the island. However, he still approached cautiously, afraid of tripping and tumbling in embarrassment during the sacred ceremony with hundreds in the audience.

The monolith loomed over Hawk the nearer he got. He could finally see the aged scarring was, in fact, carvings; etchings in a language unknown to him. The generations of rain falling on the rock had smoothed the contours of the engravings, leaving faint outlines of symbols and depictions. The huntsman struggled to interpret any of the etchings, except one: a dagger pointed directly at a monolith.

Fionn, the fount keeper, snuck up behind the huntsman. Hawk instinctively whirled and stared at the bearded older man. The white-robed man didn't return his gaze and made straight for the stone. He bent over, rummaging in the dirt. After a moment, the man stood, having retrieved a small, rusted dagger. Its blade, crooked and serrated, must've stood in the dirt since the last summoning. Then, without hesitation or remorse, Fionn lacerated his palm with the dagger.

Blood gushed from the wound while joy split the robed man's face. Dropping the dagger, he grabbed his bleeding hand and pressed it against the stone. He swiped, leaving a crimson cross on the stone. The man never winced nor cried out in pain. He simply turned around and handed the dagger to Hawk.

What have I gotten myself into? The whole ceremony was growing beyond what he wished to participate in.

"Pierce the dagger into the stone fount at the mark when I command it."

"How will I pierce the stone?" Hawk asked, but too late.

Fionn moved on to Mòrag's stone, the last to receive his mark. The three hooded figures in red robes remained at the edge of the isle. Hawk turned his attention to the center of the circles, and to the lady instead.

She'd been studying him. Her azure eyes fixed on Hawk and the rusty dagger he held. His insides twisted, and a growing unease burned in the pit of his abdomen. It took all he could muster to stifle the tingling adrenaline trembling in his hands. The lady, calm and collected, smiled at the huntsman.

"Let us begin," Fionn announced to the island.

Hawk spun the dagger blade outward. He watched the three participants in the inner circle eagerly and unflinchingly press their daggers into the bloodstain on the stone. Hawk, with no desire to further delay the ritual, turned around to face his standing stone. The bloodstain dripped, curving the drops along the etched stone. Hawk took the dagger in his gloved hands and pressed the point of the rusty blade directly into the mark. It melted into the stone seamlessly, like an icicle to a flame. The granite seemed to swallow the entire blade to the grip and, with a satisfying click, locked the dagger in place. Hawk let go and took two paces backward, unable to believe what he'd just done. He spun, looking around to see if it had happened to the others.

No disappointment here, he thought as six daggers locked in the stones. Six daggers ringed the central fir stump as the Lady of Caledonia approached it.

She stood at the midpoint, towering over the stump. She bent over next to the stump and regally lifted a red deer pelt with spread arms. She slid her hand under the hide. In a single, swift motion, she swept out a sword. She discarded the deer pelt, placing both hands on the sword's hilt. The polished blade appeared a near reflective silver in the glimmering sunlight. More than sunlight glowed from the blade, however. Runes blazed violet along the blade's fuller. Hawk stood too far away to read them, but the color looked strikingly familiar.

The lady raised the sword into the air with both arms, then rapidly spun the blade point toward the stump. With the sword hilt above her head, she peered at the ritual's participants, finding Mòrag last. The lady winked before promptly plunging the sword into the wooden stump.

A bone-rattling reverberation echoed through the glen, bouncing off the hills and up into the blanket of clouds. The Lady of Caledonia released the sword, satisfied with her work. She floated back toward the island's edge and those gathered on the opposite bank.

Is the ritual complete? She seems ready for an address, Hawk noted, *and damn it, how did that sword make such a noise?* He stood, stunned. The sword remained illuminated in the stump, a purple torch amongst the gray stones. It even seemed to stare back at him through the bright blue gem embossed into the pommel—a sapphire.

"Magic. Oh, God . . ." Hawk whispered under his breath. "Could it be?"

He looked at Mòrag, but she seemed unaware of his gaze. The Lady of Caledonia enraptured her. Hawk had to call out to her. She had to know that the sword, the one driven into the wooden base, was Claidheamh-mòr an Adhairc, the sword of Clan MacTarbh.

Hawk opened his mouth but froze. In his periphery, a flash of light sparkled in the loch behind the island. It penetrated the depths and rose to the surface of the dark abyss. It drew his gaze.

"Good day," said a voice from beside the bridge.

Hawk knew that voice, that cunning prominent tenor. The violet engravings, Mòrag's clan sword—it all whirled through the huntsman's mind, clicking into place. The Lady of Caledonia was Lady Phillipa NicNeev. He spun to hear her speak.

The lady continued, orating and boldly gesticulating with every sentence. "Clan chiefs of the Scoti. Brothers and sisters, you've heard my calling. I sent the golden eagle to each of you, sacred and noble, as it happened in the ages past. I summoned you here to bear witness to the changing of one nation, and to witness your history. Because, make no mistake, history is occurring. You've traveled far, over great distances. Some have sailed, others riding with all haste. I thank you, for your horses will surely not."

A murmur of laughter swept through the gathered crowd.

The water behind the huntsman bubbled, no, boiled, sending steam rising into the air through a cascade of venting water. A rush of heat flourished past him. No one except for Hawk seemed to notice.

"I'm glad to see you've all come," the lady went on. "Clan MacTamhais, Clan MacDòmhnaill, and even Clan Ogilvy, right? That's quite a distance you've come, then. Well, I assure you it wasn't in vain, all of you, for I've called you all here to heed my council and decide your fate. A power rises before you and threatens your very way of life. King David, seated on the throne of Edinburgh, wishes to rule over you all. He wishes nothing more than to subjugate you, remove your clans, your identities, and your way of life, in an effort to *unite* you. He believes his new continental influence will modernize the land and that his new spirituality will help you. But it will only bring ruin and death, stripping you of everything you hold dear. He brings forth a great tyrannical evil. Verily I say unto you, do not cast your sword with the likes of King David."

"Why the bloody hell not?" shouted a man dressed in an adorned breastplate armor. He carried the sigil of Clan Druimeanach. He thumped his steel chest and went on, "I and my clan serve under King David. My father before me served his father before him. He's noble, and his cause is just. This is blasphemy. Tell me, oh Lady of Caledonia, why should I listen to this drivel?"

Others appeared to agree, reinforcing the sentiment with their shouts.

"Are ye asking us tae decide whether or nae tae go tae war?" asked Graeme MacTarbh. "'Cause, if that is the question, oh Lady, then the answer is obvious. There will be nae war for my clan. I will send naught tae war with those who make nae war with me. And King David sits far away on his throne in Edinburgh."

The shouts of agreement rose once more.

"King David doesn't sit idly on that throne, MacTarbh," shouted Ceitidh, standing with the leaders in front of the crowd. "His armies are spreading north like a plague, even now. They've marched on our lands, and when they're finished, they'll march on yers. I can assure ye. War will come tae ye."

"As if I would take any advice from a Moravian here," cried the plated man in service to King David. "I'll hear no more of these bold accusations and lies."

The Lady waved for silence before she spoke again. "If you'll not listen to that, listen to this." She lifted a single hand skyward, purple sparks shooting from it. "Rise, Uilepheist. Come serve your master."

The boiling water behind Hawk erupted. He swiveled about, no longer able to ignore the sound. Out of the penetrating light and water slithered an enormous serpentine head unlike anything Hawk had seen before. The head and neck slid along the island shores before four stout reptilian limbs emerged from the water and crawled onto the island. Dark green patches of algae camouflaged its cobalt scales. The ground beneath Hawk quaked with every step the behemoth took, gripping the island with its sheer immensity. Hawk backpedaled out of the creature's way as it passed him. The serpent shook like a wet dog, raining water in every direction and drenching the isle. Steam rose off the isle from the water, reeking like low tide on a sun-drenched shore. Then the creature opened two bat-like wings that jutted from its torso.

They spread out, flinging to either side and, as if to leave no doubt of their function, swung toward the ground, expelling a gust of wind to either side. Hawk put a hand up to shield against the burst. He watched in awe. A veritable dragon stood in front of him.

"Do not be afraid," the lady shouted over the gasping and shuffling crowd along the bank. "Uilepheist and I, Lady Phillipa NicNeev, the Lady of Caledonia, will lead you together against the tyranny of King David and his continental push. Together, we shall unite as one under the Caledonian banner. You've gathered here as the leaders of your clans. Now, step forward so we may hear your voice. I ask those who stand in the front to kneel. Kneel, and you and your clan shall be safe. Kneel, and join me. Kneel, and we shall save Alba from the puppet who plays at being a king."

For a moment, no one moved, not even a twitch. Then Hawk couldn't believe his eyes.

Ceitidh kneeled, pressing her knee into the wet grass at her feet and her sword in front of her. The chief of Clan Sruidh kneeled next, and, like a dam bursting, others kneeled in kind, laying their swords before them. Soon, half of the leaders along the shore placed themselves on the ground. But only half.

"Is there no one else?" Lady NicNeev cried out.

"I see nae reason tae. Why would we trade one tyranny for another?" MacTarbh's chief roared. "Why would I lay my sword before ye and bring my clan tae war?"

"Aye," agreed the plated leader of Druimeanach. "Why would I join you, *O' Lady of Caledonia*, when these Highland scum are on your side?"

"I'm nae on anyone's side. Watch who yer calling scum, ye English-loving bastard," Graeme retorted, challenging the plated man with a gesture Hawk considered inappropriate.

NicNeev raised her hand once again from the island's edge. Violet bolts of lightning shot from her fist. They flew like strangely lit arrows across the water and landed on the leaders kneeling in the grass. The bolts must not have hurt, for none flinched as they struck. They didn't move from their spots, but soon the violet glow washed over their bodies. They shone purple, and then the hue changed to blue, before finally a dull gray. Hawk watched as Ceitidh, leader of the Moravians, transformed into a solid stone statue.

"What is this devilry?" Graeme shouted out in disgust.

"Some of you have led your clan for too long," the lady began. "The old ways of clan rivalry, constant bickering and in-fighting, must end. Watch what'll happen to those who oppose us. It's time to put the past in the past!" Lady NicNeev raised her fist once more.

The dragon raised its wings into the air. They spread out and heaved with all their might to the ground. Uilepheist beat its wings until it took flight. The gale of wind below pushed the huntsman back. He quickly restabilized his footing and shielded his face again. A rush of wind sounded from the dragon. Suddenly, fire belched from its jaws. The fire jettisoned across the water to the crowded bank. The first row of onlookers had no time to react. A fiery inferno whipped across the shoreline, scorching the clan leaders.

CHAPTER TWENTY-EIGHT

"Oh no," Hawk blurted, not aware he was speaking out loud. "What's happening?"

The dragon flapped harder, lifting into the sky. It soared upward and banked in a circle around the isle. Screams rose from the field along the shore. The dragon swarmed the fleeing crowd and herded them back to the water like sheep. Hawk couldn't move. He stood rooted in his spot on Eilean Na Mòine, watching the terrible spectacle.

He chanced a glance at the other stones. Two of the ceremony participants had leaped into the water, fleeing the isle. A third pressed against the stone as if to blend in and disappear. Across the isle, hands behind her head, Mòrag's eyes locked with the fiery shore. She moved toward the connecting bridge.

A branch cracked beside Hawk and broke his stupor. The Lady stood just in front of him. Her youthful features returned to the familiar, wise, and aged face of Lady NicNeev. Her grin remained elegant and disarming. Hawk's instincts failed him. His legs rooted to the ground like the surrounding menhirs.

Lady NicNeev grabbed his hand and removed the glove and pressed her hand to his. A violet shock arched between them.

Hawk snatched his glove back and recoiled, but Lady NicNeev's smile only widened.

She licked her lips as if the shock whetted an appetite. "It's happened already. I told you the time would come, did I not? Magic has burst out from you. Now is the time, Huntsman," she said, extending her hand toward him again in a humble offering. "The offer I gave remains, but only for this moment. Here and now, join me, Hawk. Yes, great magic is all around you. Together, we can unlock that power. Harness it. Join me."

"What?" he replied.

The sight of her stirred up his brewing cinders of anger toward the woman who had deceived him, deceived his friend—the woman who was raining death and destruction on innocents.

"What are you on about? Did you just kill those people?"

She sounded mildly agitated. "The rabble? I'm doing what's necessary. David is a fool, I told you. I will unite this land. Join me, and we can bring peace. We'll bring peace, with Uilepheist and our power, together. We can bring death to those who oppose us. We can even bring death to the Norsemen. Together, Hawk. Join me."

She shook her hand in earnest.

"Death to the Norsemen?"

"They're here. I warned you, only I could help you bring an end to Blåveis. That's why they're here. For you, Hawk. Revenge is sweet, I assure you."

The Lady NicNeev threw her hands toward the edge of the isle, unleashing a gust of wind.

Hawk thought his eyes deceived him. The men clad in the red hoods revealed their shaggy mops. They shuffled back-to-back to protect themselves. Blåveis's blue-colored eye leered at the huntsman.

Hawk's worst fears had occurred. He had hoped none survived Loch Ness. But the chaotic fray must've blinded him to their escape. The sight of them should have ignited something in him. It should've taken hold, like countless nights before. It should've fueled that pit of misery inside of him, an unbridled desire for revenge. But no misery rose to the surface—no rage manifested.

"How? How did they get here?" Hawk could only ask.

"Please, I'm the Lady of Caledonia. I've brought back magic to this land. I heard the whispers in the wind of your exploits at Urquhart. They begged for their God's mercy on the loch's shore, and, well, I answered. I conjured them here in a trance, knowing you'd follow that stupid girl to the summoning. This is your last chance, Hawk. I've brought you the chance for revenge. Take it!"

Hawk looked away from Blåveis and his piercing blue eye. He met NicNeev's stare, unflinching.

"They'll not haunt me anymore," he growled. "I've moved on."

She scoffed. "Please, you don't believe that. Think of what Blåveis did to you. It's what your journey was for. He took everything from you. Don't deceive yourself."

"You deceived me at Urquhart. You lied to Mòrag and me the entire journey. All so you could have the sword. For this?" He gestured to the chaos still churning around them.

Through the gaps of fire on the shore, Hawk could see people running about in terror. Some stood in defense. The dragon bellowed above as arrows darted past it. Wind rushed the fire into tumultuous blazing spirals blocking his view.

"Of course I lied. I know everything about the sword and the clan that keeps it. Pathetic, losing the sword. I did what I needed to return it—the great sword of the horn—to its proper place on this island. The sword calls on the power of Uilepheist." Her voice turned low and seductive. "I could show you that power."

"For this? You burned innocent lives for opposing you. You're herding them like cattle to slaughter, and you expect me to join you? What are you thinking? I'll not join you and help this madness."

"Madness? Madness, you say? That king conscripting slavers is madness. Is David with his Christianity any different?" She grunted with contempt. "I'll bring peace. Can't you see that? No? A shame, Hawk, that you'd choose destruction over peace. Your death over unlocking your true potential. Death over—" Lady NicNeev abruptly halted, tackled to one side and slammed into the fir branches on the ground.

Mòrag bounced up off the cushioned firs and readied for another attack. She couldn't have prepared for what came next.

"You ignorant wench," muttered Lady NicNeev.

With a violet swish of her wrist, she tossed Mòrag end over end into the loch.

Lady NicNeev rose, her elegance abandoned with the grime of the island ground on her dress. She brushed off the needles that clung to her.

Hawk wasted no time and removed his tomahawks in a flash. Lady NicNeev wore a malicious scowl and turned to face him. Hawk raised the black steel to attack, but hesitated.

Behind Lady NicNeev, Uilepheist landed with a crash. The lady shook her head in disgust. She raised her arms and rose into the air with sparks of purple energy. She floated over Uilepheist's scaled back and rested between the dragon's shoulders. Lady NicNeev gripped the dragon with one hand and pointed at the huntsman with the other.

She paused for a moment, delaying what appeared to be an attack.

Does she think I might still join her? Or is she trying to figure how to inflict as much pain as possible before killing me? He took in a deep breath. He knew she might be at his end.

At that moment, arrows rained down on Uilepheist and Lady NicNeev. They struck the dragon's scales, bouncing off like pebbles on a boulder.

Violet rage burned in Lady NicNeev's eyes. The dragon launched into the air with the Lady of Caledonia mounted like a demonic rider. They headed for the banks of the loch.

Cowering in the center of the isle, almost forgotten, kneeled Blåveis and his two companions. Their fear of the dragon left them vulnerable for an easy strike by Hawk. The last of the Norsemen slavers wallowed in their own doom. But Hawk no longer feared the Norsemen. He returned the tomahawks to his back, turned his attention away from Blåveis, and didn't look back. They'd no longer steal anymore of his life.

Hawk, still on the isle, darted toward the edge where Mòrag was tossed so brusquely. A wave of relief hit him when he saw her already climbing out of the water. Mòrag reached from hanging branch to branch.

"Mo, give me your hand," Hawk shouted, extending his own to help her to higher ground. She crawled about the edge of the isle as the huntsman lifted her to him. Getting her boots planted underneath her, she stood upright.

"That sorceress bitch," Mòrag cursed, ringing out her hair dripping with water.

"Are you alright? That was quite a spin." Hawk was pleased to see she could stand.

A roar echoed across the loch from the dragon. Before she could answer, he grabbed her hands and urged her on.

"C'mon, we've got to run!"

"Make for my da! We must help him!" Mòrag shouted over the roar of chaos.

They raced across the island to the wooded bridge. The fallen fir needles propelled their every step like tiny springs. Hawk rushed headlong for the bridge path, but movement in the center of the isle drew his attention. Blåveis and the two Norsemen careened toward the bridge's entrance. Hawk was fast, once outsprinting the legendary draugr of Orm Odinsson's burial site. But the enemy moved quicker. Blåveis blocked the entrance to the wooden bridge, halting Hawk's and Mòrag's escape.

"*Red boy*," shouted Blåveis's hoarse voice. "*A little creature of Vinland, so long ago. You're some kind of warrior now? But you'll always be that slave, boy. Time to send you home to meet your family.*"

The Norsemen approached Hawk and Mòrag. With swords drawn, Blåveis raced toward them, flanked by his two brethren.

Mòrag, never conceiving of a battle amidst an ancient ceremony, had no bow to defend herself. Hawk brandished the obsidian knife and thrust it handle first toward her.

"Mo! The one on the right. Take the one on the right."

Hawk reached behind and unsheathed his black tomahawks. He let out a deep breath and took a step forward, finding his footing by tapping against the ground. He stepped again, finding a rhythm with his boots amongst the fir branches. Blåveis's bright blue eye drew closer. Hawk moved, impelled by unknown music, feeling the vibration of the ground as the Norsemen approached, their swords raised.

Blåveis shouted and, finding the right branch on the ground with his tapping, Hawk launched himself off of the ground into the air. He spun to his left in a powerful dance, using the momentum of his spin to fling his ax. The tomahawk catapulted into the nose of the left, flanked Norsemen, cutting him down with one blow.

Hawk landed his spin and immediately fell into step, dodging the furious swipe of Blåveis's blade. Blåveis whirled around, wasting no time, and swung at him again. Hawk, still in his rhythm, dodged repeatedly. Blåveis came at Hawk with thunderous strikes, but each time, the blade was wide of the mark. Hawk flowed around the swipes, transfixed by his demon's attack. The towering brute seemed to be like a fire, and Hawk found his place dancing around its lashing flames.

The moment he waited for came. An exacerbated swing of the sword came down and struck the ground. Hawk swiped his ax at the flat of the sword blade and sent the sword backward, drawing Blåveis off balance. The huntsman moved in, slashing at Blåveis's unprotected waist and stepping through to his opponent's other side. The torn skin enraged the Norseman, and with a renewed zest, he raised his sword to attack Hawk.

The huntsman's focus shattered at a sound that turned his

blood cold. He knew that war cry, that aggravated scream of intensity. *Mòrag.*

Hawk glanced at her. She flailed on top of the third Norsemen as they wrestled for possession of the obsidian knife. He couldn't see who had the upper hand.

Hawk's eyes wavered too long. A blade ripped down his buckskin kilt before he saw it. The sword cut through the thick hide, pulling Hawk to the ground as it sliced into his thigh. Hawk's knees met the ground. His free hand instinctively went to press against the wound. It stung, lashing like a cruel bite in his thigh. Hawk met Blåveis's strange, haunting eyes as the brute readied his next attack.

The sword came for Hawk's exposed neck. With a last effort, Hawk leaned back, missing the force of the blade. As the tip of the sword passed, it grabbed the beads of his wampum necklace, slicing through the string.

Time seemed to slow. From adrenaline or something more, the huntsman couldn't tell. The beads scattered through the air. Each purple and white bead shimmered as they flung into the fir needles. The memories each piece of wampum held struck the soil like lightning. His tribe. His mother. Ayaksak, his sister. They all were in those beads at that moment. With each bolt that landed, a fire ignited inside Hawk.

Crimson flames burst from Hawk's hands, surrounding his palms and fingers like a warm, sparkling glove. The flames passed through his grip into the tomahawk, wrapping the ax in a red glow. Hawk nearly dropped his weapon in surprise.

Blåveis lifted his colossal sword and swung at Hawk. Still, time seemed slower to the huntsman. The edge of the Norseman's blade approached. Hawk rose to meet it. The red steel of his tomahawk moved to parry the blow, steel on steel, but no clang of metal sounded. The red ax sliced the steel blade in half like a hot knife through butter. Blåveis staggered from the block, his sword melted and steaming.

Hawk raised his fiery crimson hand and drove the tomahawk

into Blåveis's singular blue eye. It singed, sizzled, and burned its way through the Norseman's skull. His screams resounded over the isle, but soon were muffled in the searing of flesh from the tomahawk. Hawk wrenched the ax out and, for the last time, looked into Blåveis's dark eye. Hawk ended the nightmare with a single crimson swipe of his ax.

He turned to help Mòrag. But it wasn't needed. She wrenched the obsidian knife back from the fallen Norseman and plunged it through the man's fleshy chin. The man hemorrhaged and coughed his final breaths.

Hawk let out a long sigh. His body felt like he'd climbed a mountain—winded and drained. The fire once sprouting out from his hands receded, his ax black once more.

It's real. Magic is real. That was incredible. Hawk held up his hands for inspection, but nothing had changed. He didn't know how the magic had sprung forth, but he remembered Lady NicNeev mentioned she took time to recover from its bouts.

Pain bit at his leg. Hawk brushed aside his torn buckskin to examine the spot. Cut, but not serious. He wanted to sit, but the roar of the dragon brought him back to his senses.

Hawk only had time to gather his tomahawks; the rest would have to wait. He sheathed the axes and turned to Mòrag.

"Are you alright?" he asked.

"Bugger it. C'mon," Mòrag replied.

They ran onto the bridge's branches. They hurried, stepping lightly and assuredly across the twisting wood.

Shielded by the canopy of the bridge, Uilepheist landed at the end of the bridge as if from nowhere. It gulped, taking in an airy breath.

"Jump," Mòrag cried, grabbing Hawk's shoulders and yanking him off the bridge.

They tumbled into the cold water below as a ball of flame raced past where they had once stood.

The water was ice. It chilled to the core, causing Hawk to inhale reflexively, choking on water. Pain like tiny ice-like nettles dug into his chest. Disorientated from the fall, he sunk under the weight of his armor. He instinctively tried to get his boots beneath him and to swim upward. Brushing against the rounded rocks below, Hawk pressed with all his strength to launch toward the surface. He emerged from the water and cleared his lungs with a sharp hacking cough. It was then he noticed how deceptively shallow the waters were, only reaching as high as his chest.

Mòrag breached the surface already and waded toward the shore. The huntsman grabbed the reeds on the edge of the bank and hurled himself onto the grass. He had no time to catch his breath.

Fire spread all around the field, feeding the chaos. Hawk struggled to look past the charred bodies strewn in front of them. Panic gripped the glen. A wall of flame, surging from Uilepheist's jaws, poured over those attempting to flee. A hellish inferno consumed the field, and Hawk crawled his way into it.

The huntsman rose to his feet, removed his tomahawks from their sheaths, and, with his first step, stumbled over a fallen bow. Mòrag seized the bow and grabbed the fallen arrows.

"Her, aim for her," Hawk roared. "Don't waste any on the dragon's scales. You must aim for her."

"I have two bloody arrows!" Mòrag cried, crouching on the ground.

She shuffled along to take cover next to a stony figure kneeling in the grass.

"Here she comes!"

The wind howled around them as the dragon's wings parted the skies. A shadow rushed over Hawk as the tremendous canopy of Uilepheist flew overhead. Mòrag whirled over the stone statue and, with steady aim, fired at the circling serpent. The arrow whizzed over Lady NicNeev's golden-crowned head. The dragon banked in the air, tearing across the clouded sky, and ripped toward the scorched terrain below. It landed with an earth-rattling boom, vibrating the ground beneath Hawk's feet.

A volley of arrows rushed toward the dragon and its rider.

The clansmen on the shore did their best to stop the dragon, but it proved of little use. One brave man dashed at them, sword in hand, but was quickly snatched up by the dragon's jaws and tossed into the loch. Lady NicNeev, with a flick of her wrist, burned the arrows flying toward her in a rage of violet.

We'll never defeat a dragon and a sorceress. We're trapped, Hawk silently cursed.

As if it could sense his defeated attitude, the dragon turned to Hawk. There was no escaping Lady NicNeev's burning violet eyes. But then she blinked, and with that blink, weariness crept across her face. The sorceress was tired.

Uilepheist slithered, galloping across the field at Hawk and Mòrag. The huntsman dropped one of his tomahawks to the ground and raised the remaining blade above his head with both hands. He exhaled a deep breath and aimed. Only one chance remained—one desperate attack. Hawk gathered every bit of strength left and transferred it into the ax. As he concentrated, the black steel took on a crimson hue again. Finally, he hurled the ax end over end toward his mark.

Time slowed, the ax cutting through air and smoke toward the target. Lady NicNeev raised an arm of purple sparks, ready to defend against the rapidly approaching ax. But at the last moment, an object glinted in Uilepheist's eye. The dragon lurched to avoid Mòrag's approaching arrow. In doing so, it arched its back, thrusting Lady NicNeev forward and into the tomahawk's blade.

It struck hard and true, gripping Lady NicNeev's sea-foam green dress's tight-fitting shoulder. Blood burst from the ax's new home. No, it couldn't have been blood Hawk saw, as it illuminated, bursting into crimson flame around the lady.

NicNeev screeched, falling from her mount, no longer able to grip the dragon. She crashed to the ground with a resounding thud, still caught in the red-ember tangles of flame. Uilepheist, frightened, took to the skies again. He went higher than before, breaching the gray clouds and disappearing into the wondrous snow-white air.

Lady NicNeev wrenched Hawk's weapon from her shoulder and tossed it aside. The huntsman picked up his second ax from the ground and, with renewed gusto, volleyed the blade at Lady NicNeev's golden crown. It never reached its destination, as a burst of energy and violet flames consumed the lady's body. The ax collided with the charred earth and ricocheted wildly, bouncing twice before rolling to a final rest.

Hawk dashed to the where the sorceress had fallen. Mòrag, rushing too, bumped into Hawk's back. They stared at the blackened circle of the field where nothing but a single, black-steeled tomahawk remained.

CHAPTER TWENTY-NINE

They arrived from the forest's edge. Always in pairs. Deliberately. Unerringly. They moved with playful glee, child-like in height and rhythm. They skipped from the forest, arm in arm. A dozen emerged from the wood across the field. They cared not about the scorched earth. They cared not about the charred remains. They hung on to their pointed hats with their free hands and, without concern, stopped to twiddle their wiry whiskers.

"Brownies," Mòrag gasped, wiping sweat and ash away from her brow.

They reminded Hawk of the Makiawisug from long ago.

The fairy-like creatures strolled and hopped across the field to the loch's bank. They had but one purpose. They stopped next to kneeled statues. They were always in pairs. One brownie wore a knitted green hat and buttoned vest, alongside his partner, a blue-hatted toad of a brownie.

They stood next to a stone-faced woman, kneeling with her eyes facing the island in the loch. A granite statue, carved with life-like detail that no chisel in the world could've made, watched over the loch. The stony figure, which the green- and blue-hatted brownies stood next to, bore an uncanny and incredibly accurate depiction of Hawk's friend Ceitidh.

The brownie in the green hat gave a tooth-filled grin. He reached a hand toward the sky, then across to hold the hand of the blue-hatted fairy. They placed their free hands on the statue.

A crisp pop leaked from the statue. Steam rose and hissed from the rock sculpture, and then, like snow on a warm spring day, the stone melted from her pale face.

Ceitidh gasped for air.

———

"What do we do now?" Cailean, son of Ciaran of Clan MacFhionghuin, asked the gathered group. "What do I tell my family?"

"What the devil even happened here?" cried Bhaltair of Clan MacTarbh. "I saw the lad ride back in terror. He bawled for help. Then me, the wolf, and the lads came, quick as a fox, and we've come tae this? Who set fire tae the earth? What were ye doing here? Whatever ye were doing here, clearly it got out of hand."

"I'll say," piped the tall, long-haired boy from MacFhionghuin. He hawked and spat onto the ground. "Ogilvy is dead, charred like the others. Twenty-two clan leaders dead. The others? Heh, they'll carry those burns and scars for the rest of their days."

Mòrag stood taciturn amongst the circle of anxious men and women. Hawk noticed she didn't look at who spoke, but studied her hands instead, turning over her gloves in some kind of detailed inspection. She didn't grimace at the boy from MacFhionghuin's words. Hawk imagined Mòrag knew her father, though alive, would carry those scars for eternity. Neither did she smile with joy, knowing her father lived when so many other fathers had not.

Mòrag stroked the black fur atop Tiree's scruff. The wolf sat in hushed reverence, the only presence not consumed with the day's events.

They collected in mass on the field where it all happened, overlooking the isle Eilean Na Mòine and its summoning stones. Some had fled, immediately gathering their host and fleeing, the ceremony and torturous aftermath too much to bear. Those who remained tried to pick up the pieces. Some watched the skies, fearing the return of the dragon, and others tried to decide what came next.

"Hang on, lads," said the ashen-covered man from Clan Capallcoille. Hawk wouldn't have recognized the pattern of his purple-and-blue tartan were it not for the clean area over his shoulder where his shield had rested.

"We're going in circles now. It's like we've already said. The Lady of Caledonia summoned a dragon from the stones. She threatened tae kill us if we didnae join her, and when we refused, she sent that *Olly-fish* to task on us."

"Uilepheist," Hawk corrected reflexively, remembering clearly NicNeev's words. "She called the dragon Uilepheist."

The Capallcoille man brushed Hawk off. "Aye, that's what I said, lad. This is the dragon's work. All of this around here, the charred earth, that was its doing."

"Nae, it was the Lady's work. She controlled the dragon," replied Cailean. "I stood behind my father. I saw her cast the spell, and the dragon moved tae attack. My father died in that fire. I think I bloody know who we have tae thank for that, Capallcoille."

"Aye, that bloody witch. It's good she's dead now."

"Aye, dead is true," Cailean added, "I saw it with my own two eyes. The huntsman here made sure of that. Yer ax fell the Lady, err, witch. She burst in tae red hot fire, like the fiend she were."

"Aye, thank God for the huntsman." The Capallcoille man nodded in Hawk's direction. Murmurs of agreement flickered through the gathered people. Hawk put on his best attempt at gratitude. But he didn't share their sentiments. He wasn't as easily convinced that Lady NicNeev's disappearance equated death.

"I thank you for your kindness, my good people, but don't

put forth your thanks in haste. I don't believe she's dead. I don't believe it."

"What do ye mean?" Cailean sniggered in surprise. "Come now, Huntsman. She burst in tae flames. Yer ax found its mark true, and the witch perished."

"Yes, you're not mistaken. But I've seen her burst into flames once before, and nevertheless, she returned today."

"Ye cannae speak truly. The Lady of Caledonia has nae been seen for hundreds of years, Huntsman."

Hawk scoffed. "The Lady of Caledonia she may be, but last week she titled herself simply Lady Phillipa NicNeev. I saw her at Urquhart castle. She walked around the courtyard as you or I would. Dressed as any noblewoman would and talked as any noblewoman should. But . . . Well, when it was just me, I'd seen her take possession of that sword she held today and burst into flames of her own accord. She must've transported herself and those robed men here with some kind of magical power. But it was the same then as it was today. The fire, the heat, and then, not a single trace of her remained."

The Capallcoille man couldn't believe it. "Truly? Ye kent the lady before today? Where does she live? Where could she have gone?"

"I don't know. I don't know if I ever really knew her, and I don't know where she is or would've gone."

Hawk remembered his travels with Lady NicNeev. He spent so much time on the road with her, yet she remained a mystery. *How did she know I was magic almost from the beginning?* The hints she gave him were clear, but it's hard to believe anything she said, knowing how she lied about everything else. Hawk spat at the ground.

"Well, what do we do now?" Cailean asked Hawk.

The huntsman, however, didn't reply. He had no answer, and, for a moment, his mind betrayed him, unable to come up with the words to say.

"Mourn," Mòrag replied in a terse command. "Mourn those

who fell. Then go home. Go back tae yer lands. Back tae yer families and loved ones and remind them they're indeed loved. Ye dinnae ken when they may be lost tae ye. There's nae sense staying here."

Cailean agreed somberly. "Aye, she's right. My da . . . Too many were lost this day."

"Many clans will need new leaders," said the man from Clan Capallcoille. "My brother is dead. Now I must fill his place. And those who kneeled at the feet of the bloody witch stand here unblemished."

Ceitidh, who had remained quiet during the circle's arguments, cringed at the mention of the kneelers.

"They should be punished," he added in rage.

Concurring cheers split those who gathered.

Ceitidh tried defending herself. "Punished? For what? For believing in the Lady of Caledonia? For choosing what I believed was best for my clan?"

The man from Capallcoille pressed harder. "Ye chose tae fight against King David of Alba and his good graces. Ye chose tae side with a witch. I wonder if ye're nae a witch yerself?"

"How could I ken what she was, or who she was? I kneeled tae the Lady of Caledonia for my clan. I kneeled for what I thought was right for them."

"Ye've kneeled for a witch. Ye should pay for it, with yer lives. The others, may God rest their souls, sure paid for it."

Ceitidh slid her hand down to the sword tied into her belt. "And I suppose it's goin' tae be ye who'll make me pay for it, aye?"

Grunting and turning red, the man barked, "Aye, someone should teach ye . . ."

"Enough!" Mòrag cut in, stepping into the center of the circle between Ceitidh and the Capallcoille. "Enough of this! This bickering and clan rivalry is stupid. Always fighting. We're playing right into the Lady's hand. Enough of this. We came here for peace, did we nae? So let it remain. Let us decide what tae do with that peace. Decide what we do with the dragon and be done with it, eh?"

Hawk remembered Lady NicNeev on the isle. She, too, wanted peace. How long would the peace last?

Ceitidh nodded fervently, breaking eye contact with the man who had threatened her.

She coughed and spoke, "What do ye propose, Mòrag?"

"Well, surely the dragon must be stopped, aye?" Mòrag responded like the answer was clear to everyone. "Before it can bring destruction again."

"Aye, how though?"

Silence blanketed the crowd. Then, something unexpected happened. A voice, tired and strained, spoke. One that longed for sleep and a simpler life of traveling and hunting.

"I'll go to hunt the dragon," Hawk said wearily. "I've fought nothing like it, but I shall try my best to help you, all of you."

Cailean stepped into the circle. "The huntsman defeated the lady. It's fitting we call on him tae defeat this dragon."

"Aye," the man of Capallcoille agreed, "we should help the huntsman defeat the dragon. We'd gladly pay for his support."

"I've fought beside the huntsman in battle, and I can think of naebody more clever and capable of taking on such a task than Hawk," Ceitidh shouted, grasping her sword and thrusting it out toward him.

Cailean removed his hatchet and followed suit.

Hawk looked at Mòrag for support. She wore a wicked smirk, like a child tossing a leaf in a campfire to watch it burn.

"Ye truly are the best hope for us," Ceitidh pleaded.

"Thank ye, Huntsman!" Cailean rejoiced. "God thank ye."

"Aye, bless ye, lad," delighted another in the circle. All around, praises sounded.

Mòrag shouted once more. "Alright! Ye heard him. Now it's time tae go. Away with ye and get ye home. It's best nae tae linger here any longer than we must. It's time tae leave."

The crowd dispersed slowly and steadily, like dissipating

smoke from the cinders of a dying fire. Conversations withered and finished, then drifted away. Hawk remained unable to bring himself to leave. He shook hands with the brothers from Rùm, an isle of the western coast, whose father was lost at Uilepheist's hands. With tears in their eyes, they thanked him. He grieved with Beasag, widow of the clan chief of MacDiarmid. They came to him one by one in admiration and appreciation until only four remained: Ceitidh, Mòrag, Tiree, and Hawk.

Ceitidh reached out and grabbed the huntsman's shoulder. "Hawk. That's twice now ye've saved my fate. Thank ye. And thank ye, too, Mòrag. If ye didnae quell those men back there. I dinnae ken what might've happened. Monsters they were."

"Nae monsters, just afeared of the unknown. We all are." Mòrag pulled Ceitidh closer in a squeeze.

Ceitidh returned in kind, tightening the embrace and resting her chin on Mòrag's black hide mantle. Ceitidh's tears proved to Hawk that, after the blistering events of the day, what Ceitidh desired most was Mòrag's humanity.

"Aye." Ceitidh sniffled. "Well, thank ye all the same. I must get my people out of here before there's trouble. Soon, I think. We shall head back through the Great Glen to Urquhart. Continue our struggles onward. No doubt we'll find Lulach along the way, late tae his own party, the bastard."

"Farewell, Ceitidh," Mòrag said. It was her turn to wipe her eyes. "Look after yerself until we meet again."

"The same as well tae ye, Mòrag. I trust we *will* meet again. Huntsman, take care of yerself, and good luck with the dragon. I wish tae see ye again in one piece."

Hawk stifled a laugh. "I will. Thank you, Ceitidh, and safe travels."

Ceitidh smiled and before that smile could fade, turned and hurried east toward the tacked horses and Glenfinnan.

They stood there alone, the huntsman and the warrior from Clan MacTarbh.

"Do ye think we'll nae see her again?" Mòrag asked the huntsman.

"Never say never, right?"

He grinned but stopped at the sight of Mòrag wiping away streaks from her emerald eyes. She fell into him. Whether from exhaustion, stress, or just a need for support, Hawk didn't know. He caught her, holding her against his body as she wrapped her arms around him.

"Are you okay?"

"Aye, just glad yer still here," she said into his chest.

"I'm glad you're still here too," he replied, leaning his head against hers. "I'm glad your father is alright as well."

"Aye. We should head back to him soon."

Mòrag's father had left, taken on horseback as soon as possible to Glenfinnan and the campsites. It must've been hard for Mòrag to watch her father ride away, but Graeme asked her to stay and speak for Clan MacTarbh.

"Soon, yes."

Then Hawk remembered. He couldn't believe he'd almost forgotten. Their journey—the entire reason they had banded together, the reason they had ventured there.

"The sword. Mo, your sword. It's still in the stump on the island, is it not?"

"Aye. So it is. C'mon."

They walked together over toward the edge of the shore overlooking the island. The bridge, which once connected the shore to the small plot of land in the loch, stood no more. With the end of the Lady of Caledonia's presence, the magic of the bridge had disappeared.

"We'll have to swim there. Tiree, stay where ye are," Mòrag said, sliding down the edge of the land. She looked back at Hawk, who hadn't followed.

"Ach, c'mon, ye already went for a swim once today."

She wasn't wrong.

They waded across the gap of water to the island and climbed up the steep side, using the fallen fir branches as a ladder.

Hawk reached the top first. The summoning stones remained, silent and ominous, undisturbed as they were for thousands of years. And in the center of those monoliths stood a stump with a bright shimmer protruding from its surface. The sword remained fastened in place, still blade down in the wood.

They moved closer, timid and cautious, as if the stones could come alive at any moment. Hawk took a moment to kneel and gather the wampum beads amidst the needles on the ground. He placed them in his pocket and paid little attention to the Norse bodies nearby. Hawk stepped on and past them, moving toward the center of the isle.

The sword drew nearer. Hawk could make out the runes engraved on the steel surface of Claidheamh-mòr an Adhairc clearly. They were dark, etched with some great god's charcoal pen.

Mòrag stepped up to the stump and placed a foot on top. She removed her gloves, slipping them into her leather belt. Sliding her fingers around the sword's grip, she clenched it with both hands. With a swift jerk, she thrust the sword up from its resting place, pommel skyward. The sapphire gem caught the dimming sunlight over the hills and created a dazzling display of cobalt light across Mòrag's face. The blue light sparkled across her eyes, melding with the green and shifting into indescribable splashes of turquoise.

Mòrag spun the hilt, and the blade whirled through the air with a metallic hum. She sighed with serene relief.

"Finally. After so long on the path, after I've done so much, I have it. I cannae believe it. Ach, look at it, Hawk. It's just the way my da said it would be. The handle. Look at the way it shimmers. And such fine steel." She turned the blade over, laying it out flat in her palms to read the inscription. "*Adharc bàis an tairbh.* Beautiful."

"You deserved to find it. To hold it, truly, you do," Hawk said in sincerity.

"Thank ye, Hawk. For helping me, I mean. From Rosslyn to Urquhart to Glenfinnan. I would've been lost without yer help. I would've gotten swallowed by that werewolf, nae doubt." She laughed.

"No, I should thank you. For, without you, I'd be dead, lying in a cesspit in Inverness. I would've been killed at the hands of Gospatric's men, and for that, I have you to thank. For everything, really."

"Hawk?"

"Mo?"

"Can ye hold the sword while I tie a wee loop in my belt for it tae rest?"

Hawk, expecting a different question, was surprised. He wasn't ready when she pressed the sword at him, hilt first. Taking the sword from her, he stepped back and checked the weapon's balance. It felt impeccable. A master smith must've forged it.

Sunlight glared across the steel, and Hawk adjusted the blade's angle. The sword's dark runes emitted no light. He removed his glove to examine the contour of the engravings. He brushed his fingers across the steel, and bolts of red sparks flew from the blade. Hawk, caught off guard, dropped the sword, but reached for it with his bare hand reflexively and grabbed the hilt.

Power raced through Hawk's arm, tingling every nerve and fiber of his body. The hair on his arms rose on end, matching the spiked raven mane of his head. The etching on the blade, *Adharc bàis an tairbh*, glowed crimson with fury.

"What the . . . What just happened?" Mòrag stammered.

"I don't know . . ." Hawk replied truthfully.

But Lady NicNeev's words rose from the depths of his memories. She had sensed the magic in him. He'd seen it in Loch Ness's waters. He'd seen it again on the island. Magic. In him.

"It must be some remaining magic from Lady NicNeev when

she drew the sword and plunged it into the stump," Hawk deflected.

He couldn't understand why he lied to Mòrag. Perhaps it was because Hawk himself hardly grasped what his magic could be. He wasn't exactly sure what had happened. But more than that, he didn't want her to be afraid. Especially not when, moments ago, magic brought such destruction in the form of violet flames. He'd tell her eventually once it was clearer to him. The time would come, but not yet.

"The sword did nae such thing when I touched it. What does it mean?"

"I don't know. Here. You take the sword," Hawk said, proffering the sword back to Mòrag.

She took the sword, and surprising no one, the glow ceased.

"Thanks," she said, "although I think it likes ye better."

"You came all this way, and now you have the sword back."

"Aye, now we have. Just dinnae let me go bursting into flames, will ye? I've had enough of that for one day."

"Tell me about it." Hawk smiled, stepping closer. "But I don't plan on leaving your side soon."

"Until ye hunt the dragon, that is?" Mòrag asked with a sheepish grin.

"Well . . ." Hawk started, mustering his courage. "I hoped . . ."

"Ye thought I'd come with ye tae hunt that thing? Uilepheist? Nae chance. It's a bloody dragon." The huntsman's face dropped slightly before Mòrag burst with a giggle. "I'm only joking. I would've helped ye. I mean, I will help ye, if ye want."

Hawk's mouth tugged toward one ear in a smirk.

With his bare hand, Hawk snatched Mòrag's. He drew her in close, pressing her gently against his leather-bound chest. Hawk was astonished she didn't move with his heart pounding out of control like a mighty hammer. Her emerald eyes bore into his. He leaned his head toward her and instinctively closed his eyes. He found the soft edge of her lips. The huntsman kissed the Highland archeress.

He broke off, opening his eyes once more. *Perfect*, he thought.

"Perfect," Mòrag whispered. She smiled with joyful longing. Hawk brightened.

"C'mon," she said, "let's head back across tae the other side and grab Tiree. The sun will be setting soon."

"We'll need to eat and get some good rest tonight if we're to track this dragon."

Hawk headed toward the island's edge, brimming with joy. He'd waited ages for a moment of peace like he would have that evening.

Mòrag beamed. "Aye, for we'll be making a start at the greatest hunt of our lives."

Hawk couldn't have known just how right Mòrag would be.

Acknowledgments

This book represents the culmination of an idea I had in 2018 while in veterinary school. Growing up in the Mohegan Tribe of Connecticut, I lived and learned of the rich and magical culture my family shared as a community. While I was in Scotland, I became enamored with my wife's Celtic origins and the history of her nation. I found myself wondering, what would a story look like if our cultures collided?

I must thank my wife, Sarah, for being my first fan and critic. Thank you for humoring my writing side project. I hope you love the series as much as I do. This book is for you.

I could not have been here without the help of my editors, Cate and Laura, whose insights and inputs helped turn a mess of thoughts into a novel. Thank you all so much for your guidance. To the big man himself, Gavin, thank you for taking the time to test read my book. I appreciate you. To all the beta readers who have critiqued my manuscript, your love and hate polished my story beautifully. Thank you all.

To anyone who read this book and took a moment to research an aspect of Indigenous culture or Scottish history, I thank you. This book was written for you.

PLEASE LEAVE A REVIEW

If you have enjoyed this book, it would be amazing if you could leave a review wherever you purchased it.

Reviews help bring my book to the attention of others who may enjoy reading them too.

Thank you!

THE STORY CONTINUES IN THE HUNTSMAN OF ALBA SERIES

The Huntsman of Alba - Book 1

Abducted as a child from his tribe in the New World, Hawk has spent the last fifteen years traveling medieval Europe as a huntsman for hire. All the while, he hopes to find and enact revenge upon the Norsemen raiders who murdered his family. This quest brings him to twelfth century Scotland's Kingdom of Alba where he is propositioned by the king. In exchange for slaying a mysterious beast, the king will share information about Hawk's kidnappers.

The Cleek Creek Forest - Book 1.5

Recovering from his recent battles, Hawk takes refuge in the Highland village and clan of his partner, Mòrag. While out on a hunting trip, they are beckoned into the haunted Cleek Creek Forest by a frantic traveler. But not all is as it seems, and Hawk and Mòrag must decide whether to defeat the evil beast within the dark woods or protect themselves and escape. Will the huntsman conquer the monster, or are some dangers too powerful to overcome?

Get a FREE copy of the novella, *The Cleek Creek Forest,* if you sign up for Dr. Doug Chapman's Reading Club at www. drdougchapman.com

Caledonia's Dragon - Book 2

Hawk has successfully avenged the murder of his family, but his quest is far from over. Now stalked by an evil sorceress, Lady NicNeev, after thwarting her plans of conquest, he and his partner, Mórag, must set out to slay the lady's dragon to protect the ones they love.

Out of options, the pair journeys through the Highlands and isles of twelfth century Scotland seeking to unlock a power strong enough to defeat Lady NicNeev's beast. But her dangerous mythological creatures stand poised and ready to strike along the way. Meanwhile, Lady NicNeev is not the only sorceress in the land, for another one rises to power. Confronted with the destruction of his home village, Hawk must decide whether to finally wield the magic that runs in his veins.

Will the Huntsman master his abilities or sacrifice it all for the ones he loves?

———

The Spirits of Samhain - Book 3

Coming soon!

Also by Dr. Doug Chapman

A Sweet Veterinary Life

After his mother dies, Tim Daniels must graduate from veterinarian school, find a job, pay-off his loans, keep his girlfriend content, and try to keep his head...all while removing a designer purse from a dog's stomach. Just another Tuesday morning...

Anxiety has always been Tim's annoying friend. Embarrassing him in middle school, preventing him from taking chances, but lately, Tim's *friend* has become a looming enemy. Faced with the loss of his mother and the stressors of medical school, the young vet has reached a breaking point.

In the wake of her death, Tim's mother left him a lump sum to follow his dream of finishing vet school in Scotland. Tim thought the toughest challenges were now behind him. Instead, the fire in his belly leaves a wake of uncertainty. Pushing away the pain of loss and failure, Tim tries to save the lives of his animal patients but wonders if he can save his own.

Buy A Sweet Veterinary Life

ABOUT THE AUTHOR

Dr. Doug Chapman graduated from the Royal School of Veterinary Studies in Edinburgh, Scotland. Dr. Chapman grew up learning and appreciating his culture as a member of the Mohegan Tribe of Connecticut. He now works in New Hampshire as a veterinarian with his wife, and dog, Tiree. When he is not working, you can find Doug running through the woods and streets as an avid ultra-marathoner, or hiking through the white mountains with his loving wife. You may even catch him trying to vacation back to Scotland when he can.

Discover more at www.drdougchapman.com

Made in the USA
Middletown, DE
02 August 2023

36070574R00203